Praise for Akosua Busia and
THE SEASONS OF BEENTO BLACKBIRD

"Solomon is the kind of man any woman could fall in love with. Frankly, I did too. . . . Busia really understands her characters. She gives Solomon, Miriam, and Ashia their full humanity, evoking their beauty and their flaws and their rage. We get to see what's inside their hearts."

—Bridgette A. Lacy, *The Washington Post Book World*

"Akosua Busia poetically connects the past to the present. . . . When Solomon is spiritually awakened to the questions in his life, we have turned the last pages of a novel that is literary, political, seductive, spiritual, and contemporary."

—Rita Coburn Whack, *Chicago Tribune*

"Akosua Busia's brisk, descriptive first novel is alive with sensation. Readers 'see' the vivid blue Caribbean sky and ocean, 'touch' the red earth of the Motherland, and 'smell' the consecrating rains that announce the blackbird's awaited homecomings. The author says she hopes to take readers 'on a trip' with *THE SEASONS OF BEENTO BLACKBIRD*, and she does, making the scenery come alive. Akosua Busia's suspenseful tale of love and wanderlust kept me eagerly turning the pages to its satisfying and surprising conclusion."

—Wendy Robinson, *The Christian Science Monitor*

"Written with a wide-eyed eagerness. . . . Akosua Busia's sprawling first novel maps the physical, erotic, and spiritual. . . ."

—*Publishers Weekly*

"The language of Akosua Busia's first novel is as lush as the Caribbean island of Cape Corcos, the home of protagonist Solomon Wilberforce. . . . Busia has set up an intriguing situation . . . [and a] complex romantic plot."

—*Library Journal*

"An ambitious first novel . . . magnificent prose . . . reminiscent of Toni Morrison's *Song of Solomon*. . . . There is a majesty to the story line of Solomon Wilberforce searching for his identity and his people. . . . There is a timeliness to the topic of a black man searching for his place in the world."

—Evelyn Martin-Anderson, *Austin American-Statesman* (TX)

"A debut novel that could be a movable feast of blackness and love as it moves across cultural and geographical boundaries. . . ."

—*Kirkus Reviews*

"A highly ambitious first novel that . . . clearly identifies Busia as a writer to watch."

—*Booklist*

"*THE SEASONS OF BEENTO BLACKBIRD* rolls on waves of passion and creates a romantic epic that bridges the diaspora."

—John Singleton, director of *Boyz N the Hood*

"Busia manages to describe each location in a colorful way, incorporating myth and romantic love."

—Patti Thorne, *Rocky Mountain News* (Denver)

"I was so impressed with *THE SEASONS OF BEENTO BLACKBIRD* and its fascinating characters. What extraordinary talent the author has! Read it!"

—John Schlesinger, director of *Midnight Cowboy*

"Busia's ability to convincingly transport the reader from Caribbean sunsets to the lures of West African customs and cuisine to life in Solomon's Harlem brownstone is impressive."

—*Vibe* magazine

"From its stunning opening scene of a Caribbean island, Akosua Busia's novel, *THE SEASONS OF BEENTO BLACKBIRD*, entices us into a world so fully lived-in that we have no choice but to submit to the care of this remarkably told story of personal migration and the price we pay to be anywhere."

—Wesley Brown, author of *Tragic Magic* and *Darktown Strutters*

The Seasons of Beento Blackbird

A Novel by

Akosua Busia

WASHINGTON SQUARE PRESS
PUBLISHED BY POCKET BOOKS

New York   London   Toronto   Sydney   Singapore

WSP

A Washington Square Press Publication of
POCKET BOOKS, a division of Simon & Schuster Inc.
1230 Avenue of the Americas, New York, NY 10020

Copyright © 1996 by Akosua Busia

Published by arrangement with Little, Brown & Company

ISBN: 0-671-01409-9

First Washington Square Press trade paperback printing December 1997

10 9 8 7 6 5 4 3

WASHINGTON SQUARE PRESS and colophon are registered trademarks of Simon & Schuster Inc.

Cover design by Brigid Pearson
Cover art by Phil Boatwright

Printed in the U.S.A.

This book is dedicated

To Mama, Mrs. Naa Morkor Busia—
my greatest inspiration and the love of my life.

To Papa, Dr. Kofi Abrefa Busia—
who taught me before he passed on
that dreams are dreamed to be lived by the power of God.

To my Heavenly Father—
without whose Spirit, I am nothing but dust.

In Acknowledgment for Love, Generosity, and Encouragement

✦

A HEARTFELT EMBRACE to my amazing sister, Abe, otherwise known as Dr. Abena Pokua Adompim Busia—who God in his wisdom sent to earth before me to hold my hand and accompany me up the great mountain of life. Thank you, big sister, for teaching me my alphabet, how to read in my head, and other such valuable skills that eventually led to the writing of this book. Thanks to my big brothers, Nii, Kofi, and Yaw, and to their devoted wives, Dinah, Carol, and Monica: your solid marriages are an example and encouragement that love can conquer all.

To Mr. Gordon William Snelling—my primary-school teacher who read to me from "Cider with Rosy" and taught me the poetry of words—thank you, I have never forgotten you.

Sincere gratitude to: Fredi Friedman, my editor—for such unyielding dedication to my work and for thought-provoking me to reach for my highest; Harvey Klinger, my literary agent—for the education and the laughter; Chuck Hurewitz, my attorney and friend—for setting goals and protecting my interests; Lanz Alexander, my business manager, and Eva Richards—for dealing with reality for me while I create.

A special thank-you to: Claudia Wells—for all the faith, devotion, and investment spent on me while working on this book; Khalid Hafiz—for believing so strongly in this story and encouraging me to write it down; Panther, for prompting me to publish; all my Monday night prayer sisters, and Dr. Mardra Paredes—for teaching me how to move onward and upward; Camille, Chip, and Johanna Mitchell—for all the family dinners and for proving to me that Vancouver is also a great place to write; members of C.E.F., especially Segun Oyekunle and Najee Williams—for the hours you gave so freely, installing my programs and troubleshooting me through my varying technical mishaps; Denise Edmonds—for giving me your home computer after mine was destroyed in the earthquake in Los Angeles; my girlfriend Gail Grate—for securing my front door after the shake-up so I could remain in writing hibernation; my pray-sisters, Andi Chapman and Wanda Vaughn, for cutting short our wonderful conversations and encouraging me to "get back to work"; Segun, once again; and Janette Richter-Addo—for retyping my words.

Thank you, thank you, thank you to Bishop Charles E. Blake and Sister Mae Blake—for uplifting me week after week with your graciousness, your caring, and your messages of hope. You bless my life so enormously. I thank God for you.

*   *   *

To all my friends—like stars in the sky you have become too numerous to mention, but know that the light of your love brightens my path, illuminates my soul, and ignites my imagination . . .

May your fountain be blessed,
And may you rejoice in the wife of your youth.
A loving doe, a graceful deer—
May her breasts satisfy you always
May you ever be captivated by her love.

Proverbs 5:18, 19

The Seasons of Beento Blackbird

BOOK ONE

✧

Winter

The Final Season

Chapter 1

✦

*T*HERE IS NO BLUE like the blue of the Caribbean Sea. No rhythm like the rocking of her waves. No taste like her salt-sea tongue. No touch like her soft warm wetness. Every time the fisherman hit dry land, he missed her—the lullaby of her call, the lapping of her hypnotic laughter as she stretched herself across the horizon. People called her the Caribbean, but to him she was Cara, Cara the beautiful. Away from the sea he was empty, a deep well with no water; but in her aquamarine presence, to the depths of his soul, he was full to overflowing. "My love is wide," he used to call out to the soaring seabirds, "deep and wide like Cara."

Digging his feet into the damp sand, the fisherman dragged his old battered boat to the water's edge and jumped inside. Cara licked the bottom of the boat, coaxing him away from the shore into her arms. Safely floating on her waters, the fisherman wiped his wet fingers on his frayed shorts and removed his sack from his shoulder. The *stranger of no words* had broken his silence, asking him to deliver a "very important package" to the post office. Reaching inside his sack, the fisherman carefully removed the package. He had no idea what was wrapped so carefully in the thin beaten tree bark tied with ropy vine, but whatever it was, it had caused the *stranger of no words* who lived in darkness to emerge into the light, to open his mouth, to speak. The wonder of that alone was reason to handle the package with care. Dangling it away from his body so as not to soil it against his sandy legs, he lowered the package into a small water-proof container at the back of the boat and closed the lid tight. Satisfied that it was safe from harm, he leaned back and rowed away.

*   *   *

Solomon stood alone on the beach, his tall sculptured body completely naked except for the faded African cloth wrapped around his waist, and a charm and locket on a leather shoestring knotted around his neck. His smooth, shiny, earth-brown skin reflected the sunshine like a mirror. His jet-black baby dreadlocks pointed up to the heavens like a proud peacock's crown. With a growing sense of excitement, he watched the fisherman row toward town. *Finally*, he thought. *Finally I can live again.*

Everyone on Saint Germaine resided near town on the south side of the island. Besides a thin strip of sand leading into the sea, there was nothing on the north side except rocks and caves. It was considered the bleak portion of the island, but Solomon liked it for its deserted quiet.

Peace was right, there was a sacredness in silence. In the five months that he had followed Peace's example by doing away with speech, Solomon felt more at one with himself and his Creator than he had ever felt in his thirty-eight years of life. Still, he didn't regret breaking his silence. He had known for nearly a month that this day was approaching. When he woke and saw the early morning sun piercing its rays through the mouth of his cave, he had known immediately that this was the day—it was time. Time for him to emerge. Time for him to speak. Time for him to reach out across the ocean and gather unto himself the pieces of his self he had left behind.

Stepping into the daylight, he had looked for the only person he had seen since first arriving on the island: the fisherman, his unspoken friend. Venturing out only at night to bathe in the moonlit sea, Solomon had often noticed the fisherman casting his net in the darkness. The fisherman would wave to him from a distance; Solomon would wave back. The gentle communication of those waves was the only human interaction Solomon allowed himself in his months of isolation.

One night at the beginning of Solomon's second month in hiding, he dragged his canoe from the cave and joined the fisherman in the water. Without saying a word, the fisherman threw Solomon a bag of bait and allowed him to fish by his side. It was as if he understood that Solomon was not yet ready to speak. Toward 3 A.M., when the weather turned cooler, the fisherman had taken off his jacket and tossed it to Solomon. It was an act that sealed their friendship. After that night, on the rare occasions when he didn't go out with the fisherman on his nightly jaunts, Solomon would stand in the mouth of his cave and whistle to let his friend know that he was alive and well.

Solomon watched the fisherman heading for a cove of rocks. Having finally spoken that morning, he realized he hadn't asked the fisherman's name, or given his own. "Hey!" he shouted across the waves, even though he knew the fisherman was too far away to hear him, "My name is *Solomon!*"

Solomon smiled at the pleasure of hearing his own voice. "Solomon Wilberforce," he said, introducing himself to himself. "Nice to meet you, Solomon," he replied politely, amazed at how completely himself his own name made him feel.

The fisherman rowed his boat around the curve and disappeared behind the rocks. Solomon felt confident that his package would soon be safely on its way to England. He purposed in his heart to do something good for the fisherman in return for all his kindness. Perhaps send him money as soon as he returned to *civilization*, or better still, buy him a brand-new boat, a houseboat that he could sleep on, a home . . .

Solomon's mind wandered back to the package. It should reach its destination by the end of the month, and around then he would send the fisherman to Cape Corcos. Then what? It was too much to think about now. All he knew was that when he had awakened that morning, it had been crystal clear to him that it was time to return to his life.

*   *   *

Stepping through the door of the small dilapidated post office in the center of town, the fisherman did his best to ignore the stationed security guard, who was staring at the fisherman's bare feet as if the sand falling off them onto the old tile floor could cause some kind of permanent damage. Swiveling his sack off his shoulder, the wary fisherman removed the package; and holding it in front of him as carefully as a child holds a ring pillow at a wedding, he walked ceremoniously to the back of the line.

Twenty minutes later, when it was finally his turn to be served, he placed the package on the counter and handed the clerk the note written by the *stranger of no words.* The clerk read it, sucked his teeth in irritation, picked up the package, and disappeared into a back room.

The fisherman stood, nervously wondering what had happened. It was his first time in the post office, and he felt very much out of place. Below the din of car horns and bicycle bells, below the distant throbbing of reggae music, he could hear Cara calling him, the soft murmur of her waves beckoning him home. Were it not for the importance of his mission, he would have turned around and left.

Just as the fisherman was contemplating how to question the surly-looking guard as to what was going on, the clerk came out with the package neatly wrapped in brown paper and tied with string. Pasting on the handwritten address from the bottom of the note, the clerk weighed the package, plastered the surface with brightly colored stamps, dropped it in the overseas mail, and rang up the register.

*   *   *

Solomon knew the package was in motion. He felt it. Like a sailing inside, the lifting of a weight. The release of what could not be contained. It was the kind of sensation he used to experience when addressing a crowd or launching his latest book. Remembering the pleasure he used to derive from knowing his words were reaching out into the world, Solomon was struck by the revelation of how aiming to reach one solitary heart could be so important to him, so exciting, so vital to his well-being.

He tilted his head and looked up at the blazing sun. Showered by its rays, he was intoxicated by daylight. After months of darkness he had thought the sunlight would dazzle him blind, but instead it seemed as though his body were made of it, as if he and the sun were merging back together. Sunbeams embraced his naked torso, and he laughed at the tickle of their touch. "I'm alive!"

Stretching his long, brown, muscular arms above his head, Solomon reached to touch the scorching yellow glow. Hot sweat ran down his fingers, down the back of his hands, trickled onto his broad shoulders, slithered down his solid chest, caressed his smooth taut stomach, slid down his thighs, and seeped into the warm sand. The sensation was delicious. For the first time since his seclusion, he allowed his mind to recall the sweet sensations of his yesterdays . . .

the euphoric scent of a body not his own . . . soft supple contours not his own . . . a voice not his own . . . stirring him . . . crying out . . . moaning his name . . .

"Solomon." He called himself into remembrance. Yes, it was time. Time for him to reach across the ocean and gather unto his self the pieces of his self he had left behind.

Chapter 2

✦

OLU DID NOT SHARE most Ghanaians' fascination with England. If it wasn't for Ashia, he'd be out of there—and home to Ghana—on the next available flight. He stepped off the bus, turned up his collar against the cold November drizzle, and strode down the dreary section of London's Shepherd's Bush Road.

He had learned to keep his eyes small and unfocused, blurring the people's somber faces, the dark sooty buildings, and the cloudless colorless sky. Why anyone would willingly trade the vibrant beauty of a West African sky for this dull gray coldness was beyond him. Of course, if you came to get a degree and then return home, like Ashia, then there was some point. Although certainly Ashia's college work was elementary compared with what he had to study to get the same degree from Legon University in Ghana. But having a foreign degree had status; so from that aspect, Ashia's endeavors were worthwhile. He was proud of her, and proud of the way he had coached her into this scholarship. A village girl with a dream.

Olu ran down the steps into the London Underground to ride the two stops home. He never used the escalators, neither up nor down. He was six feet tall and twenty-five years old. He wasn't vain, but he liked the way his body felt: firm and in control. As far as Olu was concerned, health clubs were too Western and too expensive, so he exerted enough energy in his daily life—like pounding up and down the stairs, racing the escalators—to keep his legs empowered and his lungs strong. Water was his favorite drink, and like many Ghanaian men, sugar was not big on his menu—a combination which helped keep his skin flawless.

The smoothness of Olu's face gave it that open quality that

women trust. At college he had never been Mr. Dangerous, that devastatingly good-looking guy who infatuated women. He had always been the "nice guy." The one women talked to, the faithful friend who assisted them with their studies, listened to their woes, and helped them get over Mr. Dangerous. Once healed of their heartache, the women would turn all their attention to Olu, the "nice guy." Suddenly aware of his manhood, they would wonder why he had never made a pass at them, never tried to kiss them. Thinking he was too shy or too honorable, they would make the first move. And the second. And the third. Until finally he would succumb to their wishes.

That's how it had always worked for him—slow, easy, effortless. The only woman he ever had to work hard to get was Ashia. And, even now, he could not be sure that she was completely his.

Olu rounded the corner into the empty Underground tunnel. A lone busker sang, desperately twanging his guitar, vigorously shaking his head, as if some terrible memory clung to the roots of his wet stringy brown hair. Finally reaching the entrance of the platform, Olu ran up the stairs and headed for the farthest bench to get away from the noise.

The half-empty tube train roared toward the platform. To finish work at 6 A.M., before the rush-hour crowd came spilling out like frenzied mice, was about the only thing Olu liked about his job at VVMC; other than that there wasn't much good he could say about cleaning vending machines. He looked up at the clock as the train came to a standstill at 7:13 A.M. If he hadn't had to pick up a package for Ashia from her old apartment, he would be home by now.

The doors slid open, and Olu stepped in and sat down next to a fellow Ghanaian. He could spot them immediately. He liked to sit by his fellow countrymen because whether or not a conversation started, there was usually a look exchanged that said, *How goes it my friend? I know what you are going through.* The camaraderie of that unspoken exchange comforted his homesickness in London's gray and barren land.

Olu looked down at the feet of the Ghanaian woman he sat beside. Her thick black socks poked awkwardly through her open-toe leather sandals. The hem of her traditional, brightly printed, ankle-length skirt was soggy, darkened with rain. Glancing up her body, he noted how she had squeezed an oversized sweater underneath her matching thin cotton top, creating an odd bulkiness. Yards of matching cotton fabric were piled high on her head and tied with abandon. Long fake-gold earrings dangled down her neck, dancing with the movement of the train. Her clothes were bright, but her eyes and face were downcast and weary. A cold, crushed, beaten-down look emanated from her eyes. Olu looked away. It pained him to see his women like this. He wanted to claim her back from England, transport her onto rich African soil. He felt a sudden urge to tell her to go home. He imagined her as she was supposed to be, free from the worries of the West, sashaying down a hot dusty road in Ghana, her hips swaying, her shoulders bare and glistening in the sun.

The train came to an abrupt stop; the woman stood up, gathered her shopping bags, and shuffled off the train. As the train pulled away, she turned and smiled sadly at Olu through the glass. Waving good-bye, he vowed once more that as soon as Ashia graduated, he would take her home to Ghana before the cold could infiltrate her soul or eclipse the sunshine from her eyes.

That was the plight of many Ghanaians. Stuck in mediocre jobs, working year after year, laboring in positions far below their education *(as he did)*, being underpaid *(as he was)*, slaving in vain for that elusive financial windfall. And at the end of their quest, instead of returning home rich as they had envisioned, many would die in a cold foreign land, with the sunshine knocked from their eyes. If Ashia and he stayed on in England, Olu feared that would be their fate, so he was determined that they return home as soon as Ashia got her degree.

That is, of course, if Ashia would come with him.

Olu pulled the package out of his damp raincoat and studied the colorful Caribbean stamps. He guessed it must be from Jezz since she was the only one who wrote to Ashia from over there—although Jezz had Ashia's new address, and this had been sent to her old one. Luckily, Ashia's former landlady had been kind enough to call and let her know that a package with her name on it had been sitting on the hall table. Olu shook it close to his ear, but the sound gave him no clue as to the contents. Placing the bundle on his lap, he noticed for the first time that it was addressed to "Ashia Wilberforce," a title that Jezz never used in reference to Ashia. A bitter teaspoonful of nervousness rose in Olu's gut. Drumming his fingers on the crumpled wrapper, he tried to tap down the acrid discords as they clamored out of his stomach, crept up his veins, and crawled into his heart.

Stepping off the elevator, Olu passed the door of his small bed-sitter and headed straight for Ashia's one-bedroom flat at the other end of the corridor. Keeping his own place was a complete waste of money, since he spent all his free hours at Ashia's, but some misguided sense of loyalty and her decency made her insist on living without him until everything was legally settled. He suspected it was all part of her guilt. He knew that, even though she denied it, Ashia still feared she had let *Selfish* (as Olu frequently called him) down, maybe even caused him to kill himself. Olu knew it was Ashia's goodness that made her think so. It was, of course, not Ashia, but *Selfish* who was the guilty party.

Despite the fact that she was twenty-three, there was something childlike and innocent about the purity with which Ashia made her decisions. To her, living together without being married would be a sin, and to force her into doing what she considered sinful would be to break her spirit. And it was Ashia's spirit that Olu loved most of all.

Olu opened the door with his key. The best part about entering Ashia's apartment was the smells. First there was the constant aroma of cooking. Ashia loved the steadiness of a low oven, so she baked everything for hours, causing the aromas to ooze out slowly and linger long. Soft plantain bread and roasted peanuts. Cassava leaf stew in red palm oil. Rosemary chicken smothered in dried shrimp pepper. Yellow pound cake with lemon butter icing. Then there was the powdered fragrance of Amankwa, the cleanest little infant in the universe. That munchy-baby-toe-sucking clean that only scrubbed little children can produce. Then, of course, there was Ashia herself . . .

Olu inhaled deep, trying to hold in the intoxicating scent of her silky dark skin oiled with sandalwood, cedarwood, lavender, and a touch of patchouli. Ahh . . . He let out a breath and inhaled her soft cocoa-butter hands, the coconut oil of her long black braids, and ahh . . . mmmmm . . . her full, plump, succulent, nibble-them-up, mint-tingle lips.

He placed the package on the little telephone table in the entranceway and removed his wet raincoat. Before Olu could hang his coat on the hook behind the front door, Amankwa came crawling toward him at full speed, crashing into his long legs like a fist into a punching bag. Olu swooped the little boy high into the air, making him squeal with excitement. Ashia shouted from the living room, "Careful, don't play rough." No one, not even Ashia, knew why she bothered to say it. Olu never heeded her caution; in fact, despite her warnings, "rough" was the very reason Ashia was so grateful to have Olu around Amankwa. Someone to throw him in the air and treat him as a father treats a son.

Olu entered the living room still tossing and catching Amankwa. Confined in the cramped dining area, Ashia continued working, without looking up. She liked to pretend that she wasn't excited to hear Olu come through the door. Feigned indifference was an act that disappointment had taught her. Demonstrative love had turned out to be such a painful open road that she had learned to keep her love hidden. Olu understood the reserve of Ashia's affection. He knew that he was paying for another man's behavior.

Ashia sat writing at the dining table piled high with books and papers. Placing Amankwa on the floor by the sofa, Olu walked over and kissed the top of her bent head. Mmmmm . . . there it was . . . that hint of coconut. He nuzzled his face in her hair. Oh, to just squeeze his hands around her tiny waist, lift her out of the chair, and carry her off to the bedroom. He inhaled again . . . and moaned softly. Ashia shivered as the warm breath from his nostrils spread across her scalp and rippled through her body.

"Don't disturb me, Olu, I've got exams tomorrow," she said, pulling away from him, but Olu could tell by the soft yield of her body that the move was not easy. He fought the urge to distract her and left her alone, appeasing himself with the thought that the quicker she graduated, the quicker they could go home.

Drawn by the smells, he wandered into the kitchenette and eased open the oven door. Heat steamed out, misting his face into tiny beads of sweat as he peeked in pots of oxtail stew and corned beef hash. "Can we eat? I'm starving."

"I just want to finish taking notes on this article, then I'll make us some breakfast. I've already baked some egg and mushroom pie; it's on top of the stove. If you want, you go ahead."

Olu closed the oven door. The commune of eating together was one of the rituals Ashia delighted in, and he knew she wanted him to wait for her. "It's okay, I'll wait. Will the TV disturb you?" he asked, passing back into the living room and making himself comfortable on the couch.

"No, just don't talk to me."

Olu flicked the remote control, keeping the sound on the television low. Amankwa pulled himself up and played with the coasters on the coffee table, lost in his own little world. Like his mother, he was resourceful. That was one of the many things Olu loved about them: their ability to be content with very little.

Olu looked over at Ashia. Busy as she was, going to school during the week, braiding customers' hair on weekends in order to supplement her funds, she still found time to raise her son, keep her house clean, cook for all of them, and keep him company. Unlike many of the Westernized African women, she did all this without even uttering a word of complaint. No, Ashia's closed heart was not his doing, but if assuming the debt would bring her closer to him, then he was glad to pay the price.

Chapter 3

✦

SOLOMON WAS AMAZED at how many beautiful flowers he had managed to find growing in the cracks of the rocks and on the trees and bushes sprinkled behind the lighthouse. Picking them in the dark to avoid being spotted by people on their way to the ferry, he had not really seen how vibrant the colors, how detailed the petals. Now that he could see them clearly, as he knelt in the sand entwining the flowers around the fisherman's boat, he marveled at the artistry of God. Elucidated by the light of the rising sun, each bloom belied the simple description one would have given on first glance. Like the blossom he was holding, what had appeared to be a plain pink petal was in fact a cacophony of crimson, canary, lilac, and white, with a delicate pink veil drawn across the surface.

Like life itself, Solomon mused as he scattered some of the flowers on the inside of the boat. *The truth is always right there in front of you, all the colors you should see. But in stormy times things appear clouded. You must look toward the light. For it is only when the sun shines through the rain that you see the rainbow.*

He had thought he had found the ideal way to live: a little rain, colored by some sunshine. It suited him—he loved them both. But in mixing them together, he had not been prepared for the turbulent weather his lifestyle created. It was only now that he had stepped out of the darkness into the light that he was beginning to see how they could salvage a rainbow out of it. If only the sun and the rain were willing.

Solomon stepped back and inspected the boat. It looked, as he had hoped, like a basket of flowers. *Will she come? What shall I have him tell her? Shall I send a note? . . .* Solomon debated . . .

He had a few hours to think it over and find his answer.

* * *

Weary from rowing, the fisherman let the tide drift him ashore. Gentle raindrops danced on the surface of the water, almost lulling him to sleep. Just before reaching Cape Corcos Island, he splashed seawater on his face to refresh himself. Surveying his surroundings, he focused on an isolated Spanish-style adobe house a few hundred yards from the shore. On the sea side of the house was a sprawling outdoor dining room set, on a magnificent Italian tile floor that stretched out into the expanse of surrounding sand.

The *stranger of no words* had been talking to the fisherman for the past few weeks, and everything was exactly as the stranger had described: the curve of the shoreline in front of the adobe, the outdoor dining room, the flagpole adorned with multicolored wind chimes, the clothesline anchored in the sand—everything. The fisherman had no doubt that he had come to the right place.

Seeing a figure moving in the distance behind the clothesline at the side of the house, the fisherman stood up in his boat. Masked by a thin white sheet billowing in the rainy breeze, the moving figure flashed in and out of his view—like a whisper he could hear but not understand. Before too long he realized it was a woman, head thrown back, arms outstretched, spinning naked in the rain. Airy as a vision, she spun round and round and round. As he watched, he wondered if it was her, the one for whom the stranger had intertwined his boat with flowers, the woman he had been sent to fetch.

Not wanting to embarrass her by interrupting, the fisherman decided to lie down in his boat and wait for her to finish before making his presence known. Leaning his head against the side, he closed his eyes. The salt-sea breeze, the smell of the moist sand, the scent of the flowers wafted past and heavenly, gently, carried him away.

Chapter 4

✦

*A*SHIA WASN'T WATCHING the television or consciously listening to the sound when they made the announcement. Yet the news was so stunning, it hit her like a transfusion running through her veins.

"Meanwhile, in the Caribbean, on the island of Saint Germaine, a man living in a cave has been identified as Mr. Solomon Wilberforce."

Before Ashia had a chance to assimilate the information, her body was already in motion. She rose from her seat at the dining table and walked toward the static rays of the television. She needed to be right there, within reach of the screen, right where the voice was coming from, the voice that had uttered that name: *Solomon Wilberforce.*

"A local businessman from the neighboring island of Cape Corcos recognized Mr. Wilberforce and snapped this photograph of him, which he turned in to the authorities earlier this week. A former resident of Cape Corcos Island, Mr. Solomon Wilberforce was reported missing five months ago when he went for a jog on a Cape Corcos beach and never returned."

Ashia's heart hammered hard against her breast, pulsated through her stomach, reverberated down her legs, and quivered in her feet. She felt as if she were swooning and flying at the same time, yet everything was at a complete standstill. Everything except her racing heart and the constant movement of the news anchor's ruby red lips. Red jellyfish lips blowing word bubbles that floated out of the television and popped against her brain. In response to the attack of all those bursting Anglo words, Ashia's brain reverted to its own language. Suddenly English was all too foreign, unscramblably confusing. Was Olu listening? Was he grasping it? Could he explain it to her?

She turned and saw Olu perched catlike on the edge of the sofa. He was watching her watch the television—studying her every move. The news that Solomon was alive made her raw, nakedly herself, charged with emotions that could not be contained. Everything she was, everything she felt, was unprotected and easy to read. Hoping to escape Olu's probing eyes, she turned back around and focused on the screen.

A blurred photograph of a black man filled the frame. He was standing in the mouth of a cave, naked except for a piece of African fabric wrapped around his waist and a charm and locket on a leather string knotted around his neck. Ashia studied the picture as the voice continued.

"Mr. Wilberforce is preventing the authorities from dynamiting the area. His refusal to evacuate the cave is obstructing government construction of a bridge to link Saint Germaine with the mainland."

"My gosh! Unbelievable! How do you think—"

"Shhhh!"

Ashia cut Olu off more harshly than she had intended. Her eyes were still riveted to the ruby lips, and she had to concentrate very hard to grasp what the news anchor was saying.

"Mr. Wilberforce, who wrote under the pseudonym Beento Blackbird, is the author of the widely acclaimed bestselling novels The Adventures of Beento Blackbird. *Beento Blackbird books, which were originally targeted at children, garnered international acclaim when the books also became bestsellers in the adult market, winning the author a Pulitzer Prize in fiction—which he declined to accept, preferring to preserve his anonymity. It was not until his disappearance late last year that the author's identity was made known. Until this recent sighting, Mr. Wilberforce was missing, presumed dead."*

The screen divided into facial close-ups of the past and present Mr. Wilberforce. Amankwa pointed at the latter picture with the crown of dreadlocks sticking up in the air and laughed.

"Stop it, Amankwa!" Ashia snapped. Amankwa was so taken aback by the unfamiliar harshness of his mother's voice that he crinkled up his little face and cried.

"Hey there, little man," Olu comforted, tickling him under the arms, "you want to go to the playground and play swinging space-ships?"

"Good idea," Ashia encouraged, the edginess still apparent in her voice.

"Great, let's all go," Olu enthused, wrapping his arm across her shoulders, causing them to tighten. "Relax yourself, everything's going to be fine," he said, gripping her protectively with more firm assurance than he felt.

Ashia was tense. She wanted to shrug Olu's arm off her shoulder. It was all weight and no comfort. She could feel the misalignment of his being: he was nervous about their future, and his nervous affection heightened her tension.

"I'm telling you, I don't think it's him," Olu continued. "And even if it's him, so what? Obviously, he likes disappearing—so let him stay lost! But I'm telling you, I don't think it's Solomon."

"It's him," Ashia replied with a certainty that Olu did not dare contradict. She disentangled herself from his comfortless arm and sat down on the couch, her two feet planted firmly on the floor, her back straight as a bamboo shoot.

Despite her rigid posture, Ashia could feel herself slipping away. She was trying not to, but she could feel the slip. Like an untied barge following the current of the river from which it came, she was drifting away, and there was nothing she could do. She could feel Olu pulling at her, trying to draw her back, but she couldn't fight the current. She had prayed for news, good or bad, to sweep away the shadow of uncertainty over her life. She had hoped that the news would be the final link to join her and Olu together. Instead, here she was, drifting away from him, treating him as if he were an irritant, a fly to be swatted away. She knew he wanted her to speak, to assure him that she was with him, that even if Solomon was alive, she wouldn't leave London and go to him. She wanted to speak but didn't know what to say.

Just as she conjured up the perfect words to express herself, the waters of her heart welled up, forcing her to hold still as the overflow pivoted precariously in her throat. Tugging on her soul, she held back what she was about to utter, realizing that if she opened her mouth to let out the words, a dam of tears would flood out in their place.

"Let's go to the playground; we'll talk about all this while Amankwa runs around," Olu suggested again, muting the sound of the television. Ashia didn't answer; she didn't even look in his direction. She sat staring at the silent screen, unblinking, motionless as a garden statue. Olu scooped Amankwa onto his shoulders. "Ashia, come on, it's stopped raining. You don't have to be at college till two; let's take a nice walk. It will clear your head, and we can talk this over."

Ashia had turned to stone. Whatever garden she was gracing, Olu knew it wasn't his. Despite the very best of his nature that he had steadfastly planted around her, she had gone. With Amankwa riding high on his shoulders, he strode out, slamming the front door behind him. A thin bright-red twinge of temper lingered in the living room, right above the spot where he had stood.

Ashia clicked off the television, tossing the remote onto the coffee table. She reflected on all her countless days of guilt, of waiting, of heartache. And all this time he was alive! Solomon Eustace Wilberforce was alive!

She tried to whip up anger toward him, but it wouldn't come. Tears, but they wouldn't fall. Laughter . . . perhaps; bitter, bitter laughter—burning as anger, wordless as tears—welling in her heart.

Absentmindedly she turned her wedding band round and round on her finger. *"Till death do us part,"* she remembered. And down it poured: scorching hot laughter, silent and lethal.

Chapter 5

✦

*I*T WAS A WINTER-BRIGHT New York morning. Gazing out her window at the chilly sunlight, Sam stood next to the stove so she could turn the kettle off as soon as the water boiled. She didn't want it to whistle, for fear it would wake Lawrence. She had a hunch that if he woke before she dressed, he would feel obliged to attempt to make love to her. She knew there was a part of him that still believed they should get married, and from what he said last night, he was between girlfriends again.

Sam couldn't remember all the reasons why she had broken up with Lawrence, but one of them was definitely their lack of physical chemistry—strange, how the very thing that used to put her off him was now the very reason she could allow him back into her life. Lawrence was good male company. She could take him into any crowd and know they would both have a good time without *owing* each other anything. When she needed him to mingle, he mingled; when she needed him to help her out of a boring conversation, he was right there, telling an amusing anecdote or leading her away to meet someone more interesting on the other side of the room. He was kind, not overly possessive, financially stable, and clever. In fact, as her girlfriends kept remarking, he was excellent husband material. For Sam, there were only three drawbacks: she wasn't attracted to him, she wasn't in love with him, and she wasn't looking for a husband.

"Everybody's looking for a husband," her best friend, Cheri, insisted. "If you're older than thirty and alone, you're looking for a husband!"

"You're in denial, Sam," Marsha added. "Thirty-five is getting up there. You need to wake up and smell the coffee."

"Leave her alone," Eula piped in. "It's 'cause she's in love with what's-his-name. You know, that mysterious client of hers—no one knows his real name. That Beento Blackbird guy. She'd marry him in a minute! That's why no one else ever seems good enough, 'cause she compares everyone with him."

"Who?" Charlaine asked enthusiastically. "Sam's got a man?"

"No," Cheri asserted emphatically. "Having a crush on a client who's only around a couple of times a year does not qualify as having a man!"

That's why the moment Sam got home from her weekly night out with the girls, she had called up Lawrence and invited him to the party the following Sunday. Had she gone unaccompanied, the girls would have spent the evening trying to fix her up with some eligible bachelor, and she wasn't in the mood to go through the motions of being politely responsive, giving only her answering service number to ensure that she could not be reached. It was much more relaxing to appease her girlfriends, and keep other men at bay, by walking in with Lawrence on her arm. Besides, she hadn't seen Lawrence for a couple of months, and they were due one of their "let's stay friends" outings.

Sam heard the whistle about to blow and snatched the kettle off the fire. *Strange, though,* she thought, as she poured boiling water into a small teapot, *how I never miss having a man in my bed, until there's a man in my bed.*

To Sam, there was no lonelier feeling in the world than waking up beside a man she knew in her heart was not for her. When she slept alone, which was nearly every night, she felt fine. She slept soundly and woke up happy and full of purpose. It was only on those rare occasions when she permitted a man to stay over that she would wake up feeling the acute lack of significant male companionship.

She had tried one time to convince herself to get married. She had even let him move in with her. *Bob. Bob Grandville.* She could still remember the night she knew it was not going to work. They had come back from a great day, reading poetry and playing Frisbee in Central Park. One of those laughter-filled afternoons that reminded her of her childhood Sundays, playing with cousins in her granny's backyard. She was in the den, drawing the shades, when Bob came up behind her and stroked her hair. Twenty-four hours earlier the same motion had aroused her so recklessly, her impassioned response had started them on a sexual escapade that lasted several hours. "Wow!" he had exclaimed when it was over, throwing his arms above his head on the living room carpet. "Wow! That was . . ." He grinned at her, lost for words. "That was incredible!"

So here he was again, fingers in her hair, stroking it, waiting for her to purr. As if she were a cat. Stroke, stroke, stroke. It irritated her. "Worked yesterday," he complained as he followed her into the bathroom, sulking in the doorway as she took a pee.

She tried everything. She couldn't bear to belittle the spontaneous fervor of the day before by mimicking a repeat performance, so she tried everything to get his mind on something else. "I'm not in the mood," he kept saying as she suggested watching a movie, playing cards, listening to music, or simply talking to each other.

Finally, around midnight, looking at his hostile body turned away from her on the bed, she moved across the sheets and curled herself against his back. He turned around and kissed her. She apologized. She wasn't quite sure for what, but it was her way of expressing that she wanted things to be good between them. "You're forgiven," he said, in his smooth addictive voice. And then he took her by the wrist and led her into the living room, to the exact same patch of carpet he had lain on the night before. He even went back into the bedroom to fetch the same lingerie she had worn, and directed her to put it on. He stood over her with his arms folded, waiting for her to obey him. *It's dirty*, she thought, wanting to refuse him; but something in his assertive manner choked her. When she had put on the skimpy garment, he lay down, sat her on top of him, closed his eyes, and waited for her to rock his world. She did.

Wedding's off, she thought as she left him satiated and asleep on the living room floor—and nothing, absolutely nothing, could make her change her mind.

No more sleepovers, Sam promised herself as she pinned her long slick black hair up into a smooth chignon. Having a man in the house made her reflect too much on the male species. That's how she got herself into bad relationships in the first place, especially in her twenties—by reflecting on men too much and sacrificing too much to make them happy. She applied her mascara and tried to push the memory of Bob out of her head. She was annoyed with herself for having conjured it up again: the image of herself sitting on top of him in her dirty see-through underwear—her teeth gritted, her mind screaming—praying he would hurry up and climax. And the strange thing was, even though he opened his eyes and looked right at her, he hadn't even noticed the tears that were streaming down her face. "Good job," he had said and gone to sleep. It made her furious—furious and ashamed.

"I'm off." Sam placed her hand affectionately on Lawrence's forehead.

"What's the time?"

"Eight-fifteen."

"I'll be leaving soon myself. Got a client at noon. Just close the door, right?"

"Yeah, make sure the lock's pushed in."

"Okay, will do."

Sam picked up her briefcase and walked out. Somewhere between taking her shower and buttoning up the jacket on her tailored pink-and-gray suit, she had wondered whether she was expecting too much out of life, out of people. Thinking of Bob and his utter selfishness highlighted Lawrence's good qualities. She had gone into the bedroom to wake Lawrence up, wondering for the umpteenth time what would be so bad about having him as a life partner. He had just reminded her. *Absolutely no chemistry, no music whatsoever.*

Sam had trained herself to think of New York City traffic not as an inconvenience but rather as an opportunity to spend time planning and projecting what she would like to accomplish that day. As one of the most successful agents in the literary department of International Artists Agency, or IAA as it was commonly known, she had a salary such that she had managed to buy herself a comfortable apartment in a secure building with its own restaurant on Forty-eighth Street, between Third and Lexington Avenues. Walking through the flower-filled courtyard, heading out to flag down a taxi, she felt thankful, as she often did, that no matter whatever else was going on in her life, her job remained a constant source of gratification.

Sam had worked hard to get where she was. As founder and editor of *Mental Hors D'Oeuvres*, a short story college-campus magazine she began in Atlanta two years before her graduation, she caught the attention of Andréa Du Pois, one of New York's leading literary agents. Impressed by the quality of writers Sam managed to discover for the magazine, Andréa offered Sam a standing invitation to come work for her. Sam graduated, moved to New York, and joined Andréa within a week of her arrival. She had been at the agency ever since, working her way up from receptionist to personal assistant to junior agent to agent extraordinaire.

I'll close the Brooks deal by lunchtime, Sam determined in her mind as she stepped out of the taxi onto the pavement in her gray stiletto heels. *I know Jean will accept my offer.* Jerry, the doorman, greeted her with his flirtatious wink. In her more militant days, when she was rebelling against her Miss Teen Maryland beauty-pageant stigma, Sam would have found his wink derogatory, along with the *Hey pretty mamas, What's your names,* and *Yo baby, come over heres* that perpetually trailed her as she walked. But time had mellowed her, and she no longer took such things to heart, either as validation of her looks, as she had done in her school days, or as a slight on her intellect, as she had done at college.

"Good morning, Jerry," she said, greeting him in response to his wink as he opened the door for her.

"It is now," Jerry replied covertly. Sam smiled graciously and headed toward the elevator.

The second she walked into the reception area of IAA, her spine seemed to lengthen and her muscles seemed to move in a more fluid powerful way. It wasn't something she did on purpose; it happened automatically whenever she prepared to immerse herself in her work. Discovering, encouraging, shaping, and selling literary talent gave her a charge that made her grow in strength and stature. Whenever she discovered writers who were good, ones that she felt could be marketed, she passed them on to one of the junior agents. But on the rare occasions that she discovered writers with talent— true, raw, God-given talent—she kept and represented them herself. Like Gail Alexander, the promising new writer for whom she had recently managed to close a phenomenal first-book deal.

"Did Gail Alexander's package arrive?" Sam asked Lisa, the receptionist, as she passed by her station.

Clutching the revised draft of Gail's manuscript, Sam shut her office door and got to work. She had barely finished her first phone call when Debra, her assistant, opened the door and poked her head into the room.

"Can I come in?" Debra asked as she stepped gingerly into the office.

"What is it, Debra?" Sam asked, hoping to get her to come quickly to the point.

"I wasn't sure if you'd seen this," Debra replied, tentatively edging up to the desk.

"Victor's terrible review?" Sam asked nonchalantly, noticing the newspaper Debra was clutching in her hand. "Yes, I have. They're wrong. Just keep a copy in the files." Dismissing the subject, Sam went back to making notes on the deal she had just been negotiating.

"Not Victor's review," Debra said quietly, slipping the paper onto Sam's desk. "This."

Sam gave the paper a sideways glance. "What?" she asked, getting a little irritated.

"They've found Solomon. He's alive!"

Sam got up slowly and walked over to the window. She didn't know why, but she needed to look out. Maybe because looking out at Manhattan from sixteen stories high made her feel on top of things. Or maybe she looked out so Debra wouldn't be able to see her face and read the thoughts running through her mind. Or maybe she just needed to look out because she was afraid of what she would find if she looked inward.

"Thank you, Debra." Sam's voice was polite but dismissive.

Debra took the cue. "I've left the paper on the desk," she said, closing the door behind her.

Sam kept on looking out the window. *He's alive!* The words slid into her warm as her granny's tongue on her wounded knee or as her daddy's hot-chocolate special on a cold January morning. *He's alive!* Of course he was. She always knew it. She knew it because she had never felt him leave. And she knew that if Solomon were dead, she would have felt him slipping forever out of her universe.

Chapter 6

✧

*M*IRIAM BELIEVED that if you had never seen the beauty of a Caribbean sunset, you had never seen God at his best. Some argued that since she had never set foot outside the Caribbean (not even off Cape Corcos Island, where she was born), she was not qualified to make such a statement. "How you know other skies not more beautiful?" they would ask. "Or a mountain in Kenya? A forest in Brazil? A waterfall cascading down a rock in China?"

"Look up," she would reply. "Look!" She would tilt her head up to the crimson sky, her heart bursting through her eyes. "See," she would say, spreading her arms wide. "The crowning of God's creation, right above our heads. Me no know how you can doubt it!"

In her forty-seven years on earth, there were only three things in life Miriam truly believed in: birthing babies, that the Caribbean sky was the most beautiful sight in all the world, and Solomon.

Exhilarated from dancing in the raindrops, Miriam spun to an abrupt stop and turned toward the insidious hiss in the sand. When she saw the police car speeding toward her, her stomach took a leap and wouldn't come back down. It fluttered around her mouth like a frightened bird teetering over the ocean searching for a place to land. It was not so much the worry of being caught outside naked in the rain that alarmed her, but rather the memory of the last time a police car had come dust-flying across the sand in her direction. That last occasion precipitated such devastating repercussions on her life that she was still trying to sweep away the ruins from her mind.

Sergeant Vincent, a young dark-chocolate man of few words,

jerked the vehicle to an abrupt halt, spraying sand from the spinning wheels like water from a garden sprinkler. It was an unnecessarily dramatic entrance, but to Sergeant Vincent, drama was what police work was all about. Captain Morrow, an imposing military officer in his midthirties, stepped out of the passenger side and moved cautiously toward the wooden stablelike doors at the side of the adobe, through which Miriam had disappeared.

Peeking out at the captain through a slat in her bedroom door, Miriam could tell by his measured footsteps and concerned expression that he was anxious not to startle her. She realized he had probably heard the much-believed rumor that, since Solomon's disappearance, she had gone mad.

The madness theory began when a few passersby reported that they had seen her dancing naked in the rain. If they had asked her, she would have assured them that she was not mad at all, that she did it because feeling the raindrops caress her naked body was simply the next best thing to having Solomon touch her. Rain was the blood of their covenant. It was the signal they had prayed for from God, to let them know that it was right for them to join together and become one. When she felt Solomon's absence most, she comforted herself by letting it wash over her. Rain. She needed it. That's what she would have told them if they had asked her, but nobody asked.

Miriam threw on a long flowered chiffon dress and then opened wide the big wooden doors. With a congenial smile, she welcomed Captain Morrow to her home, offering him her hand. It was a gesture so archaically normal, she could tell by his reaction that it only served to confirm his suspicions of her instability.

The Islanders rarely saw Miriam like this, at home, in her own surroundings. Her beautiful, thick, curly jet-black hair, usually pinned up or wrapped in a scarf, cascaded freely down her shoulders. In her thin pastel dress, free of the many layers of flowing white robes that she wore when on her midwife rounds and that usually hid all her shapely curves, she looked less like a saint and more like a seductive angel.

Captain Morrow stared at her as if transfixed. Staring back at him calmly, she used her left toes to brush the sand off her right foot while she waited for him to pluck himself out of the pull of her smile and tell her why he had come.

Speeding back along the sand in the police car, nobody noticed the fisherman asleep in his flower-covered boat, not even Miriam, who usually noticed any unfamiliar sights near her adobe. She was too busy breathing in the information to focus on her surroundings. Solomon was alive! The news filled her like air in a balloon. For the first time since his disappearance, she grew spacious again, weightless, able to ascend. Joy. God-thanking joy was her only emotion. The sensation made her laugh. Captain Morrow turned around at the sound of her laughter and was drawn back into her smile.

"You happy," he said. "That a good reaction. Many women get mad when they man disappear and found again."

"He alive!" Miriam exclaimed. "I give thanks."

Miriam tried to keep out of her mind the fact that they were going to put her in a helicopter. She wanted to bask in her happiness as long as possible, and the thought of flying terrified her. She had only agreed to fly because Captain Morrow had assured her that speed was of the utmost importance, forewarning her that in the time it would take to sail across to the neighboring island of Saint Germaine, things could get out of hand. Solomon was inside the cave. Until they got him out, the cave could not be blasted, and the bridge could not be built. Realizing that his refusal to move was also protecting the wildlife, conservationists were marching up and down, chanting antigovernment slogans in Solomon's support. The ferrymen who had feared that a bridge to the mainland would render them redundant cheered on Solomon from their boats. Local nationalists vehemently opposed to being linked with Saint Germaine held up placards and shouted for Solomon to stay where he was. Everyone was in support of him except the government, which had dispatched armed military forces to carry out the bombing of the cave, regardless of the fact that Solomon was inside. Once Solomon had been identified as the missing famous author, Captain Morrow had convinced the military that if anyone could talk Solomon into coming out of the cave peacefully, it would be Miriam.

Miriam looked out the car window at the rooftop balcony of Cape Corcos Airport looming in the distance. Her mind traveled back two years to the last time she had stood up there, watching, excited, waiting for Solomon's arrival. That was when things were still in rhythm. Before everything had tilted precariously.

Two years to the day, and she remembered that night as though it were yesterday . . .

Chapter 7

✦

*W*ILL SHE REMEMBER? Solomon wondered as he added more paper to the fire. He watched his penmanship curl into spitting red flames, rise, and disappear smoke-white into the walls of the cave. Months of writing, years of his life, going up in flames.

When he had first entered the cave, the happiness of their life together had been difficult to recall. He had been amazed at the ugly creatures he had found as he overturned the stones along the pathway of his mind. Sequestered in the darkness, timeworn from playing events over and over again, Solomon let his thoughts trudge through the jungle of his past, like a hefty elephant stripping down the foliage of better days, leaving him a wasteland of regrets.

But now, having grieved, written, read, prayed, waited, and rejoiced, Solomon let vivid images of the joy they had shared ripple refreshingly through his mind. . . . His hand in hers, struggling up the rocks, pushing against the flow as they climbed up a waterfall. "Don't climb beyond that rock what look like a dagger," the guide had warned. Paying him no mind, they had climbed way beyond it, high up, where tourists fear to tread. Their feet slipping, they had caught each other, pulling and pushing all the way to the top. "This is it!" she had exclaimed. "Paradise!" She lay her body on the flatness of a big rock, defying the water to carry her away. The water took on the challenge, and she screamed as she felt it dragging her across the smooth mossy surface. Solomon caught her by the ankles. She laughed. "You can't get me now," she taunted the cascading water. "My Solomon got me and never letting me go."

If she remembers those days, Solomon thought encouragingly to himself, *then there's hope.*

By his calculations, the fisherman would return in three or four hours. In an hour or two he would go sit near the mouth of the cave and look for them. He wanted to see her, coming over the horizon, floating toward him, surrounded by flowers.

Did she get into the boat? Of course she did. Stretched out on a mound of dry seaweed, sinking into semiconsciousness, Solomon tried to put out of his mind any doubts of her arriving. *There's no way she would turn down the fisherman's request. But when she arrives and finds she was tricked into coming, what then?*

She'll understand, Solomon assured himself as he drifted into sleep. *Miriam always understands.*

BOOK TWO

✦

Winter

Sea Blue Island Rhythms . . .

Chapter 1

✦

*L*EANING BACK in the police car on her way to the airport, reflecting on life before Solomon's disappearance, Miriam let her mind slip back two winters, easy as a child slipping down a slide. All she had to do was let go and there she was, on the exact same route, headed to the airport on the evening of Solomon's arrival: seeing it, smelling it, living it, all over again . . .

*   *   *

It had been one of those hot windy Corcos nights. God was blowing down mercy that swept across the island like a fan. Miriam loved nights like this one. Nights when you could lean against the wind and let it carry you. Her long soft white clothes billowed around her body like the masts of an old-fashioned sailing ship. She was sailing on the wind.

Propelled by its currents, she arrived on the outskirts of town and anchored her body against a pillar of the old courthouse to catch her breath. Many childhood remembrances skipped up and down its formidable steps. Left to crumble, the courthouse had been long since deserted, except by curious children, wandering dogs, and Miriam, who never deserted anything. Gathering her skirts into her knees, she slid down the pillar into a squat to savor the wind-directed drama of the evening. Everything visible was playing a part. Even the deep-rooted palm trees swayed as though preparing to fly. The only things not moving were the stars. Miriam looked up at the sky and sensed him—Solomon—blowing toward her. Excited, she rose, and continued walking.

*   *   *

Drawn by the wind, the musky smell of travelers whooshed past Miriam as soon as she opened the door of the small airport building. Pushing against the current, she leaned her way in through the glass door, closing it behind her.

The room was crowded. The habitually late local aircraft that shuttled inhabitants from one island to the other was, as usual, "lost in the air." "The plane will get here just as soon as it arrive," the announcer declared. Miriam wove in and out of the stranded passengers, who, understanding the implications of the announcement, dragged their suitcases and cardboard boxes in search of enough floor space to curl up and sleep. Passing the duty-free counter, Miriam stopped and bought a bag of French bonbons as a treat for Cassie. They were Cassie's favorite sweets, and the airport was the only place you could buy them. Unless it rained before morning, Miriam would be unable to make her usual delivery of bread to the hotel, so Cassie would be sent to collect it. Cassie, at only seven years old, was a very hard worker. In appreciation, Miriam liked to give the girl a treat whenever she came to the house on an errand.

There were only three levels to the airport building: the ground, the first floor, and the rooftop, where Miriam was headed. The air on the rooftop always seemed sweeter than the air down below. Miriam strolled to the retaining wall, leaned over the edge of the rail, and looked out over the island. Lights glimmered everywhere. Lanterns twinkly as earthbound stars glowed in the nearby marketplace. Yellow headlights flashed as scooters wove their way along the narrow streets. Over to the far left, spotlights beamed across sculptured gardens, illuminating opulent swimming pools in La Grandiose Bay, the richest section of the Island. To the right, flickerings of moonglow shimmered across the surface of the ocean, highlighting the white foam tips of the waves as they tossed and crashed in and out of the night black Caribbean Sea.

She looked up at the sky, thinking how amazing it would be if, just for once, right when Solomon landed, it rained. If it rained immediately, she wouldn't have to wait, wouldn't have to hide from him on the rooftop. She could run out onto the tarmac and embrace him, and he could sweep her off her feet and carry her home to bed. She looked away from the windy cloudless sky and reflected that it had never rained on the very first day of Solomon's arrival, and yet had never failed to rain on the second. It was as if God wanted to allow Solomon to rest from his journey before coming to her. The very fact that it always rained within twenty-four hours of Solomon's return was a yearly affirmation, she thought, that God and the elements approved of their union.

Thinking about Solomon, Miriam keyed up with anticipation. There were only two flights left to arrive that night, the lost local and the international flight from the United States. By the excitement of the other people waiting up on the roof, Miriam judged that they were also waiting for friends and family on the latter flight.

A small boy dressed in his Sunday best sidled up to her and tugged on her long skirt. "Me want to see," he pleaded in a plaintive voice, stretching on his tiptoes. Miriam lifted him in her arms. His face beamed as he gasped at the sight of the island. "Pretty!" he exclaimed, curling one hand around her neck, clapping the other against her cheek with his sticky fingers. Miriam wasn't sure if he meant the view or her face; either way, it pleased her. He bent his head into her softness and made his body at home against the melody in her heart. Swiveling her hips from side to side, she rocked him in rhythm to her silent song. Gripping her neck with his toffeed fingers, he shuddered in contentment.

Miriam hugged and stroked his tiny back in an attempt to soothe her longing. If she could have just one. Just one God-sent child of her own. She used to want eight; by the time she reached her midthirties, she had halved it to four; when she hit forty she decided that since many childbearing years had passed her by, she would probably have time to bear only two. On her forty-fifth birthday she had narrowed it down to one. One miracle baby. A living testament of their love. That was her deepest desire.

A light twinkled through the darkness. At first it looked like a shooting star, but soon Miriam realized that it was Solomon, up there, gliding toward her. Sensing her elation, the little boy, who had fallen asleep in the rock of her arms, woke up and followed her upward gaze. Calling out to his big brother, he pointed up at the plane. "Wook! Airpane! Airpane!" he shouted, wriggling to free himself from Miriam's arms. She lowered him and he ran off.

Group by group, people hurried down to await their arriving parties, until Miriam was the only person left on the rooftop. She was glad. Savoring the moment of Solomon's arrival was always more potent when she could witness it alone.

The aircraft landed. There was a thrill in the wind, sending a cool ripple that circled the imprint of the little boy's hot sticky fingers on the base of Miriam's neck. Licking her fingertips and touching them to the spot, she rubbed away the traces of toffee he had left behind. The sudden loss of his warm pudgy body made her feel surprisingly lonely. She became anxious that for some reason Solomon had missed his flight. With her eyes fixed on the landed aircraft, she gripped the railing, leaned forward, and waited.

A broad-shouldered six-foot-four silhouette headed across the tarmac like a panther on the prowl. She would recognize that walk anywhere. Focused. Upright. Full of power. How could any one man be so magnificent? Stopping to adjust his hand baggage, his eyes cutting through the darkness, he looked straight up in her direction. She moved backward, covering her face with her shawl to avoid his possibly spotting her.

*   *   *

Solomon shifted his bag onto the other shoulder and continued walking. He needed air in his legs, and walking across the tarmac felt good. Although a frequent flier, he never got used to the feeling of confinement. Flight attendants always did their best to make him comfortable, often allowing him to pace at times when passengers were clearly requested to remain in their seats. It wasn't as gratifying as striding across open spaces, but he appreciated their bending the rules on his behalf. But then again, Solomon was used to being allowed to do the forbidden.

Heads turned in admiration as he entered the dimly lit airport building and marched straight up to the familiar officer supervising the passport control desk.

After thirteen hours of flying, Solomon looked as fresh as a man who had just bathed and dressed. There was not a crease in his clothing, not a hint of travel-worn weariness about his being. You only had to look at him to know he was special. He was handsome, but that was not the point. His earth brown body was as smooth and sculptured as a marble statue, but that was not the point either. And yes, his full pink-brown lips could smile you out of the vilest of moods and kiss you into Heaven, but still, that was not the point. To get the point, you had to look into his eyes. They were the eyes of the gifted. Alluring. Inspiringly alive. Focused. He used them openly, unafraid. To him, everything was a miracle of creation. A nose. A cheek. A tree. A fly. He had traveled the world over, yet still maintained the innocence of a curious child. It was that childlike curiosity that invoked in others their youth. The joy within. And for that they loved him. When he held them in the brightness of his gaze, they became kaleidoscopes held up to the sun. Looking into Solomon's eyes, people saw the shattered pieces of their lives change nature. Old wounds and tragedies shifted from ugly painful scars to beautiful carvings of life fully lived. Through Solomon's eyes they saw that they were rich. Colorful. Changeable. A kaleidoscope. Solomon's eyes made them love themselves. Made them reach inside and re-ignite themselves. Inspiring. Alluring. Alive. Solomon's eyes. The eyes of the gifted. A gift.

Chapter 2

✧

CAPTAIN MORROW did not need to look up to know that Mr. Solomon Eustace Wilberforce was standing before him. It's not that the captain had any special sixth sense. It was, after all, November 21, the beginning of Solomon's winter season, and it was the only flight arriving that day from America. And then inevitably there was that scent. That excited female scent that frothed from women whenever Solomon was around, rather like champagne bottles popping their corks.

"Mr. Wilberforce, on time as usual," Captain Morrow said jovially, stamping Solomon's passport and standing up to offer him his hand.

It was common knowledge that Solomon was a major financial backer of Mr. Kawasaki, who was buying up Cape Corcos Island property at a remarkable rate. Thus, the two of them were on the military's "A" list of important persons. For that reason, Captain Morrow stood up to greet Solomon, a courtesy he usually reserved for beautiful women or heads of state.

Solomon gave him a warm handshake, smiled his good-to-see-you-brother smile, and walked on. For Solomon to befriend him would be considered a political statement, and Captain Morrow was aware that Solomon didn't involve himself in local politics. He left that to his two Island buddies, Toussaint Joseph and Mr. Martin Thomas (or Mr. Kawasaki, as he was more commonly called, because of his first financial venture—importing Kawasaki motorbikes onto the island for sale). Solomon was too busy with politics on a grand scale to get involved locally, or so he claimed. "The global black experience as an interconnected family . . . Retwining the threads that bind the black families of the world . . . Coming together as one force, one nation"—Captain Morrow had heard Solomon speak on these and other such impractical-sounding concepts at various Island functions. *But what does it all mean,* he wondered as he watched Solomon's receding back, *if you don't rub your brother's back and acknowledge an extended hand? I honored him by standing up; the least he could have done is taken a moment to exchange a few pleasantries.*

Captain Morrow chastised himself for making the mistake of thinking of Solomon as one of them. Solomon may have been born on the Island, raised on it till he was thirteen, but things like this, like his not understanding local Island etiquette, reminded the captain that Mr. Solomon Wilberforce was, indeed, an American.

*   *   *

Solomon sat in the backseat of the taxi, leaning comfortably against his black metal trunk covered with airport stickers from all over the continent of Africa. He gazed excitedly out the window; for him, even in the darkness of night, Cape Corcos had a special charm. "Careful," his mother used to warn him, "don't love it too deep. Always remember, Solomon, home not a people or a country—it the shelter within your own soul." She would stare into his eyes and try to put reins on her heart. "Don't love any one person or place too much, Solomon. Love but don't attach to anyone. Love widely. Don't let no one person confine you. Don't let this island swallow you up. Break out. Broaden your horizons. You a strong black boy; your race need you. The world need you. Break out, son, and don't never look back."

He missed her. Missed her achingly. Missed her tender broken heart that tried to teach him not to hope for neverending love, not to trust a person's words, and never to be beguiled by beauty. When she was fifteen, tempted by beauty, she had bedded with appearances—and Solomon was the result. The day she told Solomon's father that she was pregnant was the last she saw of him. Wounded and betrayed, she vowed never to love or succumb to a person or place ever again. The hour Solomon was born, she broke that vow when she looked into his eyes. This new baby stole what was left of her

fragmented heart, and there was nothing she could do about it—
nothing except warn him to make sure her history didn't repeat
itself. "Love but don't attach to anyone, Solomon. Love but don't
attach."

He missed her. It had been twenty-three years since she passed
away, yet he never went a day without missing her. Missing her was
as familiar a sensation to him as his heartbeat. It underlined everything he did. "Break out," she had said, "the world need you." So in
honor of his mother, he had covered the globe. He had tried to take
her with him in his mind, yet whenever he landed back on the Island
he knew that this was where she was, where she had always been, on
Cape Corcos Island.

Solomon realized the cabdriver was studying him through the
rearview mirror. Sensing he had been caught, the driver slipped a
tape of a live rap concert into the deck and focused on the road ahead.
Solomon rapped along with the tape. "Turn it up," he requested after a while. Only too pleased to oblige, the driver turned the music
full blast.

"Where you from, man? If ya don't mind me askin'."

"I'm Cape Corcon," Solomon replied.

Surprised, the driver turned around. "Me had you figured for an
American, you know!"

"No, I'm Cape Corcon," Solomon asserted in an American accent
and continued to rap along with the tape.

"That great, man." The driver's demeanor brightened. In a burst
of enthusiasm, he reached his arm over the top of the seat and shook
Solomon's hand. "They call me Headley."

"Solomon. Solomon Wilberforce."

Headley checked Solomon out again in his rearview mirror. "You
accent confuse I, but then I say to meself, it be real strange for a foreigner to be clued in to someone as grassroots as Leo Rap-A-Tap, and
him not even recorded. Me pirate this tape, you know, from one of
him concerts. So what you do in America? You a rapper, man? Me
can tell you real famous!"

Solomon was about to answer, but Headley continued talking.
"Me like meeting people like you. Locals what gone to the States
and come back rich. It let me know me dream possible. Soon as me
save up me money, me heading for the States meself, you know?"

Headley pressed his foot on the gas pedal, explaining to Solomon that no offence, but the quicker he dropped him off, the quicker he could pick up another passenger, the more money he could make that day, the quicker he could get to the States, the quicker he could return home rich. "Yeah, man!" he said, swerving the car abruptly to avoid a large branch that the windstorm had blown into the middle of the road. "Me was planning on going to the Rap-A-Thon tonight but, cha man, you inspire me to miss me concert and work double shift. Me gonna work all night, make big bucks! Thanks, man!"

Realizing the driver's incessant chatter had come to an end, Solomon refrained from gazing out the window and brought his attention back into the car. Bemused as to why he was being thanked, he smiled graciously at the driver beaming at him through the rear-view mirror and said, "You're welcome, Headley."

The taxi pulled up into the circular driveway, and Solomon stepped out of the car. Headley turned off the engine, and the night became still. Solomon stood in the quiet, marveling at the hotel. The transformation was incredible. A converted colonial mansion in the center of town, it had been repainted pale salmon with lime green trim. The old window shutters had been stripped to their original wood, and the ornate wrought-iron balconies had been lacquered in a shiny black paint. Spotlights had been placed in the flower beds surrounding the building, their soft amber glow beamed fifty feet high, coating the whole area in an enchanting shimmer.

The air was sweet, perfumed with exotic fruit trees that had been transplanted onto the grounds. A colorful mural depicting Toussaint L'Ouverture's victory in Santo Domingo was painted across the entire span of the garden wall. For those who thought the building was still owned by the British embassy, Kawasaki had erected a flagpole on the roof to fly an African flag at all times, changing the countries according to his whim. Solomon looked up, and the Ghanaian flag was flying high, in honor of his arrival.

"This the new hotel," Headley announced with a sense of national pride as he dragged Solomon's trunk off the backseat. "She a beauty, no?"

Solomon resisted the urge to say, *Yes, I own half of it*, saying instead, lovingly, "Yes, she's a palace."

He looked up at the freshly painted sign, HOTEL L'OUVERTURE, with a deep sense of achievement. It had been eighteen years since his first return to the Island from boarding school in the States, when his best friend, Martin—now known as Kawasaki—and their former soccer coach, Mr. Carl Joseph, and he had tried to enter this very building, to celebrate his homecoming at the fancy Club Britannica. They had been turned away without explanation in front of a crowd of disdainful Englishmen. That night, standing on the graveled driveway, they vowed one day to buy the place and name it "The L'Ouverture" in honor of their hero, Toussaint L'Ouverture, the black man who in 1791 had led the first successful slave uprising in Santo Domingo. The next morning Carl Joseph changed his name to Toussaint Joseph as a reminder to the young men of their vow. Now, eighteen years later, the place was theirs. *Childhood dreams are sweet*, Solomon thought, *especially the ones that come true.*

He stroked the head of one of the two life-size jade lions posted on either side of the entranceway, pushed open the wide glass doors, and stepped inside.

Solomon liked the click-click of his heels against the marble floor as he crossed the grand lobby to the front desk. A large black marble statue of Toussaint L'Ouverture graced the center space. Gold gilt-framed portraits of Haile Selassie, Nelson Mandela, Marcus Garvey, Martin Luther King Jr., and other honorables covered the walls. Busts of Nefertiti, Cleopatra, and Tutankhamen were displayed amidst flags of African and West Indian countries. Ashanti stools, Congo drums, and large Egyptian jars were arranged around the lobby. Kente and other richly woven fabrics hung on walls and draped over velvet leopard-skin chairs and pale salmon raw-silk sofas. Eight tall leafy palm trees in big oriental pots cast shadows across the opulent splendor from the four corners of the room. *Champa*, Solomon thought, inhaling as he walked, *my favorite incense.*

Reaching the front desk, he was surprised to see Joan Joseph, Toussaint's plump teenage daughter, working by herself. He was even more surprised to see her wearing makeup. *How old is she now?* He tried to calculate in his head. *Thirteen? Fourteen?*

Joan, who was usually pleased to see Solomon, treated him with cool reserve. "Hi," she said, sucking in her stomach, arching her back, and pushing out her breasts.

"Hey," Solomon replied, a little surprised by her cool coquettishness, "how's my baby girl?"

"Grown," Joan retorted with an edge to her voice. "Cassie's your baby girl."

"I stand corrected," Solomon said, amused.

"I'm grown," Joan repeated emphatically.

"So I see."

Solomon didn't actually *see* until after he'd said it, and now that he was looking, he felt uncomfortable. Her breasts had grown large for a girl her age, and her top was too low and too tight, her skirt much too short. Solomon made a mental note to suggest to Toussaint that his daughter dress more appropriately for the front desk of the hotel.

"Where's your papa?" he asked, hoping the word "papa" wasn't as offensive to her as the word "baby."

"He sail with Mama to Barbados to visit Grandpapa for the night. They be back tomorrow."

"You need a ride anywhere else, Solomon Wilberforce," Headley interrupted, handing Solomon an old white card with a handwritten number on it, "you call me. That me sister's phone. Just tell her you need Headley, she come get me, no problem."

Solomon tipped him generously for dragging in his heavy trunk. Headley smiled, thanked him, and walked back out across the lobby, with a spring in his step.

*   *   *

Joan was relieved when Solomon went up to his suite. She hadn't realized he was flying in that night. The first night in months that she was free of her parents, and he had to show up. He would probably tell her papa how she was dressed. She could see it in his eyes—he was shocked and ready to snitch. Typical! Then her papa would probably guess that she had been dressed up to sneak out to the Rap-A-Thon, to which he had forbidden her to go.

Joan slumped down onto the high stool behind the desk. *Me probably shouldn't go,* she reasoned, *but me promised Leo, so busted or not, I going.* She reached down to retrieve her mother's black evening purse from under the counter and enhanced her pink lipstick with a layer of gold gloss. *Look out, Leo Rap-A-Tap, 'cause here me come*, she thought. Much to her surprise, instead of Leo, the image of Solomon leaning across the front desk came looming into her mind. His big broad shoulders, his eyes—his sparkling eyes—roaming all over her.

Chapter 3

✧

*D*AWN HOLDS SECRETS. That was Miriam's firm belief. So she rose each morning around 5 A.M. to heed what nature was saying. The wisdom Miriam learned at dawn she passed on through her hands to laboring women as she stroked their aching pregnant bellies, and to newborn babies as she guided them safely out of their mother's womb from water into air.

Miriam eased out of bed, draping a silk kimono around her strong sensuous body. This morning was a dawn of dawns. Solomon was on the Island—she had witnessed his arrival the night before—so she knew rain was sure to fall. When the rain fell, Miriam would be ready.

In rhythm with the roll of the sea, she swept a rush broom over her bedroom floor. She enjoyed the sound of the dry rush against the red clay tiles as she brushed the dust out of every nook. Out from under the bleached pinewood bed. Out from under the little cream dresser with tiny peach flowers. She even lifted her antique treasure chest onto the bed so she could sweep under the Persian rug.

Satisfied that the floor was thoroughly clean, she unbolted the big stable doors at the end of the bed and flung them wide open to let in the morning. There it was, the view she could never leave—soft limitless sand sweeping into deep blue waters as far as the eye could see. She looked out at the sun creeping over the pink-blue horizon and whispered wishfully, "Rain."

*　　　*　　　*

Traders, mostly fishmongers, passed by the Hotel L'Ouverture on their way to market. They slowed their pace to admire the colorful mural on the wall, proudly noticing all the little details the local artists had included. The hotel was still the talk of the town, so people liked to say they had seen the wall, eaten in the restaurant, or even slept in one of the palatial suites.

A schoolteacher stopped her crocodile swatch of uniformed toddlers as they passed by, to point out and explain the scenario on the mural. Holding hands in their crisp, white, clean-for-an-hour shirts and their navy blue shorts or pleated pinafores, the children tried very hard to listen and understand what she was saying because "Teacher Cambridge" was young and pretty and they liked her. Behind the mural, delicate as a fairy castle in a cloudy mist, the pale salmon walls of the hotel blended against the early blue-pink sky.

The poetry of the morning was wasted on Joan. She couldn't believe she had stayed out all night. At the open-air Rap-A-Thon beneath the stars, she had felt like a seductive goddess. Now, without the covering of night's blackness, she felt naked and panicked. Being given a leg up by Leo Rap-A-Tap through the storeroom window was an embarrassment. Afraid that the hotel staff would realize she had been out all night and report her to her father, she had decided not to take the risk of walking through the front lobby or the back kitchen door, but instead to sneak in through the storeroom.

Preparing to drop from the high window to the floor, she caught sight of a sack of rice that, if slipped below the window, would lessen the impact of her fall. "Cassie!" she bellowed with all her might, praying that Cassie was up early helping in the kitchen. There was no response. "Cassieee!" Joan hollered again. "Cassieeee!" she screamed, feeling angry and disobeyed. She began to think of ways to punish Cassie for not being at the right place at the right time. Just when decapitation was springing to Joan's mind, Cassie cracked open the storeroom door and peeked inside. Seeing Joan's torso dangling precariously, she ran to help.

Leo saw the last of Joan's legs slip through the window and took off racing across the grass to a chorus of giggles and the schoolteacher's futile efforts to quiet the children.

Joan sat on a big box of tinned milk, licking her scraped hands. The fact that Cassie had managed to struggle the heavy sack of rice below the window didn't enter Joan's mind, nor did she thank Cassie. She was too busy eyeing her with hostility to appreciate the little girl's effort, too busy contemplating how she was going to intimidate her into not tattling.

Cassie looked up at Joan with her big green eyes as if to say, *Please, don't be mad at me.* Joan hated that look. That look alone made her mad. It was almost as irritating as Cassie's constant desire to please everybody. If there was one thing Joan despised, it was a people-pleaser. That's why she hated working at the front desk: people expected you to please them.

Joan slid her scraped finger into her mouth. "Do it hurt?" Cassie asked with concern.

"Course it hurt," Joan answered crossly.

"Sorry," Cassie said with genuine sweetness. "Maybe rub some plant on it. That what I used to do when I was out by meself."

Joan hated when Cassie made mention of her homeless days. She still couldn't imagine how such a young girl could have survived almost a year out there on the streets all by herself. She didn't like Cassie to mention it, because it made her feel sorry for Cassie, and somehow envious, and a little ashamed of herself for not treating her better.

Cassie loved to do all the things Joan hated to do, which were all the things Joan's mother had desperately tried to teach Joan—sewing, cooking, cleaning, and serving. What was the point? As far as Joan was concerned, there wasn't one. After all, where would that take her in life? Straight to the steamy kitchen of some hotel, or a small sunless outhouse at the back of a vacation villa for some rich foreigner who rents it out by the week to other rich foreigners, who lie around in the sun and watch you clean out the pool, pick up their clothes, make them cocktails and "good old West Indian food," all of which they pay the owner a fortune for, while the owner pays you just enough to buy your daily bread.

No way! Just to ensure that she would never be able to take such a job, Joan had decided never to learn to do anything domestic. If Cassie wanted to get up early and train to be a slave, that was her business. Cassie was born to be a worker. You only had to look at those bare feet and that wild unkempt hair to see that she'd always be a worker. Besides which, Cassie was so thankful to be saved from the streets, of course she'd do anything to stay off them.

Joan licked her grazed hands like a cat. That's it! Of course! She knew exactly what she would say to make Cassie keep her mouth shut. This was going to be easy.

Chapter 4

✦

*U*P THE STAIRS, two storeys above the storeroom, in the Alexander Dumas Suite, Solomon lay fully dressed on the bed in a deep sleep. Fatigue from his travels had hit him as soon as he entered the room. He had lain down intending to rest before taking a shower and had remained in that same position all night.

Only here on Cape Corcos did he sleep with such complete stillness. Even so, split seconds before the approaching feet came to a stop outside the door of his suite, he woke up. Years of sleeping out in the open had keened his senses. Keeping his body perfectly still, he opened his eyes.

He hadn't bothered to turn on the light the night before, so he was seeing the room clearly for the first time. Fleur-de-lis wallpaper covered the walls. Fabric of a matching motif had been made into curtains, chair covers, bedding, and a wastepaper basket. A fencing foil, plumed hat, cape, and mask hung on the far wall, and miniature wooden horses with a sheet of glass across their saddles served as a coffee table. Solomon smiled. The room had been decorated in honor of Alexander Dumas, the famous eighteenth-century author of *The Three Musketeers*. A hotel full of black legends, everything they had ever fantasized—sweet, sweet dreams . . .

There was a light tap on the door. Solomon closed his eyes, reached out his arm, felt for his leather satchel beside the bed, pulled out a large illustrated children's book, *Little Girl Lost* by Beento Blackbird, whispered, "Morning, Cassie," and sank back into sleep.

"Uncle Solomon," Cassie called out tentatively from behind the door. No response. Carefully balancing the breakfast tray on one hand, she used her free hand to slowly lift a key from a big chain hooked around her waist and unlock the door. "Uncle Solomon?" she whispered, pushing the door open with her bare foot. Cautiously she crept inside.

Cassie liked this suite best of all. Maybe because she had been told it was decorated especially for Solomon. It was to be used only by him, so while he was away, when she felt sad or afraid, she would sneak in to talk to him. It was a safe place to be because no one came inside except Pernella, the maid. Pernella was always nice to her. She would dust around a little bit and leave her be. And Pernella always kept her promise to Cassie, not to tell anyone that she was in there. Cassie believed that whenever she talked to Solomon from his suite, even though he was far away across the ocean, he could hear everything she was saying. Sometimes she would pick up the telephone and, without dialing any numbers, talk to him in America. Other times she would just sit in the big armchair facing the window and talk to him in her head. Either way, she believed he could hear her.

Breakfast tray in hand, she tiptoed over to the bed, leaned over, and peered at his face. *Him asleep or him just pretending?* She guessed he was just pretending but waited quietly because if he was really asleep, it would be naughty to wake him, and Cassie was determined not to be naughty. If she could just behave good enough, maybe she would be allowed to keep sleeping at the hotel—or better yet, maybe Solomon would stay forever.

"Boo!" Solomon's voice so startled her that she almost dropped the tray of food, but she was so afraid of doing things wrong that she managed to hold on tight and not even spill a drop of tea.

"What you got on that tray?" Solomon asked, laughing.

"Jasmine tea, hot bread, banana fritters, and Auntie Miriam's mango jam," Cassie replied, trying to calm herself from the fright.

Solomon opened his eyes and smiled straight into Cassie's big, beautiful, flashing-white-around-translucent-green eyes. "Good morning, gorgeous. Did you miss me or did you forget all about old Uncle Solomon?"

"Sometimes me thought you was never coming back," Cassie responded sadly.

"Course I was coming back. I promised you, didn't I? I never break a promise," Solomon said emphatically.

"Please, Uncle Solomon, don't go away again," she pleaded, creeping a little closer to the bed. "Me want you to stay."

"What's up, Cassie?"

"Just don't go away, please," Cassie begged, nervously backing away again. She was afraid that if she said too much, or said things the wrong way, everything would come to a terrible end.

"Come back here," Solomon coaxed. "Tell me what's up." Cassie shook her head no. "Come on," Solomon beckoned. "Come here, give Uncle Solomon a big hug and tell him what's up." Solomon sat up in the bed and opened wide his big irresistible arms.

Cassie tried not to go to him. She was afraid that if she went into those tree arms, she would break down and tell him everything. She knew she mustn't tell him, even though she was tired. Tired from trying to hold all the don't-forget things in her mind and keep all the nasty street things out. Tired from not sleeping, because maybe she still needed to keep her eyes on the night. Tired from thinking up funny things to say so Mama Emelia and Papa Toussaint would like her. Cassie was so very tired, yet her little body tried to resist those oh-so irresistible arms. So when she felt Solomon's big warm hands scoop her up into a cuddle and knew she didn't have to try not to anymore, she let all the big tears that had been choked up in her must-be-good little heart come splashing down her face.

Solomon didn't say a word. As soon as he felt Cassie's hot little fingers gripping the flesh of his forearms, he knew not to speak. Lifting his hand onto her soft wet face, he leaned her head against his chest and waited. He didn't look at her eyes. None of them had ever seen Cassie cry before, yet his instincts told him that if he looked at her eyes, she would dry away her tears and try very hard to smile. Solomon knew that a crying heart beneath a smiling face was a poisonous combination. So for life's sake, he let Cassie sob in his arms without trying to stop her.

When Solomon first set eyes on Cassie, she was begging in the marketplace. He had presumed that someone had put her up to it: a jobless father, a crippled grandparent, or a poor homeless mother. He

had dropped a few coins into her open palm and was about to continue walking when a look in her flashing-white-around-translucent-
green eyes captured his attention. She moved to run away, but before
her legs could gather momentum, Solomon caught her by the wrist
and asked her who she was. She yanked her wrist out of his grasp
and ran off.

At first, Solomon thought she was protecting someone. Street
hoodlums had taken to soliciting children from Patta Town, the
poorest section of the Island, and hiring them to beg. The children's parents received a small percentage of the day's intake in
exchange for their child's services. Sometimes these men had as
many as twenty children working for them at once. In some in-
stances the parents didn't even know their children were being used
as beggars, for the men would round them up in trucks and deposit
them back home before the parents returned from work. In those
cases the men kept all the money and the children agreed not to tell
their parents in exchange for candy, a luxury their parents could not
afford.

Solomon had presumed that the little girl was one of those hired-
for-candy kids until he noticed *that look* in her eyes. That faraway
deserted look. That look of desolation. Of grief, of resignation to suffering. He had seen that look before in the eyes of young widows
whose husbands' premature deaths had left them begging on the
roadside with their children, struggling for survival, or in the eyes of
the old and dying whose families had long since forsaken them. But
he had never seen that look in the eyes of a child.

People watching him sprint through the market like a racehorse
thought he was chasing a pickpocket. He didn't shout for help, and
they couldn't see who he was chasing, so they moved out of his way
and carried on with their trading. When he reached the entrance of
the market, Solomon was relieved to see the little girl wandering
down the alley. He stopped running and walked quickly, determined
to catch her but anxious not to frighten her.

Like a hunted animal, the little girl sensed that she was being stalked.
Despite all the other people walking behind her, she knew as soon as
she turned around and saw him that the man who had given her the

coins was after her. She walked as fast as she could and hoped that he would go away. She knew she mustn't run, because whenever she ran, people chased her and beat her up before she could tell them that she hadn't stolen anything, that it wasn't her, that it was one of those spitting boys from Patta Town.

The thought of those boys made her mad. Whenever a vendor noticed something was missing, Patta kids would stand around looking innocent, fingering food they had no money to buy, and no one would beat them or ask to see their pockets. Instead, they would go chasing after her or some of the other homeless market children, swishing sticks at them or throwing dirty water. She was tired of getting beaten and smelling like peepee, so nowadays she did like the Patta boys—she never ever ran.

Fast as she was walking, she could feel the coin-giving man getting closer and closer. Her legs were hurting and she was hungry. All day she had been dreaming of getting enough pennies to buy some of the soup lady's roasted peanuts. She peeked over her shoulder. With a few more steps, the coin man would be able to touch her. He was so big. Even bigger than the other one had been. Her heart beat so fast, she could barely breathe. She didn't want any more bad things to happen. She took another peek over her shoulder. It was no use. There was no escape. She stopped, turned around, and waited for him to catch up with her.

When Solomon got an arm's length away, she stretched out her hand and offered him the coins in her palm.

Solomon was stunned. It was an image he would never forget. The sight of this tiny undernourished green-eyed waif, covered in dirt, her blondish brown hair a tangled mass of uncombed curls, her thin tattered dress tearing away at the waist, her little brown feet black with filth, standing there, offering him his money back.

"No, no, keep it. You keep it," he said, lowering his body to face her eye-to-eye. "That's yours; I don't want it back."

They remained that way for a long time, reading each other's face, the little girl with her arm outstretched, Solomon crouched down on his knees in front of her.

Alley vendors haggled all around them. Colored fabric flew in the air as yards were measured by the span of an arm. Imported canned goods, their selling dates long since expired, were peddled off at "discount" prices. A feebleminded man banged his metal spoon on his corroded tin cup, keeping rhythm with his madness, hoping for an occasional coin. Skinny ribbed dogs ambled aimlessly, lapping water from dirty mud puddles, panting perspiration through their sweat-slicked fur. Amid all this activity, locked in a world of their own, Solomon and the little girl heard and saw nothing but the compassion in each other's eyes.

Without saying a word, the little girl lowered her arm, stepped forward, took Solomon by the hand, and led him to the end of the alley. Standing on the corner between the alley and the street was the soup lady, with her wheelbarrow full of peanuts and her heated metal trash can full of soup. The little girl bought a bag of peanuts in their shells, poured them onto the ground, divided them into two equal portions, put one portion back in the bag, and gave the bag to Solomon. "Eat," she said with a smile that could make a sinner shout hallelujah.

By the time they reached Miriam's adobe, Solomon knew that the little girl's name was Cassie, that her parents had died when she was "much littler than now," and that her aunt and uncle had left her in the market "to play" and had never come back. She didn't know how long ago it was that they had left her in the market, but it was when they were digging the holes for the toilets. Solomon calculated that she must have been living in the market for over a year, because he knew that the toilets had already been erected by the time he arrived on his previous trip to the Island over a year ago.

When he put her on the back of his bike that afternoon, he had no idea what he was going to do with her—he just knew that there was no way he could leave her all alone begging in the market. It was quickly decided that Toussaint and Emelia Joseph were the perfect couple to look after her. They were kind, stable, and had an only child, Joan, who needed a sister. Miriam had been a possibility, but her adobe was so isolated, and she spent so much time caring for the pregnant poor that she was hardly ever at home. Cassie would have had to spend too much time out there by herself, and everyone agreed that after what she had been through, Cassie needed as secure and routine a family environment as possible. So when Solomon had left the Island, he had entrusted Cassie to the loving protection of his childhood friend. It had seemed the perfect solution.

Cassie's hiccuping cry subsided. Still snuggled against Solomon's chest, she played with his fingers, crossing and uncrossing them, piling them up one on top of another. Solomon figured that she had cried herself out and that it was a good time to talk.

"What's up?" he asked, looking her in the face. Cassie pursed her lips tight, like children do when they want to stitch a secret inside of them. "Hey, this is Uncle Solomon," he said, as if he were amazed she would even dream of holding something back from him, "keeper of secrets, remember?" He tickled her under her chin. "Speak up, little birdy."

Cassie's eyes welled up with tears again. "Joan say if I not good, they go put me back out on the streets. She say if she tell them, they go drop me off in the market tomorrow."

"Who? Uncle Toussaint and Auntie Emelia?"

"Yes!" blurted Cassie, sobbing, as if the very sound of their names could make it happen. "I no want to! I no want to go back to the market!"

Solomon was perturbed. Joan had been such a sweet girl—a little moody at times, but never mean. He had put her present coolness down to puberty. But this was just cruel.

Cassie gripped his forearm, her fingers scrabbling like a cornered mouse. "And she say . . . and she say . . ." Her little chest heaved up and down as she tried to breathe through the horror of it all. "She say she know all the bad things me done, and if she decide to tell, then they going to put me out for sure."

"What bad things?" Solomon asked, trying to shed more light on the situation.

"That the point," Cassie burst out. "Me can't remember!"

The bad thing that she was so terrified Joan may have discovered, Cassie remembered only too well. Sometimes she remembered it in her mind, other times it slipped from her mind and became that scared thing in her heart. She didn't know how Joan would know about the market man, but Joan had a way of finding things out— and Cassie figured that must be it, because it was the only bad thing

Cassie could think of. His stinky breath. His nasty hurting fingers in her private places. He came out of the night and vanished into the night. Just before he disappeared, he had squeezed her face hard in his rough hand and told her she had been bad. "Very, very bad." They were the only words he spoke that she could understand, and she believed him, because for a long time after that night, she couldn't look anyone in the face. For days and days she couldn't really look at anything at all. Except the night. She kept her eyes on the night to make sure nothing else bad came out of it.

"No one's putting you out," Solomon stated, angrier than he had realized. "No one's ever putting you out on the streets again."

Cassie looked down, uncertain. If only she could believe it. Sometimes, even when sleeping at the hotel, she dreaded the outside darkness so much that she still watched it. She was afraid that was how Joan had found out. That maybe Joan had caught her watching the night and had figured out why. Suppose when Solomon left, Joan carried out her threat. What then?

Solomon gently lifted up Cassie's face so she could see the promise in his eyes. "Listen to me, Cassie," he said softly, wiping away her tears. "I promise you, I'll always make sure you're all right. Blood promise."

Solomon reached for his satchel and scribbled on a sheet of his notepad:

I, Solomon Wilberforce, do hereby solemnly promise that sweet little Cassie will never be left homeless again. Witnessed by us two, Cassie and me.

He removed a small silver blackbird pinned to his shirt pocket, squeezed his finger with his thumb, and pricked the tip with the pin. Cassie watched, her eyes wide with wonder, as a drop of dark red blood rose to the surface of his skin. Solomon spread the blood over his thumb and signed the paper with his bloody thumbprint.

"Blood promise," he whispered.

"Blood promise," Cassie replied, her voice filled with awe. And then she smiled the smile Solomon had been waiting for. A smile straight from her heart.

Chapter 5

✧

*M*IRIAM STOOD OVER the kitchen sink, holding a freshly boiled egg under a running tap. The gentle coolness of the water in contrast to the steamy hardness of the shell made her fingers tingle. She dried the egg with a clean towel and carefully placed it with eleven others in a cloth-lined tin. She always took a dozen boiled eggs to hand out to the family of a newborn child, and to pass out to the less privileged children on her midwifery rounds.

Eggs were special to Miriam. Standing in for her mother, Miriam delivered her very first baby when she was only nine years old; she had run home giddy, triumphant, and ravenously hungry. The only things in the refrigerator ready to be eaten were two hard-boiled eggs, which she devoured with shaking fingers and a trembling heart. From that day on, as far as Miriam was concerned, there was no taste more comforting or celebratory than the taste of a hard-boiled egg. Since then she had birthed over a thousand babies, but nothing ever came close to the exhilaration of that very first delivery, and the taste of those two boiled eggs.

He had slipped out quiet and easy. His mother thought he was dead because he was born so still. Turning her head away from Miriam, she cried for what she vowed would be the last time. She had spent her entire pregnancy in tears, and she was determined that these would be the last ever to fall from her eyes. God was punishing her for the circumstances of her baby's conception: there was no other explanation for the depths of her misery. She felt deserted. Deserted by the baby's father, who had disappeared off the Island as suddenly as he had appeared. Deserted by her parents, whom she had not seen in months. Deserted by Miriam's mother, the midwife who was nowhere to be found. Deserted by her newborn baby, who had decided not to stay in this world with her as his mother. And deserted by Almighty God who was obviously displeased with her: her baby was stillborn; she knew it, and that was that.

Miriam believed otherwise. She held the lifeless baby in her hands and played her mother's voice through the memory tapes of her mind, searching for some direction. What to do with the umbilical cord? What to do about his not breathing? Keeping hold of the baby, she willed herself to remember until it came back to her like a flood, her mother's voice carefully explaining:

"Cut the cord, you have to cut the cord. Tie a string along it, nice and tight, six inches from the baby, like so . . . then another string, an inch away from the first, to cut off the flow you see, protect the mama, like so . . . then you cut in between the two strings, nice and neat, Miriam, like so . . ."

Miriam placed the baby still attached to its mother on the bloody bedsheet and raced to the main house to look for a pair of scissors. Everyone said some force bigger than her must have guided Miriam, because she managed to cut what later became a perfectly shaped belly button.

Holding the still-lifeless baby in her arms, she pondered what to do next. Spontaneously, she leaned over and kissed the baby's lips. His eyes flew open. Miriam trembled with excitement as she held new creation in the palms of her hands. She kissed him again and he gasped, gulping air, his tiny, wet, sticky body beating warmth through the center of her palms. His big black eyes explored the room. Finally, they settled on her face, unblinking. She stared back at him in amazement as he inspected her eyes, her mouth, her neck. She wanted to say, *Welcome*, but she didn't dare speak. They gazed at each other, and then at only three minutes old, he reached out his fingers, touched her cheek, and smiled.

Later, when Miriam told the grown-ups all that had happened, they told her that most of it was impossible. "For instance," they explained, "newborns don't barely know how to see, let alone focus." "And me never see no newborn come out smiling." The women laughed good-naturedly at Miriam's dramatic account, especially at the part about her kissing the baby to life. "She'll be a griot when she grow up," one of her aunts said, chuckling. "She a real storyteller."

"That for sure," the aunt's friend added.

"Nonsense!" Miriam's mother cut in. "Miriam going to be a midwife; she got the gift of birthing in her hands."

The baby's mother had been so busy turned away in tearful sorrow that she couldn't confirm or deny Miriam's story, except to say that when he came out, her newborn was dead, and when Miriam handed him to her, he was alive. Whatever had happened in those few minutes, the mother was so grateful to Miriam for delivering what turned out to be a healthy baby that she asked her to choose a name for him.

Miriam had taken the honor of naming the baby boy very seriously. She had sat alone on the beach for hours, munching on her eggs, pondering a name that would fit him. He was so brave. No tears, no punching arms, no wriggling legs. He was completely different from all the babies she had watched her mother deliver. Holding him was the most alive she had ever felt. Sitting there she could still feel his heartbeat pulsating through her hands. Even before he smiled at her, she knew he was special, a king. A king! Miriam jumped up off the sand on her gangly nine-year-old's not-yet-a-woman legs and ran back to the house.

"I have it," Miriam announced proudly, standing in the shaft of light in the open doorway. "I have his name!" She bounced about, clapping her hands for joy.

The mother lifted her head off the cot in the corner and peered at Miriam, standing in the entrance, framed by the afternoon sunlight. "What you name him?" she asked weakly, grateful that finally someone was talking about her baby with excitement instead of tragic regret.

"He a king," Miriam explained, moving toward the shadowy images of the women standing around the bed. "Me know he a king 'cause me birth him and him so strong and quiet, so we got to call him by him kingly name." She smoothed out the cotton of her short flowery dress and stood up a little straighter.

"Come on, Miriam, hurry up and tell us," her mother urged, amused but a little embarrassed by her daughter's theatrics. "What you name him?"

"Solomon," Miriam declared proudly. "King Solomon."

The room fell silent with approval. Nothing could be heard save the sudden sound of raindrops . . . dancing on the roof.

A saucepan of mango jam bubbled on the stove in a low thick whisper, bringing Miriam back to the present. She shifted the pan onto the cool countertop just before the bubbles erupted. Stirring the jam with the wooden spoon, she soothed it into stillness, then covered the saucepan with a damp rag to keep it just the right consistency. Licking the spoon clean, the sugary tartness creeping along her inside jaw in a bittersweet sensation, she pondered whether it needed more maple syrup. Deciding it didn't, she washed the spoon and stood it in the drying rack. Picking up her cloth-lined tin full of boiled eggs, she placed them in the refrigerator to keep them fresh and headed for the bathroom.

Kneeling down on the floor, Miriam removed her best bedsheets from the bathtub, where she had left them soaking overnight in water perfumed with drops of lime-blossom oil. Taking tender care not to wring them, lest she damage the soft thin white cotton, bordered with hand-embroided silver crowns, she squeezed the water out by pressing the sheets gently in her hands. The sheets were made from one of the many beautiful fabrics Solomon had brought her from his travels throughout Africa.

He had gifted her with fabrics from Benin, Botswana, the Congo, Cameroon, Senegal, Sierra Leone, Egypt, Kenya, Nigeria, the Sudan, and, of course, his beloved Ghana. Miriam had these fabrics sewn into every kind of article she could think of: bedsheets, napkins, tablecloths, dresses, skirts, scarves, petticoats, blouses, and lace-trimmed camisoles. Many of the fabrics Solomon gave her were white. He knew she loved the cleanness of it; it made her skin feel happy. Whenever she went on her midwifery rounds, she wore only white—soft, long, and flowing. Like a uniform, it let people know she was on duty and made her feel good.

Satisfied that the mustiness was washed out of the sheets, Miriam let out the bathwater and headed outside.

Eyes closed, his long cascading dreadlocks covering his face like a veil, Peace, her unofficial watchman, sitting cross-legged on his mat outside her bedroom door, continued his meditations as she stepped around him. She hadn't set eyes on Peace since she came running home through the windstorm the night before. She usually saw him when she opened her bedroom doors at dawn, but this morning he had already moved from his mat, perhaps to stroll along the beach or take one of his rare trips out into the sea to catch fish.

Shaking out the sheets, Miriam hung them on the clothesline anchored in the sand. Smoothing her hands along the top, she pulled each one taut along the rope, securing them with wooden pegs. Before long she knew the damp cotton would soak up the fresh sea air and, stretched out on her mattress, would turn her bed into an ocean. Pressing her nose against a sheet, she inhaled lovingly and pictured herself riding on its waves. *Soon*, she thought, *very, very soon.*

She lifted a white chiffon scarf from her shoulders and draped it over her head. Walking toward town across the sparkling sun-bleached sand, she turned back toward Peace and called out in her singsong voice, "Pray for rain."

Chapter 6

✦

CASSIE WAS RELISHING THE DAY. Solomon had let her fall asleep snuggling in his bed while he washed, shaved, and dressed. Then he had let her go with him to Lumbly's Bar to say hello to some of his friends. Mr. Lumbly had sat her up on the counter and made a big fuss of her, telling Solomon what a good girl she was, how she ran errands for everybody and never asked for free sodas or money like the other kids. Then Mr. Lumbly did something he very rarely did: he let her have a whole glass of Fanta Orange all to herself. He even tossed in a colored straw and one of the pink paper umbrellas that he usually saved for expensive cocktails.

As if all that weren't special enough, Solomon had then taken her to Miss Milicent's store and bought her a pair of sky blue silver-buckled sandals—which, of course, she wouldn't wear, because she preferred bare feet, but could keep in her treasure box along with her Beento Blackbird books and her fancy white dress from Mama Miriam.

Now here she was, back on Solomon's bed in the hotel, listening to him read her his brand-new story. Nobody but nobody had heard it yet, only her 'cause she was special. Solomon told her never to forget that. "You're special," he kept saying. "You're special, Cassie, don't you ever forget it." With him around, how could she possibly ever forget? . . .

Solomon stopped reading. Cassie had fallen asleep. Andréa, the head of his literary agency, had told him that when testing his books on children, it's a good sign if the children fall asleep. "Parents read to their little ones at night to put them to sleep. When they talk, it's bad; when they sleep, it's good," she had asserted in her strong French accent. "When they sleep, it means the story transported them, up, up into another world."

Cassie had lasted barely a page. *I guess that's high compliment*, Solomon thought, closing up the manuscript. He smiled to himself at the sight of Cassie all curled up with her new Clark sandals strapped to her wrists like bracelets. Lifting her head, he eased her into a more comfortable position on the pillow.

There wasn't a blessing in life Solomon wouldn't exchange for a child of his own. With all the orphaned, homeless children in the world in need of love, he sometimes felt blameworthy for the intensity with which he desired one from his own loins. He wanted one with a passion that he felt could move mountains, but in all these years he had not managed to spawn a child. Yet he still had hope.

Solomon stretched out on the bed, crossing his arms behind his head. *Yeah*, he thought, faith rising in his heart, *I need to be with Miriam tonight. Time to bring down the rain.*

Toussaint Joseph was back and in residence. No one needed to tell you he was back on the Island, you could sense him; and if you were anywhere in the vicinity, you could certainly hear him. Everyone considered Toussaint to be one of those "warm-spirited Islanders" that made Cape Corcos famous for its congeniality. He was loud, he was round, and he was fifty.

"Pappy," Joan cooed, catching her father as he walked through the hotel lobby. "Mama say, please send Cassie over to Miriam's to fetch the jam."

"Miriam sick?" Toussaint asked nonchalantly, pretending not to notice that she had called him "pappy," an endearment he had not heard her use for almost a year and which was a sure sign that she was guilty of something.

"Solomon arrive last night, so she won't come over."

"Uncle Solomon to you," her father corrected.

"How come he always got to come same time every year?"

"How come you always got to ask so many questions? Why you can't mind you own business?" Toussaint complained.

"Mama say he breaking the law and she crazy to put up with him, say you'd have married her yourself if she take you."

"Married who?"

"Miriam!" Joan retorted so loud and harsh that it made Toussaint cringe. He didn't like to hear Miriam's name mentioned unless spoken with the soft tender lilt it deserved.

"Hush your mouth," he scolded. "When you get so grown to be talking with your mama in me business?"

"Baby Joan, what you doin' in your daddy's business?"

Toussaint looked up in the direction of the voice and saw Solomon looking down at them from the door of his suite.

"Morning, Solomon!" he shouted cheerily, hoping Solomon hadn't overheard Joan's comment about Miriam. "Welcome, welcome, welcome," he greeted effusively, covering up his embarrassment.

"Morning." Solomon beamed, filling the lobby with his vitality as he descended the stairs. "Toussaint Joseph, my main man." He opened his arms wide and embraced Toussaint. "You getting too wide, man, you need to slim," Solomon teased, breaking loose and patting Toussaint's round belly.

"You getting too tall, boy, you need to shrink," Toussaint teased back. "You like you room? We had to make you a bed special."

"Alexander Dumas! It's perfect."

"Nobody believes me when I tell them he a black man and him write *The Three Musketeers.*"

"Place looks good!" Solomon exclaimed, admiring the lobby in daylight.

"The Kruiser Club jumping, the old motel packed, and we killing it here on the restaurant alone." Toussaint leaned into Solomon confidentially. "Serious profit, man! Your money in good hands."

"'Specially with a manager what don't pay his employees!" Joan interjected in a complaining voice.

"Child, you know your money saving. When you grow, you thank me. Now get busy and don't talk fresh."

Joan cut her father a saucy look, flashed a flirtatious smile at Solomon, retrieved her romance novel from behind the counter, and headed for the storeroom, where she could read in peace.

"You see the abuse me have to put up with?" Toussaint complained as Joan departed. "It a hard thing, a daughter; you blessed to be childless." The word *childless* shot through Solomon like the sting from a bee. "We having some powerful sun lately," Toussaint continued, oblivious of Solomon's injury. "Look like you be sleeping here awhile."

"I'll be out of here by tonight," Solomon retorted, recovering from the bite.

"Weatherman say you lie."

"Fifty bucks," Solomon challenged confidently.

"You going to pull rain out a clear blue sky?"

"Fifty bucks says it'll rain by sunset."

"How come you always so sure?"

"Desire, it can move mountains, it can bring down the rain."

"If it simply a matter of desire, Solomon, me would have won."

"You never stood a chance, Toussaint. I took my first breath and claimed her."

"What you on about, boy? Me not talking 'bout Miriam. Me not thinking about that old stuff."

"So what you talking about?"

"Last year's bet 'bout the rain."

"I won."

"I know, Solomon, that what me talking about. We was betting for food, remember? So if it was simply a matter of desire, me would have won."

The two men stared at each other and laughed. The kind of laugh that says, I know you know that I know you.

"Food! We need food," Toussaint declared suddenly.

"Don't tempt me," Solomon implored. "I just had lunch in my room."

"Nonsense," Toussaint bellowed, slapping Solomon cheerfully on the back, "that was two hours ago. Come."

Toussaint headed for the dining room and Solomon followed. Even though Toussaint essentially worked for him, Solomon still felt a certain obedience toward the man, partly because Toussaint was fourteen years his senior, but mostly because he still remembered Toussaint as the fatherly but very demanding soccer coach he played for in the Corcos Junior League, just before going off to America.

Taking their seats on the restaurant patio, Toussaint looked up at the sunny blue sky and chuckled. "Me doubling the bet. Hundred bucks. One hundred bucks say it not going ta rain by sunset."

"You're on," Solomon said with a smile.

Chapter 7

✦

SOLOMON HURRIEDLY put the key in the door to his suite, unlocked it, and stepped inside. A rush of adrenaline surged through his blood. His body was charged. He was about to bring down the rain. God would be gracious to him one more time. He could feel it in every bone in his body. It had been a beautiful sky-blue day; it was a warm cloudless night. Not a drop of rain in sight. That made the challenge all the more thrilling. "No way," Toussaint and his friends had challenged. "You may be charmed, but no way it gonna rain tonight." Solomon could already feel the sweet water trickling down his neck. Charged as he was, it might even thunder.

There was a sudden loud banging on the door. "Mr. Rainmaker!" Toussaint shouted as he continued to bang. "Me see the sun setting but me no see no rain, you losing you touch, man!"

Solomon sat on the edge of the bed, nibbling on a toothpick. Toussaint banged again. "Mr. Rainmaker, if you no have hundred bucks to pay the bet, me willing to take a *raincheck!*" Toussaint laughed at his own pun. His heavy footsteps and boisterous laughter trailed off back down the atrium stairs.

Solomon remained perched on the edge of the bed. He continued gnawing on a toothpick as he focused out the window. The heat of the reddening sun blazed through the glass onto his face. He rolled the toothpick around his mouth with his tongue and waited.

Moments later, the sun's last rays crept their way through the open shutter slats, frailed through the glass, shimmered across the floor, and showered him in a final burst of light. Solomon rose and went to the window. He was a part of the elements. Herald of the moon. Brother of the dying sun. Caller of the rain. He pictured

Miriam's face before him and slid his fingertips down the pane. A slow gentle slide. Smooth skin on smooth glass easing on down. Coaxing. Tender. Yearning. The spirit of desire. Have mercy, Heavenly Father; bring forth your tears. Weep love. Drop joy. What God approves, he waters. What God waters, grows. Of all the varying things Solomon had believed in his lifetime, he believed unwaveringly in that one fact.

Chapter 8

✧

*R*AIN. Miriam was awakened by the call of raindrops drumming on the roof, knocking on the door, splash-tapping against the windowpane. She had taken a nap in order to be strong for Solomon's coming, and was awakened by the sweet cadence of rain. At the sound of the first drops, her heart surged like the waves of the sea rising to meet the sky. Rain! It was raining. *Hurry.* She could taste him, sense him, feel him running toward her.

She jumped out of bed. Stripped off the sheets. Rolled them. Tossed them into the treasure chest. Grabbing one of the clean embroidered ones off the dresser, she flung it open, high across the bed, its essence of sea and sunshine filling the room. Lightly it descended, float-kissing the mattress in a billow of white. Smoothing and stretching it tight, she folded and tucked, folded and tucked. So much to do. He was racing, rushing toward her, his feet pounding the sand, his breath gusting through his lungs, scattering the wind. He was running, soaring maybe—he had wings, her Solomon, wings to fly. So much to do, so much to do. *Heat water. Fill bathtub. Pour oils. Burn incense.* Checking the list in her mind, she spread the second sheet on the bed and hurried into the kitchen.

"Solomon," her heart burst through her mouth. "Solomon. Solomon." Rain, rain, rain! He was on his way.

*   *   *

Running, spinning, leaping across the sand, Solomon was joy in flight. His laughter rose and tickled the raindrops as they burst out around him—wet silvery-see-through drops, pouring down from a pitch-black sky, drenching him clean. With his sleeves rolled, shirt open, chest bared to the downpour, he embraced rain's baptism with open arms. "Glory!" he whooped as he sprinted along the shore. "Glory! Glory!" His voice skimmed across the surface of the waves, sinking into the deep blue sea, where schools of brightly colored fish leaped in his honor. "Glory!" he whooped again, swinging a boot in each hand, his arms spinning like windmills as he raced, raced, raced along the shore.

Straining through the darkness, the lights of Miriam's adobe reached out almost imperceptibly, thin flashing needles crisscrossing in the distance. Solomon saw them, took a breath, and flew.

Panting and exhilarated, he slowed as he neared the back stable door of Miriam's adobe. Camouflaged by the darkness, Peace sat before him, cross-legged on his mat, sheltered under a big black umbrella. Dressed in long Arab robes, his head draped in cloth, Peace remained perfectly still as Solomon approached.

"Peace?" Solomon called out in a breathless rasp. Peace rose majestically from his mat. Moonlight flashed against the metal handle of his umbrella, illuminating his face.

"Evening," Solomon said excitedly. Peace inclined his head in recognition and stepped away from the door. Solomon's wet slippery fingers fumbled with the latch. Opening the bottom partition, he crouched down and stooped inside, closing the door behind him.

Miriam lay on the bed in the moonglow, naked between the thin white sheets, freshly bathed and scented, with her thick, black, curly hair threaded out across the white lace pillow, like algae on a lake of water lilies. Solomon stood by the door, laughter-tickled raindrops dripping down his body onto the floor. He slid his eyes along the contours of Miriam's form, feasting himself on her shapeliness. Inspired by her curves, he peeled off his rain-soaked shirt and stepped up to the bed.

Clutching the sheet, Miriam rose to her knees, touched her palm against his smooth wet chest. Her soft lips a whisper away from his own, he could feel her warm breath blowing across the ridge of his mouth. "Behold King Solomon in all his glory," she praised, spreading her fingers open across his chest like a fan.

Solomon shuddered at the tenderness of her touch. A thrill of excitement rippled through his body as it responded to the attention of her stroking hand. "Beautiful," Miriam moaned as she trailed her fingers across his chest, off his flesh, and lay back down on the bed. "Beautiful, beautiful King Solomon."

Solomon looked down at Miriam sprawled before him on the bed. There she was, rib of his rib. He had traveled the world over, and no one had those sensuous heavy lids half-masted over hazy hazel eyes, surrounded by those lashes that curled and reached for attention. Or that gypsy-wild black hair, framing those high cheekbones. Or that wide inviting mouth that could hold you prisoner in its smile. He peeled away the top sheet, revealing her creamed-coffee curves that beckoned him come. Easing his eyes over her naked body, he ran the top of his middle finger slowly down her forehead, her nose, her lips, her neck, through the center of her collarbone, stroked it between her heavy breasts, tickle-traced it down into the dip of her belly button—Miriam gasped, held her breath as he wiggled the top of his finger in the little hollow, then rotated it in tiny circles, around and around, wider and wider, over the smooth curve of her stomach, down into her thick curly hairs. She gasped again, letting out the faintest trace of a moan. Solomon smiled, unbuckled his belt, and stripped naked.

By the time Solomon rose up out of the bed, all signs of the previous night's rainstorm had disappeared, and Miriam, who was singing out on the patio, had already returned from a full morning's work in town.

Clutching a tiny jewel in his hand, Solomon wandered naked into the second bedroom on the other side of the bathroom to hunt for something to put on. Furnished with only a bed and small side table, the room's grandest feature was a pair of wall-length glass doors that offered an unobstructed view of the sea.

Solomon riffled through a closet full of his clothes, picked out a calf-length Indian shirt, slipped it on, placed the jewel in the top pocket, and stepped outdoors to join Miriam, seated at the patio table. Smiling her just-for-you smile, she reached out her hand and offered him a baby coconut. Standing beside her, Solomon took a sip of the sweet milk and placed the shell back on the table.

"Close your eyes," he entreated. Compliant, Miriam closed her eyes. Removing a tiny emerald-crusted palm tree from his pocket,

Solomon added it to the gems on the charm bracelet around her wrist. "Open."

Miriam opened her eyes. "Oh! Oh, beautiful!" she said, admiring it. "Where this one come from?"

"I got it in Dakar."

"It really beautiful. Thank you." She puckered up her lips, Solomon bent, and she kissed him lightly on the cheek.

"You're welcome, honey," he declared as he took his seat at the glass-topped iron dining table, encircled with matching chairs.

Leaning back and stretching out his legs, Solomon soaked in the sun, basking in his tranquil surroundings. He looked around contentedly. The patio was a fully furnished dining room, complete with crystal lanterns that sprouted out from the adobe walls, a life-size marble sculpture of King David flanked by two stone-carved footstools in the shape of kneeling angels, and a big overstuffed deep-yellow velvet sofa that faced the sea. It was all mounted on a surface of beautifully hand-painted tiles from Italy, stretching far out into the sand, giving the adobe the appearance of a roofless edifice, like the ruins of an old Roman castle.

Solomon yawned, stretching his arms to the sky. A light sea breeze tingled the tips of his fingers, the sensation awakened his memory to the tingle he felt the night before while touching Miriam's skin. *Remember last night?* his eyes flashed. *Mmmmmmm*, Miriam's eyes replied sensuously.

"I always forget how peaceful it is here," Solomon said, the serenity of sunshine sighing in his voice. "Think I'll just stay here forever and grow old."

A shadow passed through him. He knew the instant the words left his mouth that he should not have said them. Staying on the Island forever was a topic that was best left alone. He hoped Miriam would not pick up on it, but she did.

"You serious, Solomon?" Her raised hopes tremored in her voice, fragile as the windblown skeleton of an autumn leaf. "You think you ready to stay here forever?" The leaf fluttered and landed delicately at his feet. Solomon hesitated; he knew he had to tread lightly or Miriam would be crushed . . . "Don't say what you don't mean, Solomon," she said to his hesitant silence. "You get my hopes up."

"Maybe I do mean it."

Solomon looked away. He had walked this forest many times in his mind without ever reaching the meadow beyond. *I need to settle*, he thought, *to reach that meadow beyond the trees. The meadow in my dreams.*

"What about Summer?" Miriam's voice was hushed, as if breathing a secret she was keeping from herself. "If you mean to stay forever, then what about Summer?"

There it was—the inevitable question. The sky Solomon gazed up to for help was cloudless blue without even a seagull to distract him from answering. *Summer.* He hated the way Miriam always called her "Summer." Never using her name created a barrier that he wanted to tear down, but didn't know how.

"Eat," Miriam said, saving him from the awkwardness of his silence. She slid over a large dish of rice with two whole grilled red snapper sitting on top. "Mrs. Shackelton fry you the fish this morning, special."

"She knows I'm back?" Solomon asked, grateful for the change of subject.

"She say she see it in my eyes."

Solomon gazed into Miriam's eyes. "I didn't know I looked that good."

"Better," Miriam said, meaning it.

This time the silence that settled upon them was not the awkward silence of unanswered questions, but the soothing silence that cradles lovers. The sea sang them a sweet song, and Miriam closed her eyes to the lullaby. *She's a good woman, my Miriam*, Solomon thought as he scooped himself a large plateful of food. Miriam opened her eyes. "Bon appetit," she smiled, seasoning his food with her love.

Chapter 9

✦

GAZING OUT of the wide-open bay windows of Miriam's kitchen, Solomon marveled at how time flew and sometimes crawled within the confines of its unchangeable rhythm. Each day had passed with a relaxing steady easiness; yet nearly five months had come and gone so fast, it seemed unbelievable that he was already preparing the final dinner of his stay.

Chip-chop, chip-chop, he diced the garlic on the wooden cutting board into tiny chunks. Solomon loved to cook, but the mood had to be just right, he had to have a taste for something, or something had to inspire him, as it did today.

He had gone to the market to pick up wooden carvings of the African saints, Saint Bernard and Saint Augustine, which he had commissioned one of the local artists to make as a gift for Andréa and Sam. On his way back through the stalls, he had spotted a mound of the most scrumptious-looking shrimp on earth. That had started him off. By the time he left the marketplace, his arms were piled high with food.

When he reached home, Miriam was nowhere to be found. It was Saturday, or "Cassie day," as Miriam called it. Cassie day was the one day a week that Miriam devoted to spending fun time with her little friend and sometime helper. Solomon knew they would eventually turn up to tell him all about their escapades, and to eat. When they did, he would be ready with a feast.

One of Solomon's culinary prides was the art of preparation. When he cooked, it was not just the taste of the food that was important to him, it was the organization, the design. The kitchen looked like the cover of a gourmet magazine or cookbook. He had

washed and placed everything decorously in piles: two purple
eggplants here, a yellow pepper there, three red hot chilies over here,
a pile of white pearl onions over there. Up on the window ledge
he had perched a cutting board of pink lamb and plump spicy
boudin sausage, next to it a big metal colander full of rainbow-
colored shellfish: mussels, prawns, crab legs, and, of course, the most
scrumptious-looking shrimp on earth.

Solomon lay on the bed sipping a glass of champagne. The only sign
of his having cooked was the heat coming from the kitchen and the
smell of fish emanating from the oven. Through the cracked-open
stable doors, he watched the pale pink promise of dusk fringing the
corners of the sky, waiting to darken and unfold in a blaze of crimson
orange. Peace passed by in the light of the glow, causing a momen-
tary eclipse. Solomon sat up, calling out to him.

"Peace, excuse me, have you seen Miriam?" His voice was polite,
uncharacteristically formal. Even though they were much the same
age, Peace always managed to make Solomon feel restricted, self-
conscious, as though he needed to be on his best behavior. It was as
though Peace somehow had the right to watch Solomon, watch how
he treated Miriam, make sure that he was worthy of her love.
Miriam was Solomon's wife, and Peace no kin to either one of them.
Nevertheless, Solomon still gave Peace the fatherlike respect he
silently demanded.

"I was wondering if you know where Miriam is," Solomon asked
again. Peace pointed in the direction of the tide, to an old canoe way
off down the shoreline. Solomon leaned out of the door and saw two
bodies he reckoned must be Miriam and Cassie stretched out inside.
"Thanks," he said to Peace's shadow as it disappeared around the side
of the house.

Peace never stayed in Solomon's presence for long. It made it hard
for Solomon to get to know him. On first appearance Peace had
looked simply like a wayward wanderer, a poor fisherman who
drifted onto the Island in need of shelter. But there was more to
Peace.

Most of what Solomon knew about Peace he got from Miriam.
Since that first day nearly two years ago when Peace had appeared
and laid a palm leaf full of baked fish outside Miriam's kitchen door,

he had never left her adobe, except to stroll along the beach, practice T'ai Chi at the edge of the waves, or sail out in the old canoe to catch fish. Miriam had taken to feeding him, and he to feeding her. Whenever he baked his fresh fish seasoned with seaweed outside in the sand, he would leave some for her by the kitchen door. She in turn would cook and place a dish of food for him beside his mat. Apart from a few garments she occasionally had tailored for him in town and the odd plate of food, she gave him nothing but the freedom to be, without making any demands of him or asking him any questions. In return for her kindness, Peace gave her the quiet safety of his devoted protection. He had never stepped inside the house. He spent each night outside, sitting on his straw mat, guarding her. He had never harmed her. Never touched her. Never spoken to her.

Asking around town, Miriam had discovered some of the sorrow in Peace's silence. There was much talk of a wife, a child-bride named Rafael. Rafael was a legendary beauty on the island of Balanique, from a rich and powerful family. Rumor had it that Rafael had run away from home to join Peace in hiding in the woods, where he was the leader of a trained militia dedicated to the overthrow of the ruling dictatorship. Peace, besotted with Rafael, had married her, and they had lived hidden among the trees, in a close-knit community of the other families whose husbands or wives were also fighting for freedom. Although seventeen, Rafael had the sweet face and disposition of a child, and she played and laughed in the woods as though Peace's peaceful dream for the world had already come to earth.

One day Rafael decided to surprise Peace by preparing the thing she knew best how to make: chocolate rum cake. She sneaked into town to buy the ingredients and noticed her husband sitting on the patio of an exclusive restaurant with a group of four men. His comrades watched nervously from their posts along the street as she headed toward his table. Deep in conversation, his back to her, Peace didn't see her coming. With his defenses always on the alert for combat, when Rafael covered her hands over his eyes with the intent of asking him, "Guess who?" he chopped his hand across the neck of his attacker before she had a chance to finish voicing the question.

Four grown men jumped up in awestruck silence as her lifeless body hit the ground. Her neck broken like a bird, the smile of surprise was still on her lips. *Guess who? Guess who?* Peace looked down and felt what he perceived to be his spirit slip out of his body and lay beside her on the ground. Before he could utter even a groan, his comrades came running from all directions. Guns drawn, they snatched him out of his chair and backed him out of the restaurant into a waiting car.

Days later a group of comrades eased Peace's limp body into a boat, instructing him to sail to another island, where he should say, they told him, if asked, that he was a poor fisherman looking for work.

"We can't just put him out to sea; he not well enough yet," one of his loyal comrades objected.

"Well, we can't keep him here. Police looking for him—he a liability." The rough voice was firm, unsympathetic.

"Man not even talk yet. Least we could wait to hear what he got to say, after all he done for us. It don't seem right," a third comrade continued to plead.

"It the price he pay for playing with expensive trinkets. Me warned him to stick with his own class, me knew that girl going to cost too much." The firm rough voice was twinged with envy.

"But look at him," the loyal one pleaded. "He no speak, he no eat, he could die out there."

"He already dead," said the firm-voiced man as he shoved Peace's boat out into the water and walked away. One by one the men turned and followed their new leader back into the trees. They concerned themselves with the fate of the populace, not the individual. It was the way Peace had trained them.

Solomon looked out again to where Peace had pointed, and wondered if the food was ready enough to call Miriam and Cassie to come inside and freshen up for dinner. Strolling back into the kitchen with his glass and bottle of champagne, he stuck a fork in the top of the bottle to keep it fizzy and placed it back in the fridge. He rarely drank; whenever he did, he was reminded that it was only the sound of certain drinks that he liked, not the taste: he much preferred fruit juice. Testing the food, he decided dinner was at the peak of its perfection and that instead of calling Miriam and Cassie to come eat, he would take it to them outside. Carrying a picnic basket with a large silver-domed platter balanced on top, a white tablecloth folded across his arm, he headed across the sand.

Sitting in an old canoe moored at the edge of the waves, their faces to the water and their backs to the setting sun, Miriam and Cassie were so engrossed reading Solomon's latest book that neither of them noticed him sneaking up behind them.

Just then two bully boys from Patta Town stole away the little girl's money. Down Beento swooped, pecking their naughty ears until they dropped the money and scampered away.

Cassie turned the page, and Miriam continued reading aloud.

"Oh, thank you, birdy!" smiled the little girl bright as the sun.

"Look, Auntie Miriam," Cassie interrupted, pointing excitedly at the illustration of the little girl. "See, she look just like me!" Miriam read on.

"Follow me," said Beento, flapping his wings. "Where to?" asked the little girl. "Just trust me and follow me," Beento replied. "Why?" asked the brave little girl. "Why should I trust you?" "Because—"

"—I am Beento," Solomon cut in from behind, taking over from Miriam by memory. "Beento Blackbird, freedom flier from the Ashanti gold mines of Ghana, West Africa, and my mission is to protect, enlighten, and inspire all the underprivileged and misinformed children of the world."

Cassie leaped out of the boat, clapping her hands. "Uncle Solomon, Uncle Solomon!"

"At your service." Solomon bowed, placing the basket in the sand. The white tablecloth still thrown across his arm, he looked more like a waiter from an expensive restaurant than a renowned author of children's stories. "Zee dinner is served," he announced in his best Continental accent.

Cassie lifted the large silver dome off the platter and peeked inside. The giant shrimp lay garnished on top of a mound of rice like jewels in a crown. "Look, Mama Miriam!" Cassie squealed. "Uncle Solomon make your favorite Spanish thingy."

"Paella!" Miriam exclaimed joyously.

"*Por la bella*," Solomon said, flinging open the tablecloth, which Miriam caught by its corners and helped spread out on the sand. Once the silver platter was placed in the middle, they all sat down, opened the basket, and laid out three place settings—complete with three tall champagne flutes trimmed with gold—and a silver bucket of sparkling apple juice on ice, which Solomon immediately popped open to pour them each a frothy glass. Lifting his own up in the air, he made a toast to their continued love. Miriam touched her flute against his. "Come on." She reached her drink toward Cassie. "Toast. You have to touch your glass to ours, Cassie, and drink to the toast."

Cassie knelt in the sand, staring down at her champagne flute filled with apple juice. The setting sun shed fiery sparks in the delicate trumpetlike crystal. Light as a feather, she reached out her finger to touch the reflected flames. "Like magic, only prettier," she said shyly, running her fingertip around the thin gold rim. And for a while nobody spoke, as the grace of the evening descended upon them like shimmering sand.

It was the perfect supper. The perfect evening. Feasted and full, Cassie lay fast asleep among the half-empty dishes, satiated as a cherub at a heavenly banquet. Solomon and Miriam lay intertwined in the boat, lost in the comforting waves of their familiar passions: new but enduring. Safe but adventurous. Steady but dizzying. Solomon licked the tip of Miriam's nose. She crinkled it, tilting up her face, and he brushed his lips against hers and kissed her thoughts away.

Yes, it was the perfect evening. Perfect. Nobody mentioned that tomorrow Solomon would be returning to his other life.

BOOK THREE

✦

Spring

With the Energy of Green . . .

Chapter 1

*T*RUMPETING HIS RETURN, Solomon's black metal trunk echoed as he dragged it six flights up the concrete stairs of his 1930s apartment building on Riverside Drive and 118th Street, just on the tip of Harlem. "It's bust," he panted to the young mother standing by the sixth-floor elevator with her two small children. "The elevator, it's not working. The doorman is trying to find the superintendent to let him know."

Happy to be near his apartment door, Solomon dragged his trunk a few more yards and searched his satchel for his keys. The irate mother looked at him, then looked disgustedly back at the immobile elevator before heading down the stairs with her children. Solomon sympathized with her. One of the few drawbacks of living in the charming landmark building was that the mahogany-paneled elevator with the elaborate iron gates periodically refused to budge.

Entering his foyer, which divided his living room from his dining room, Solomon reflected that the view from his wall-to-wall living room windows, overlooking the river, was one of the joys of living in Manhattan. Standing on his Persian rug, surrounded by antique African artifacts, earth-tone easy chairs, and a Moroccan tapestry couch, Solomon gazed admiringly out the window. No matter what time of year it was, the view always inspired him. He had lived for short spells in the Village, in Brooklyn, and on Central Park West, but nothing compared with Riverside Drive near Harlem.

The trees that lined the roadside were speckled with buds, ready to spring out and shower the boulevard with their Easter bouquets of brilliant green leaves. In the distance, an old tugboat floated down the Hudson River, as the beckoning bells of Riverside Church rang through the air, calling the devout into remembrance.

Remembering the red flashing lights he had left blinking on his double-parked rental car, Solomon dashed to the window and looked down to the street below. "No!" he exclaimed as he charged out of the apartment and raced down the six flights of stairs.

By the time Solomon burst out onto the street, the traffic warden had written a ticket and driven away. Irked by a group of youths who stood around laughing, Solomon removed the ticket from the windshield wipers of the car and stuffed it in his pocket. Unlocking the doors, he unloaded the rest of his luggage onto the curb, ran it up the stairs with the help of the doorman, came back down, and backed the car one block down a one-way street before turning and heading to his parking space in an all-night garage, four blocks away. *No doubt about it*, he thought as he passed the derelicts huddled under the bridge linking the elevated subway, *I'm definitely back in the U.S. of A.*

Solomon's study was his sanctuary. It was the only room that never looked abandoned, no matter how long he had been away. In times of chaos or loneliness, he stilled in its comforting arms and pondered the meaning of his existence. Relics of his life were scattered all around. Framed Beento Blackbird book jackets and photographs of children of all nationalities covered the walls. Sentimental knickknacks and precious artifacts collected in his travels were all mixed up together, strewn across the window ledge or sprinkled along the bookcases stacked full of copies of his published stories in languages from around the world.

He stripped off his leather jacket, exchanging it for a worn woolen cardigan hanging on the back of the door. Feeling more at home, he lifted away the small airline blanket that he used to protect the computer on his desk. Sitting in front of it, in his antique leather chair, he ran his fingers lovingly across the keyboard as if it were a grand piano. He was eager to get started. He had a story running through his veins that didn't want to wait. Digging into his trouser pocket, he pulled out some notes he had scribbled on the airplane and laid them on the desk. Turning the computer on, he jumped up and went over to a giant Year-At-A-Glance calendar hanging on the wall.

Solomon took a thin black marker hanging next to the calendar and wrote *arrived back* under April 5. The calendar was divided into color sections according to his personal seasons. Six weeks, from April 5 through May 21, were blocked out in green and labeled SPRING. May 22 through October 4 was blocked in yellow and labeled SUMMER. October 5 through November 21 was shaded in orange and labeled FALL. And November 22 through the end of the year, plus January through April 4, was left white and labeled WINTER.

Under May 21, Solomon wrote *Deadline: Baby Ghost — 1st draft*. Satisfied, he sat back down at the computer and started to write. A small note taped to the side of the screen caught his eye. He leaned in close to read, *Listen to memo on your machine*. Solomon smiled, reached out, pushed MEMO on his machine, and continued to write.

"Hi, Solomon." The accent was distinctly New York.

"Hi, Zelda," Solomon mumbled back as he squinted at his notes, trying to decipher his own handwriting.

"Welcome back," Zelda's voice continued. "Just wanted to remind you that Chester and I are off for three weeks to rekindle the old flame, so the first Tuesday I'll make it in is on May second. All your mail is under your desk. I opened everything that looked like business—most of it can wait till we get together. Nothing is scheduled in your two weeks of quiet, but after that, don't forget Thursday the twentieth at three P.M., you're addressing the Senate Black Caucus Subcommittee in Washington, D.C. And Saturday the twenty-second at six P.M., you're the keynote speaker at the Bedford Hills Correctional Facility. By the way, Maryland Penitentiary called to say fifty-two of the sixty inmates who volunteered, completed and passed your Power Program, so they'd like you to come for their graduation ceremony next month. Sunday's clear, then Monday the twenty-fourth, seven P.M., you're master of ceremonies at the United Nations International Women's Day. Details of all the above are in a memo on the notice board in the kitchen. I think that's it for now—all your other engagements happen after we get together on the second. Wish me luck, it's the first time in three years that Chester and I are going away without the kids. We're hoping for romance—ugh, the pressure! Sometimes I think you've got the right idea: no routine, no kids, no commitment—what bliss! Page me if you need me; otherwise, see you May second. Did I say, 'welcome back'? Welcome back! Ciao, Zelda."

Hearing her voice, Solomon realized that's who he had tried so hard to remember when he was buying presents for people during his last two days in Cape Corcos. He knew there was someone he had forgotten to put on his gift list. *How could I forget hardworking Zelda?* he chastised himself.

Zelda had started off as his once-a-week housekeeper, but with her initiative and diligence had become more of a personal assistant, coming in weekly—even while he was away—to clean up, sort his mail, pay his bills, and respond to the calls on his answering machine. Solomon made a mental note to look through his personal things for something special to give her.

Settling in to write was hard. Solomon realized he was cold and hungry, that he craved a bowl of oatmeal, or *brain food* as he often called it. *Raisins*, he thought, as he headed to the kitchen. *I forgot to buy raisins.* Driving in from Kennedy Airport, he made his usual stop at Food-N-More to stock up with goods for his two-week writing hibernation, which he always embarked on after arriving back in New York. He had bought enough oatmeal to feed the U.S. Army but had forgotten the most important ingredient: raisins. Glancing out the kitchen window at the darkening windy sidewalks, he decided to head back out before he got too comfortable.

Walking down the crowded shopping aisles, Solomon tried to fathom what it was about America, and especially New York, that always pulled him back to it. Certainly, it couldn't compare in peacefulness and beauty with most of the places he wrote about in his books: countries full of savannas and forests, wildlife and rivers, deserts and lush vegetation. Tranquil countries where people didn't kill one another for the crime of being from the wrong neighborhood or for wearing the wrong color clothes or for simply walking down the street. Perhaps it was the potency of New York City that pulled him back. Perhaps he was seduced by the pace, the rhythm, the fascinating tapestry of cultures, the opportunity to succeed, to speak out, to right wrongs, to make a difference. Perhaps it was the excitement of being in a nation that other countries looked to for influence, a nation that had come such a long way and yet had such a long way to go. Perhaps it was his conviction that his contribution was of value. Or perhaps he needed the vibrant inescapable energy of Manhattan to charge and inspire him. Whatever it was, no matter where in the world he traveled, he kept coming back.

Staring at the shelves stacked in front of him, crammed full of raisins of all types, colors, and origins, Solomon was suddenly overwhelmed by the choices. He missed the simplicity of the Cape Corcos market, where food was fresh and choices limited, where companies didn't bombard you with their brightly labeled claims: the *best of*, the *don't miss*, the *bigger than*, the *cheaper than*, the *new*, the *improved*, the *fat-free, salt-free, sugar-free, cholesterol-free, low-calorie, low-sodium, high-fiber, high-energy, processed, unprocessed, seedless, cost-less, 2-ounces–4-ounces–6-ounces, free-free-free-free!* Solomon was frazzled. Choosing a brand because it had the only raisins sealed in a tin, he pulled down three cans and headed for the checkout line.

The frail white cashier, who looked old enough to be his grandmother, rang up the few groceries more quickly than most cashiers half her age. Solomon studied her as she worked. The harsh fluorescent lights shone straight through her thin dyed-strawberry-blond-over-silver-gray hair, which was teased out to its fullest. He noticed the little roadways of exposed pink flesh where her teased-up hair was not thick enough to cover her scalp. The ash gray–pink of her scalp matched her powder-puffed face, her faded pink blouse, and her grayish pink apron. It even matched her long milky-pink nails that were busily clicking away at the register.

"Eleven dollars and forty-eight cents," she said in a monotone, tearing off the receipt and handing it to Solomon. Realizing that he had only foreign cash left in his pocket, Solomon pulled out his checkbook and rested it on the counter. "Do you have a pen, please?" She handed him one from her pocket. As he reached to take it, her eyes flashed up to him for the first time and instantly registered apprehension. Taking a step back, she watched him write out a check. It was an almost imperceptible little step, but Solomon noticed. Signing the check, he tried to hand it to her, but she was too busy beckoning for the supervisor. Solomon turned in the direction of her gaze and saw a balding officious-looking man headed in their direction. Satisfied that help was on its way, the cashier turned her attention back to Solomon. He handed her the check and his driver's license.

"This your license?" she asked, holding it up in the air.

"What's the problem?" the balding supervisor asked, eyeing Solomon warily.

"Wants to pay by check," the cashier clucked, cutting her eyes to Solomon as if paying by check was a low-down thing to do.

The supervisor inspected the check and the driver's license, and asked Solomon if he had any other identification.

Solomon looked down the long line of cashiers tinkling on their tills, servicing customers—at least two of whom he had seen pay by check without being questioned. "Not on me, but I live around the corner. I shop here all the time," he answered patiently.

"Don't remember ever serving him," the cashier quipped.

"Whether you've ever served me or not, I've been shopping here for more than four years."

"And I've been working here for nineteen," the cashier retorted in a snippety voice, "and I've never seen you. Not once."

"Which doesn't change the fact that I've been shopping here for more than four years," Solomon responded calmly.

"You wouldn't happen to have a store credit card then, would you?" the supervisor asked, as if that would prove who was lying and who was telling the truth.

"If I had a store credit card," Solomon articulated as if talking to a child, "I'd have used it."

"Well, I'll just get this cleared then, sir. It won't take a minute," the supervisor said, heading for the telephone at the customer service desk.

"I'd like to see the manager," Solomon called out after him.

"I am the manager," the supervisor shouted back without bothering to turn around.

The frustrated shoppers waiting behind Solomon changed into faster-moving lines. The cashier pulled out a little plastic purse from her apron pocket, took out a nail file, and concentrated on shaping her fingernails.

A black man who had been watching from two checkouts away shook his head and called out to Solomon. "Brother, you just a black man living in America. What can I tell you, ain't nothing but a stinkin' conspiracy. We should boycott this racist joint like we did that fishhouse up the road." His voice was startlingly loud and unafraid, one whose very being reeks of revolution.

Aware of the uneasy atmosphere, the supervisor hung up the phone and hurried back to Solomon. "Here we go," he said, handing Solomon his license. "Accepted," he said to the cashier as he signed his initials on the top of the check.

"What was the problem?" Solomon asked, tucking his license back into his wallet.

"Standard procedure, sir."

"Well, how come people have paid by check since I've been standing here and you haven't gone through any kind of standard procedure with them?"

"If you would like, sir, you can fill out an application for a store credit card."

"You didn't answer my question."

Lost for words, the supervisor glared at Solomon.

"Have a nice day," Solomon said, scooping up his groceries and striding out of the store. Eager to get back to his writing, he deemed the incident not worth his time or the energy of his indignation. It was the same old story. Incidents like this one happened over and over again, not just to him but to many of his nonwhite friends, especially the men. Different scenarios, but the same underlying cause: racism. Every time he came to the States, he hoped things would have changed. Sometimes it appeared as though they had, but invariably something would happen to remind him that racial harmony in America was still an elusive dream.

Thinking about the disharmony of the races, Solomon was even more avid to write. *The Baby Ghost* was screaming inside of him, pushing to come out and tell the children of the world the truth about all that sweet young African blood shed on the castle steps of a Senegalese island in the middle of the Atlantic Ocean, of all the tender human flesh squandered and raped on the slave ships, forced to breed more little bodies to be used as labor to grow America great.

So great that now, centuries later, it could deem their heirs dispensable, labeling them as useless black youth not worthy of the cost of an adequate education. Or dangerous men, not to be trusted, not even for the price of a tin or two of raisins.

Walking up the slight incline of Riverside Drive, the streetlights streaking across the pavement, the tin of raisins clutched under his arm, Solomon reflected on how the incident in the store had served to remind him of what he was doing with his life and why. "Beento," he whispered to himself, "Beento Blackbird, freedom flier from the Ashanti gold mines of Ghana, West Africa. My mission is to protect, enlighten, and inspire all the underprivileged and misinformed children of the world."

Solomon quickened his pace. His inner child was eager to come out and show him how to lead the children into a bright new world. Plotting the story that he was rushing home to write, he reflected on his most recent trip to Senegal. He had spent his last night on Goree Island, at the enchanting Goree residence, visiting his friend Zaimann. Standing with a group of tourists at The Door of No Return, looking out to sea, Solomon found the view from the old slave castle so serene, it was hard to believe that at that very spot hundreds and thousands of men, women, and children from all over Africa had been shuttled onto slave ships, never to return. As he stood there in the open doorway, surrounded by the eerie beauty, he was filled with a sense of urgency to write about it in a way children could understand.

Having been to Goree many times before, not wanting to listen to yet another guided tour, he had waited for the tourists to leave, then moved to the small room where little children had been herded in and kept in conditions far worse than for cattle. A handwritten inscription over the doorway read: "*Innocent enfant loin du sourire et du pleur de ta mère* (Innocent child far from laugh and the cry of your mother)." Once alone inside the room, Solomon had slid down, leaned against the stone wall, and grieved over all the children who had died in that very spot. *If only walls could speak*, he thought, knowing he would never really know the depths of the degradation inflicted upon those children. Haunted by his own history, he closed his eyes against his vivid imaginings. That's when he heard it, that's when he knew: *Walls do speak*. Solomon took out his pen and pad and wrote down what he heard, whispering, whimpering, weeping out from the walls.

It was 4 A.M. by the time Solomon thought to look at his watch. Saving his work, he switched off the computer and just sat for what he intended to be a second, to muster up enough energy to wash and go to bed. Two hours later, he woke up cold and ravenous. Lying in his king-size bed, with a printed Kente bedspread and mud-cloth pillows, eating a bowl of warm oatmeal and raisins, Solomon flicked on the television to watch the early morning news. Having sat through the entire program, he felt a surge of personal insult at the network's failure to mention the previous morning's death of the longest-governing president in history. Could it be because the president happened to be an African, ruling an African nation, that his passing was deemed not worthy of mention? Was that why his death was less important than a cat stuck in a tree? A cat whose story was not only reported but whose rescue was filmed with close-ups of the cat being petted and returned to its basket. Solomon realized with disgust that despite having listened to several news broadcasts in the past twenty-four hours, had it not been for three of his African friends leaving their various messages on his answering machine to inform him of the president's passing, he still would not know. He flicked off the television in dismay, determined not to watch it for the remainder of his two-week hibernation.

By the end of the two weeks, Solomon was ready to immerse himself in the bustle of life. After two weeks of not talking on the phone, not watching television, not eating out, not communicating with human beings; two full weeks of no radio, no music, no sounds save the running—the flushing, the splashing, the boiling, the pouring—of water, the rustling of paper, the dragging of a chair, the drone of his computer, the spring of his bed, his footsteps on the wooden floor; two weeks of hearing, yet not experiencing, the city streets; two weeks of discipline and self-denial—Solomon was ready to plunge into the heart of New York City.

Chapter 2

✧

*H*I."

"Hey!" Solomon stood up from the table and gave Sam a hug.

"How's it going?" she asked, slipping off her short cashmere coat and sliding along the wooden bench.

"Good." Solomon replied, sitting back down on the bench opposite her. "You look great."

"Thanks." Sam smiled. "I feel great. Nice restaurant," she admired, looking up at the straw baskets full of sausages and garlic dangling from the ceiling, the red-and-white-checkered tablecloths, and wooden picnic benches. "I feel like I'm in a village in Italy."

"Have you been to Italy?" Solomon inquired.

"No," Sam admitted. "But this is exactly how I picture it."

"You should see it sometime," Solomon said in the most inviting of voices. "It's every bit as romantic as they say."

"I'd love to," she responded, thinking how pleasurable it would be to see it with him as her guide. "It's one of those countries I want to experience with the right person."

"There are places in Africa you should see first, though," Solomon encouraged, "much more beautiful, much more romantic, and a lot less touristy."

"Well, I'm a willing traveler—anytime you want company, just say the word," Sam said, picking up the menu to distract him from the hint of longing in her voice.

There was a charged silence as they each looked over their menus. At least to Sam it was charged, but she could never tell if Solomon felt the same powerful energy between them that she always experienced when they were together.

"I can't recommend anything," he apologized, "it's my first time eating here, but according to its great write-ups, everything on the menu is excellent."

"I'd never even heard of this place," Sam said. "It always takes you coming in from out of the country to show me all the fashionable new in spots."

"That's because you're so busy up in that agency, making us writers rich, you don't have time to keep up with what's going on in the streets." Solomon smiled.

Those eyes! Sam thought, averting her own back to the menu. *Boy, it's good to see those eyes again.*

By the time the food came, Sam had settled down a little. Even though it happened every time she saw Solomon after one of his long trips, it still threw her how much she was affected by him. Her body always came so alive that she felt sure he must be able to sense her every desire. It wasn't just the physical attraction that stirred her, it was something else, something indefinable. Talking with him—discussing work, the latest headlines, the future of the country—was always deeply gratifying. He listened to her ideas, never becoming intimidated by her convictions or by the passionate way she conveyed them. Other men criticized her for "talking too much," for being "overbearing" or "overambitious." "You think too much," they often complained. "As pretty as you are, you should act more feminine. You're much too independent." Solomon made no such accusations. He embraced her style of expression, her passion, her intelligence. Being with him was a comfort, an encouragement, an affirmation that she didn't need to change who she was—only who she associated with.

Finishing dinner in good time, Solomon suggested that, if Sam were willing, they walk to the theater instead of taking a cab. Dressed for the evening in her favorite black cocktail dress and her black cashmere coat, Sam was glad she had decided against the stiletto shoes she usually wore with that outfit, in favor of her black patent-leather flats. "I'd much rather walk," she said honestly.

It was a beautiful walk. Strolling through the streets of New York, they admired the tops of the buildings: the intricate ironwork, the lovely stone carvings. They had passed them many times before, but somehow tonight they noticed them. Sam lingered in front of store windows she would never ordinarily have the time or inclination to peruse, pointing out embroidered tablecloths from Taiwan, ceramic cats, yapping electronic dogs. Solomon took her by the hand when walking her across the streets, sometimes keeping hold of her after they had reached the other side. His hand was warm—firm—protective. She missed it whenever he slipped it away to point up at a building or to make a gesture emphasizing his conversation, not offering it again until he led her across another street.

"Had Andréa seen the show?"

"She's not a big fan of musicals," Sam replied, not wanting to admit to Solomon that she hadn't taken his suggestion to ask Andréa whether she had been to the show they were about to see. Unless it was necessary, Sam preferred not to tell Andréa about her outings with Solomon. Even though she and Solomon nearly always discussed work at some point, somehow their outings seemed less business, more intimate, when they took place without her boss's knowledge.

The show was entertaining in a flamboyant New York way: all glitz and elaborate sets and sequined dresses. The plot was simple and sweet, staged in a railway station in Berlin and a villa in Vienna— from rags to riches, from loneliness to love. Sam and Solomon whispered and laughed conspiratorially throughout the entire two-and-a-half-hour performance.

Bursting out of the theater with the crowd, they argued playfully about whether one of the lead dancers was a woman or a man. Sam was sure it was a woman; Solomon insisted that it was a man in drag.

They waited casually for a taxi, letting the heavy theater crowd flag theirs down first. Solomon bought two bags of hot chestnuts, and they stood by the side of the road, peeling off the brown slightly charred shells, eating the soft warm nuts, as they discussed the political undertones of the show. "Hitler was never mentioned," Solomon noted, "but it's pretty obvious which tyrant all those wealthy Europeans were fleeing."

The crowd thinned. Solomon hailed Sam a taxi. Holding the door open for her as she slid inside, he kissed her on the cheek and told her they should do it again soon, catch another show or have dinner.

"Sure," Sam said, debating whether to give him a quick *friendly* good-night kiss.

"I'll messenger the new story over in the morning," Solomon assured her. "But don't forget, I don't want anyone else to see it yet. Let me know what you think."

Opening his wallet, Solomon slipped the cabdriver a twenty-dollar bill. "Take her to One sixty East Forty-eighth Street, between Lexington and Third, and don't pull away until you see the doorman buzz her in." The driver turned off his meter and pocketed the money. "Let me know you got home safely," Solomon instructed Sam as he closed the door and headed off in search of another taxi.

As soon as she arrived home, Sam stripped off her clothes, put on her negligee, lay across the bed, and telephoned Solomon. His machine picked up. Disappointed, she hung up without leaving a message. Wandering into the bathroom, she wondered where he was. *Maybe he had another date—a late-night rendezvous with some lady friend.* The thought that Solomon might now be with another woman saddened her. It had been such a wonderful evening, she wanted it to end with the two of them lying on their respective beds, talking each other to sleep. It surprised her, as she washed the makeup off her face, how hurt she felt about his not being home. She was suppressing it, but being honest with herself, she had to admit that she felt the urge to cry. Maybe her friend Eula was right. Maybe she was denying to herself the depths of her feelings toward him. It was so hard, balancing it—the business and the pleasure of their relationship. She was always afraid of losing one by pushing the other. Or worse still, of losing both.

The phone rang, interrupting her thoughts. Sam hurriedly splashed water on her eyes, grabbed a towel, and ran into the bedroom.

"Hello?" she panted.

"Sam?"

"Solomon?"

"Yeah. Weren't you supposed to call me and let me know you'd got home safely?"

"Oh, yes, I forgot. I mean, I was going to."

"When? After I'd sent the police out looking for you?" Sam didn't reply. "Bad girl," Solomon continued.

"I'll remember to call next time," Sam said, smiling to herself as she eased down onto the bed. "Did you just get in?"

"No, I've been sitting here working. That wasn't you that rang and hung up a little while ago, was it?"

"No," Sam lied. There was a brief silence. Not wanting him to hang up, she made small talk. "So, did you find another cab easily?"

"Yes."

"Good. That was a superb restaurant tonight. I'll have to remember it."

"Yes, good food."

"Great ambience, or maybe it was the company," Sam said, braving it. Solomon didn't respond. Sam could feel him about to say bye and hang up. "What's your favorite restaurant in Italy?" she asked, scrambling for something to say to keep him on the line.

"Ahh!" Solomon sighed in blissful remembrance. "There's this great hotel just outside Florence. It's an old converted monastery I discovered by accident on my way driving back to Rome. I'd rented this little antique car . . ."

Sam lifted her duvet and snuggled contentedly down in bed. She had done it. She had managed to get him off on one of his stories. By interjecting well-placed questions, she knew she would be able to keep him on the phone for a while. Long enough for her to enjoy the deepness of his voice, the quickness of his mind, and the romantic touches of his observations.

By the time they said good-night to each other, nearly forty minutes later, Sam felt as though she had strolled with Solomon through the flower-filled woods of that old monastery, helped him pick and sauté the tastiest wild mushrooms in Italy, and sat with him on the balcony of his suite and listened to the pealing bells ring in the end of the day. With her eyes closed, she could believe there were fresco angels painted all over the bedroom walls, just as he had described. "Sleep tight," she said dreamily as she placed down the receiver.

*   *   *

Solomon listened to the dial tone for a few seconds before hanging up the phone. He had a feeling that he had talked Sam to sleep.

Probably didn't hear a word I was saying. Either that, or she was making notes on how I could turn it into a book, he thought with a smile. *Beento Blackbird makes pasta with mushroom sauce and flies it to starving children in Somalia.* Solomon turned off his computer. All jokes aside, it had been a good night. A New York night. Sam was good company. He always had a great time with her.

Stripping off his clothes, he gazed out his bedroom window at the city that never sleeps. "Sleep tight, Sam," he mumbled. *Strange,* Solomon mused as he always did after an evening out with her, *how an attractive, intelligent, successful woman like her is still single and living alone. But then again,* he speculated as he climbed into bed, *maybe she likes being alone. Seeing friends, dining with whomever, whenever she pleases, working as much or as little as she feels like. After all, she seems to get whatever she wants in life; so I guess if she wanted a husband, she'd have one by now.* Solomon turned off the light. *Still, for some man, she'd be a really good woman . . . ,* he supposed before he rolled over and went to sleep.

Chapter 3

✦

"OKAY, LISTEN UP," Solomon boomed through the microphone, "I know y'all want me to hurry up and get outta here,
but before y'all get busy with the music and comedy and all that, I
need you guys to do me a favor."

The more than five hundred black and Hispanic youths continued
talking and moving around the Brooklyn Youth Gymnasium as
though Solomon were nonexistent. They had come to watch and
participate in a competition for rappers and comics, and they were
not particularly interested in anything else.

Amid the din of activity, Solomon was more overwhelmed than
his voice conveyed. He wasn't getting through to them, that was obvious. He put the microphone back in its stand, took a step forward,
and stared out at his unruly audience. Noticing that his voice was no
longer booming across the room, many of the kids turned toward the
makeshift stage to see why he'd stopped talking. Solomon motioned
to the ones nearest him. "Sit down. All you guys, sit down on the
floor," he instructed covertly. To his relief, the children obeyed. The
room got quieter, as more and more of the youths looked to see what
was going on. Solomon continued to signal them down onto the
floor, until two-thirds of the children were sitting. He stepped back
to the microphone. "I'm going to tell you something you may not
know about these kids sitting on the floor. But first I want you all to
come up here, stop talking, and take a good look at them." The gymnasium went quiet, as the rest of the children slowly edged forward
and came to a standstill around the stage.

"If things in this country don't change," Solomon continued, thankful that he finally had their attention, "one year from now, in this city alone, the number of you in this room sitting down on the floor will all be dead."

Kids yelled and twirled their fists in the air victoriously, while others nudged each other and laughed. With lightning speed, Solomon reached under his sweatshirt, pulled out a gun from the waistband of his pants, and pointed it at his raucous audience. Looking out, he noticed more than twenty children had pulled out their own guns and aimed them in his direction. There was a brief clamor as some of the children who were standing hit the ground, and then the room fell deathly quiet.

Solomon kept his gun pointed out, his arm steady. "Oh, I guess I must have been wrong," he said in a smooth calm voice. "Sounded to me like y'all thought dying was funny."

"Fool, ain't nothin' funny 'bout dyin'. It's jus' reality."

Solomon shifted his eyes toward the kid who had spoken. A lean muscular-looking brother in a long plaid shirt and oversized pants, with a head of curly slicked-back hair, held in his gold-ringed hand a gun pointed straight at Solomon's head.

Solomon felt a rush of adrenaline flush through him. He wished momentarily that he had not consented to Sam's coming with him. He always felt safer when he was alone in these situations. Maneuvering solo, he could gauge the atmosphere and be ready to move swiftly, if necessary. He could also do whatever he felt necessary to get his point across. Having someone else to protect limited his flexibility.

Solomon looked toward the far edge of the room where Sam was standing. She looked concerned, but calm. The handful of uniformed guards around the gymnasium were keenly watching him and the kids with guns. One of the guards surreptitiously lifted a walkie-talkie to his lips. Spotting him out of the corner of his eye, Solomon stopped him. "Hold up, brother, it's cool; we're just talking here." Solomon passed his eyes over the kids in front of him. "Right?" he asked in a pleasant voice. "That's all we're doing, isn't it? Just talking." Solomon put his gun away and waved his empty hands in the air. "I'm not about to shoot anybody. I don't need to. I'll just do like the government: sit back, fold my arms, and watch y'all shoot yourselves."

Solomon looked out at the stunned children. Many who had drawn their guns put them away; a few kept them pointed at him. "Y'all want to shoot me, huh? For what? For trying to keep some of you off the streets and out of jail? Or for pulling my water gun on you? Or maybe you just want to shoot me 'cause you feel like it," Solomon continued. "Go ahead. Shoot me." Fear and compassion tremored together in the pit of his stomach. Looking out at the kids, young enough to be his children, Solomon felt the urge to step down off the podium and embrace them. If he could only hug away their problems, he would. But he knew that for most of them, what they needed went far beyond the compassionate embrace of a virtual stranger. His empathy and concern for the danger and hardships they had to endure would not in itself make their lives any better, so he forged on, prepared to do whatever it would take to get their attention, and affect them enough to make them want to take that first step toward a better tomorrow. "Come on," he goaded them, spreading his arms wide in submission and closing his eyes. "Go ahead, shoot. I'm just another black man living in America."

Solomon heard footsteps coming toward him, heard someone climb up on the box—step onto the stage—come to a stop beside him. Then he felt the muzzle of a gun against his temple and heard a threatening voice say, "An' I'm jus' another nigga livin' in de ghetto."

Solomon opened his eyes. With his peripheral vision he could see the gun in the gold-ringed hand belonging to the slick-haired youth who had called him a fool. Solomon spoke to him in almost a whisper, "Not to me, brother. That's exactly why you don't want to do the man a favor by taking me out. To me, you're not just another kid in the ghetto. To me, you're a strong black man with a mission and a purpose who hasn't realized his power yet. The kind of power that doesn't need a gun to prove itself."

It seemed like an eternity before Solomon felt the muzzle of the gun move away from his temple. "You ain't no fool, brother, you crazy!" the slick-haired boy declared, giving Solomon a fist handshake. "Talk your talk," he encouraged as he jumped off the stage, "we listenin'."

It always surprised Solomon how one minute a kid would appear cold-blooded and impenetrable, and the next minute he or she would be shaking your hand, asking you questions, thirsty for knowledge. The tougher the neighborhood, the hungrier some of them appeared to be to change their lives, grateful that somebody still cared enough about them to give them a little time and understanding.

"Okay," Solomon proceeded. "Since you spared my life, I'm going to share something with you. Power. Preparing Ourselves With Every Resource. P.O.W.E.R. POWER! That's what you get when you take what you're gifted with and sharpen it against what's available. If you're interested in more than drugs and dying, then get with the Power Program. Me and other committed people in the program, many of whom started out worse off than you are today, will help you find what's available to help you get where you want to go in life. Power starts with the basics. Almost any profession you might dream of being in is going to require you to read, even if it's just the contract or your bank statement. So that's where we start, by helping you with your reading skills. But Power doesn't stop there. Power helps you deal with everyday living: how to respect yourself and others, how to handle your conflicts, your parents, teachers, gangs. Where to go, and someone to mentor you if you need to get free from an addiction. Or maybe you keep getting busted by the cops, and you need to turn your life around. Power helps you find what you're gifted at and shows you how to make that gift work for you. It's time to get paid instead of punished. Don't be like the hustlers out there, learn to make some money you can live long enough to enjoy. If you graduate Phase One of the Power Program, you'll be eligible for our free weekend seminars, where a variety of professionals, from well-known basketball players to computer analysts to beauticians to doctors to famous rappers, will come and talk to you about what they do and how they became successful at it. Everybody has a dream. If your dream is positive, Power will help you create it. If you wanna be a winner, come see me in the far corner over there, I got some books and pamphlets I'd like to give you, and I'll answer any questions. While you're thinking about it, I asked a few of my homies to come with me this afternoon and drop something on you you need to hear. They're D.J. Dove and the Righteous Rebels, a group made of rival Los Angeles gangs: Bloods, Crips, and Ese's; and they're touring the country to let kids know it's time to stop the killing. They're some of the baddest rappers around, so don't just move to the beat, check out the message. If you think you got what it takes to make it in this world, I'll be over there, waiting to sign you up."

One Hispanic and three black youths jumped up on the stage and paced across the surface with raw compelling energy. Rhyming into cordless microphones, they chanted a hard-hitting rap with a message of hope. The kids leaped to their feet, cheering, pumping their fists, and moving to the beat.

Solomon stepped down and headed for a table at the far end of the gymnasium that had been set up with information and a sign-up sheet for his Power Program. Children flocked toward him. Some of them wanted to play with his water gun, which he pulled out and squirted at them, while others wanted to ask him questions or simply slap him five and let him know that they thought he was cool. Many children signed up, and even though he was aware that by the end of the year, 50 percent or more of them would have dropped out, for those that remained, Solomon knew from the program's track record in seven major cities that being a part of Power would be a life-affirming commitment for them. One that helped them stay in school, obtain jobs, raise their own kids, and maybe, just maybe, help other people in their communities.

Sam headed toward him from the far side of the room. "You do it every time," she marveled, shaking her head. Then she whispered, "You had me scared to death. We've got to talk about that water gun stunt you pulled; it's way too dangerous."

Solomon looked up and grinned at her like a naughty little boy. "Got everybody's attention though, didn't it?"

"You're incorrigible," Sam smiled. "I've got to run—I'm meeting Cheri and Ernest at B. Smiths for dinner. Feel free to come join us for dessert if you get out of here in time. Thanks again for letting me come; I'd forgotten what an incredible speaker you are. It was good seeing you in action again."

"Thank you for coming," Solomon responded to Sam as she walked away. "Make sure one of the guards walks you out and waits with you till you get a cab."

"I will," Sam promised. "See you later."

"Hey, Sam?" Solomon called out as he lifted a small boy onto his knee. "Where are the giveaway books?"

"I left them with the guard over there," Sam shouted back, pointing to a burly-looking man who was watching over a box of Beento Blackbird books as though they were bars of gold.

"Great. Thanks." Solomon waved. "Take care."

Some of the male teenagers whistled and cracked jokes as Sam walked across the gym to the exit, her heels clicking loudly on the polished wooden floor, her hips swaying in her stylish jeans and short suede jacket. A guard held the door open for her and accompanied her out.

"Man she fine!" one of the boys commented.

"That your bitch?" another one asked.

"She's not a bitch, she's a woman," Solomon corrected. "But if you mean, Is she my wife or my girlfriend, the answer is no, she's not. She's my agent. My literary agent."

*   *   *

Solomon was tired. Completing his book; making speeches; visiting schools, prisons, and youth clubs; and still making time to see his friends had worn him out. He was ready to leave the crowded cacophony of New York City, car horns blasting, sirens screeching, people yelling—"Taxi! Taxi!" Solomon stepped into the middle of the street, to distance himself from the clashing voices and tried again. "Taxi!" A yellow cab swerved toward him and sputtered to a standstill at the very tip of his toes. Opening the door, he tossed his knapsack across the backseat, threw his duffel bag on top, and quickly scooted in.

"Fifty-sixth and Madison," he said, leaning forward, infusing just enough rush into his voice to let the cabbie know that he was in a hurry.

"You got it," said the Mideastern-looking cabbie, barging his way across the road and speeding off down a side street.

Solomon leaned back, checked his watch, and calculated how much time he had before his flight. If he didn't stop to talk, he had just enough time to drop off his manuscript and hightail it to Kennedy Airport. He had never missed a deadline yet, and this time he had also included his own illustrations for the book. As opposed to the strong vivid paintings of his usual illustrator, he felt his light, watery, water color paintings would be more in keeping with the wispy quality of Goree Island, which he had described for the children in great detail in the text but which he also wanted them to see as close to reality as possible. Pale green, soft beige, and creamy yellow buildings; tree barks and tree roots twined into walls, twisting all the way up to the top; delicate fuchsia-colored blossoms hanging off branches, decorating window ledges, dangling through shutters—he wanted the children to see it all. Solomon slipped his painting pad out of his satchel and flipped through. Yes, there it was: Goree Island. He had done a good job. He tucked the pad back into his satchel and turned his attention to his last sights of New York.

"Stop here," he directed at Fifty-sixth Street and Madison Avenue. The cabbie pulled up outside a tall high-rise, and before the meter had stopped, Solomon had jumped out, his bags clutched in his hands. "Five minutes, don't move. I'll be right back," he called out to the cabbie as he headed for the big glass doors.

"So leave your bags!" the cabbie shouted crossly out of the window. Solomon kept on walking, nodded to Jerry the doorman as he entered the building. Furious, the cabbie jumped out of his car. *"Hey! Pay me now!"*

The elevator stopped on the sixteenth floor and opened out onto the reception area of the literary department of IAA. Lisa, the receptionist, was percolating on the phone over her new "I can't tell you now girl but, oooo, wait till you see him, he's so unbelievable" boyfriend. Solomon slapped his manuscript down on the desk in front of her, startling her back to reality.

"Oh! Hi, Mr. Wilberforce," Lisa said, hanging up the phone.

"Morning, Lisa. Make sure Sam gets this right away—and these." He slipped the paintings out of his satchel. "They're the originals. I added one more to the ones she chose. Tell her I need her to make me some excellent copies of all of them before she sends them out." With that, he headed back to the elevator. "And I've told you before, Lisa," he said, pushing the button, "you don't have to call me Mr. Wilberforce. My name's Solomon."

"Oh, wait a minute!" Lisa suddenly remembered. "Sam told me to make sure you drop by her office."

"Tell her I'm running late for my flight," Solomon said, pushing the elevator button again.

Lisa surreptitiously picked up the phone. "Sam, he's here. Hurry up, he's leaving." The elevator arrived and Solomon stepped inside. "Mr. Wilberforce, wait two seconds, she's on her way out. She made me promise not to let you leave without . . ." The elevator doors closed and Solomon was gone, plummeting back down to the lobby.

Seconds after Solomon left, Sam came rushing into the reception area. "He's gone," Lisa said, nervous because she hadn't managed to detain him.

"Darn it!" Sam lamented. "I really wanted to see him! I told you to call me, Lisa."

"I tried," Lisa pleaded.

"I can't believe you let him go!" Sam complained, straightening her navy blue coatdress that had twisted slightly off-center in her rush. "Darn it," she grouched. "He's going to be lost to the world for the next five months."

"Where does he go?"

"That's the whole point, Lisa. Nobody knows. He won't tell us; we can only communicate with him through Zelda, his assistant, and that's why it was so important that I talk to him before he left," Sam expounded, suppressing the urge to run down after him and at least see his face and say good-bye.

"Something tell me you an honest man," the relieved cabbie chattered as they crawled through the Midtown Tunnel on their way to Kennedy Airport. "Usually I don't wait, but something tell me you honest."

"Told you I'd be five minutes," Solomon said, starting to get excited about his trip.

"Yeah, but in New York? New York people crazy, you know; you can't trust nobody in New York. Where you from?"

"Me? New York—Harlem."

"Yeah?" The driver took another look at Solomon through his rearview mirror. "I was thinking you were an Island man, Jamaica or somewhere like that."

"No, I'm American," Solomon said, a hint of Cape Corcos still lingering in his voice.

"Where you going to at the moment, if you don't mind my asking?"

"Air Afrique."

"Yeah, I know, you tell me that already, but where you going? I mean where you fly to?"

"Ghana. Ghana, West Africa."

BOOK FOUR

✦

Summer

To the Yellow of the Sun ...

Chapter 1

✦

*T*HE RED DUSTY EARTH scattered through the air as the crowded coach wound its way along the deserted road from Accra to Kumasi. Solomon's body rocked back and forth as it yielded to the motion of the wheels plummeting and jumping over the many potholes and slopes along the route.

The coach had fallen quiet, the talked-out passengers resting their tongues. Bending over their cloth-covered bundles, or leaning against the dust-caked windows, they had nodded off one by one into a semiconscious sleep. Even the tied-up chicken stuffed in a basket at Solomon's feet had finally ceased its clucking.

Sensing the coach coming to a stop, Solomon opened his eyes and sat up to see where they were. Leaning over the young pregnant woman sitting beside him, he peered out the window. Thick, lush, green vegetation, peppered with red earth, spread out to the horizon and into a forest of trees. Way in the distance he could see a lone farmer with a herd of sheep, reclaiming the road that he had temporarily surrendered to the oncoming coach. Solomon often wondered where these men were going when he saw them like that, barefooted, stick in hand, steadily walking in the middle of the road in burning sunshine, miles and miles from any visible habitation.

The driver picked up a flask and stepped off the bus. Figuring that the bus couldn't go anywhere without its driver, Solomon decided to get off and stretch his legs.

Stepping onto the ground, he felt a sense of well-being. Removing one leather sandal, he rubbed the sole of his naked foot back and forth across the surface of the dusty earth, letting the gritty goodness scratch against his skin. A wave of rejuvenation rose up from the earth and flooded through Solomon's body in a surge of energy so powerful, he almost keeled over. Overwhelmed, he squatted to regain his balance.

The driver unzipped his trousers, stepped up to a cluster of foliage, and urinated the red dust off the surface of the leaves, revealing the primary brightness of their green. He poured a little water from his flask onto his fingers, dried them on the leg of his khaki trousers, and stepped back onto the bus.

Solomon hurried on after him. He didn't want to be left behind. He had been left behind once before, on his maiden trip to Ghana, so he knew better than to linger outside after the driver had taken his seat. On that memorable occasion, when he had come to do research for his very first book, the coach had stopped to let off a passenger in what appeared to be the middle of nowhere. Looking out the window, Solomon had noticed a funeral taking place in a nearby field. The driver had dismounted, and Solomon had followed suit. Moving in close to take photographs of the mourners, Solomon had become so engrossed that he was unable to tear himself away, and the coach had taken off, leaving him stranded. Invited by strangers to spend the night in their compound, he had gladly accepted. The journey he ended up taking that day, both physically and emotionally, had dramatically changed the course of his life—to what he believed was a better way. However, despite the fruitful outcome, he didn't want to be left stranded again.

"Are you feeling fine?" the driver asked as Solomon took his seat, slipping his sandal back onto his foot.

"Yeah." Solomon smiled. "It's summer—I always feel fine in the summer."

Solomon was the first to step off the coach when it finally arrived in Kumasi. Passengers poured out behind him, jostling him as he turned to help the young pregnant woman who had been sleeping beside him down the steps. Steering her safely out of the crush of people, he handed her the basket with the chicken, nodded down to her rounded belly, and said, "Take good care of it." The woman smiled, thanked him, and merged into the Kumasi city bustle.

Solomon tossed a cap on his head to shield him from the sun, slung his knapsack on his back, clutched his bags, and headed toward a cluster of rickety-looking three-toned red-yellow-green taxis circled underneath a big shady tree. Before he could reach them, he was surrounded by young peddlers pushing their wares.

"Fan milk."

"Cola nut."

"You want orange? I peel it nicely for you."

"How much? How much you want to pay? This is fine, fine radio. How much you want to pay me?"

Detecting that Solomon was not in a buying mood, the more astute peddlers backed off, giving him the space he needed to reach for the door of a taxi and jump inside. As the vehicle struggled away, Solomon rolled down the window and handed out a few coins to some of the smaller children. A bright-eyed boy with a basket full of sugarcane balanced on his head pointed at Solomon's New York Yankees baseball cap. "You give, I give you sugarcane; you give, I give you sugarcane," he pleaded with longing in his eyes as he ran alongside the taxi. Solomon pulled the cap off his head and held it out to him. Before the sugarcane boy could get it, a small girl with thin sticklike legs sprinted up to the window and snatched the cap out of Solomon's hand. The other children chased her as she tossed it in the air triumphantly. The sugarcane boy caught the cap midair and slammed it down firmly on his head. Placing his basket in the dirt, he ran after Solomon, a long stick of cane in his hand, and speared it through the open window. Laughing, Solomon dodged out of its way as it flew past his face and landed on his duffel bag.

"Thanks," Solomon shouted to the boy as the taxi turned onto the main road and accelerated away. Ripping away the tough skin with his teeth, Solomon peeled the sugarcane like a banana. Biting into the juicy sweetness, he crunched down hard into the firm center, releasing the tasty liquid into his mouth and down his thirsty throat. He was so pleased with the world that he smiled broadly.

"What takes you to Aburanoma village?" the taxi driver asked. "It's far, you know? Have you seen it before?"

"I live there," Solomon replied without a moment's hesitation.

Chapter 2

✦

THE OLD, CHIPPED, baby-blue battery clock hit 11 A.M. and sounded its alarm with a rapid persistent clanging. Without opening her eyes, Ashia reached her naked arm through the curtain and clamped her hand over the two shiny silver bells on the top of the clock. With the button to stop the ringing long since broken, she held her hand over the bells until their muffled vibration came to a halt.

It was unusual for Ashia to be in bed this late in the morning, but she had needed some more rest. In her excitement, having gone to bed around midnight, she had jumped up at 3:15 A.M. and busied herself with cooking, cleaning, threading and rethreading her hair. Finally, around 9 A.M., she had lain back down, setting the alarm for eleven.

Veiled behind the mosquito-net curtain drawn around the brass four-poster bed, her slender body curled on top of the sheet, she slowly opened her eyes. The see-through white haze of the curtain gave the room a shimmering quality that Ashia liked because, when she woke, it always made her feel as though she were still partly in her dreams. She looked around the shiningly clean room with a sense of satisfaction. Eight brand-new white candles stood in their three-foot-high wrought-iron candleholders at the four corners of the bed. A large Bible on a wooden lectern in the shape of an eagle with wings outstretched stood in the center of the floor, as if primed to protect her. Rolling off the mattress onto her knees, Ashia buried her head in her hands and prayed.

Wrapping a piece of faded fabric around her naked body, she stepped out of the bedroom through the thin lace curtain covering the open doorway and walked into the courtyard. A solitary tree that had seen many decades curtsied in the center of the open space. Its trunk bent low with age, it reached out its entwined and twisted branches, offering sun-dappled shade to all who passed its way. It was Ashia's favorite place to be. She could be most often found sitting beneath its boughs, braiding her customers' hair, cooking food on a small open stove, or studying for English tests that Olu would give her on his frequent visits from Accra, tests to help her fulfill her dream of one day attending a college in London.

Jumping up and grabbing hold of one of the limbs of the tree, Ashia pulled it low and removed a piece of lace that she had hung out to dry the night before. Letting the limb spring back into place, she carried the lace into the living room on the other side of the courtyard. The only room in the house besides the bedroom, the living room was kept tidy at all times, even when her little house was crowded with relatives—which it most often was, except when they evacuated for the summer season. Even so, clean as it was, Ashia had still managed to spend time that morning making sure the room was absolutely ready. One of the specific tasks she had done was to wash the yellow lace, which she now returned to its position on the back of the brown leather sofa.

When she pulled away from draping the lace, her arm accidentally knocked crooked the picture hanging on the wall. It was a framed poster of the book cover for *Little Ashia, Don't Cry* by Beento Blackbird, with a picture of her at fourteen, dancing in black funeral clothes, tears streaming down her cheeks. She was proud of being the subject and cover of a book, despite the fact that even though the picture had been hanging there for years, the memory of the day it was taken released such intense emotions within her that she hardly ever looked at it. Eight years since her father's death, she still missed him too desperately to dwell on. And yet, but for his death, but for their deciding to have his funeral beside his favorite river, but for the Accra coach driver being so impatient, she might never have met Solomon. Averting her eyes from the picture, she straightened it and hurried out to complete her preparations.

Squatting down behind a waist-high semicircle of stones in the open courtyard, Ashia scrubbed her body with a loofah until it tingled. Dipping a tin can into a bucket full of clean water, she poured it over her shoulders and down her back, her arms, her legs—running the soapy suds off her skin into the red earth that surrounded the rubber mat under her feet. Satisfied that all the soap was washed away, she closed her eyes, picked up the bucket, and poured the rest of the water over her head. The cool rush revived her from her sleepiness. Patting herself dry, she wrapped the damp towel across her chest, hung the tin bucket on the tap sticking out from the wall outside her bedroom, and went inside to dress.

Even though she had expected it—waited for it for hours—the sound of Kummaa's excited high-pitched seven-year-old's voice shouting, "Auntie Ashia, Auntie Ashia, he is coming, he is coming," as he tore through the front of the house into the courtyard, sent a thrill through Ashia that froze her to the spot. Had it not been for Kummaa's hot sweaty little hand pulling at her, his body slanted forward against her weight, dragging her past the tree, up the step, through the living room, and out into the dusty front yard, she might have remained frozen in front of the mirror, retying the new outfit that her grandmother, Nana Serwah, had sewn for her so she would look "pleasing when the Big Man arrives."

Her little brother, Kummaa, who called Ashia *auntie* in deference to her age, even though she was his half-sister, had come to her house early that morning with all his friends and preteen relatives, who loved nothing better than to be on lookout duty for an expected visitor. It was a far more enjoyable chore than scrubbing cooking pots, fetching fire twigs, sweeping, or running to buy something from the market for whatever grown-up might happen to pass by and decide that the children were hanging about idle and in need of a task. Lookout duty could also be lucrative. The expected visitor, happy to have finally arrived at his destination, would often hand out candy, leftover drinks and biscuits, or coins and occasionally even bigger shop-bought gifts, which would be distributed among the gleeful welcoming committee.

In excited expectation, Kummaa and his friends had frolicked the morning away on lookout duty. Gathered outside Ashia's house, they had started off by playing *asow:* arranging themselves in a horseshoe-shaped curve, standing snuggled together, singing and clapping, they had taken turns being the one in the middle, the one who got to dive backward into waiting hands, to be caught and thrown forward, dance a little step, and dive backward again, flinging, falling, flailing through the air to the rhythm of the claps, this way and that, that way and this, everybody's eyes, ears, arms, fingers, all on the alert to catch and throw the child in the middle, back and forth, back and forth, the surrendered body being let drop lower and lower until it almost touched the ground.

"*Pre-pra-pre-pra,*" Kummaa had shouted—and everyone had changed games, hopscotching along squares drawn in the dirt. After a while, Abena had pulled out a ropy vine twisted by her brother, the lanky boy who helped her circle the rope over the girls' heads as they jumped, clapped, hopped, turned, jumped, clapped, hop-shuffle-turned, shuffle-hop-shuffle-turned. Clap. Clap-clap. Clap. Clap-clap.

"What is all this noise? What are you small children doing?" Papa Freempong had grumped, his beady eyes quickly counting all the idle hands he could put to better use.

"Helping Auntie Ashia watch for the Big Man himself," Kummaa answered bravely, as his friends scatter-ran behind him like the dust up the dirt road. That's when Kummaa had first noticed it, the distant circling dust and the faint signaling horn of the oncoming car. "Excuse me, Papa Freempong," he had garbled as he rushed inside to alert Ashia.

Standing there in her bright traditional robes, a light sweat beaming on her forehead, Ashia watched the approaching dust cloud wrapped around the red, yellow, and green taxi that was honking its way to her house. She wiped the sweat off her face with the back of her hand and let loose the little laugh that had snaked all the way up from her belly into her mouth. The children laughed too, in sweet anticipation. There was nothing more promising than a laughing grown-up and a gift-bearing visitor come all the way from America.

*   *   *

Having sucked his sugarcane dry, Solomon was ready for some real food. The very thought of it made his juices flow. There was not a mountain he would not have climbed to reach his destination. Maybe the myth was true—maybe there were certain African women (wherever on the globe they had been dispersed to) who could cook you into compliance, pound you into putty, and sauce you into utter submission.

Passing the yellow schoolhouse that marked the beginning of Aburanoma village, he had been so engrossed in his oral fantasy that he had almost forgotten to tell the driver to start beeping the car horn, a ritual he performed in order to signal the children to gather round, not realizing that his arrival was such a major event that they had typically been gathered since morning. As the taxi pulled into the final stretch of his journey, Solomon, unmindful of the dust, rolled down the window to get an unobstructed view of the beauty before him.

Nothing could have made him mistake the grace that was Ashia. Standing poetically still amid the clamoring children, her hands respectfully folded in front of her, her head slightly bowed, she magnified his manhood by the very womanliness of her being.

Solomon opened the door before the driver could bring the car to a complete stop. Leaping out with his arms outstretched, he burst through the curtain of Ashia's shyness, lifted her off her feet by her waist, and spun her round and round while gazing up into her eyes. Unable to return his gaze or allow herself to hold on to his oh-so-chiseled back, Ashia cast her eyes toward the ground, leaving her hands dangling by her side like a defenseless rag doll until the sheer power of Solomon's spin forced her to grip onto his shoulders, her loose robes flying up in the air like wings.

The children cheered at the sight of their flying aunt and crawled into the taxi like ants on a crumb. Pooling their strength, they unloaded Solomon's bags and produce he had bought along the roadside, holding them as high as they could to prevent them from dragging in the dirt. Five or six children to a piece, they marched in formation as they wrestled them into the house.

Feet safely back on the ground, Ashia redrew the invisible lacy curtain around herself, took a step back, and reached out her hand. *"Akwaaba,"* she greeted in her native tongue, stooping into a small graceful curtsy.

"Akwaaba," Solomon greeted in return. *"Wo ho te sen?"*

"I am well, thank you," Ashia said, unable to repress the smile that had been hovering at the corner of her lips. It was always funny to hear Solomon speaking in her language. Even though these few responses were virtually the limit of his repertoire, he spoke them with such bold confidence that it gave the illusion of fluency. His bravado tickled Ashia, although she had a feeling that one of these days he would surprise her by breaking out into the most eloquent, perfectly pronounced Twi. He could, after all, speak fluent English, French, Spanish, and Swahili, while English was her only other language. But then again, Solomon was a genius, so learning things was easier for him than it was for her.

The taxi driver honked his horn, summoning their attention. "May I fetch him some refreshments?" Ashia asked Solomon quietly, considering the driver a friend for having delivered Solomon safely to her door.

"Sure," Solomon said, not really wanting to lose sight of her so soon. "Hurry back. I'll pay him his money."

Solomon leaned his arm along the open window frame of the taxi, counted out a pile of cedi notes, and paid the driver his fare. "I was hoping to drive you back to Kumasi," the driver said, a note of disappointment in his voice. "If you want, I stay some few hours. Me, I don't mind to wait."

"Thanks, but that's okay."

"To get back to town is a very long way," the driver persisted. "If you try to call up there to have taxi come get you, nobody go come. Make I wait and take you back. It's not a problem."

"Thanks, but I really don't need a ride back," Solomon insisted politely, handing him a few extra cedis.

"You're going to stay in this place?" The driver asked, surprised, slipping the money under his seat.

"I told you," Solomon said, straightening himself fully, "I live here. This is my home."

Ashia headed back toward them, a tray of refreshments in her hands. The driver scrutinized the modest house, the rural surroundings. "You live here?" he asked incredulously. "In this here house?"

"Yeah," Solomon said, affectionately placing his hand on Ashia's shoulder as she sidled up beside him. "This is my wife."

Solomon's bags were spilled open in the courtyard like split piñatas at a Latin festival. The delighted children showed off their gifts to one another, each believing he or she had been handed the very best toy. Colorful jigsaw puzzles, spinning tops, paint sets, and other age-old amusements now demoted in the minds of American children in favor of computer games were passed around like found treasures from a sunken ship. Happy to share with one another, they kept an eye on what was theirs, lest children wander off forgetting they still had a borrowed toy in their hands; unless, of course, they were a relative—in which case they had a blood-born right to keep it for as long as they pleased.

The only toy that was off-limits was a stuffed kangaroo with a pouch containing a solid sterling silver heart, inscribed, TO ASHIA, MY BELOVED WIFE. FOREVER YOURS, S. W. Wrapped in yellow cellophane, tied with a big silver bow, the kangaroo had been placed outside Ashia's bedroom door.

Solomon was seated on a wooden stool in the sun-dappled shade of the big tree, restfully watching the children. Ashia walked up, her tiny feet silent as a whisper. Placing one foot carefully behind the other, she bent her knees slightly and wordlessly offered Solomon a calabash of cool water to wash his hands. Using the slice of lemon floating on the surface, Solomon rubbed the red dirt and dried cane juice from in between his fingers. Soaking his hands in the bowl, he never once moved his eyes from Ashia's face. Even when she looked shyly away, he continued to gaze, offering her shyness no mercy. Slowly he slid the towel off her shoulder, dragging it across the tip of her breast, sending her a message so clear that she felt as though he had already stripped her naked.

"You must eat something," Ashia said, trying to reclothe herself for the sake of the children.

"What do you have in mind?" Solomon asked suggestively, ignoring the curious eyes of the little ones.

"Let me bring you," Ashia smiled, hurrying away to rearrange herself.

Solomon dried his hands on the towel, raising it to his nose to sniff the scent infused into the cotton where it had brushed against Ashia's naked neck: sandalwood, cedarwood, lavender, and a touch of patchouli . . . His shoulders relaxed, his muscles easing at the familiarity of her smell. He stretched out his legs and peeled off his sandals, using one foot and then the other. Loosening his belt, he untucked his T-shirt from his jeans and slipped it off over his head.

Dappling down through the branches of the tree, the sun twinkled on his naked back like diamond light dancing on a shadowy wall. Scrabbling his toes in the hot earth, Solomon closed his eyes to savor the sensation of warmth encompassing him from above and below. Home . . . He was home . . . The only true *home* he had ever known. Not a people, place, or country, but a settlement in his soul. He could be walking down the streets of Harlem or sitting by the sea in Cape Corcos or, like today, in a sun-dappled courtyard in Ghana, and he would realize he had arrived—in the settlement of his soul: he was home.

Carrying a small clay oven, Ashia rounded the corner from the back of the house and stopped. The sight of Solomon's strong, brown, naked back took her breath away. Not wanting to disturb him, she moved quietly to the side of the tree, placed the oven on the ground, fanned the coals with her hand until she was satisfied that they were still alive, and went back behind the house to fetch the food.

Solomon kept his eyes shut, his head tilted up to the sky. The red of the sun, shining through his closed lids, the warmth of the soil, the laughter of the children, the smell of Ashia—these things he prayed he would remember at the time of his death, so that bliss would be his last sensation on earth.

"Let Uncle Solomon eat in peace," Ashia appealed to the encroaching children as she placed a pot of bubbling chicken palm-nut soup on top of the oven.

"No, it's okay. Come on, come eat," Solomon invited, opening his eyes and seeing the children edging toward the food. "Come on, come on over here, come eat," he called out, beckoning the more reticent ones who had stayed on the fringes of the courtyard. "Where's Amamaa?" he asked, realizing that he had not yet set eyes on Ashia's little sister.

"*Kummaa ko fa wo nua.*"

"Yes, Auntie Ashia," Kummaa responded.

"Wash your hands," Ashia commanded the rest of the children, as Kummaa ran off obediently to fetch Amamaa. "Uncle Solomon says you can eat with him." The children cheered and went pushing and shoving to wash their hands at the tap sticking out from the wall.

Ashia set a big oval plate heaped with fufu on a pile of bricks by the small clay oven. Patted to perfection, the rounded fufu balls stuck together in a huge sticky mound like jellied mashed potato. Dipping a serving spoon into a bowl of clean water so the sticky substance wouldn't cling to it, she used the wet spoon to separate one of the balls, scooping it up and dropping it into a deep serving dish with an experienced flick of her wrist. Holding the dish over the oven, she filled it ladle after ladle full of palm-nut soup, brimming with whole okras, meaty land snails, flat water crabs, garden eggs, dried fish heads, pepper, onions, tomatoes, and pieces of the chicken she'd killed and plucked early that morning.

With a certain reverence for the goodness of God at allowing her the privilege to afford such tasty ingredients, and for the honor of being able to present the nourishment seasoned and cooked to such a deserving man, she handed the dish to Solomon. *As for this here soup*, she thought as Solomon reached to take it from her, *it will be the best he has ever tasted.*

Carefully, as if handling communion wine, Solomon placed the bowl on the ground between his legs. The mound of fufu poked up through the orange-brown liquid like a butter-colored whale in muddy water. He leaned over, pinched off a piece of the sticky goodness with his fingers, dipped it in the soup, put it in his mouth, and surrendered. It was the best he had ever tasted. "I'm yours! Whoo, Ashia! Glory hallelujah, I'm yours!"

Satisfied that her husband was taken care of, Ashia busied herself arranging the children in a circle at the other end of the courtyard. Making sure their hands were clean and cautioning them to help the little ones, especially the two- and three-year-olds, she placed a large bowl of food in the center of the circle for all of them to share.

"Sit," Solomon compelled, before she could busy herself with anything else. Ashia dragged over another wooden stool and sat opposite him. Solomon fed her food from his hand, enjoying her plump lips as she closed them over the tips of his fingers, sucking off the fufu. Dipping her hand in the bowl, Ashia offered him food in return. He accepted, savoring the morsel. Catching her hand as she pulled it away, he cleaned the soup off her fingers with his tongue, dragging it up the side of one finger, circling around the tip, sliding it down the other side, licking in between and up the next one, until each finger and her thumb had been given his personal attention. Reluctant to release the sweetness of Ashia's flesh, Solomon popped all four of her fingers into his mouth at once and sucked.

The warmth of Solomon's mouth, the nakedness of his chest, the softness of his tongue, ignited feelings inside Ashia that she had done her best to bury in the many months of his absence, marking her sexuality with a tombstone that read DO NOT DISTURB. Feeling that tombstone come crashing down, the soil of that shallow grave erupting, she tried to pull her fingers out of his mouth, to stop the ghost of her resurrected feelings from revealing itself in the open courtyard.

Solomon gripped Ashia's fingers with his teeth—not so hard as to hurt, but firm enough to prevent her from slipping them out of his mouth. He knew her being was shaken by the way she was wriggling on the stool, knew it by the little undulations that rippled up and down her spine and traveled along her hand through her fingertips into his mouth. He did another revolution around her fingers with his tongue and released them. "Delicious," he smiled, his voice loaded with intent. "Absolutely, delectably delicious."

"Thank you, I am glad you are enjoying it. I cooked it early this morning," Ashia replied, her eyes full of innocence, her smile full of mischief.

Chapter 3

✦

*B*Y THE TIME Solomon and Ashia walked across the grassland to greet her parents, the sun had already subsided into a late-afternoon glow, casting shadows through the long dry yellow-green grass that tickled weightlessly around their calves. Holding hands, arms swinging gently back and forth, they sauntered along, teasing each other in easy honey-coated voices—carefree as high-school sweethearts strolling home.

Kummaa had retrieved his nine-year-old sister, Amamaa, from their grandmama Nana Serwah's pampering and was leading her with a long stick a few yards ahead of the two grown-ups. Amamaa, who had been blind since birth, loved to teach her little brother all the stories she had memorized. Holding on to the long stick by which Kummaa led her through the grass, she chattered away, reciting to him one of the fables Nana Serwah had told her.

Solomon let the two children get a little ahead of them before pulling Ashia by the hand, slowing her to a standstill. Bending down, he planted light delicate kisses all around her lips. Her sweetness got to him and before he knew it, he was probing deep into her mouth, his tongue writhing as if trying to convey all the secrets in his heart that words could not express. Ashia listened, making her mouth available to his innermost joys and sorrows. Moved by what he revealed, she placed her hand on the back of his neck, pulled him in closer, and spoke back. *I hear you*, she responded through her slowly moving tongue. *You are not alone. I feel it too.* They were just about to turn their heads into another position, delving deeper into their conversation, when Kummaa's voice pinned them down to earth.

"Uncle Solomon," he interrupted. "Don't you want to hear the rest of Amamaa's story?"

"Go ahead," Solomon allowed, pulling himself out of the liberating world of Ashia's mouth.

"Finish the story in English," Kummaa instructed his sister. "So Uncle Solomon can understand."

Amamaa was delighted. With no blind school close enough for her to attend, she was tutored by the family. English, which she studied with Ashia, was her favorite subject.

"So the white man shouted at Queen Yaa Asantewa, I do not care about your native king. I am Sir Frederick Hodgson, British governor of the Gold Coast, and I order you to bring me the Ashanti Golden Stool that I may sit on it."

"Only we don't call our country 'Gold Coast' anymore; the British stole all our gold, so now we call it 'Ghana,'" Kummaa interrupted.

"But this happened on March twenty-eighth, nineteen hundred, when we were still the Gold Coast," Amamaa explained.

Finding it hard to concentrate on anything except Ashia's lips and the voiceless conversation they had been sharing, Solomon, seeing the children's backs were turned as they walked slightly ahead again, pulled Ashia back to him and resumed their kiss.

"Are they kissing?" Amamaa asked.

Kummaa spun around. "Why are you doing that to my sister?" he demanded in a protective voice.

"Kummaa, don't be rude," Ashia reprimanded. "You are too young to be asking Uncle Solomon such questions."

"How does she know?" Solomon whispered to Ashia. Amamaa smacked her lips in response, making loud kissing sounds that made Kummaa and her giggle.

"Stop it, don't be silly," Ashia said, feeling embarrassed. Amamaa let go of the stick she was being led by and clasped her hands over her mouth to try to contain her snickers. Kummaa joined her and hid his face in her neck as they attempted to control themselves.

"Kummaa, Amamaa, stop it! Kissing is not funny!" Ashia admonished.

Amamaa's hands flew off her mouth into the air, and Kummaa's head sprung up out of its hiding place in the crook of his sister's neck as they fell backward together onto the ground, laughing uncontrollably.

*   *   *

Akua Gyamma did not want to be seen, so she laid low and kept very still. Resting in the grass, under the shade of a guava tree, she watched her children laughing and frolicking on their way to her husband's home. She did not consider it her home, although she slept there every night. To her, this was more her home—this guava tree, this patch of grass where she came to sit and remember. That's why she laid low, so her children would not see her: so when they were sent to find their mama who had disappeared again, they would not come and disturb her memories.

Separating the blades of grass with her hands, Akua Gyamma peeked out at her three children and son-in-law as they passed by. Solomon looked well; she was glad. If there was one thing she prayed for her daughter, it was that her husband would be granted good health and long life. They looked happy together. Ashia and Solomon, Solomon and Ashia. And look at Kummaa! Were his legs that long when she woke him up this morning? When she shook him from his mat to get up and sweep the veranda, was he already such a man? And Amamaa—dear God, why did Amamaa have to have her papa's eyes? Blind, unfocused, every which way, but still they were her papa's sweet, sweet eyes. Sometimes Akua Gyamma felt that if she could just get Amamaa to look her square in the face, then *he* would be looking at her too. Oh, if *he* could only look at her, then she would know she was still alive. She had tried it, tried to hold Amamaa's face in her hands at such an angle that their eyes would be looking into each other's, but every time it seemed as though it were about to happen, Amamaa's eyes would suddenly roll back, showing more milky whiteness than iris, and Akua Gyamma would know *he* could not see her—*he* just could not see her.

Akua Gyamma knew it was not Amamaa's fault that Amamaa could not grant the honor of turning her husband's sweet, sweet eyes in her direction. Pregnant at the time of her first husband's death, Akua Gyamma blamed no one but herself for Amamaa's blindness. She firmly believed that the grief and bitterness she had festered in her belly over her husband's passing had turned to poison and blinded the fetus in her womb. Poisoning Amamaa was the guilt she added onto the guilt she already felt for not being a loving affectionate mother.

All her life Akua Gyamma had been raised to believe that when the time came, she would honor, respect, and obey her husband and not to be disappointed if her love for him did not compare with the affinity she had for her own family. "Don't you worry," Nana Serwah had assured her. "Always be loyal to your husband, do not be quarrelsome, take good care of him, lay with him whenever he desires, and in return you will receive your reward—children; blessèd children—who you will love more than you do your husband, more than you do me, your mother, more even than you love life itself."

Akua Gyamma had believed her mother with all her heart, until God sent her such a strong, dark, white-toothed sunshine of a man that she couldn't help loving him beyond anything she had ever known. More than she loved her brothers and sisters, more than she loved her father, more even than she loved her own mother. So when she became pregnant with her first child, feeling so strongly for her husband, she just knew that the mother-love-beyond-all-others that the women talked about so much would literally flood her soul.

Still sweaty from labor, she propped herself up against the pillow, held her firstborn against her nipple, and waited for the rush. Nothing came. Mother's milk, but nothing else. As the days passed, she rocked Ashia, fed Ashia, changed Ashia, bathed Ashia, felt kindly toward her—often affectionately amused—but that mother-love-beyond-all-others never came. If the situation should ever have arisen, she would have traded little Ashia's life in exchange for her white-toothed husband any day of the year. She loved him beyond rival, and she declared so. This, her sister had informed her, was not only unnatural but sinful.

Chastised by the women for her abnormal lack of motherly instinct, she was overcome with a burning sense of guilt that crawled up inside her brain and never left. So when fourteen years later she became pregnant with her next child (everyone said it had taken her so long to conceive again because of her lack of motherliness), she vowed to love the new baby better than the last. She talked to it inside her womb; stroked her belly constantly to soothe it; and in the

seventh month, encouraged by the women, she even promised it that
when it was born, she would give it some of the potent love she had
only ever lavished on her husband.

When she heard that her husband had collapsed in the cassava
field, blood dripping from the corner of his mouth, Akua Gyamma
knew without anyone telling her that he was dead. Sending up a wail
that made not only the women but the dogs howl, she beat her stomach, pounding it so hard with her clenched fist that the older women
stopped their crying and leaped to restrain her, lest she pound her
unborn child to death. "I killed him. I killed him. I killed him," she
screamed, as the women lowered her bucking body to the ground.
Pinning her arms above her head, they tried to uncurl the fury
pumping through her fists.

"Uncurl your fist, uncurl your fist," Nana Serwah commanded,
pulling at her daughter's knuckles, knowing that if the anger wasn't
broken quickly, it would turn in on itself and eat her daughter alive.

Akua Gyamma kept her fists clenched for thirteen days. Despite
the doctors at the hospital telling her it was cancer that killed her
husband, she was convinced it was not cancer at all—but rather the
threat of her sharing her love for him with the unborn child—that
had sent him to his grave. He had always told her, "Akua Gyamma,
your love keeps me alive." In the rough times, when crops had failed
or when his mother had died, he swore that it was the enormity of
her potent love that pulled him through. In her quest to love her unborn child, she had threatened to steal some of that love away, and
the threat alone had killed him. Even though he had never heard her
say it, she believed that speaking it aloud had broken the protective
wall of love she had built around him and had allowed the enemy of
life to walk right up and steal him away.

"Forgive me," she said as she washed his clothes. "Forgive me,
forgive me," as she starched them, pressed them, folded them away.
"Forgive me," as she beat her head, beat her head with her fist.

The women told her to take her mind off her dead husband and
think of the child in her womb. She did. And as she did, resentment
churned in her stomach, causing her to keep her mouth closed for
fear of breathing its foul poison onto those who came to offer their
condolences. Regretting ever having opened her mouth to promise
her unborn child anything at all, she secretly cursed it, vowing in her

heart to avenge her husband's death. She would have let the fetus rot and die, but her mother, Nana Serwah, realizing that Akua Gyamma was not eating, in order to vindicate herself for her husband's death, whispered quickly in her ear, "Perhaps he has given you a son, exactly like himself." Shortly after that, Akua Gyamma could be found in the storeroom, gobbling up dried cassava in the form of gari as if her life depended on it.

When Amamaa was born, the midwife placed her in Akua Gyamma's arms and said, "Congratulations on a beautiful daughter." Without looking at her, Akua Gyamma passed the baby over to Nana Serwah, rolled over, and went to sleep.

"She is blind," Nana Serwah pronounced sadly, looking at her granddaughter's eyes. "Like her mother, who cannot see her own blessings."

Fifteen months after the death of her husband, Akua Gyamma became the second wife of Mr. K. K. Opoku, a respectable man from Aburanoma who had worked as a land surveyor in Kumasi and had settled back in his home village to live comfortably for the remainder of his days.

Mr. K. K. Opoku's proposal had come as a complete surprise to her. Believing she would never love again, Akua Gyamma had agreed to become his wife because by all reports he was a decent man, with a decent household in which to raise her two daughters. After the death of her first husband, she had aspired for nothing more than to farm and sell enough cassava to be able to help Nana Serwah feed and clothe Ashia, Amamaa, various relatives, and themselves. When Mr. Opoku offered to assist by making her his second wife, urged by her mother not to turn him down, she accepted.

When Kummaa was born at the end of that same year, the depth of her love for her newborn son shocked her. The son of a man she had not much feeling for, Kummaa awakened in her the motherhood she had tried so hard to muster for her daughters. That's when she blamed herself for Amamaa's blindness. Blamed herself for having sent down all those vengeful thoughts. Knowing now what mother love was like, Akua Gyamma did her best to make it up to the little two-year-old girl she had never really looked upon. But Amamaa was already attached to her grandmama.

Turning her attention next toward Ashia, she found that her

daughter, who was then nearly sixteen, had matured much more than she had realized and was madly in love with a visitor from America. It was the third time he had flown over to visit her, and Akua Gyamma, who regretted never having given Ashia much affection, was glad to see that her daughter had inherited from her and her natural father the one important fact of their lives together: that beyond custom, beyond duty, beyond respect, it was possible to love a man, to love a woman, with all your heart, with all your passion, with an inexplicable unshakable devotion. Ashia believed in romantic love, and Akua Gyamma was glad.

When she saw how Ashia looked at the visitor, talked to the visitor, waited eagerly for the visitor each time he promised to return to Ghana, when she saw Ashia wrap the visitor with that same thick blanket of love in which she herself had wrapped her first husband, Akua Gyamma went into motion.

Her first mission was to persuade one of her sisters to hint to the visitor about marrying Ashia. When the visitor agonized over the fact that he was already married, Akua Gyamma encouraged him to go back and ask his wife's permission to take Ashia as his second wife. Judging by the fact that the visitor could afford to travel back and forth all the way from America, and from the expensive gifts he showered on them each time he arrived, Akua Gyamma felt sure he could afford a second wife. She therefore explained to him how even though he was married, Ghanaian custom allowed that he could still marry Ashia, provided he could fulfill the necessary requirements to be granted another wife. On taking another wife, she explained, a man has to have enough social standing and wealth to be able to afford another family, calculating that each wife could possibly produce ten children. He would also need to get the approval of the elders of both his own and his intended's families, and preferably the approval of his existing wife or wives. As a second wife herself, she talked with him about the advantages of more than one wife—for all concerned. She even got Mr. Opoku's first wife, Afua, to advise him on how to approach his wife, what to say to her to make her understand and give him her approval, without which, they both explained, it would be unadvisable for him to proceed if he wanted a peaceful home. Akua Gyamma suggested that if he met with any resistance, he bring his first wife to Ghana with him next time so that she could talk to her, woman to woman, and introduce her to Ashia and the rest of the family. She was sure that if his wife met Ashia, she would see the benefit of having such a good woman as a part of their household.

When the visitor returned at the beginning of the following summer, he came without his wife but told Mr. Opoku that he was ready to marry Ashia. As a foreigner, the visitor did not know how to implement the customary procedure. He also apparently had no family members that could fly to Ghana to represent him in the proper fashion, so instead of turning him away for coming alone and empty-handed (which was considered an insolence), Mr. Opoku was merciful and recommended a decent local family with knowledgeable elders who might be willing to come and ask for Ashia on his behalf, in the appropriate manner.

The following Saturday three elderly men and seven women came from the Mensah clan, bearing gifts of palm wine, yams, two live chickens, and two pieces of cloth, to perform the *Agoo*, the knocking on the door of the Opoku family on behalf of Mr. Solomon Eustace Wilberforce.

Mr. K. K. Opoku invited the delegation into his living room, giving them a *bresuo nsa* to wet their dry throats and welcome them to his home. When they had drunk, he asked them about their mission. The oldest of the three elderly men informed him that they represented the Wilberforce clan and would like permission to come and ask for Ashia, to give to their son, Mr. Solomon Eustace Wilberforce.

Rising up an hour later, shaking his hand, thanking Mr. K. K. Opoku for his hospitality, the three men and seven women slipped on their thong sandals, which they had left outside the door by the veranda, and headed back down the dusty road from which they came.

Mr. K. K. Opoku called for Akua Gyamma to "come quickly."

Hiding behind the dining room door from where she had watched the whole proceedings, Akua Gyamma, who was not usually so easily accessible to him, appeared before her husband within seconds. "Go and fetch our eldest daughter," he said, attempting to hide his pride and happiness at the prospect of their daughter's fine match.

Akua Gyamma came back full of excitement, holding Ashia's hand. Ashia looked down demurely at the ground as Mr. Opoku waved his hand over the gifts lying on the floor: the fresh palm wine, the brightly spun cloth, the tied-up brown-and-white chickens clucking and flapping at his feet. "These have been delivered on behalf of Mr. Solomon Wilberforce and his people. They want to come and ask for you for Solomon. Tell me, Ashia, would you like for us to accept these gifts?"

"Yes, Papa, I would like it," Ashia said shyly, unable to contain her bloom, which was opening and spreading all over the room. Akua Gyamma not only witnessed her daughter blossoming before her very eyes, she could smell her, as the fragrance of Ashia's flowering love perfumed the air.

"Very well then," Mr. Opoku said, surreptitiously breathing in the sweet aroma, "we will send a delegation to inform them that we have accepted their gifts, and let them know on what day they may come and ask for you."

At the *Asradee* later that month, when the Mensah family gathered to officially engage Ashia on Solomon's behalf, they represented the Wilberforce family in grand style, making sure they presented the necessary symbolic gifts to show Solomon's high esteem for Ashia and her relatives.

Solomon was both nervous and intrigued. Over forty of the Mensah family members and more than eighty members of Ashia's extended family—consisting of members of her mother's family, representatives of her deceased father's family, elders from Mr. Opoku's senior wife's family, and, of course, many members of Mr. Opoku's immediate family—all met in the open grassland at the back of Mr. K. K. Opoku's house.

After the prayers and the *Otu won apo*, Mr. K. K. Opoku, believing that God and the ancestors had been duly acknowledged, asked the Opoku spokesman to ask the Mensah spokesman to ask the Mensah clan why they had come. "He is letting them know we have come to ask for Ashia on your behalf," Mr. Kwesi Mensah's grandson interpreted for Solomon, as the Mensah family spokesman answered the question. The purpose of the Mensahs' visit having been clearly relayed, and the Opoku spokesman having relayed acknowledgment of the Mensah clan's intent, the gift-giving began.

Mr. Opoku received drinks, *adanta* pants made out of fine handwoven fabric, and a gold coin. "The coin is in place of what used to be a large monetary or goods offering," the grandson explained to Solomon. "Mr. Opoku wanted it clear that they are not *selling* their daughter to us; she is, of course, priceless. He says that there is no way that we can pay for all the love, years, and money it has taken to cultivate such an exquisite jewel. So we should bring only one coin as a symbolic gesture, in respect for culture."

Next, Akua Gyamma got her *Obatan Kete*, a bedding mat. "What's that for?" Solomon asked, whispering to his helpful new friend.

"It is to replace the space that will soon be left when Ashia removes her bedding from her family house to her new home. And the cloth they are now giving her is her *shamombo*, or mother's urine cloth. It is for Ashia's mother to make herself a clean garment. Ashia as a baby must have urinated on her mother's clothing, so now that Ashia is grown and to be taken away, we bring a clean new cloth for Akua Gyamma to reclothe herself."

Abusua for the clan, and *bedwafoo* for the gathered witnesses, was given in the form of cases of drinks, palm wine, black-and-white neck and wrist beads, matches, and salt. "Salt? Why the salt?"

"You see, Mr. Solomon, in this part of Ghana, as inland tribes living far from the sea, salt was historically prized by our ancestors," the grandson educated. "Now that there is plenty of salt, I do not know why we keep these things up. We must seem very backward to you. I suppose it is just tradition."

"No. No, I don't think it's backward; I think it's good. I love your traditions. I think they're wonderful; you must hold on to them. You mustn't get like we are in the States. Once you let go of culture and tradition, there's nothing to replace it," Solomon educated back.

While the plentiful beads were being distributed—one for each person—Ashia's older brothers, the adult sons of Mama Afua, Mr. Opoku's senior wife, stepped forward and challenged Solomon, "*Ma me adee na me nkye wo adee.*" Solomon looked nervous.

"They are saying, 'Give me something so I give you something.' They cannot be expected to give us their beautiful sister for free." The grandson laughed.

"Maybe we should send you away and look for another husband. Our sister is only seventeen, so we have plenty of time," one of the brothers threatened Solomon playfully. Hearing him speak

English startled Solomon. He was tempted to reply, but he had been instructed not to speak on his own behalf unless addressed by one of the two spokesmen, so he held his peace. The brothers were given a case of drinks and a large piece of fabric to share as appeasement for taking away their sibling. Even little Amamaa and baby Kummaa were given a string of beads to wear around their ankles.

With all parties satisfied, two young women were then sent to fetch Ashia from the house. Solomon turned to look at her as she came out—she was stunning. Beautifully adorned in a blue-and-silver cloth that Nana Serwah had stitched by hand, she stood by the door with her hands folded in front of her, her eyes cast down, until the older women beckoned her forward. Escorted by the young women who had been sent to fetch her, Ashia picked her way across the ground in her bare feet. Her slender ankles accented by gold and silver beads, she moved toward the gathered clans gracefully as a doe.

"Is this the girl in question?" the Opoku spokesman inquired of Solomon.

"Yes," Solomon answered softly.

The Opoku elders noticed the way Solomon was looking at Ashia, his eyes full of love and desire. And even though she kept her eyes down, they could feel Ashia receiving him into her skin as his manhood rose and spread over her like a sheen. They feared *mpata* for *kwaseabuo* might be necessary. They continued to scrutinize Ashia, trying to see if their fears were right. Was *mpata* necessary? Had the visitor exploited their daughter? Had he taken advantage of her innocence? Had he taken her before asking? Or was she still a virgin? They could not tell. They could not see into Ashia's eyes, because she kept them lowered to the ground, never once looking up at them, so it was hard to judge her expression. Was it one of bashfulness? Or shame?

When questioned by the Opoku spokesman whether he had already made love to Ashia, Solomon replied in a calm emphatic voice, "No. Absolutely not." His answer was pure and simple, and he was purely and simply believed, so without further delay, Ashia's gifts were handed over to her mother. Seven pieces of differently colored and textured fabric, a white leather Bible, a gold necklace made of linking *adenkra* symbols of peace, with a matching bracelet and earrings. A wooden trunk, inlaid with brass and ivory. "To pack the things she will need to bring to her new home," the grandson explained before Solomon could ask. And a diamond engagement ring, which was the only item Solomon had brought with him from America. "So you are now our son," Mr. Opoku said to Solomon. "I think you will agree, my son, that we are bequeathing you with a most exquisite jewel."

"Thank you," Solomon said through the Mensah family spokesman. "I cannot begin to tell you how much this afternoon has meant to me. *Me da wa si*—I thank you," he said again, his voice cracking with emotion.

Watching the betrothal proceedings, Akua Gyamma was so moved that she cried for the first time since the year of her first husband's death. "Ashia," she whispered, touching her daughter's slender wrist. "You have the greatest treasure life can gift you, the love of a man you truly cherish."

Passing into the house to check on the meat for the feast— chicken, pig, goat, lamb that had been slaughtered, plucked, pounded, seasoned, boiled, stewed, skewered, roasted, and garnished that morning—Akua Gyamma turned to her soon-to-be son-in-law, who at thirty-one was only five years younger than she, and with tears in her eyes whispered in Twi, which she knew he could not understand, "Give my daughter the love I failed to give her. Love her like the mother I never was, like the father she lost too soon, like the husband she dreams you to be. Love her like God loves her. She deserves it, for truly she worships you." Not sure exactly what she had said but moved by the spirit in which she had spoken, Solomon replied, "I'll never let her down. I promise you, Mrs. Opoku, I'll never let her down."

Despite the sweet sincerity of his voice, Akua Gyamma was washed in a sudden wave of sadness. She had enjoyed the blessing of having her first husband all to herself, of his loving her so deeply that he had refused to take on another wife despite his family's plotting to the contrary. She wondered suddenly if she should not have insisted on the same luxury for her daughter. She had let Ashia down by not loving her enough when she was born; was she letting her down now by giving her away to an already married, traveling foreigner?

She shared her concern with Nana Serwah, who having borne four daughters and seven sons to a man who barely spoke to her, reminded her daughter that her idyllic first marriage was not the lot of most women. She also reminded her that Ashia had in Solomon a man who would take good care of her, speak to her gently, a man whose eyes danced excitedly when they looked upon her, a man who treated her like an angel. Apart from his comings and goings, Nana Serwah asserted, Solomon was a dream of a man come true.

She cautioned her daughter that if she dwelled on the sadness of Solomon's absence, Ashia might start to dwell on it too—and that would lead to unnecessary discontent. She should instead look forward to the wedding day. "Rejoice and be glad."

Akua Gyamma heeded her mother's words and put the issue of Ashia's loneliness out of her mind. Later that summer, seeing Ashia's elated face, her bridal head adorned in gold, she believed in her heart that Nana Serwah was right. Only occasionally, in the years that followed, when she saw her young daughter sitting alone in her courtyard studying under the tree, the thought would reenter her head that maybe she should have made Ashia wait for someone who would be with her nightly, touching her tenderly and making her laugh—not just in the season of summer but every day that God gave her breath.

*   *   *

Looking at Ashia now, holding hands with Solomon, laughing as they strolled through the grass, Akua Gyamma comforted herself with the thought that her daughter's marriage to Solomon was at least preferable to her own marriage to Mr. K. K. Opoku. Her own union had been so passionless that by the time Kummaa turned one, Mr. K. K. Opoku had gone back to favoring his first wife, giving Akua Gyamma the rest and solitude she had hoped she would find, knowing that her family was well provided for. Being the most successful of his clan, Mr. K. K. Opoku had several dependent relatives, many of whom lived at, or at least helped around, the house, which minimized Akua Gyamma's duties. Apart from checking on her cassava fields and playing with Kummaa, there was not much required of her, so Akua Gyamma spent much of her days sitting under her favorite guava tree, relishing memories of a strong, dark, white-toothed sunshine of a man that was only ever a thought away.

His feet—that's what Akua Gyamma was reminded of as she lay hidden, watching first Kummaa's feet, then Amamaa's a stick-length behind, then Ashia's, then Solomon's, crunching past her through the dry grass just a few yards away from her face—her dear deceased husband's strong, dark, surprisingly soft feet caressing her skin as he slid them up and down her legs, whispering, white teeth flashing, laughing sunshine into her ears. "Sorry, am I keeping you?" he would tease as she tried halfheartedly to wriggle out of the tangle of his legs and stand up. "Little woman, where do you think you are going?" She would reply that she needed to go see to the baby, or stir the food she had left on the fire. Then his soft foot would melt down her calves, peeling open her legs, and she would know that for quite a while she was not going anywhere . . .

Akua Gyamma wished she didn't have to get up from the grass but she knew that Solomon and Ashia would soon arrive at the house, and that shortly afterward she would be summoned by Mr. Opoku to come and do her wifely greeting. When her children had gone far enough ahead for her not to be seen by them, she rose to her feet and followed in slow pursuit.

Chapter 4

✦

MR. K. K. OPOKU had done well for himself. When he was a land surveyor, his honest thorough reports had saved many builders and contractors millions of cedis. In gratitude, they had promised to help him build a house whenever he needed one. When they heard he had retired to his home village and was taking a second wife, a group of them paid to send builders from Kumasi to Aburanoma to renovate his existing house and build on four new bedrooms, a bathroom, and a storeroom, in order to accommodate his new family.

Mr. Opoku's renovated house was the grandest in the village. It sat on nine acres of grassland, much of it growing wild and unattended at the back of the house, where the women cooked. The front of the house was more organized, with a natural-looking but well-tended garden divided by a long gravel driveway that led up to the steps of the palatial veranda. The veranda surrounded the entire perimeter of the extended white house, which boasted sliding glass doors all along the living room in front. When not reading in his modest bedroom, Mr. Opoku could most often be found sitting outside the living room on the veranda amid the lush vegetation and opulent flowers that leaned in from the garden over the low wall, their colorful heads craning like curious spectators. On May 22, their curiosity was never disappointed.

Since morning, all the household chairs had been lined up on the veranda in preparation for the welcome. A young boy put two fingers in his mouth and whistled loudly. In a flurry of commotion, the alerted company gathered round.

*　　　*　　　*

As soon as Solomon stepped up on the wide veranda, leading Ashia by the hand, her waiting relatives rose to greet him. The way they always assembled to welcome him home gave him a humbling sense of importance, with a deep sense of family belonging that he had never experienced prior to his marriage to Ashia. Marrying Miriam had been a very private affair. The decision had been made by just the two of them and God, whom they asked to send down a rainfall by midnight as a sign of his blessing and approval. It rained; they married. It was as simple as that. Just the two of them, Kawasaki, a priest, and a stranger off the street who stepped in as a second witness when Toussaint Joseph failed to show up. Miriam's people were like his own, dead or estranged, so his life with her was like his childhood: quiet and, for the most part, devoid of any family interaction. Not until marrying Ashia and being embraced by all the extended branches of her family did he discover the comfort of being loved and claimed not just by an individual but by a whole clan.

When Ashia became his wife, she had brought him the most priceless of dowries, an ancient bloodline of which he could be a part. He had first come to Ghana in search of more African history than the little he had been taught, hoping to find the missing link within himself. To his delight, he had discovered not just a link but a whole rich chain of culture that enveloped him like a coat of armor. The shield and warmth of family was a sensation he had longed for all his life. Being a part of Ashia and all she represented protected him. It made him stronger, taller, richer, more powerful—more himself.

Solomon passed by each assembled person, shaking him or her by the hand as he bid hello. "*Akwaaba*," he said, inclining his head slightly in deference to the more elderly relatives. "*Akwaaba. Akwaaba.*" He traveled along the line, making hand and eye contact with each person, enjoying the feel of warm palms, the smell of scented talcum powder and fresh sunbaked sweat. He could close his eyes and know he was in Ghana.

When the handshakes were complete, Mr. K. K. Opoku, a short powerful-looking man in his late sixties, ushered Solomon into a large wicker chair. The back of the chair rose into a large oval canopy, like a great royal throne. Cognizant that the chair was Mr. Opoku's personal seat, he attempted to decline the offer, but Mr. Opoku insisted, assuring Solomon that it would be an honor to have him sit

in it. It was a ritual they performed to demonstrate their mutual respect for each other, and ultimately Solomon always complied with
his father-in-law's wishes and sat down in the treasured seat.

The entire company of people then filed past Solomon to shake
his hand and welcome him back from his travels. Solomon feasted on
the array of rainbow-colored fabric that waved in the air as they
gathered, hitched, tossed, and tucked their attire when they rose,
greeted, passed by, and sat back down. Old men wore yards of woven
cloth, or printed cotton, draped stylishly over one shoulder, leaving
the other shoulder bare like polished ebony proudly on display.
Many of the younger men favored long embroidered robes with
matching pantaloons and caps. Women wore brightly printed tops
with long tight matching skirts and headdresses, with an extra piece
of fabric tied loosely around their waist or draped over their shoulder, or long flowing boubous, elaborately embroidered. Some of the
less affluent men of the group were clad in much-worn cotton un-
dershirts and old trousers, the women with faded cloths tied across
their breasts.

Whatever their clothing, it was evident to Solomon that all had
put on their best to receive him, except for Mr. K. K. Opoku, who
wore a plain short-sleeved khaki suit. "Forgive my casual attire," he
had once remarked with a laugh to Solomon on his arrival, "but you
are my son. A father does not need to impress his son—a son should
rather work hard to impress his father." The point had been well
taken, albeit jokingly said, and since that occasion, when going to
greet his father-in-law and the rest of his family, Solomon had never
again left on the jeans and T-shirt he wore for the dusty coach ride
from Accra.

Solomon passed his stuffed duffel bag to Mr. K. K. Opoku, who
in turn passed it to first wife Mama Afua, standing dutifully just
behind him. She held it carefully and waited for instructions.
Mr. Opoku pointed for her to take it to his eldest brother, Papa Fofie
Opoku, who was sitting at the front of the line of chairs. Fifteen
years senior, his eldest brother had never gone to school. Working
alongside their father, farming cocoa to help support his younger
siblings, Papa Fofie had remained illiterate and financially unsuc-
cessful. However, by virtue of his age, he still had seniority over his

more prosperous younger brother, even in his younger brother's house.

Papa Fofie placed the duffel bag on the ground and stood up. After years of observation Solomon knew that the bag would not be opened until more important matters had been attended to. Two small boys ran inside at Papa Fofie's bidding, and seconds later they came back out with a glass of water, an empty glass, and a bottle of gin. Papa Fofie indicated for the glass of water to be given to Solomon.

When Solomon had finished drinking the water, Papa Fofie welcomed the traveler back home in Twi, and Mr. Opoku's second-eldest brother, Nana Darkua, stood up to translate into English so Solomon could understand. Having welcomed Solomon, Papa Fofie gave an account of how the family had fared in Solomon's absence, as is the custom, relating that they had suffered the loss of a young child—the niece of one of their sisters, whom Solomon had met—but that apart from that, everything was well. When he had finished, he asked Solomon to recount how he had fared on his travels, and how their distant families were doing.

Solomon spoke to the second-eldest brother, Nana Darkua, who translated his response for the company at large. He assured them that all was well, that his travels were successful, and that he had come home to spend time with his wife Ashia. The company smiled and nodded with approval. Papa Fofie then poured a generous portion of the gin into the empty glass. Some of the company bowed their heads, while others looked straight ahead.

Papa Fofie held the glass high and then tipped it, pouring a trickle of the gin over the low veranda wall into the garden. He called on God to look after them all, to deliver them from any ill health, and to bless them with prosperity; and he thanked God profusely for taking good care of Solomon, their son, who had just returned home. Then he poured more of the clear liquid onto the ground and called on Pano, the god of the river; Sakumo, god of the lagoon; and Naye, god of the sea. For each god he tipped the glass, letting the libation seep into the earth.

The ritual always gave Solomon a sanguine sorrow. He listened as the old man called on the spirits of their ancestors, *Nana Pokua, Papa*

Abrefa, Kofi Amenyangpong, Abena Pokua, Yaw Owusu, Akosua Gyamma. The company moaned at the mention of each name.

Do any of the ancestors know me? Solomon wondered. *Have they in their spirit forms kept an eye on their children's children's children to see who we are and where we have been scattered?* "Wilberforce," he murmured under his breath, hoping one of the spirits would recognize him by name and send him a message from the other side. "Solomon Eustace Wilberforce, son of Charles Franklin Whittman and Annetta Anika Wilberforce." Surely the ancestors knew. Surely they had seen it all. Seen how his forefathers were captured. Witnessed where they were all sent. Surely there was a spirit who could trace his family tree, direct him to his roots, reunite him with his fellow branches. He was doing his best to honor them all, to reconnect with all his ancestors in Africa, America, and the Caribbean. But without guidance, it was hard.

"Watch over us," Papa Fofie implored. "Papa Kofi Abrefa, watch over us all," he prayed to their long-deceased father. Pouring the final drops of the libation into the thirsty soil, he shook the glass and refilled it. Touching it to his lips, he passed it around for all the adults to take a sip.

Shadows from the surrounding foliage and miniature palm trees danced and played on the absorbed faces of the family as they sipped in quiet communion. Solomon held the glass to his lips and tipped it slowly, sending a thin line of heat trickling down his throat. *I'm alive and in Ghana*, he marveled as he passed the glass on, thanking God one more time that groping unknowingly through the maze of his life, he had managed to stumble his way home.

Important matters now having been dealt with, Papa Fofie put the glass to the side and opened up the large army duffel bag. Amazed faces watched as the old man pulled out gift after gift for the assembled relatives. Radios, alarm clocks, two small tape recorders, pure linen shirts, men's and ladies' wristwatches, a calculator, bottles of perfume, tinned gourmet delicacies, a silver harmonica for Amamaa, a bundle of rolled T-shirts, and an envelope stuffed full of ten-dollar bills to be handed out to make sure everyone received a present.

Mr. K. K. Opoku instructed the children to arrange the goods neatly on the veranda wall and then join the grateful throng as they rose once more to file past Solomon and shake his hand in thanks. The women did a little curtsy, placing one hand on their knee as they bent, like graceful dancers.

"Kummaa!" Nana Serwah's voice bellowed from the back of the house, cutting through the jubilant voices of thanks. "Kummaa ba!" Kummaa leaped up from where he was sitting at Solomon's feet and ran to see what his grandmama wanted. Mr. K. K. Opoku stood up and took the floor. The veranda fell into a respectful silence.

"We are glad and thankful to have our illustrious son Solomon return to us in good health." He turned to Solomon with fatherly pride. "Ghana, Aburanoma village, and last but not least, we the Opoku family, welcome you back home with our whole hearts. We thank you for your liberality and generosity in bringing us these thoughtful gifts. I will not detain you with long-windedness, as I am sure you are desirous to go home and rest with our dear daughter, your beloved wife Ashia. Solomon, my son, may you and our daughter Ashia . . ." Mr. Opoku looked around and saw that his stepdaughter was nowhere to be seen. Solomon could see the irritation on his father-in-law's face.

"Where is Ashia? And where are my wives?"

First wife Mama Afua stepped forward. She was a plump woman with a smooth, shiny, round face that belied her fifty-seven years. Despite her weight, she moved with a little skip-trip every time Mr. Opoku called her name. She hopped forward from behind his chair, appearing by his side before he had a chance to even look for her.

"Come, Mama Afua, greet Solomon." Smiling at her politely, Solomon shook her hand for the fourth time that afternoon. "Where is Ashia's mother?" Mr. Opoku asked, slightly irked at having to wait for his second wife.

Just as Mr. Opoku was about to send one of the children out to look for her, Akua Gyamma came up the steps from the back of the house, moving with a slow sensuous sway of her hips that made Mr. K. K. Opoku regret that he could not get her to be more responsive to him. She never fought his advances—she yielded dutifully—but despite his authoritative manner, duty was not what he desired from his wives. Love, respect, affection—these were the things he was after—especially from her. He had showered her with gifts and compliments, but nothing seemed to pry open her passion; so he had taken to leaving her alone, except on rare occasions when, driven by her swaying hips, he couldn't help but lay with her just one more time . . .

Akua Gyamma greeted Solomon with the same reserve with which she treated everyone except her son, Kummaa. The first time Solomon set eyes on her eight years ago at her husband's funeral, he had known she was a woman of great passion. A dancing fury in the wilderness, her black mourning cloth flapping wildly in the haze, her powerful lament shattering time and space—he would never have believed she could become this distant woman standing before him. *Somewhere caged within this flaccid hand*, Solomon thought sadly as he shook it, *there is vibrant life*. Akua Gyamma removed herself from Solomon's probing eyes and took her place in back of her husband's chair.

"Awuradjua," Mr. Opoku shouted. He turned to look at Solomon, a proud gleam in his eye. "Life has been good to me, Solomon, so I have taken on a third wife. And may God be praised, she has given me another son. Awura Adjua!" he shouted again, a self-congratulatory smile on his face. When Awuradjua emerged, her infant son tied in a cloth on her back, Solomon could see why Mr. Opoku was so pleased with himself.

Awuradjua was a beauty. A lithe blue-black beauty, with limbs like a gazelle's and the eyes of a baby giraffe. At twenty-six, she was forty-one years younger than her husband, younger than several of her stepsons, and only four years older than her stepdaughter Ashia. Mr. Opoku told Solomon in a hushed voice that he had spotted Awuradjua two years ago at a local durbar, and having asked permission to marry her, had waited to make sure she could conceive before going through with the final ceremony.

"This is your son-in-law," Mr. Opoku said, throwing Awuradjua a teasing smile. "Do you approve?" Awuradjua nodded timorously and moved away. Solomon watched her as she slid behind Mr. Opoku's chair next to Afua, his first wife. Afua shrugged her arm, wiping the spot where, in moving beside her, Awuradjua had accidentally brushed against it. Immune to wifely rivalry, Akua Gyamma, standing on the other side of Afua, gave Awuradjua a smile of encouragement.

In the distance, Solomon noticed Nana Serwah pass a small wooden object to Kummaa, who gripped it in his hand and went running furtively across the grass toward Ashia's house. Nana Serwah came careening onto the veranda like a big bird of prey, her arms open wide, her feet sliding along the smooth surface in a joyous dancelike step. Slip-slip, slip-slip, she swayed across the polished stone, cheering jubilantly. "Welcome, welcome, welcome," she cooed in a chirpy voice. Alighting in front of Solomon, she leaned back, inspected his face, laughed, swooped forward, and enfolded him in the loose comforting fat of her arms. "*I am a grandmama,*" she liked to say to those eager men who, mesmerized by her swaying hips, periodically inquired if she was interested in having them fill the empty space on her bed left by her deceased husband. "*I am a grandmama, you know,*" she would say and walk off, hips swaying in that hypnotic seesaw that both her daughter Akua Gyamma and granddaughter Ashia had inherited down to the very last syllable.

"Nana, where is your granddaughter?" Mr. Opoku asked, a slight accusatory note in his voice. Solomon looked at Nana Serwah's face as she pulled back from embracing him. It was hard to believe, looking at that unassuming smile, that she controlled the entire household, as Mr. Opoku often claimed. But Solomon had to admit that on several visits he had noticed that unless Nana Serwah approved, any plans or decisions for the household were not taken seriously.

"Ashia!" Mr. Opoku shouted, losing his patience. "Where are you hiding yourself? Come and stand by your husband. I was making my speech." He looked around for a dependable child to send to go find her.

"Ashia, come," Nana Serwah summoned quietly. Instantly, Ashia appeared in the doorway.

"Yes, Nana," she said with a smile as unassuming as her grandmama's.

"Your father wants you," Nana Serwah said as she slip-slipped across the veranda and disappeared around the side of the house.

There was a slight pause as Mr. Opoku watched his mother-in-law's retreat. "Where was I?" he asked, a little flustered. "Ah, yes! Solomon, my friend, may you and Ashia go in peace. We, your elders, wish you celebration, recreation, and above all, procreation! It's

time you two had a child. If an old man like me can still be pro-
lifically populating, I know you can manage it. Go forth and mul-
tiply. Strength to your elbow!"

The company laughed in agreement, adding their friendly advice.

"Concentrate."

"Concentrate on your beautiful wife."

"You have to put your foot down and insist she give you your
child."

"Ashia, why are you being so stubborn?"

"Don't let her wriggle out of it, Solomon."

"Squeeze her harder."

The men continued to tease, their pupils dilating with lustful
thoughts.

"Ashia, don't mind these men," the women replied in defense.

"It is not your fault. A man has to bring himself."

"As for we women, we are always ready; men are the ones who
have to make ready."

"A woman can not impregnate herself, Solomon, you must stay
home until you have completed your job successfully."

Everybody laughed and Solomon laughed with them, hoping
they would not notice the sense of failure that crept through his
body into his soul.

Chapter 5

✦

SOLOMON FELT they were not alone. He thought he saw a shadow moving in the darkness, but as soon as Ashia lit the first candle, the eerie feeling he had when walking into the room was replaced by the thrill of seeing her illuminated by the light of the flickering flame. She cupped her hand around the wick to steady the fire and then circled the four-poster bed, carefully lighting the rest of the candles. The mosquito-net curtains draped across the bed's brass rails shimmered in the glow like a delicate spider's web in the center of a fairy ring.

Solomon started to undress. Ashia averted her eyes. After nearly five years of marriage, it amazed Solomon that on the first night of his return, she was always almost as shy and hesitant with him as she had been on their wedding night . . .

Having gone through all the phases of the traditional wedding, they had left the three-day festivities to come back to the two rooms and a courtyard that Ashia had requested Solomon have built, in order to live independently from her stepfather's house.

Lying on the bed watching the sun set through the lacy curtain hanging over the door, Solomon had nibbled Ashia's ears and talked love into them, hoping to abate the frightened look in her eyes. Stroking her body, he had taken minutes, hours even, to circle his fingers ever so slowly to where they really wanted to be—soft, warm, private places. "Perfect," he had moaned, his fingers finally feeling what his mind had only dreamed of. "You're perfect, Ashia."

Never having been with a man before, Ashia had flinched nervously under his probing fingers, so he had circled them back up her body, stroked her neck, nibbled on her ears, and pampered her until dawn. Finally, at dawn, having whispered every prologue, played every prelude, and conducted every overture his heart and mind could think of, he had rolled on top of her and entered her.

As gentle as he had tried to be, it was not until he had rolled off her body and kissed her into sleep that the look of apprehension had finally dropped from Ashia's face.

The same look of apprehension was on her face tonight as she wandered around the room self-consciously, looking for things to do besides undress herself. Having lit all the candles, she stopped by the lectern, turned the Bible to her favorite chapter, and read aloud.

"I am black and lovely, oh ye daughters of Jerusalem. I am the rose of Sharon, the lily of the valleys. Winter is past, the rains are over and gone, the birds sing. Yes the season of summer is here."

"What's that?" Solomon asked, moving to stand behind her, his tall earth-brown body now completely naked.

"The Song of Solomon," Ashia said, shifting slightly at the touch of his body against her back. Solomon peered over her shoulder and read on.

"You have ravished my heart, my lovely one, you have ravished my heart with one look from your eyes, with one turn of your beautiful neck."

Solomon could feel Ashia's breath change rhythm as his naked body moved against her. Pressing himself into her firm fleshy buttocks, he pretended not to notice the effect he was having on her as he continued to read.

"Your lips, O my love, how delicious your lips, sweet honey drips from your tongue."

"Mmm . . . I like that!" Solomon said, stooping down and kissing the back of Ashia's neck. Picking her up as easily as if she were a rag doll, he carried her to the bed and placed her down on her feet beside it. Parting the net curtains, he leaped onto the covers, lay with his hands behind his back, and said with a charming naughty-boy smile, "Take your clothes off and come here."

"All of them?"

"Yeah, all of them," Solomon commanded, feeling like the king he was playing.

"Please wait for me to take everything off," Ashia said, peeking coyly at him through the curtain.

"What all have you got on under there?"

Ashia lifted up her arms, slid the long flowing boubou she was wearing slowly up over her head, and dropped it onto the floor.

Solomon laughed in astonishment as Ashia's sublime naked body came crawling across the bed toward him. "You mean you didn't have nothing on under that dress all day? No panties, no bra, no nothing?"

"Well, my lord and master," Ashia said, giggling, pulling at the sheet they were lying on, in an attempt to cover up her nakedness, "when you call, I do not like to keep you waiting."

"Is that a fact?"

"Yes, it is a fact." Ashia's voice was barely a whisper as Solomon pulled her on top of him.

Pressing his hands on her shoulders, he pushed her into a sitting position so he could admire her. Bashful, Ashia tried to lie back down on top of him, but he kept her sitting up by the sheer force of his hands on her shoulders. "Let me look," he whispered hoarsely, his eyes loving all over her.

Involuntarily, Ashia's body catered to his admiration, her back arching like a cheetah ready to pounce, her breasts seemingly reaching out toward him, begging to be touched.

"Yes," Solomon encouraged, cupping them in his hands. "Yes, yes, yes." He rolled on top of her, fingers probing, surprised— always surprised—by how wet, how warm, how completely his she was as he guided himself into her. "My Ashia . . ." he exhaled as soon as he could retrieve his voice, "Oh, Ashia, my Ashia . . ."

"I've missed you," Ashia sighed, her eyes dripping tears she had been saving for a hundred years. "I've missed you, I've missed you," precious wet diamonds falling out of her big brown eyes onto his face, diamonds tinkling out from between her legs, rolling down his thighs onto the bed.

"My jewel." Solomon raised up his torso, bore his weight in his arms, bearing down on her he pushed, bearing down, bearing down. "My jewel, my jewel." Bearing down, he looked into her eyes, a treasure chest full of diamonds, shaking her body, shaking them out, shaking them out from her eyes, shaking them out from between her legs, shaking out the diamonds that lived inside Ashia. The more he shook, the more diamonds she made, showering him, showering them with her jewels. He lifted his torso a little higher, sending all his power running down to the base of his spine. "Oh, my love." He gripped her hair and pushed. "My love, my love." Holding on to the top of her head—"Oh, Ashia . . ."—he ground his body deeper. "Ashia . . . Ashia . . ." Her body moved his body—deeper—his body moved her body—deeper, deeper—her body moved, his body moved— his body moved, her body moved—deeper, deeper—dazzling diamonds. "Ashia . . . Ashia . . ."

"I've missed you."

"I've missed you."

"Oh, Solomon."

"All mine."

"Yes, I am yours."

"I am yours too."

"Oh, Solomon, I am yours, I am yours."

Yes mine

Yours is mine

Mine is yours

All of it mine

Yours . . . yours

Take it, please take me

You deserve it all

You

You

Take all of me

Here — there's more

You keep filling me up

I keep filling up

More — more

I give you rivers

I swallow the sea for you

I dig the earth for you

I scratch the sky for you

Do you feel that?

Yes — yes, I feel it

Do you feel that — do you feel that?

Pouring out all over
Like monsoon rain—
Pouring—pouring
"Oh . . . Ashia . . ."
Pouring—pouring—pouring
I cannot stop it
Drench me—drench me
Love me for an eternity
I will never stop loving you
Love me for an eternity
I will never stop loving you
Say it—say it—
Oh, please . . . please
Say it—say it—say I will love you for an eternity
Yes—yes, I will
Say it, Ashia! You have to say it!
"Oh—please—oh, Solomon, please."
Say it—say it—say it
Stop! Stop! I am going to fly
Say it
Oh, stop! Please, I am going to fly
Say it, Ashia—say it
I am going to fly, stop—I am going to fly away
I love you too much to stop
I am going to fly away
"Wait . . . wait for me . . ."
I can't help it—I am going to fly
"Wait."
Blue skies—blue skies—blue skies
"Wait . . . wait, Ashia . . ."
Oh, come see
"I'm coming, I'm coming . . ."
Look—look—come—oh, come
Where, my darling? Where?
Up here . . . way up here
Oh, my darling
Come . . . higher . . .
"Oh, my darling."

Higher . . . higher
"Oh . . . oh, Ashia . . ."
"I will love you for an eternity."
Blue skies . . . blue skies . . .
Blue skies . . . blue skies . . . blue skies . . .

Chapter 6

✦

*S*OMEWHERE IN THE NIGHT, love had been made and then made again. Vibrating faster and faster, their bodies were so stimulated, it seemed to Solomon that Ashia and he had simply ceased to be.

Ashia wriggled her arm, and Solomon realized he was lying on it and moved. They opened their eyes simultaneously and smiled recognition. The love in Ashia's smile was so exactly how Solomon felt that for a moment he thought he was looking at himself. "Mirrors don't have arms," he muttered, still in a half-sleep. The sound of his own voice and the amused puzzlement on Ashia's face woke him up fully. "What did I say?" he asked, confused by his own words.

"You said, 'Mirrors don't have arms.'"

"No, but I do," he said, hugging them around her and rolling her roughly over the bed. "Arms that ain't ever gonna let you go."

"Auntie Ashia," Kummaa's plaintive voice called out from the courtyard, cutting into Ashia's laughter. "Nana Serwah says to come and put this in your fridge."

"Come on in," Solomon invited, much to Ashia's embarrassment. They were both still naked, and Solomon laughed as Ashia dove under the sheets just before Kummaa entered carrying a large bowl of raw, red, freshly slaughtered goat. He lowered his eyes as he crossed to the back of the room, his little twiglike body stooping under the weight of the meat. Placing the bowl on the floor by the fridge, he sneaked a furtive peak under the bed. Straightening up, he looked bashfully at Solomon out of the corner of his eye, deliberately avoiding looking at his sister, who was lying with the sheet pulled up under her nose.

Solomon could tell by Kummaa's evasiveness that the boy knew something very private had gone on in the room. It intrigued Solomon how children always seemed to know when sex had taken place. "What you been up to, little man?" he asked, hoping to put Kummaa at ease.

"I have not been up to anything, Uncle Solomon," Kummaa said defensively as he squashed the bowl of meat into the already packed refrigerator. "I have been helping Nana Serwah."

"Wanna do something fun today?"

Kummaa nodded yes, his eyes still avoiding looking up on the bed.

"Okay," Solomon said, standing up and stretching his naked body unashamedly. "Let me and Auntie Ashia get dressed, and we'll find ourselves some trouble to get into, maybe even borrow Uncle Kwesi's Jeep and drive out to Auntie Pokua's peanut farm."

"Can Amamaa come too?"

"Course."

"Yaaay!" Kummaa cheered jubilantly, clapping his hands as he ran out of the room. "We are going to the farm, we are going to the farm, hooray! Hooray for King Solomon!"

Solomon stopped midstretch as a sharp pang shot through him. For a moment he couldn't think what had caused the pain; then it came to him. Kummaa's words, *King Solomon*, had reminded him of Miriam.

Easing his body up straight, Solomon wondered wistfully what Miriam was doing. Was she in the kitchen boiling eggs? Or making mango jam? Was she sitting in her outdoor dining room, gazing out to sea? Or lying in her copper bathtub . . .

Stop! Solomon put a halt to his wandering mind. Longing for one season while in the midst of another was against his own rules. *Live in the moment the moment you live it.* That was his creed in life. "Never lust for the future nor long for the past," he would tell his friends. "Don't wish away your life, suspended discontentedly between that long-gone yesterday and that never-attained tomorrow. The present is a present from God. Accept and enjoy it."

Solomon hated to see people cheated of the beauty of the present. It frightened and enraged him. He had watched his mother waste away her life, forever clinging to the past, forever deluding herself about the future, secretly waiting for his father to return to prove to her and the entire population of Cape Corcos that he had meant all those lovely things he had told her, that she was his sweet little thing, that he would take care of her, that she need never worry because he knew what he was doing. She believed him, trusted him, so how could her pregnancy have been an accident? Surely he had given her a baby on purpose so he could come back and be with her forever. "One of these days"—that was what his mother had waited for all her life. To wake up "one of these days" and find Solomon's father, Charles Franklin Whittman, returned to the Island so she could show him what a wondrous son she had borne him, so they could all live happily ever after. "King Solomon," she would say, practicing the moment of introduction as she lay in her sick bed. "This is precious King Solomon, birthed, saved, and named by the daughter of a midwife, little nine-year-old girl by the name of Miriam, come from a long line of midwives, going back four generations deep, ya know. Look at him, Charles, did you ever dream of such a son?!"

Near the end, after her mind had slipped but before the tumor impeded her speech, Solomon had heard his mother tell it over and over again. "Look, Charles, he taller than you now," she would say dotingly, struggling out her words. "Miriam's miracle baby. And he taller than you now—you ever see the like? Look, Charles, look. Say hello to your papa now, Solomon, say hello to your papa. Come, Solomon, be nice—he didn't mean no harm, say hello to your papa."

"Hello, Papa," he had finally said to the empty air, just to please her. "Nice to meet you, Papa."

His mother had smiled and closed her eyes. Despite the smile, Solomon could still see the sadness etched across her face. She made it to her thirtieth birthday, as she vowed she would, despite the doctor's prognosis. "Happy birthday, me," she croaked early that morning, falling back asleep as soon as she had spoken. Solomon painted her a birthday card covered with pink hearts and left it beside her on the pillow. When she woke hours later, the lump in her throat had grown so large that she could not form any more words. *Live only in the present*, she scribbled on the back of the card. By the end of the month, she was dead.

"How you gonna send him off to a man what didn't even come see him?"

"The boy need to be with his father."

"In America?!"

"It what she would have wanted."

"Over her dead body!"

Live only in the present. In the midst of the grown-ups arguing over his future, with his mother cold on the bed, Solomon had vowed over her dead body to live only in the present . . .

Ashia's arms sliding around his neck startled him. "What is the matter, Solomon? What are you thinking about?" she asked sweetly.

"Nothing much. I was just trying to think what to do today," he lied.

Ashia jumped off the bed, wrapping a piece of cloth around her and grabbing a towel. "Well, I will leave you to think," she said, avoiding his eyes as she headed out into the courtyard.

Solomon could tell by her hurried movements and the timbre of her voice that Ashia knew he had just lied. Whenever Ashia felt he was displeased or troubled, she moved herself out of his way in case she was the cause of his disquiet. She would busy herself elsewhere, leaving him space to spin around on the island of his mind, until he was ready to swim back to her on the mainland. It was one of the things Solomon loved about her, the unneediness of her giving.

Ashia had left the room to be considerate, but her absence made Solomon feel uncomfortably pensive. He didn't want to think anymore; he wanted to just be. "Ashia!" he called out, a hint of panic in his voice. The encroaching weight of his thoughts were stifling his joy, and he missed the easy lightness of Ashia's being.

"Ashia!" Solomon threw a towel around his waist and headed out of the room. *Swim back across,* he thought as he passed through the thin lace curtain into the sunlight. *Come on, Solomon, winter is over, swim back across, spring into summer,* he chastised himself as he walked across the courtyard to the semicircle of stones. *Don't think it, just do it. No more yesterdays, spring into summer.*

Solomon tossed his towel across the wall and squatted down next to Ashia's soapy body. *This is summer,* his mind coaxed as Ashia dipped her metal cup into the bucket of water and poured some over his head. "Ahhhh," he sighed, closing his eyes as Ashia continued to scoop and pour, scoop and pour, letting the water flow down his body in a gentle stream. "Mmmmm," he moaned as she used her loofah to scrub away the last vestiges of winter clinging beneath his skin.

"All clean," she celebrated, lifting the bucket and whooshing the remainder of water over his head. Solomon shivered as the dregs of winter washed off his body and seeped into the earth like melted ice.

"All clean," he echoed warmly, his body tingling with delight. "Ashia," he extolled, as they wrapped themselves in their towels, "it's so great to see you. It's so great to be home."

His towel wrapped around his waist, Solomon wandered through the courtyard, through the living room, to the front of the house. Sitting on the step, he looked down the deserted dusty road that had brought him home just twenty-four hours earlier. A skinny chicken pecked its way toward him, stopping occasionally to cock its head and listen for a sound in the silence. In the distance through the long yellow-green grass, Solomon spotted a lone goat tethered to a bush. He watched it, watched it sniff the dry grass, watched it taste and spit, watched it turn on the bush and chew off the few newly budded leaves, watched it strain its back legs and drop tiny round brown pellets of dung as it continued to chew with a nonchalant expression on its face. Solomon's heart sighed with relief, grateful to be back in the simplicity of life. He had made it, living in the present; he was home. Somewhere inside the house Ashia sang a native song. *Nyame edu, Nyame edu, God be praised, God be praised.* Solomon's mind danced to the music of her voice, danced with the freedom of springing into summer.

Chapter 7

✧

*I*T WOULD BE YEARS before Solomon would find the calendars that Miriam kept hidden in the bottom panel of the kitchen cabinet. At the same moment that he was sitting on the step of Ashia's house, basking in the simplicity of life, Miriam was scribbling a complicated twist of twirls with a thick lead pencil, desperately filling in the empty box beneath May 22. *Ashia, Ashia, Ashia,* she wrote in every conceivable type of lettering, over and over and over again, until the tiny box was an illegible black mass.

Miriam leaned back in her chair, her breathing labored. The first day was always the hardest. It was strange. Each year she told herself that she didn't mind anymore, that she had evolved to a higher form of being, that May 22 would come and go like any other day. She had almost made it. Almost let it pass without regard. She had been on her way to bed, feeling perfectly content. Content and at peace, she had stepped into the bathroom, caught a glimpse of herself in the mirror, and the next thing she knew she was rushing into the kitchen, scrambling around desperately for something to write with, delving into the cupboard for her calendar in order to eradicate May 22. She wanted it gone. *Gone.* Removed from her sight.

Day one.

It was the end of day one.

The pencil still gripped tightly in her fingers, Miriam looked down at the blackened square. Flipping through the calendar, her eyes traveled over the sea of empty squares to the big tick she had marked across November 22, passing by the small **X** across October 4. One hundred and thirty-six more Ashia days to go.

Sitting perfectly still in the dim dawn-lit kitchen, Miriam waited for the sun that had already risen in Ghana to rise on Cape Corcos and light up her world.

Chapter 8

✦

SOLOMON FELT like Kummaa looked, and Kummaa looked stuffed. Balanced on his strong sticklike legs, Kummaa's usually flat tummy was pushed out, full to capacity with peanuts and the sweet white sticky pulp of cocoa pods that he had eaten and sucked to his heart's content. "Look, Uncle Solomon," he said proudly, lifting up his shirt and displaying his protruding tummy. "Even though I ate and ate and ate, I still picked three big baskets full of nuts, all by myself." Kummaa held up three stubby little fingers to emphasize his point.

"I saw you," Solomon said, impressed, guiding Amamaa onto the backseat of the Jeep. "You beat all of us. I think I ate more than I picked."

That was about the only conversation that the four peanut-stuffed beings could muster as they set off on their long ride back to Aburanoma. Amamaa slept on the backseat. Kummaa sat in the luggage compartment at the rear, gazing through the backdoor window at the star-studded night. Ashia leaned against the passenger door at the front, surrendering her body to the rattle of the road as Solomon careened and bumped the Jeep along the potholed surface.

"Uncle Solomon, where are we?" Kummaa asked, as the hypnotic hum of the Jeep's engine came to a halt. "Uncle Solomon, why are we stopping?"

"To visit an old friend," Solomon said, reaching over and gently shaking Ashia awake.

A narrow river ditch made it impossible to drive any farther into the terrain without detouring around the river, way into the bushes, which Solomon did not want to risk in the pitch blackness; so with Amamaa on his back, he led Ashia by the hand and jumped across the narrow divide onto the other side. Kummaa, who had stopped to relieve himself, was suddenly spooked by the eerie stillness and, still shaking himself dry, ran after Solomon, leaping across the ditch like a baby goat.

Standing inside a cluster of trees and bushes that hid them from the road, Solomon felt as though he'd stepped back into the previous century. As he looked at the small circle of mud huts lit by kerosene lamps surrounding him, something ancient within him made him yearn to stay there forever, far from credit cards and calling cards and all the other plastic entrapments of the modern world.

"Knock, knock, Nana Abrewa," Solomon called softly.

"Aaay, Solomon, come, come, come," Nana Abrewa beckoned joyfully in her native tongue.

Solomon stooped through the opening into the small dark hut, his eyes straining to distinguish the moving shadows. Nana Abrewa rolled up into a sitting position on her straw mat and flipped the cloth she was using as a sheet across her shoulder. She ran her gnarled and wrinkled hands down her face as if washing it awake, then clapped them together like an excited child. "Solomon," she chuckled. "Aaay, Solomon."

Ashia and the two children entered the hut, searching in the darkness for a place to sit. The moon, the stars, and the few lanterns dangling on sticks outside the huts made it brighter outside than in.

"Aaay!" Nana Abrewa said sharply, lifting her fist to her mouth in shock and delight. "Welcome, welcome, welcome," she ingratiated, spreading her thin ropy arms to include everyone. Feeling for the box in the dark, she struck a match that hissed and went out. Solomon was glad to see her warm smile and sparkling eyes as they spread across the darkness like a shooting star. She struck another match and this time managed to light a lantern before the spark snuffed out. Solomon could see her clearly now, sitting bolt upright, her short thin legs sticking straight out under her cloth like an old fragile wooden doll.

Each time Solomon left Ghana, he was afraid she would not live until his return. For seven consecutive years she had proved him wrong. She not only lived, she thrived. A hundred and twelve years of being alive, and the glassy twinkle in her eyes shone brighter and brighter as the years went by.

Sending her young great-grandniece who was lying beside her to go fetch the company something to drink, Nana Abrewa invited Solomon and Ashia to sit down on the mat opposite her. She then asked Ashia to translate for Solomon that she was overjoyed to see he had returned safely from across the waters and that she was very honored by his visit. Solomon said he was overjoyed to see her too and that she looked gorgeous. He then leaned over and shook her hand. Nana Abrewa clasped her bony fingers around the back of his head and embraced him, cradling his head like a long-lost child. For those few seconds, with Nana Abrewa's potent fingers gripped in the tight of his curls, Solomon felt as though nothing bad could possibly happen in his life, ever again.

As soon as he pulled away from the safety of her arms, he missed them. Nana Abrewa chuckled, clapped her hands for joy, folded them in her lap, and settled into the contented silence of one who has no need to talk.

Amamaa and Kummaa, tired from the long drive and lulled by the sweet smell of the sunbaked mud walls of the hut, curled up together and fell asleep. Ashia leaned forward, shook Nana Abrewa's hand, expressed a few words of kindness, and leaned back, allowing the room to reclaim its silence.

After the silence had its say, Solomon pulled out a small pad and pencil from his shirt pocket. "He wants more stories?" Nana Abrewa asked, squinting at the paper and pencil in Solomon's hand.

"I just want her to go back to the part in the forest," Solomon explained to Ashia. "Ask her where the British governor put Queen Yaa Asantewa, and what they did with the other women."

Ashia translated. Nana Abrewa neatened her cloth before answering, as if Solomon's pad and pencil were a camera clicking her photograph. Just then the great-grandniece returned with a calabash full of frothy white liquid. Nana Abrewa beckoned for the girl to give it to Solomon. Solomon took the calabash. Not sure of what it contained, he was reluctant to drink; but anxious not to offend, he braced himself and took a tentative sip. His lips curled back in an automatic response to the pungent tang. "Thank you," he said, quickly passing the calabash back to the young girl, hoping he wouldn't be required to drink anymore. Much to his surprise, his mouth was suddenly flooded with a sweet aftertaste, his palate covered with a sugary coat.

"Look at you drinking like a girl," Nana Abrewa teased Solomon, who couldn't understand a word she was saying. "Drink like a man!" she cajoled, taking a big swig from the calabash and passing it to Ashia. "If you drink like a man, I might let you sleep with me tonight, since you like coming to my hut so much!" Nana Abrewa chuckled until her whole body shook; then she clapped her hands and laughed so hard that tears of merriment sprung into her eyes.

"What did she say?" Solomon asked Ashia, certain that the laughter was at his expense.

"She likes you," Ashia said, amused, sipping some of the drink. "She says if you drink like a man she might let you stay with her tonight."

Solomon smiled with delight. Fixing his eyes on Nana Abrewa as if to say *I'm ready when you are*, he took the calabash from Ashia and downed the frothy white liquid in one long challenging swallow, placing the empty calabash upside down on the ground to prove his point. Nana Abrewa laughed so hard, she began to cough. Reaching for the empty calabash, she looked inside, clapped her hands over her mouth in mock horror, twinkled her eyes at Solomon, and said something to Ashia that made Ashia shy. "What she say?" Solomon asked, noticing Ashia's bashful response. This time Ashia refused to interpret.

Several of Nana Abrewa's great-grandnieces, nephews, grandchildren, and great-grandchildren wandered into the doorway of the hut to get a glimpse of Solomon. Nana Abrewa beckoned them in, and they crowded onto the mats spread out on the ground.

"What is it again he wants to know?" Nana Abrewa asked, motioning to Solomon's pad and pencil.

"What did the British soldiers do with the other women?"

The children's eyes turned in fascination to Solomon as he repeated his question. Most of them could not understand English, but they loved to hear it spoken. Ashia translated, and Nana Abrewa's merriment turned sober as she reflected on the question.

When she finally spoke, her words were clear and fluid, her voice a low stream of intensity. Of all the people Solomon had interviewed in his travels, Nana Abrewa had proved the most lucid, the most informed, and the most impassioned. He had learned more from the recounting of her memories than he had from any other human source. She recalled incidents, places, genealogy—all with amazing clarity. Throughout the years she had sent him to many people and sites to verify her experiences and the stories that had been passed down to her: historical uprisings of Ghanaians bravely fighting against gun power, sometimes being massacred, sometimes successfully freeing their captured countrymen from the slave traders' chains. Stories and battles that Solomon never heard about in the United States. Medical miracles involving herbs and plants. Inventions. Natural phenomena. The roads of Nana Abrewa's mind had led him to many a buried treasure, valuable happenings waiting to be unearthed and committed to print. She was responsible for the subjects of at least three of his bestselling books and helped him piece together the missing links in several others.

In exchange for the gems Nana Abrewa had gifted him (she refused to accept any of his money), Solomon had finally persuaded her to allow him to buy livestock for her farmlands and to pay for her three grandsons' college educations. Her children had tried to convince her to move away from the little circle of huts where she was born, to join them in Kumasi, but she had refused, stating that she preferred to stay with her two deceased husbands and four dead infant children who were buried beneath her hut.

Ashia continued to translate as Nana Abrewa pulled out a small bundle wrapped in newspaper from an old wooden box beside her mat. "She says the villagers searched for the women for many weeks, but they found only their waist beads and torn loincloths where the British soldiers ripped them off and raped them."

Rocking her body gently back and forth, Nana Abrewa carefully peeled open the frail yellowed newspaper wrapped around the bundle and laid it on her lap. As soon as the bundle was opened, Solomon thought he heard the sound of a woman wailing in the distance. As if in response, a low, pained, barely audible moan emitted from deep inside Nana Abrewa's chest. Solomon felt the urge to plunge his finger into the channel of the open wound to stop it up, but the wail of sadness seemed to come from far beyond his reach.

Nana Abrewa stretched out her feeble-looking arms and handed the bundle to Solomon. He held it carefully, fingering the contents with sensitivity. Inside was an old fragile loincloth attached to a weak, frayed string of antique waist beads the color of red earth.

"Her great-great-grandfather found these beads in the forest after the women were attacked," Ashia continued with compassion. "They belonged to his wife, Nana Abrewa's great-great-grandmother. Her great-great-grandfather kept them to put them back on her—he searched and waited for the rest of his life, but he never saw his wife again."

Solomon touched one of the earth-red beads with the tip of his finger. He imagined the tiny waist that they had been wrapped around; imagined the savagery with which they had been ripped away, scattered to the ground like so many drops of blood; imagined the white hunters knocking her down into the dirt, barking over her like hellish dogs, unbuckling their belts—Solomon's mind stopped. His brain could not continue to imagine what had happened without feeling as if he were partaking of the sin. Would history ever be able to bear to tell the whole truth of what was done to the peoples of Africa? Would retribution ever be paid? He doubted it.

Solomon listened to the wail; it was louder now—more voices, women in agony crying out. He listened. Where was it coming from? Nana Abrewa? Ashia? The children? The hut next door? He stilled himself. There it was. His ears followed the direction of the sound. He lowered his head—it was coming from his heart. The women were wailing in the conscience of his heart.

With trembling hands he passed the bundle back to Nana Abrewa. "She says these things are too painful to remember; why must you drag them up?" Ashia's voice was fainter than before. Solomon didn't know if he had heard all of what Ashia said, but he caught the *why must you drag them up?* part.

"Tell her, 'For the children,'" he replied with passion. Every time he thought his burning quest to discover his ancestry and reveal the plight of his people was quenched, it would spark up again and lead him like a raging fire to burn down the volumes of lies, to replace lies and omissions with pages of truth and facts that had been denied for generations.

"Tell her that most black children outside Africa know that six million Jews were murdered in the Holocaust, but they don't know that one hundred twenty million Africans died through slavery. And they don't know anything about Africans before they were forced to be slaves."

Solomon paused to let Ashia translate. He wanted to cry; he wasn't sure why. Anger? Love? He couldn't tell. All he knew was that he needed to write it all down. Write it all down for a world that had gone deaf to the lament of the black race. Write it down for all the children of color who have been given the false impression by the exclusion of black history in their schools—and the glorification of white history—that their forefathers' contribution to mankind is so insignificant it is not even worth a mention. *He wants more stories?* Nana Abrewa had asked. Yes, he wanted more stories, he wanted as many stories as she had mind and breath to tell. He wanted more stories before there was no one left who knew or even cared to tell the truth.

BOOK FIVE

✦

Fall

Graffiti Black—Autumn Orange . . .

THE DISTANT RUMBLE of the New York subway, mixed with the intermittent sirens whining from the police cars, was as familiar a sound to Solomon as the croak of the evening frogs and the whining buzz of mosquitoes in Ghana. Sitting in his leather armchair, with his feet up on his computer table, he munched on a bowl of oatmeal and raisins while he listened to the endless messages on his answering machine. Punctuated by the sounds of New York bustling outside his window, his messages catapulted him straight back into the hectic pace of American city life.

"Hello, Mr. Wilberforce, Vonetta Graham here," the confident voice announced over the machine. "I don't know if you remember me—I write for the *Cincinnati Herald*. I interviewed you after you spoke down here at Convention Hall last spring. I read your recent article in *Newsweek*, 'Holding the Black Mind Hostage,' and also your 'Free Our Children' essay in this month's *Essence* magazine. I was wondering if I could get a few comments from you on the recent statistics of black-on-black crime, not just in Cincinnati but throughout the country. It seems to me the current trend of black violence would indicate—"

Solomon turned off the machine, adding Vonetta Graham to his list of people for his assistant Zelda to contact on his behalf. Placing his empty bowl on the desk, he gazed out the window at the spectacular array of autumn leaves that quivered on their branches or blew along the sidewalk, flickering in the wind, to ensure that those passing would behold them in the colorfulness of their dying— green singed with amber, brown dipped in orange, yellow tipped with red. Inspired by their fiery display, he went to work, transferring his notes from his interview with Nana Abrewa onto his computer. He had two weeks of hibernation to outline the concept of his new book before thrusting himself into the thick of New York society—the good, the challenging, and the sometimes ugly.

"Kids out there need fathers!" Solomon appealed passionately, concluding his speech to the more than one thousand inmates sitting in front of him in the auditorium of Walkill medium security prison in Westchester County. "They need you to give them advice, love, hope. They're out there on their own—undisciplined, unschooled, unsupervised—acting crazy and dying like ants in a Raid spray. Momma's giving what she can; sometimes that's enough, but a lot of times she doesn't know what's going on! Some because they're too busy working to put food on the table, and others because they're too busy putting drugs up their nose. Either way, no one's giving momma the help she needs, so raising the kids alone is a constant struggle. Our kids need fathers, and you locked up in here, pumping iron and walking round in circles, it's time to seize your *power!* You have a purpose on this planet. Join the Power Program and take a step toward finding out what that purpose is."

Solomon was pleased with the prisoners' response. They opened up and talked to him about real issues that concerned them. By the end of his four-hour visit, he was gratified but taxed from answering all the challenging questions and relaying positive encouragement. Leaving home at 6 A.M. that morning, he had debated calling to cancel his appointment with Sam, thinking that speaking at Walkill and getting to her office by lunchtime would be too much of a rush. But now, walking out through the prison gates, feeling slightly drained, he was glad he had not canceled. He was looking forward to Sam's motivating company.

"It's not like a regular store," Sam explained to Solomon as they walked through the crowded streets of SoHo. "It's more like a club that happens to sell great clothes. I wish she sold things for women. I'm telling you, you'll love it; all her pieces are exotic and one of a kind, just the sort of clothes you wear: foreign and mysterious."

"I wear foreign and mysterious clothes?" Solomon asked, amused by Sam's description.

"Everything about you is foreign and mysterious," Sam replied, looking up at him, wishing he would hold her hand. "I mean, look at how you're dressed today. This handwoven jacket comes from where—Morocco?"

"Ethiopia."

"And your baggy pants?"

"Senegal."

"The *kente* scarf I know is from Ghana. Where's the silk shirt from?"

"India."

"See what I mean? Very foreign, very exotic. You have a permanent air of mystery about you, which makes everything you wear seem even more intriguing. You're an enigma, Solomon."

"And I thought I was just a nice simple guy."

"Nice, maybe. But simple? Definitely not."

They stopped at a crosswalk and waited for the light to change. *Why is it*, Sam wondered, *that if he takes my hand right now, it will pass as friendship; yet if I take his, it will seem like a pass?*

"It's not fair," she said, voicing her opinion.

"What isn't?"

"That Eula's store doesn't sell women's clothes," she said, thinking fast. The light changed color. Much to her own surprise, she reached out and took Solomon's hand as they walked across the street.

"Your hand's cold," he said casually, putting both their hands in his pocket. They continued on in silence. A few trivial comments ran through Sam's mind, but she restrained herself from voicing them, not wanting to interrupt the far more riveting conversation taking place between their fingers, sequestered in the dark of Solomon's pocket.

"You brought him!" Eula delighted as they walked into the store. "Welcome to Eula's; can I get you some coffee?" Sam knew by the mischievous gleam in Eula's eyes that the fact she had walked in holding Solomon's hand had not escaped her friend's observation. "Was that a 'yes' for coffee?" Eula questioned, looking at Sam with an I'll-interrogate-you-about-this-later grin on her face.

"Not for me, thank you," Solomon declined as he looked around at the eye-catching decor. Every inch of wall was covered with purple velvet, with tiny hexagonal mirrors sewn on top. The few clothes that were visible were draped across five-foot-high gray marble pillars, on a black-and-white-checkered floor.

"Have a seat, Mr. Wilberforce," Eula offered, gesturing to one of the purple couches hanging from the ceiling on thick gold chains. "I'll have Eduardo routine some of the clothes for you."

"Eula only hires dancers to model her clothes," Sam explained. "Get ready, it's quite a show. She calls them her 'moving mannequins.' They're all tall, dark, and foreign with unique names."

"Actually, Eduardo's real name is Eddie," Eula confessed. "But I call him 'Eduardo' in front of my customers. 'Eduardo' sounds so much more exotic, don't you think?"

"Depends on where you come from," Solomon reasoned. "If you're Hispanic, 'Eddie' probably sounds more exotic than 'Eduardo.'"

"Well, which would you prefer?" Eula asked.

"Let's go with 'Eduardo,'" Solomon smiled.

"'Eduardo' it is," Eula said, returning his smile as she pushed a button that made the couch Solomon was sitting on swing gently back and forth. "Relax, make yourself at home. I'll go pick out some clothes I think would look good on you. I'd have pulled some before, but Sam wasn't sure you'd have time to come. Sam?" Eula beckoned as she headed into the back of the store. "Come help me?"

"Shout if anyone comes in," Sam instructed Solomon as she followed Eula through the velvet-padded door, well aware, from the tone of Eula's voice, that the interrogation was about to begin.

Sam had been right. They *were* Solomon's kind of clothes. "How long did you say she's been in business?" Solomon asked her as they sat in the cab headed back to Madison Avenue.

"Six weeks. She wanted me to bring you to the grand opening, but you were out of the country."

"I think she'll do well."

"If she can get shoppers like you, she'll do great," Sam commented, looking at all his purchases piled on the seat beside them.

"Here," Solomon said, passing her one of the bags, "for you."

"What is it?" Sam asked, looking inside. "Oh no!" she exclaimed happily, as she pulled a long reversible velvet-and-satin cloak out of the bag. "I love this!"

"I know."

"But, I mean, I meant for you to buy it for yourself, not for me."

"Eula says she can have it taken up if it's too long for you."

"Gosh! Thank you, Solomon. I know this cost a fortune."

"You're very welcome. Thank you for introducing me to her store."

"What are you doing later?" Sam asked as the taxi pulled up by her office building on the corner of Fifty-sixth Street and Madison Avenue. "One of my new writers is doing a reading from her book tonight, and I thought you might like to come along. She's Chilean, and it's her personal account of the Chilean revolution."

"Sounds interesting, but I've already promised to go to the reading of a friend's play," Solomon declined. "I'll call you next week, though, and see if you have another spare lunch break."

"Great, I could see what shows we've been invited to," Sam suggested, alluding to the frequent requests the agency received to view plays. "We could catch an evening performance—or maybe a weekend matinee," she proposed as she stepped out of the cab onto the curb.

For Sam, seeing Solomon in the evening was preferable to seeing him on her lunch breaks, when her time was restricted by pressing appointments. As far as she was concerned, it would be better still if they could meet on weekends, when her days and nights were completely her own. But for whatever reason, Solomon very rarely invited her anywhere on the weekends. In fact, unless it was at her prompting, he never really suggested anything other than their getting together for lunch, although she had a feeling that if he would only stay in town a little longer, that would change. It was disconcerting that every time he came back from one of his four or five months abroad, their relationship would start off a little more formal than when he left, then just as they got close enough for their friendship to go to the next level, he would fly away again.

BOOK SIX

✦

Winter

Chilly Snow-White Winds of Time . . .

Chapter 1

✦

"SOLOMON ARRIVE last night?"
The brashness of the voice behind the question was a rude intrusion into *The Passion of Isabella*, the new romance novel that had kept Joan riveted for one blissfully uninterrupted hour. She glanced up from the front desk of the Hotel L'Ouverture to see who the obtrusive voice belonged to. *I might have known!* Joan thought, noting the scalp-short, wooly metallic-blond curls, the caramel skin, the green-lined eyes, and the trademark black mole on the left cheek.

Jezz Nicolopolous shifted impatiently from one leg to the other. "Joan, me talking to you," she asserted. "Me ask you if Solomon arrive last night."

Perched on her high stool, Joan peered haughtily down at Jezz, scrutinizing her attire. Dressed from head to toe in a tight orange-and-yellow floral print dress with a slit that went all the way up her long shapely leg to the top of her thigh, Jezz looked so maddeningly vibrant, Joan wished she could stuff her in a dark closet. Returning to her novel, she hoped Jezz would get tired of being ignored and go away.

"Joan—" Jezz began again, her voice hardening.

"He not in!" Joan snapped, hoping *now* Jezz would go away.

"Give I the key then," Jezz demanded.

"What key?"

"Solomon room key."

"Me can't just give you him room key! Who you think you is? You can't just go in him room!"

"Me always do it. You know me do."

"Me no know nothing!"

"Me warning you, Joan, give me the key."

Joan sucked her teeth insolently at Jezz and returned to her book. She knew that at fifteen, a good ten years younger than Jezz, she ought to show her respect, but she was too vexed to care about age and respect. She reentered *The Passion of Isabella* as if Jezz didn't exist.

Irked, Jezz reached across the desk, grabbed the novel, and tossed it onto the floor. Leaning in, her voice honey with a hint of dynamite, she whispered, "You know, Joan, when me see your father in the fish market this morning, me forget to tell him how surprise I was to see you at the club Saturday, and here me thinking he don't let you out nights."

"Me wasn't at no club," Joan spat out in an angry whisper.

"Me see you, girl! Late Saturday night!" Jezz taunted, raising her voice, careless of who might hear. "Flaunting around with you midriff all out! Hanging on to that Leo Rap-A-Tap boy, or do he call himself a man now?"

"You should know!" Joan hissed venomously.

Jezz laughed patronizingly. "So that why you acting all ugly! Don't worry, girl, me not interested in that puppy."

"So why you play him all night?"

"Puppies what sniff get played with."

"Maybe if you change you scent, men no sniff so much."

"You dreaming, girl. Me no wear no scent."

"Me recognize it."

"What scent you think you smell?"

"Availability!"

"What are you two conspiring about?" Solomon called out cheerfully, slicing into their venom.

"It a female thing," Jezz replied with a smile as he strode up to them from the dining room. "Actually, me came here looking for you. Welcome home," she said, hooking her arm into his. "Me need to talk to you."

"Yeah? What about?"

"It private. Joan, Solomon's key, please," Jezz urged imperiously. Joan hesitated.

"Alexander Dumas Suite," Solomon prodded. Joan obediently dropped Solomon's room key into Jezz's open palm.

"Someone drop they book down here on the floor," Jezz said, stepping over *The Passion of Isabella*. "You better pick it up, Joan, before one of the guests slip and hurt theyself."

Seething, Joan watched Jezz saunter up the stairs, clinging to Solomon as if she owned him!

Hunting through his trunk for a small parcel, Solomon was too busy thinking about the speech he was about to give to take in much of what Jezz was saying. Since his last trip to Ghana, he had intensified his quest to assist the descendants of black slaves, or what he called *the forgotten tribe of Africa*, in understanding where they came from and in advancing their position in the world. On his arrival the previous night, he had discussed it, as he often did, with Kawasaki, who had called him first thing in the morning and suggested he speak about it at the groundbreaking ceremony for the new school that very afternoon.

"So will you?" Jezz asked, her voice finally coming to an end.

"Will I what?"

"Vote him in?"

Solomon searched his audio memory to see if he could recall any of the sentences Jezz had just wafted into the air. Much to his regret, he could not recall a single word. "Who?" he asked. "Vote who in?"

"Stavos."

"In what?"

"Investment," Jezz enunciated, as if Solomon had lost his mind. "The hotel, the boat club, the new school, everything. The committee voted no, but Kawasaki say he'll let him in if you agree."

"You still hanging with Kawasaki?" Solomon asked, irritated both by the fact that she was still trying to get Stavos, her Greek husband, voted into the Cape Africa Corporation and by the fact that she was obviously still having an affair with Kawasaki.

"Let Stavos in," Jezz responded, evading the question.

"No." Solomon stood up, having found what he was looking for.

"Why not, Solomon? Stavos love the Island. He got great ideas. It not just a money thing with him; it a passion."

"You've got to be one of us. That's the whole point of Cape Africa."

"In case you'd forgotten, Mr. Big Shot, your mama and my

mama were sisters, that make me your cousin; Stavos is me husband, that make him one of us."

"In war?"

"What war?"

"We been fighting it for years."

"A war?" Jezz sat up from where she had thrown herself prostrate on the bed. "Who the enemy?"

"Foreigners," Solomon said as if it were the dirtiest word in the English language.

"Look who talking, Mr. Bourgeois, Beento Blackbird! Been-to Paris, been-to London, been-to the States and decided to stay there!" Jezz scoffed. "You not exactly a native, Mr. American! Stavos may be Greek, but at least he livin' here on the Island, not just swanning in once a year for some winter sunshine like some people I know!"

Solomon put the parcel inside his leather satchel, swung it onto his shoulder, and walked to the bed. Stooping down, he kissed Jezz on the forehead. "I'm from the forgotten tribe of Africa," he said with a quiet strength. "So are you, Cousin Jezz, but Stavos is not. Look around you, Jezz, the Island is being desecrated by cheap resorts for European tourists, and to make room for them, underpaid natives are being crammed into high-rise slums, many of them built by your husband. Cape Africa is dedicated to building single-house compounds that return us as an African people to the type of family community in which we thrive best. You don't have to be black to join us, but you have to have the same vision. I won't vote Stavos in because our visions for the Island are completely different." Straightening himself to his full power, Solomon headed out of the suite, down the atrium stairs, and out into the circular driveway.

The number of people who showed up at the groundbreaking ceremony for what would be the Island's first independently run school was encouraging. Over seven hundred citizens of Cape Corcos came to demonstrate their gratitude and support—four hundred more than had been expected.

Solomon stood on a small podium, the audience listening to him with rapt attention. "Our children," he cried out. "Our children are taught that Africa is backward and underdeveloped. For one hundred years the white man removed Africa's craftsmen, chiefs, doctors, philosophers, our women and our children, to make other nations strong, and then they called us backward. They blasted our cities and destroyed our records, and now they tell us that we had no history before the slave trade, that we were merely savages." Solomon paused for a moment to let his message affect his listeners.

"The truth is that ancient Greece's greatest philosophers had African teachers, but they are never mentioned," Solomon continued, riding on the crest of heightened awareness. "When people admire something, they want to steal it from you and say it's theirs. If you don't know any better, you believe them. The Europeans have tried to steal everything good and claim it is white. Tea doesn't even grow there, but to hear them tell it, you'd think it was English—not to mention cricket, which they learned from the Indians. And Max Factor didn't perfect makeup, neither did Elizabeth Arden—the ancient Egyptians did! But on the more serious side, how many kids who are taught about Edison are ever taught that Mr. Latimer, his chief researcher, had his own patent for a lightbulb registered before Edison; that Mr. Latimer was a black man? And do any of you kids out there know who performed the first open-heart surgery? It wasn't Christian Bernard; it was a black man. If you're younger than twelve and you're one of the first ten children to find out his name and tell me anytime before Christmas, I'll give you one hundred dollars to buy yourself a Christmas present."

"Parents, it's important that we teach ourselves and our children our history, so that others won't control our memory. Because if you control a people's memory, you control their lives."

Solomon paused, opened his satchel, and removed the parcel. "When I was last in Ghana, West Africa," he said, lowering his voice reverentially, "an old lady, Nana Abrewa, asked me why I keep dragging up the old stories, opening up the old wounds. I told her that when imperialists conquer a country, they kill the artists first, because they know it's we storytellers who carry the spirit of who we are as a people. To understand ourselves and move forward, we have to know where we come from. For that reason, I will never stop telling our story."

Solomon opened the parcel. "She understood and she gave me

this—this broken string of beads attached to an old loincloth was found in the Ahafu forest in Ghana. It belonged to her great-great-grandmother who was attacked and forced into slavery by British traders. She told me she wanted me to have this heirloom because maybe her great-great-grandmother was my ancestor too." Solomon became choked with tears as the distant wailing that he had heard in Nana Abrewa's hut rang through the air. "They split us so far apart, but she told me to tell you to '*Take courage. We are coming back together again.*' This school, the Royal Nubian, will be dedicated to raising consciousness, rebuilding family, and bridging the many gaps in our history caused by captivity."

Solomon unveiled a miniature model of the Royal Nubian that was sitting on the podium. The crowd pointed admiringly at the splendor of the white structure.

"Many of our children are princes and princesses, descended from African royalty, but they don't know it. And even those of African descent whose ancestors were not royal, they were noble. That is why we've designed the Royal Nubian like a palace, so we can teach our children the majesty of who they really are. We are the forgotten tribe of Africa and we must find our way back home, not in territorial boundaries but in the freedom and development of our minds. I know as a black man I don't have to live in Africa, but I have to know that Africa lives in me. We must remember the mighty horizons from which we came so that we can create limitless horizons for our future."

There was a silence in the crowd. A profound recognition pulled them back into the many memories etched into the very sinew of their bones. Fueled by the passion of Solomon's speech, they believed anew in the limitless possibilities of a well-informed mind. Standing on the land already measured out for the new school, they had every faith that new leaders would be "housed and nurtured under its roof," as Solomon had so confidently promised.

Solomon was the first to feel it. As if knowing it to be the voice of God, nobody moved when the initial light raindrops fell almost imperceptibly in consecration from above. Washed by the sprinkling, the leaves on the freshly buried sapling tree glistened to a bright, wet, baby green, the color of the inside shoot of a new blade of grass. Planted by Solomon less than an hour earlier, the sapling was the forerunner of a planned avenue of trees that would lead from the road to the door of the new school.

Looking at the leaves waving under the pressure of the barely visible rain, Solomon could tell by the rhythm of their movement that it was about to come down hard. Stepping from the podium, he hurriedly shook hands with the Islanders who thanked him for his inspiring speech. "Please forgive me for rushing off," he beseeched the crowd as he sprinted across the rain-softened soil and leaped onto his waiting motorbike.

Roaring along the isolated sandy coast toward Miriam's adobe, Solomon called out her name to the crashing waves. "Miriaaaam!" he bellowed—an incantation—his voice scattering through the wind like confetti over a bride. Rapt by his impassioned cry, migrating seabirds lost their formation, regrouped, and fluttered higher into the sky. Solomon leaned his bike acutely to the left, his body precariously close to the ground. The sense of danger gave his voice more power. "Miriaaaam!" he bellowed again, spreading his arms full-stretch as the wings of the seabirds flying up above. The wheels of his motorbike spun almost out of control, and he laughed, grabbed the handlebars, sloped to the left, and accelerated.

*   *   *

Alone in the quiet of her kitchen, Miriam sat at the wooden table peeling away the orange-yellow skins of overripe mangoes piled high on a plate in preparation for boiling. Their delectable aroma hung in the air. She licked the sticky sweetness off her fingers as she worked, her soft pink tongue catching the runaway juice that occasionally dribbled down her palm onto her wrist. Glancing toward the big bay windows, she saw for the first time the light rain that was falling silently from the sky.

As if moving in a trance, she floated to the kitchen door and looked out at the waves. "Welcome home, Solomon," she whispered, her soft warm lips brushing against the cool hard glass. The sticky mango on her mouth left a murky imprint as she pulled away.

Bending over the kitchen sink, she washed the sugary residue off her hands and face. Hearing the distant roar of Solomon's motorbike, she felt a leap of excitement in her stomach at the thought of seeing him. For the first time in years, she had not managed to hide up on the airport roof and watch him arrive. His flight had landed so early that by the time she got there, he had already gone. Standing over the sink, her hands under flowing water, she was suddenly unsure of where to be. Should she stay there by the sink? Or stand by the door? Sit at the table? Go out onto the patio? After so many months of being alone, she felt awkward. The first encounter was always easier when it rained at night. That way, she could wait for Solomon in the bedroom, her body stretched out on the bed, her awkwardness overshadowed by the dark. In the naked light of day, her passion seemed defenselessly exposed.

Solomon opened the kitchen door and saw Miriam still standing by the running tap, her wet hands resting on the edge of the sink, her wild hair loosely pinned and tousled on top of her head, her thin white dress juiced with mango, her clean lips dripping with water, a slightly startled expression on her face. He moved in and reached across the sink to turn off the tap, and as he reached out his arm, he could feel everything Miriam felt, smell everything she thought.

Miriam slid her hand up his forearm and curled her wet fingers around his biceps. At the urgency of her touch, time closed its eyes and canceled out the distance they had traveled in their months apart. Before they knew it, they were merged back together again, christening their reunion right there on the kitchen floor.

It would be two hours before Solomon would finally disentangle himself from Miriam's legs and finish turning off the tap.

Chapter 2

✦

SOLOMON SPENT his sudden flight back to America with his mind groping through the previous twenty-four hours, digging for any clues he may have missed. It was curious to him how the night before an unexpected life-changing event is often a calm uneventful time that in retrospect appears to be potent with meaning. Certain casual gestures or incidental remarks suddenly take on a deep significance. He asked himself whether he had experienced any important signals last night that he should have somehow decoded, any sensations that he had ignored or denied. On reflection he could think of a few.

First, even though it was the evening of his welcome-home dinner, he had felt somehow removed. He had been on the Island almost a week, and yet that relaxed feeling he normally got after being there for a day or two, that permission to unwind and mellow out, never happened. He had remained constantly on the alert.

Then there was Cousin Jezz. Her quick wit and sharp tongue usually amused him, but last night her cutting words had wounded him. He had been shaving in the bathroom with the door open to let out the steam from his bath. Miriam was in the kitchen preparing a feast with the help of Toussaint and his wife, Emelia, when Jezz arrived.

"Jezz! Welcome. How you get here? Stavos with you?" Miriam had asked in her usual friendly manner.

"No. He say if Solomon don't consider him family, then he not coming to a family dinner."

Solomon continued to shave, his ears keen to the conversation.

"Solomon and Stavos feuding again?" Emelia asked.

"Solomon won't approve Stavos as an investor in Cape Africa," Miriam explained, her voice displaying the weariness she felt over the issue.

"Why men always got to stir trouble 'fore they feel manly?" Emelia interjected softly.

"Solomon impotent, so he worse than most," Jezz snipped. As soon as her remark hit Solomon's ears, he threw down his razor, but it was too late. She had already cut him.

"Hush your mouth, child; Solomon not impotent," Miriam chided in a low voice.

"Well, him may not be impotent, but him incapable of having babies, and that just as bad in a husband," Jezz rebutted, forging on mercilessly.

"We don't know it him incapable," Miriam defended.

"Course it him!" Jezz retorted. "He got two wives and neither one of you ever been pregnant. Face it, Miriam, Solomon's sperm rotten as a dead fish."

Sitting on the plane going over it again in his mind, Solomon felt the hot flush of pain and inadequacy almost as strongly as he had the night before. It was as if Jezz's words had carte blanche to travel through his body and stick him wherever and whenever they pleased. Standing there in the bathroom, looking at his reflection in the mirror, had he not thought of his father? Yes, he had. He had thought how wretched it would be never to have a child. How wretched to have his life come to a dead end the moment he passed away, leaving behind no root of continuance, no branch to blossom, no fruit to bear. The wretchedness of such a fate had made him think of his father, made him wonder if his father ever wondered where he was, ever longed for him, ever thought of him as his continuance.

Yes, just last night, for the first time in a long time, he had allowed himself to think deeply about his father. For one intense moment he had even had the urge to call him up.

As the plane cruised through the clouds, Solomon continued to reflect on the previous night, searching for more clues.

The patio table had been beautifully laid out for dinner for eight, with a lace tablecloth, silver candlesticks, hand-painted china, crystal glasses, and a giant bouquet of wildflowers. The food in the center had been decorated with sprigs of freshly cut mint leaves and rosemary. Toussaint had turned off the lights in the adobe, and Peace had lit all the candles on the table, as well as the lanterns on the outside walls of the house. They had all indulged themselves shamelessly on Miriam's curried goat, shrimp jambalaya, crab farci, and akee and swordfish with yellow rice. Peace was clearing away their dirty plates and Miriam was bringing out the dessert when Jezz got up, paraded herself around the table, and challenged Kawasaki to a motorbike race.

Kawasaki, who was engaged to Candy Spears, a local model, had given some vague excuse why he had not come to dinner with his fiancée as planned. Jezz had blamed Solomon for the absence of her husband, Stavos, leaving her and Kawasaki free to flaunt their illicit affair without the hindrance of their respective mates' presence. Deception. Solomon hated it. He hated to see people belittle and defile love with lies and deception, leaving nasty messes everywhere. It enraged him. Watching Jezz and Kawasaki frolic on the bikes, he was incensed by them. Incensed by the lies and dishonesty with which they conducted themselves. It had reminded him of his father and *his* lies and *his* unclaimed messes, of which Solomon was one.

"Don't be so pious, Solomon, you no better than me," Jezz had said to him in response to his disapproving look, as Kawasaki helped her up from where she'd playfully toppled off the bike onto the sand. "You need more than one woman to keep you happy; I need more than one man. What's the difference?"

"The difference, Jezz," Solomon contended, "is that you're being dishonest to your husband, and I'm honest about my relationships with Miriam and Ashia, and each understands it. If you see nothing wrong with your relationship with Kawasaki, why are you dishonest about it? Why do you hide it from Stavos, the man you supposedly love *till death do us part?*"

The plane flew into storm clouds. The captain asked the crew and passengers to please take their seats and fasten their seat belts. Solomon barely heard him over his thoughts. Had he been too judgmental of Jezz? Of his father?

The plane plummeted and rose suddenly, causing Solomon to

look out the window. Dark clouds pressed against the pane, eclipsing the view. Looking out at the ominous gray, he couldn't help wondering if the bleakness of his parents' nonrelationship had eclipsed his view and blocked him from seeing who his father really was. Was his father a good man? Solomon wondered as he attempted to peer through the darkness.

Strange to think that just a few hours before, he had seen Miriam from the very same window. It was the first time he had allowed her to come to the airport to see him off. Looking out at her face, he could tell she had tried not to let her sadness show. She had waited seven months for him to return, only to see him leave less than a week after arriving. It pained Solomon to leave her. In the five years since he had married Ashia, he had never left either wife before their season together was completed. No matter what the situation, he had always stayed. Until today. Today, within five hours of receiving the news, he was up in the air, traveling midseason, leaving Miriam behind.

Broken rhythms.

Solomon wondered whether he had made the right decision. He pulled out the telegram from his trouser pocket. He had read it many times that morning before boarding the plane, hoping that if he read it often enough, the words would somehow change or lose their impact.

He opened the telegram and read it one more time.

Sorry to inform you that Charles passed away at 5 A.M. this morning of respiratory complications. Funeral services will be held on Saturday, November 29, at 2 P.M. at his home church, Saint Mark's Church of the Divine. Please do try to come. I believe brother would want you to be there. Be strong.

With love. Aunt Josephine.

Charles. Solomon stared at the name. *Charles.* It sounded so alien, like a man he didn't know. "Who on earth is Charles?" he whispered under his breath, crumpling up the telegram.

The middle-aged woman at the end of his row of seats looked at him sympathetically. "It gets to you after a while."

Solomon looked at her, a blank expression on his face.

"The dipping around. Makes you feel off-balance." She closed her eyes as the plane did another downward swoop. Solomon uncrumpled the telegram and read it again. *Respiratory complications.* He wondered exactly what that meant. Had his father been sick? Had he had the best medical attention? If his father was sick, why hadn't he been informed of his father's illness? Prewarned? His own father was sick, dying, and no one had bothered to contact him, except to inform him that he had *passed away.* Why had the telegram taken so long to get to him? Why hadn't Aunt Josephine sent a fax? Or just telephoned the hotel? If she had called the hotel, he wouldn't have had to read those cold words.

Sorry to inform you that Charles passed away at 5 A.M. this morning of respiratory complications.

Charles. Charles? It didn't even sound right. But then again, neither did "Dad," or "Daddy," or "Father," or "Papa," or "Mr. Whittman."

Solomon began to feel a sense of panic. He couldn't think of what to call him, couldn't think of a word or a name to use to refer to his own father. What had he called him? What had he called his father when he was alive? He couldn't remember. He tried to think back. Tried hard to remember. He remembered getting off the plane at Kennedy Airport on that first trip to America right after his mother died and waiting nervously for some stranger who was apparently his father to come pick him up. He remembered wondering then what to call him when he saw him. What had been the conclusion? He tried to recollect.

He had stood in that airport lounge wondering if every passing black man was his father. After an hour he had begun to fear that his father had changed his mind and wasn't coming. Propping his little suitcase against the wall, he sat on it and reached into his pocket for his bag of peppermint candy. Popping the last one into his mouth, he dug back into his pocket and removed grains of the fistful of Cape Corcos soil that he had poured inside as a keepsake. Trying hard not to lose any, he sprinkled it off his fingers into the empty candy bag. Just then he saw a short, handsome, pale-brown-skinned man in a green suit rushing toward him, a fair-complected, brown-red-headed teenage boy following close behind.

"Don't call me 'Daddy,'" the man whispered hurriedly in Solomon's ear as he bent down to pick up Solomon's small suitcase. The fair-complected teenager stretched out his hand to shake Solomon's.

"Welcome to the States. I'm Charles Franklin Whittman Junior. What's your name?"

Solomon stared, surprised. He had thought the boy was white. "Solomon. Solomon Eustace Wilberforce," he said, shaking the boy's hand.

"How old are you?"

"Thirteen."

"Neato! Same age as me! When's your birthday?"

"June eighth."

"June eighth," Charles Jr. mimicked. "I love your accent; it's really cool, man! I Rastaman," he said, doing a poor imitation of Solomon's Caribbean accent.

"When your birthday?" Solomon asked, hoping to distract him from the pitiful imitation.

"July sixteenth. So you're . . . thirty-eight days older than me . . . no, thirty-nine. Well, it depends what time you were born. What time were you born? I was born at five-forty-five in the afternoon . . ." Charles Jr. chatted on as they followed behind Charles Sr., who pushed singlemindedly through the crowd and headed for the exit.

The bad weather had subsided. Solomon could see the wing of the plane through the break in the clouds. Easing his seat into a more restful position, he continued his remembrance. He'd forgotten he used to speak with a heavy Caribbean accent. Where had it gone? Teased away at boarding school, no doubt. He closed his eyes. He needed to answer the question. He needed to know what name he called his father. Why couldn't he remember?

Traveling from Kennedy Airport to his father's house in New Rochelle on that first day, it had become clear to Solomon from the things Charles Jr. said that he had been described to his new family as an exchange student from Cape Corcos Island. "It's simpler all around," his father had explained when the two of them finally had a moment to themselves. Solomon kept silent. "Everything was so sudden," his father continued, averting his eyes from Solomon's face. "I didn't get a chance to prepare everyone. You know, about your being my . . . uh . . . you know, my son. No point in making waves."

Nevertheless, waves came. Tidal waves that could not be contained. Within two weeks of his arrival, Solomon came running in from the backyard where Charles Jr. and his three little sisters were instructing him on the art of baseball. Panting and dripping with sweat, he strode through the kitchen, stripping off his T-shirt on his way to the bathroom. Mrs. Charles Whittman looked up from the dining table, took a good look at Solomon's naked torso, and saw what she had begun to suspect. There, right before her eyes, was her husband when she had first met him: the same physique, the same vitality, elongated on a taller, deeper earth-brown body. In fact, now that she looked more closely at Solomon, even those lips were remarkably the same.

The things she shrieked at her husband that night behind their closed bedroom door were unrepeatable. Solomon was affected not so much by the words he overheard as by the tone and volume. It was hard to believe that the genteel white woman from New England who had offered him tea earlier that morning, her pinky curled in the air with cultivated perfection, was the same person as the low-swinging gut-wrenching individual whose voice was bursting out of his father's bedroom walls. Solomon lay in his bottom-bunk bed, cringing as he listened to the slanders, curses, and insults that she hurled with abandon. He wondered if Charles Jr. in the top bunk was asleep. He hoped so.

After nearly two hours of shouting, there was a sudden silence, followed by the bathroom door slamming. Solomon hoped it was all over, but suddenly there it was again—"Charles? Charles, open the door. What are you doing in there? Charles open—this—" A loud thud, the splintering of wood, and the ferocious voice was at it again.

"Do you know how disgusted—"

"Kathleen, the door—"

"—how utterly disgusted it makes me feel?"

"Are you crazy, woman, look at the door—"

"The door?! The door?! You're concerned about the door, Charles?! Do you understand what's going on here? Do you have *any* idea what you've done? On our honeymoon, Charles? On our *honeymoon?!*"

Solomon heard the toilet flush, as the voices trailed back to the master bedroom.

"And I'm supposed to raise it? Is that what you were thinking? That I would raise it for you and your Caribbean whore? What did she die of anyway? Syphilis? Did she happen to mention in her asking price the diseases she might have?"

Solomon tensed, hoping his father would rise up and defend his deceased mother. He waited, barely able to restrain himself from running in there while the slanders against his mother continued. He willed so hard for his father to come to his mother's defense that he broke out into a sweat. But hard as Solomon willed it, his father never did defend her. He defended himself, but not her.

The following morning the five children partook of breakfast with no grown-ups in sight. Not wanting to be on the wrong side of the war, the the four full-blooded Whittman siblings ate in moody silence, each eyeing Solomon as the possible cause of the problem.

Uncomfortable under the children's resentful scrutiny, Solomon returned upstairs after breakfast, hoping to spend time alone in his room. He opened the bedroom door to find his bag packed and closed at the foot of the bed. Moments later his pale harried-looking stepmother, her eyes red with crying, came to the open doorway and told him she had a scuba diving certificate. That she had been awarded it nearly fourteen years ago on her honeymoon. "Your father doesn't swim, so I took lessons by myself while he fooled around on the beach." She stepped into the room and, reaching out her arm, offered Solomon the certificate wrapped in old dusty plastic. "I'd like you to have it," she said in an eerily faint voice. "It's kind of like your birth certificate. If I hadn't gone off in search of little colored fish, you might never have been conceived." Solomon looked confused. "Take it!" she snapped. Solomon reached out quickly in a reflex action and took it. He glimpsed down through the murky plastic, his eye catching a few of the printed words. *This is to certify . . . Kathleen Grace Whittman . . . September 18 . . . Cape Corcos Island . . .* Calm again, his stepmother informed him that a car was waiting outside to take him to Aunt Josephine's, who was his father's "favorite" sister-in-law. "You'll like it over there," she said, a resigned sneer in her voice. "Charles does. Ever since his brother died, she's been a very lonely widow. This will give Charles just one more excuse to drop in on her."

"It's for the best," his father had assured him, avoiding looking his son in the eye as he helped lift the suitcase onto the backseat of the taxi. "Aunt Josephine's real sweet, and pretty too. You're gonna love her." Solomon didn't respond, so his father kept on prattling, determined to convey how things were actually working out for the best. "My little brother Bill died a couple of years back, and their two no-good children never visit, so Aunt Josephine's all alone in that big old house. You'll be good company for her; you be sure to help her out now, you hear?"

"Yes, sir."

That was it! On the rare occasions that he had called his father anything at all, he had called his father "sir."

Chapter 3

✦

SAINT MARK'S CHURCH of the Divine, situated on the out-skirts of New Rochelle, appeared less cold and severe than Solomon's memory of it. The old gray brick building with a high steepled roof looked almost inviting, dusted over with powdery white snow. A gathering of mourners, bundled in scarves and over-coats, stood in a far-off field, their heads bowed, their mouths mov-ing in recited prayer. Dotted among the tombstones, most of which were submerged three inches into the snow, the people looked like flies settled on the icing of a cake, partaking of the last bites of the flesh and bones of one of their own.

Solomon parked his rental car along the curb and walked across the snow-covered ground toward the preacher's solemn voice, which floated toward him on the frosty afternoon air. "As flowers return to the earth, amen, so the spirit of man must in due season return to the Creator who made us. Let us therefore give thanks in a few mo-ments of silence for the life and returning home of our dear friend and brother, Mr. Charles Franklin Whittman."

In obedience to the preacher, Solomon stopped in his tracks, bowed his head, and closed his eyes. The snow under his feet sent a cold chill running up his body. He shivered, opening his eyes as if awakening from a disturbing dream. From where he stood, the half-hidden faces beneath bowed heads looked ominously alien. The profile of a nose, the side of a cheek, the corner of a mouth, were all unidentifiable to him. He didn't recognize any of the brown-colored black people, pink-colored white people, or mixed-colored where-do-you-come-from people that were crowded around his father's open grave.

Were those his father's colleagues from B & W Businessmen's Association? Or were they his employees from Whittman's Electrical Supplies? Those over there were probably teammates from the Great Lion's sports club and over there, definitely blood relatives from Mississippi. And, of course, front and center, Mrs. Kathleen Whittman and children surrounded by his father's Caucasian in-laws.

Each faction stood in separate little clusters, like miniature colonies claiming various portions of his father's life. Solomon realized with creeping loneliness that he didn't fit into any of the categories. There was no portion, not even a portion of a portion of his father that he could legitimately claim to have been a part of, other than his mother's fabalistic account of the meteoric force of his conception: a beautiful man from America, she confided, had lowered her into the soft warm sand, lain on top of her, and pierced her virginity in a moment so intensely powerful that a piece of his inner light had fallen on her face and temporarily blinded her vision. By the time she could see again, the man was gone; and the only things she could recollect for sure were the seven days of his hand-holding laughter that had led her to this momentous afternoon, and his whispered promise that he would come back for her. He did. Again and again. For fifteen days in a row, he came back to lay her in the sand. One day for each year of her young life, until on that fifteenth day she told him how fortunate it was that her menstruation was five days late, how he must be performing magic on her. "Yeah," he said as he rolled off her. "Want some ice cream?" He slipped on his red-blue-and-white-striped shorts, strolled across the sand, and never returned. "But he left his light behind, Solomon," his mother insisted. "And God made you out of it."

I am the light of my father, Solomon tried to convince himself as he trudged across the snow-covered ground, hoping to reach the grave site and blend in with the mourners before they opened their eyes. Feeling out of place, he searched for what it was that had made him jump on a plane and come to the funeral. Was he still trying to invent a father for himself? The question made Solomon uncomfortable, so he determined to transform his intense emotions for his father into those of a distant acquaintance. *After all*, he reasoned, *that's all he really was.*

While Solomon was struggling to put all personal thoughts of his father out of his mind, the cold chill that had run up his body and caused him to shiver slid down his arm and attacked his naked fingers. "You gotta make a fist and blow on 'em to make 'em warm, like this . . ." There he was, his father, the day after Christmas, out in Aunt Josephine's backyard, visiting him for the first time since putting him on a train to boarding school. "No, he don't need no gloves, Josephine. Come on, sunshine boy, get tough, squeeze you another snowball. I'm trying to teach you how to win a snow fight. You too timid, like your mama. Probably what killed her, never learning to fight back . . ."

"Whoof," Solomon said quietly to himself as he steadied himself from the surge of grief. Standing behind the Mississippi faction of mourners, he planted his feet a little farther apart in an attempt to rebalance his body. *Should I have said something to my father that day? Like what?* he wondered. *It was your neglect that killed her, sir?* Whatever he should or should not have said, Solomon realized it was too late. Both his parents were dead. It was all far, far too late. He closed his eyes and swallowed painfully, as though a big sharp stone were choking his throat.

"Hear our prayer, O Lord," the preacher called out, breaking the few moments of silence. The mourners opened their eyes, lifted up their heads, and added, "And let our cry come unto thee."

"Amen," Solomon mumbled as he lifted up his head.

With her face now fully visible, Mrs. Kathleen Whittman looked older than her sixty-two years and much thinner than Solomon had expected. Her pale white skin looked ghostly under her little black hat and veil, and her thin flamingolike legs looked barely capable of supporting her body. Surrounded by her four children—little Angela now thirty years old; Charles Jr., thirty-seven; Lynn and Selimah, somewhere in between—she looked like the mother hen of a strange breed of chickens. All her children looked alike: thick, curly, red-brown hair, fair-complected coffee-with-a-lot-of-cream–colored skin, marmalade eyes, fleshy pink-brown-freckled lips, and long straight Anglo noses. The odd mix of features, taken from both the black and white branches of their family, set them as a tribe apart. Four pale-speckled siblings standing on either side of their mother, their arms linked together, impenetrable as the mesh on a chicken coop.

Just as Solomon was plucking up courage to advance on the Whittman barricade, he noticed a black flowered hat moving behind them, weaving in and out of his sight as it bobbed toward him. "God bless you, baby, God bless you," Aunt Josephine greeted him effusively. "I was afraid the message wouldn't get to you in time. Everything was so sudden. Oh, Solomon," she said mournfully, her eyes filling with tears. "I just can't believe he's gone." Solomon put his arm around her, and she rested her head against his shoulder, crushing the fresh flowers on her hat. They stood together like that in silence as the preacher pronounced his final blessing.

"Grant peace and comfort this day, O Lord, to those loved ones he left behind, most especially his wife, Kathleen, and his precious children, Charles Jr., Lynn, Selimah, and Angela; in the name of Jesus Christ our Lord. Amen."

Solomon tried not to mind his name being omitted. He didn't expect it to be mentioned. Yet it was strange to be the eldest son, to have flown so far, and not to be mentioned. With her thickly gloved hand, Aunt Josephine patted his back as if to say, "Never you mind, son," the way she used to after his father left from one of his brief visits, robbing the house of his bright suits and his bedroom laughter. *Never you mind, son, he'll talk to you another time.*

The ceremony over, Mrs. Kathleen Whittman was escorted into a waiting limousine by her speckled offspring, several of her Caucasian relatives in tow. Solomon wasn't sure if they had seen him. As he was debating whether to hurry after them to say hello, Granny Earleatha, who at eighty-eight didn't look a day over seventy, grabbed him by the arm and dragged him toward the grave site. "If you ain't a Whittman, I ain't got no sense!" she declared in her strong southern accent. "Look at you flauntin' your granddaddy Hugh's sweet Whittman lips! A woman got-ta close her eyes not-ta wanna kiss you! What you so quiet about, handsome? Move those pretty lips and make you some noise. All this morbid carryin' on. We ought-ta party when someone old go on home, like folks do in Africa. Ain't you the one livin' over there in Africa? Come on, Marky!" she called, turning to a striking ponytailed young man with a long black music case slung over his shoulder. "That there wasn't no funeral! We didn't hire no coach to drive all the way up here from Mississippi to bury our kin like he was a white pole-lit-tician. Pull out that there horn and let's see if we cain't find a hallelujah buried 'neath all this misery!"

With that, Granny Earleatha let out a wail, which other Mississippi relatives caught in the air with their voices in perfect gospel harmony, coming down together in a run of notes so sweet that it seemed they had consorted with the angels up there.

Solomon so lost himself in the singing voices that the stony grief in his throat diminished with each note, fragmenting and shrinking so small that it slipped down and became tiny pebbles lodged in the corner of his heart.

With the freedom of his unrestricted breath, he found himself sailing on the sound of the music, traveling back in a sensory memory to a place where his being longed to return. The mourning voices . . . the wailing horn . . . the resonance of *tenteben* . . .

He had never heard anything like them before. *Tenteben* long as his arm, being played like trumpets. Seven men seasoned with age stood in a row, each one wearing a deep-reddish-brown cloth draped across one shoulder, their raised naked arms holding curved and ancient rams' horns high up to the sky. Eyes closed, they blew power through their billowed cheeks, transmitting a message straight into Solomon's soul. A message he had waited all his life to hear. Urging him. Invoking him. Calling him home.

Was the compelling cry coming from some eternal spirit? Or was it coming from the souls of the skillful men? Perhaps it was the wail of the slaughtered animals, trapped in the dark hard hollow walls of their severed horns. Solomon didn't know; all he knew was that he was being beckoned—beckoned so overpoweringly, he had no other choice but to get off the bus.

Solomon's sandaled feet touched the red crusty earth. He smiled. It was his first trip to Ghana and his first ride outside the capital city of Accra. In a burst of inspiration, he had abandoned his research at the national library in favor of traveling around the country gathering oral recollections for his book. With his camera slung around his neck, he crossed the dirt road to the open field to get a good shot of the *tenteben* blowers. It was obvious by the wailing voices and the sea of black robes that he had happened onto a funeral. Strange. The funeral seemed to be taking place in the middle of nowhere. The field was surrounded by thick foliage leading up into what he later discovered was the Aburi hills. Green and lush, the hills circled upward in a rich mountainous climb that bore an unobstructed view of the valley below. *Ghana!* Solomon thought, raising his camera to his eye. This is what he had come in search of, what he had come to discover. *Beautiful, beautiful Ghana.*

Close up, Solomon guessed that the men blowing the *tenteben* were all at least sixty years old. They were blowing with such mournful intensity, he felt that to use his flash would be intrusive, so he crouched his body low and photographed them against the skyline— seven strong black ancient trees, laced against the setting sun.

"Solomon . . . Solomon." Aunt Josephine tapped Solomon on the arm. He lowered his gaze from the sky.

"The ground's cold," he murmured, looking down past Aunt Josephine's worried face, onto his wet shoes. He had been expecting warm red earth, but instead he was standing in a pool of melting snow.

"Let it out," Aunt Josephine cooed, running her hand up and down Solomon's back. "This is the place, son. You've got to let it all out."

The mourners danced in bitter release, the sweet pain Solomon had felt inside for as long as he could remember. Dark-red, brown, and black cloths sailed through the air as feet shuffled and twisted, kicking up the red earth beneath the green, turning the field into a blood-colored dust storm. Solomon wandered into their midst, shooting his camera. Turning, clicking, turning, clicking, he dodged the reeling, shaking, spinning bodies as gracefully as a matador at a bullfight.

Following the flying fabric of the women as they flapped their cover cloths through the air, Solomon spun on his heels and there she was—an apparition, the stirred-up earth veiling her in a dusty red haze . . . a woman-child . . . fragile . . . alluring . . . with the most enchanting face he had ever seen. Tears bigger than raindrops budded out of her pupils, clung to her long lashes, trickled down her cheeks. She was dancing and sweating, sweating and crying, spilling out her juices onto the thirsty red earth. Not a solitary sound passed from her lips. Not a whimper or a moan. She did not chant or sing like the other women. It was as if she were trapped in a private world of silence. Her arms twisting through the air like birds in flight, she swooped past Solomon so fast that by the time he recovered his step, she had disappeared.

Bumping clumsily into moving bodies, he spotted her, poised his camera to take a picture, and then lost her again. Craning his neck, Solomon jostled in and out of the dancers, desperate to find her. All of a sudden he found himself swimming against the tide, as a sea of women, roused by a change in the beat of the drums, shuffled in his direction, hips swaying, hands clapping, right feet stomping, stomping, stomping down their grief.

Standing in the midst of the chanting, surging women, Solomon heard the bus engine roar up. Peeking above the bobbing heads, he could see the restless driver waving him back onboard. Solomon hesitated, searching once more for the face that had taken his breath away. The bus driver honked the horn impatiently. Solomon took a step toward the roadside and there she was, dancing with the children. He crouched by the side of the grass—if he held his ground, she would pass by his way. The bus driver shouted, honking the horn again. Just a few more seconds . . . Solomon lifted his camera, focused—the undulating back of a passionate young drummer obstructed her face from his view. He heard the bus move slowly forward; the dancing drummer moved out of his eye-line. Without looking at the driver, Solomon held up his hand for him to wait just one more second. Captivated, he watched through his camera as the woman-child spun right in front of his lens—she froze in front of him, her eyes wide and glazed as a frightened antelope. Quickly he refocused, close-up: the big brown eyes, the giant teardrop pivoted on the edge of falling, the glowing ebony cheeks, the wet baby lips, the gold-bangled arm dancing in the air. Click! In a flash she was gone. He wasn't sure . . . He wasn't sure if he had got her—he prayed he had got her, but he wasn't sure.

The bus driver stepped on the gas and sped away.

After the funeral was over and the mourners prepared for their journey home, one of the drummers, noticing Solomon had nowhere to go, beckoned him to follow. He took him through the hills to the household of the bereaved family, offering him a bed for the night since there would not be another coach until the following afternoon. Despite their tragic loss, the family was so hospitable that they encouraged Solomon to stay on, which he did, for twelve unforgettable days.

As soon as he returned to the States, he developed the photographs of the funeral. Heart pounding, he held the negatives up to the light to see if he had gotten the shot. There she was in all her Nubian beauty. Her exquisite doll-like face became his most popular book cover to date. It had even been turned into a poster: *Little Ashia, Don't Cry* by Beento Blackbird.

"Solomon! Solomon! Come on up to the house with us; we're all going over to Kathleen's. Come on, son," Aunt Josephine urged.

Solomon felt cold and disoriented. Looking around, he was surprised to see that most of the mourners had dispersed and that his father's coffin had already been lowered into the ground. He didn't remember that taking place.

"You go on, Aunt Josephine, I'm going to spend a few moments alone here and then head to Manhattan."

"But we haven't even had a chance to really see you. A lot of your relatives are here, you know. At least drop in at the house on your way out and say hello to everybody," she appealed.

"I haven't set foot in that place for quite a while; it's probably best left that way," Solomon responded tightly.

"Life is a lonely road, Solomon," Aunt Josephine said quietly. "You should never throw away family. I know this family isn't an easy one for you to have been born into, and I know there have been some regrettable things done, but regrets are better than loneliness—at least they're something to write about on the blank pages of your life. There's no words to describe loneliness; it's the nothingness of life. That's what your father was afraid of: nothingness. So he lived his life reaching for something, something bright, something to let him know he was alive. He made mistakes, Solomon; people do. I know I've made enough to last a lifetime, but we all have to find it in our hearts to forgive one another and make amends. I'll leave you alone for a minute only if you promise to come and join us at the house—be with your family. Charles would have wanted it that way."

Because he believed in forgiveness, Solomon agreed. It had been twenty-four years since he had been banished from his father's house. In retrospect, he felt he should have gone back years ago, if for no other reason than to tear down the barriers and eradicate the unpleasant memories. "Yes, I'll drop in," he said softly. Satisfied, Aunt Josephine took off across the snow.

Solomon stood alone in the wintery silence. He needed to speak to his father. To utter words of closure. He could not remember when he had last spoken with him. *Was it the Christmas before last? Or New Year's Eve? Or was it on his sixty-third birthday? What did I say to him? Merry Christmas? Happy Birthday?*

Stepping to the periphery of the open grave, he fixed his eyes on the steel-trimmed coffin. "Well, I guess this is it. I know I should say something really profound but—" Solomon looked around self-consciously, making sure no one was within earshot. "I don't know—profundity fails me—I guess I'm a man of letters but no words." He smiled at the irony. The snow glistened around him in dazzling detachment. "Aghh . . ." he muttered, feeling the tiny pebble that had lodged in the corner of his heart pierce him and splinter like glass. "I . . . uh . . . I what?" he asked himself, pressing his hand against his chest to try to relieve the pain. "Well, let's see—" He tried to think of something good, to lift his wounded soul. "I've written another bestseller, you know—did you ever read any of my books? You never did mention—would have been nice, just a mention—'Well done, son'—something uncharacteristic like that.

"Yeah, sure! . . ." he muttered again, battling with his anger and his grief. "So who says you can't miss what you never had? Without you around, who am I gonna fight not to be like?"

Solomon felt the urge to run away, but he held his ground. He was determined to complete his thoughts. Hot tears flamed around his eyes. "Aghh," he moaned through clenched teeth, beating back the tears. "Guess what? I love you—ain't that a joke?"

Solomon laughed to stop himself from crying. There was nothing more to say. The man lying dead in the casket in the hole in the ground was his father and he loved him. There was nothing more to say.

He lifted up the flap of his shoulder satchel and pulled out a copy of his latest book, *The Baby Ghost of Goree Island* by Beento Blackbird. Squatting down, reaching his arm into the gaping hole, he dropped the book on top of the coffin. "Present. Read it sometime." He straightened himself to his full height and checked to make sure there was still no one around. Before walking away, he looked back down at the shiny mahogany casket for the last time. "Say hello to Ma," he instructed, his voice suddenly strong. "In case you don't recognize her, she's the one with two halos."

Chapter 4

✦

*H*IS FATHER'S HOUSE looked brighter than Solomon remembered. The wood moulding had been freshly varnished, and the winter-white paint was clean and new-looking as the untouched snow that had settled on the sloping rooftop. A double-storeyed structure along an avenue of similar houses on a quiet street in New Rochelle, the house, which his father had purchased nearly forty years ago, had weathered the tick of time with remarkable fortitude.

Walking up the neat driveway hedged in by trimmed evergreen bushes, Solomon could see through the front windows into the parlor. Paisley curtains framed a setting worthy of a David Hockney painting. Nicely dressed people sipped tea from delicate china cups and ate fruitcake off little gold-rimmed plates.

Solomon climbed up the porch steps. Before he could ring the bell, a thin white man opened the door. Stepping out onto the porch, the man pulled the door nearly shut behind him. Solomon took one look at the nose and knew this man was related to Kathleen. His high cheekbones, ginger-gray hair, and steely gray eyes could almost have been deemed handsome, were it not for the distraction of his unusually long nose.

"Um—Solomon, right?"

"Yes. Wilberforce."

"I'm Robert Lynwood, Kathleen's brother. We weren't sure you'd make it over."

"Here I am."

"So I see."

The pleasantries over, Solomon took a step forward to enter the house. Robert Lynwood's face flushed pink. "It's pretty crowded in there," he said, holding on to the doorknob.

"I guess my father knew a lot of people." Solomon reached beyond Mr. Lynwood's shoulder, placed his hand on the nearly closed door, and pushed it open against Mr. Lynwood's slight resistance. "Excuse me."

An almost imperceptible hush swept across the inner parlor as Solomon stepped into the hallway. Mrs. Kathleen Whittman sat in a large armchair by the garden window, looking faint. Flanked by her speckled offspring, Solomon could see in her focused metal-gray eyes that she was much stronger than her fragile frame suggested. Solomon's Aunts Bessie and Josephine were seated on the couch not far from Kathleen's chair. Leaning away from them, Mrs. Whittman whispered to Charles Jr. Charles Jr. patted his mother's hand reassuringly and headed toward Solomon. The level of the conversations returned to normal, as if everyone realized that whatever had created a slightly tense atmosphere was being managed.

"Look, I don't know how else to say this, but it's probably better if you left," Charles Jr. whispered brusquely into Solomon's ear.

"What's the problem?" Solomon asked uncomfortably, sensing Mr. Lynwood hovering behind him.

"Come on, Solomon, you know what the problem is," Charles Jr. said, furtively taking note of the inquisitive eyes watching them from the parlor.

"No, I don't," Solomon said emphatically. "I don't know what the problem is at all, so why don't you break it down for me?"

"Listen, I know this is a tough day for all of us. Let's not make it any tougher by being difficult," Robert Lynwood said, placing his hand on Solomon's shoulder.

"Who's being difficult?" Solomon's voice was calm.

"I'm just asking you not to create a scene." Robert Lynwood patted his hand on Solomon's shoulder as if patting down a growling dog.

"Create a scene? Is there any reason why I should?"

"Look," Charles Jr. said, spreading his legs, taking a stance like a bouncer in a nightclub. "I asked you nicely to leave. It's not a good day for my mother to be upset; she's already upset enough."

"I have no intention of upsetting your mother," Solomon assured the speckled one.

"Well, you *are* upsetting her," Charles Jr. said impatiently. "Your being here upsets her. So if you have no intention of upsetting her, just leave quietly and don't make a big deal of it."

I'll leave, Solomon thought. *I'll leave soon. But I'm not a servant who can be rudely dismissed, or a dog who can be booted out the door. I'm not a vulnerable thirteen-year-old kid, in a strange country, with no money and no one to turn to, crying secretly for my mama, trying to squeeze love from my daddy. I'm a man now, visiting my father's house. And I'll leave like a man, in my own good time.*

"Look, for goodness' sake!" Charles Jr. hissed between gritted teeth. "Mom just lost her husband of thirty-eight years! We just lost our father, d'you understand that?"

"Of course I understand that," Solomon said sympathetically. "He was my father too, remember?"

"Yeah, well there's no proof that he was actually your father, is there? I mean, he never took a paternity test or anything. How would your mom really have known?"

"Charles . . . Franklin . . . Whittman . . . Senior . . . was my father," Solomon enunciated with a predatory fierceness that took him by surprise.

"Guys, this is not the time or place," Robert Lynwood interjected, stepping in closer to the two brothers. "I think we're getting a little off the point."

"Which is?" Solomon asked, upset with himself at how angry he felt.

"The point is your leaving," Charles Jr. said, moving in a step closer to Solomon's face. "So why won't you just leave? What is it you want? You want everyone to know you're his son? You want me to tell you your mama was not a whore? Is that what you want?"

Solomon froze. The two men stared each other down, while a quarrel in their blood erupted, enraging them, beckoning them from a muddy pit beneath their feet. It was a quarrel that had stagnated inside them for twenty-four years.

He had called. As soon as the cab driver deposited him at Aunt Josephine's house, Solomon had called his newfound friend and brother to tell him that no matter what craziness was going on with the grown-ups, they could still be friends. For Solomon, brought up as an only child, his mother recently dead and buried, a blood brother was a discovery too precious to lose.

For eight days straight, no matter what the hour, morning or night, it didn't matter, whenever Solomon called to speak to his brother, his little sisters told him hesitantly that Charles Jr. had "just stepped out." At other times when he rang, the second he said, "Hello," he would hear silence followed by a dial tone. Finally, on the ninth day of his calling the Whittman home, an electronic voice informed him that the number had been changed to an unpublished number.

When his father came to visit several days later, Solomon asked him for the new number. "Probably better if you don't call over to the house till everybody settles down," Charles Sr. had answered.

Apparently, everybody never settled down, because by that September, when Solomon was shipped off from Aunt Josephine's to a small boys' boarding school in Pennsylvania, he had still not been permitted the number to his father's house, nor had he heard any word from his newfound brother.

The next time Solomon heard of Charles Jr. was from one of his Mississippi cousins who had come to spend a few nights during the Easter break at Aunt Josephine's, where Solomon spent all his vacations until he was eighteen, when he was able to work and save enough for airfare to spend his vacations on Cape Corcos.

"I hear your momma was freaky-deaky," the Mississippi cousin salivated as they hid in Aunt Josephine's musty garden shed, pawing over a *Playboy* magazine. "Charles Junior say she was one of them wild Island whores, say she drugged your daddy and forced him to have voodoo sex with her."

Solomon's fists flew. They jabbed and flew inside the shed until they knocked against the tiny cobwebbed window, rendering a family of spiders homeless as the glass shattered onto the dewy green grass outside.

"I ain't spreading no *rumors*," Charles Jr. retorted two months later, when Solomon finally confronted him sitting in his daddy's car outside Whittman's Electrical Supplies. "Your momma *was* a whore." Laughing, Charles Jr. proceeded to spout forth a litany of what "the whore" was like, describing her private parts: how they looked, how they felt, how they smelled. Solomon jumped out of Aunt Josephine's car, balling up his fists. "What you gonna do, Cape Coconut–head?" Charles Jr. taunted, springing out of his daddy's bright-green Buick.

Before Solomon could punch his reply, their father came sprinting out of the store, commanding them both to "Back off!"

"I'll call you later," Charles Sr. shouted to Aunt Josephine, who hurried out of the store behind him. Sitting next to his daddy, Charles Jr. laughed and gave Solomon the finger as the car sped away.

All Solomon could think as he stood there in the hallway, a mere breath away from his half-brother's face, was, *How could my daddy have sold out and bred a half-breed-honky-white-momma'd-punk like you?*

Solomon's thoughts took him by surprise. He had always believed that racism in any form reflected an evil or ignorant mind. He had never dated a white woman but had always maintained that it was circumstance, not racism. Now here he was, thirty-seven years old, feeling racial hostility toward the white woman who was ordering him out of his own black father's house, and her pale son whom he was ashamed to think of as his own blood relative. The shocking thing about it was not that he did not like them as people, but that he was seeing them in terms of color. Everything suddenly seemed a matter of either black or white, and he preferred black. He was a black man. He liked the way black people did things. The way they expressed themselves, the way they mourned, the way they endured, the way they loved. Yes, he was a black man. Black like his black mama. Black like his black father. The first begotten son. The real and rightful Charles Franklin Whittman Jr. He had been robbed of his father, robbed of his name, robbed of his home, and robbed of his sweet mama's reputation. Robbed by this no-good-honky-white-woman and her half-breed-no-good-honky-looking . . . Solomon stopped midthought—was Mrs. Jeannie Baker-Weiss, who had cared for him for thirty-six hours straight, without sleeping, after he suffered a concussion on the excavation sight in Egypt, was she a no-good honky? Or Rupert Toot, his best boarding-school buddy from England, was he a no-good honky? Or Lenny Cathcart, his college coach, who gave him his first car? Or Channing and Camille Jean-Claire, who typed his first book for free? And what about sweet Claudia Grace, who was always there when he needed her, was she honky-white and no good? Solomon recalled his Caucasian friends with affection and took back possession of his mind.

"I came to pay my respects," he said politely. "I don't know why that would cause such a problem but—"

"Okay, brother dearest," Charles Jr. interrupted sarcastically. "You want me to spell it out for you? Mother doesn't want to have to explain your existence. Most of her friends don't know about you. You're not exactly the kind of thing our family boasts about—you're an embarrassment. Get it?"

"An embarrassment? Who the *heck* are you to call me an embarrassment?" Solomon's loud indignant voice bounced off the walls and toppled into the middle of the hallway floor. The inner parlor fell silent, as a hundred prickly eyes focused piercingly in his direction.

Solomon stood for a moment, stabbed by the cake-eaters' stares, and then he moved. People made way for him to pass as he headed for the back of the parlor to where Mrs. Whittman sat motionless and ghostly pale. "My condolences," he said with genuine sympathy. He leaned into her, lifted her limp hand out of her lap, and shook it politely. "I know you loved my father very much. It must be a great loss. I pray time will make his absence easier to bear."

Solomon looked up at Charles Jr., who had rushed to stand beside his mother, as though Solomon's presence might do her grievous bodily harm. "Charles," he said, straightening himself up to his full height, "my mother was not a whore. When our father met her, he failed to mention that he was married. He was twenty-seven at the time, she was a fifteen-year-old virgin. Make no mistake, Charles Whittman knew he was my father. They both did."

Alone in the stillness of the snow-covered porch, the slammed door still ringing in his ears, Solomon thought he could hear a robin sing. He had forgotten about the robins. In his first two weeks in America, twenty-four years ago, when he had stayed with the rest of his siblings in this very house, he used to get up early in the morning to stand on this porch and feed the robins toasted breadcrumbs. *Are these the same robins?* he wondered as he buttoned his raincoat and

walked down the perfectly manicured driveway. *Or their offspring?*
He opened the front gate and stepped out onto the sidewalk.
Fumbling for his keys, he unlocked the door to his car. Were those
footsteps? Was someone running after him? Whose voice was that?
Aunt Josephine?

Solomon climbed into his car and drove away.

*   *   *

Crawling along the Connecticut Turnpike at less than twenty-five
miles per hour, Solomon did not have a destination. Ignoring the
honking horns and angry sideways glances of frustrated drivers as
they overtook him, he gazed ahead as if in a trance.

A loud blast, like the foghorn of a giant steamship, jolted him into
reality as an oversized truck suddenly tried to overtake him, forcing
him to swerve into a near head-on collision with a brown station
wagon in the neighboring lane. Speeding vehicles, whizzing by,
dodged one another as Solomon's car skidded across the icy surface
of the road, bumped against the dividing barrier, spun 360 degrees,
and jerked to an abrupt standstill.

Shaken but unharmed, he pounded fury into the steering wheel.
"WHY! WHY! WHY! WHY! WHY!" he wailed, pounding his
knuckles against the hard new plastic, banging them raw, as he beat,
beat, beat, rattling loose the sharp pebbles of pain lodged in his heart.
"He-was-my-daddy-too-he-was-my-daddy-too-he-was-my-daddy-
too," he protested, angry tear-colored pebbles flying out of his eyes
like hailstones.

Stunned by the eruption of his inner self, Solomon stopped still
to discern what was coming from his soul.

After many hours, passing cars no longer noticed his immobile,
slightly dented Ford sedan, wedged against the dividing barrier on
95 South. Finally, shifting forward to pull away, Solomon caught a
glimpse of his face in the rearview mirror. A small insignificant dot.
That's what came to mind as he elbowed his car into the flow of
traffic. A small insignificant dot. Alone. On a crowded turnpike.
Lonely. In a nation full of people.

Chapter 5

✦

*B*Y THE TIME Solomon reached Manhattan, he had tempted fate by driving almost one hour with the light on the dashboard reading EMPTY. He felt grateful to have made it to a familiar destination as the car sputtered up to the corner of Fifty-sixth and Madison Avenue.

The doorman stepped forward to open the car door. "Hey, Jerry," Solomon greeted, slipping him a ten-dollar bill, "watch the car for me. I'll be right out." Handing him the keys, he disappeared into the building.

"You!" Receptionist Lisa's voice was shrill but pleasant. "I'll tell them you're here," she said, reaching for the phone.

"I'll tell them myself," Solomon replied, striding down the short corridor to Sam's office. Sam was not there. Thinking she might be with Andréa, he headed for the set of double doors bearing a large plaque that read DU POIS INNER SANCTUM. Placing his hands on the brass handles, he flung the doors open, making a grand entrance.

The room was empty.

More like a boudoir than an office, Andréa Du Pois's Eurocentricity was splashed everywhere. French sofas, Italian paintings, German etchings—there was even a little brass table with a selection of Swiss and English chocolates.

Solomon heard a tap running in the small bathroom at the back and presumed it must be Andréa. Wandering over to the Louis XVI desk in the center of the room, he made himself comfortable in her large antique armchair.

"Well, if it isn't the kid himself!" Andréa's voice was like her demeanor: bold, unafraid, and distinctly French. Despite their sometimes-heated disagreements, Solomon admired her. She had come over from Paris to New York seventeen years ago, when she was in her early twenties, with nothing but brains, courage, good looks (it was often said she resembled Lauren Bacall), and an uncanny knack for discovering talent. Utilizing those attributes, she had built a small empire. After nine years of hard work establishing Du Pois Literary Agency, she had branched out to include screenwriters, directors, producers, and eventually actors, creating International Artists Agency. IAA was a hive of activity one floor below her current office. She kept the name Du Pois for the literary department, to remind herself and her employees of how IAA began and who was running the show. Andréa Du Pois was unquestionably the captain of the ship, and Solomon its number-one client.

Andréa bustled about, digging out reviews of Solomon's latest book, *The Baby Ghost of Goree Island.* "Fantastic reviews, no?" She tossed him a week-old *New York Times.* "And you should read the *Newsweek* article: white middle class has gone crazy over Beento Blackbird—they love the travel, the adventure—you're even adored by the little British royals. Congratulations, my dear, you've hit the big time."

"If black kids read my books, that's big-time. The rest is cream, and I like my coffee black."

There was an awkward pause.

"Well, like it or not, your coffee's attracting a lot of cream," Andréa said finally. "Recent figures reflect not only an increase in your book sales in the adult market, but also a greater white following. In fact, you are becoming too popular to remain anonymous, Solomon; people need to see your face."

"The kids think I'm a bird, I'm a bird. That's the way I like it: *incognegro,*" Solomon quipped. "Look, Andréa," he continued, "I didn't come here on business. I just dropped by to say hi."

Solomon felt Andréa studying him, a worried expression on her face. "What's wrong, *mon cheri?* Why so sad? So militant?" Solomon ignored the question. "What are you doing here anyway? You just flew off on one of your long trips, no? How come you are sitting here in my office? What happened?"

"Nothing."

"Yes, look at you. I know you. Something happened. Something bad, no?"

"Not at all. Just a little death and family drama," Solomon said flippantly.

"Oh, I'm sorry," Andréa empathized, despite his flippant attitude. "Who? How?"

"It's okay," Solomon assured her. "No one I was close to." His lips spread into a smile; his eyes remained sad.

"But you flew back—"

"You know how family is, you have to at least make an appearance at the funeral, or everyone gets upset."

"Not with us. My family is not close like that. We never get together, not even for funerals. You are lucky," Andréa said wistfully.

Solomon felt a twinge in his heart. He wished he had not mentioned it: the funeral, the family—he had purposed to leave it behind, scattered on 95 South.

"I know what will cheer you up," Andréa said brightly. Just then there was a light tap on the door, and it opened and Sam St. James peered into the room.

"I hear our favorite artiste is in the office."

"Now where'd you hear that?" Solomon flashed Sam a warm smile, relieved to see her.

"Oh, you know how folks love to talk," Sam said playfully. Wandering in, she perched on the end of Andréa's couch.

"We are taking him with us this evening, Sam. He needs cheering up."

"Great," Sam enthused. "You're coming with us to Pat Kelly-Moore's book party?"

"Certainly he is coming with us," Andréa said emphatically. She picked up the phone. "Lisa, call Carriageways, tell them we want to change from a town car to a stretch if it's not too late, and book us dinner at Jezebel's for nine-thirty. Tell them we need a table for ten."

"Actually, I'm not sure I'm up for a social evening, Andréa. I really just wanted to talk a few things over with Sam," Solomon said, looking at Sam, realizing what a relief it was to see her. "You think I could borrow her away for a few hours?"

"Maybe Solomon and I could go on ahead and talk at the restaurant, and you and Pat could join us there later," Sam suggested.

"Hey, Frank," Solomon shouted, leaning forward. The glass partition dividing the front from the back of the limousine rolled down.

"Yes, sir," Frank said, settling back into the driver's seat, having escorted Andréa into an art gallery where the book party was in full swing.

"Where's my luggage?" Solomon inquired.

"In the trunk, sir."

"Good. Take me home."

"One hundred eighteenth and Riverside?"

"You got it."

"What about Jezebel's?" Sam asked casually. "Andréa's expecting to come and join us there afterward. We were supposed to go there to eat."

"We'll order in." Solomon rested his head against the back of the seat and stretched out his legs.

"Is that an official invitation to dinner at your place?" Sam asked after a brief pause, her voice more liquid than before.

"Yes."

"So, I finally get to see where the maestro works."

"And eats and sleeps," Solomon added.

"Eats and sleeps? I didn't think you did mundane things like that. You mean you're a mere mortal?" Sam smiled, her eyes sparkling. *Nice eyes*, Solomon thought. *She really has lovely eyes.*

Chapter 6

✦

*I*T WAS LIKE a bad dream. Like suddenly finding himself entangled by the legs of an octopus at the bottom of the sea, understanding how he got down there but not knowing how to get back up.

Solomon lifted his chest off Sam's naked breasts in the hopes of getting some air. If he could only get some air, maybe he could disentangle himself and swim back up.

Still in the throes of desire, Sam reached for the chain around his neck to pull him back toward her. He resisted, and the chain broke under the force of her fingers.

"NO!" Solomon snapped, referring to his broken silver chain, the half-naked woman beneath him, the death of his father, his hostile half-brother, his sexual desire—everything. He reached out his hand to retrieve the antique silver locket that had dropped onto the floor, but Sam reached it first and tossed it across the room. Laughing, she rolled him over, sat on top of him, pinned down his arms with her knees, bent down, and nibbled on his nipple. In one fierce undulating move, Solomon bucked her off, leaped to his feet, and shouted, "I can't do this!"

Sam froze. Solomon looked at her crouched on his living room rug and realized that the sudden violence of his move had frightened her. Wearing only her skimpy peach satin-and-lace panties, she clutched her arm protectively over her naked breasts and waited to see what he was going to do next.

"It's okay, it's okay," he said, easing himself carefully onto the end of the couch farthest away from her to let her know he meant her no harm. "Sorry. It's got nothing to do with you. It's just—"

"Hold it." Sam crawled across the floor and retrieved her camisole. "Somehow, I think this is going to be one of those speeches I should be dressed for," she said, slipping the camisole over her head.

"No speeches. I just want you to know it's got nothing to do with you."

"Sure!" Hostility spiced Sam's voice. "Let me guess: you're gay. You don't find me attractive. You're only attracted to white women."

"I think you're gorgeous . . . I—"

"You're married," Sam continued, not giving him a chance to finish. "And we never see your wife 'cause she's in a mental institution, but you won't divorce her 'cause—"

"She's not in a mental institution." Solomon's voice cut in harder than he had meant.

Sam stood up, rested her hands on her slim hips, and stared out the window. Solomon felt uncomfortable. It was hard to read her. Studying her, trying to gauge her thoughts, he wished she didn't look that good standing there with her small breasts pushing through her peach satin camisole, her long shapely legs just an arm's reach away. Her half-naked closeness, her unreadable silence, made him more aware of the loneliness of his soul.

"The violins just stopped," Sam quipped in a sarcastic voice, focusing back on the room. "Go on," she said, reaching for her skirt, which she had slung over the back of the couch, "say what you wanted to say."

"I, uh—" Solomon floundered.

"Yeah, right!" Sam scoffed. "So you're married."

"Yeah."

"Where is this wife?"

"One's in the West Indies, the other one's in West Africa."

He said it as casually as he could, slipped it in like everyday conversation, hoping against hope that she would let it pass without comment.

"Excuse me?" Sam laughed in disbelief. "Come again?" She turned to look at him, her laughter stopping as suddenly as it began. Once more, it was hard for Solomon to read her. For a split second it appeared to him as though she genuinely found it funny, but then he saw the anger in her eyes. "So much for my too-shy, too-busy-to-have-a-woman theory," she said ruefully as she snatched her panty-hose off the coffee table. "Talk about being way off base! You've got two wives?"

"Look, I'm sorry I—"

"So what am I?" Sam quizzed indignantly, nearly tripping as she struggled into her pantyhose. "I mean, we have kind of been dating, haven't we?"

"I don't necessarily consider lunches with a business associate a date," Solomon said defensively.

"What about dinners?" Sam jabbed.

"We haven't really had that many dinners—"

"How many dinners makes a date, Solomon? Do you have a mathematical equation for it? Four dinners, three lunches, and two postcards a year equals one date? Or does it have to be five dinners and three lunches? What about three dinners, six lunches, and a let-ter instead of the postcards? Would that do it?"

Solomon knew he had to proceed very carefully. "I'm not deny-ing our friendship, Sam. I'm not denying our closeness."

"But the attraction I feel when we're together is just one-sided, right?"

"No, I'm very attracted to you," he admitted, "but—"

"But what?" Sam's look confronted him.

"But I've never been unfaithful to my wives," he said, feeling lonelier by the minute. "This is the closest I've ever come."

Sam looked at him as if he had just stepped off another planet. "Wait a minute." She moved in a little closer. "I think I'm missing something here. You've never been unfaithful to your wives? Cor-rect me if I'm wrong, but isn't that a contradiction in terms?"

"Not to me," Solomon asserted.

"Having two wives and calling yourself faithful is not a contradic-tion?" Sam asked incredulously.

"No." Solomon remained firm.

"Have these wives ever met?"

"No, they haven't."

"You see them separately?"

"Yes."

"When?"

"One in the summer, the other one in the winter."

"Fascinating," Sam scoffed. "And how long has this arrangement been going on?"

"I've known Miriam all my life. I've been married to her for twelve years. We—"

"You mean you've been married twelve years and never once thought to mention it to me?" Sam interrupted, her voice escalating. "I mean, I've asked you so many times, Solomon!"

"No, Sam, you've never once asked me if I was married."

"I did! Okay, maybe I didn't! I mean, maybe I presumed—I've known you so long, Solomon! I mean, I would have thought you would tell me! I mean, I know I definitely asked you if you had any kids or anything. You've always said no!"

"Well, I don't."

"You don't?"

"No, I don't."

"Well, how old is your wife?" Sam asked, struggling through her hurt and confusion.

"Why?" Solomon asked defensively.

"Why not?" Sam countered.

"Forty-six. She's forty-six."

"And the other one?"

"I've known Ashia for eight years. I married her five years ago."

"How old is she?"

Solomon felt he was being trapped, but he wasn't sure how or for what purpose.

"She's young, isn't she?" There was something mocking in Sam's voice that challenged him.

"Twenty-three," he answered, resenting the feeling of guilt that Sam was invoking.

"It figures," Sam spat out disdainfully. "So you just leave each wife alone for months on end?" Solomon didn't reply. "They're happy with that? Sitting around waiting for you?" Sam continued derisively.

"They lead full lives of their own. They don't just sit around waiting for me. They have friends, family, ambitions. They're both incredible women. It's a choice," Solomon asserted. "The way we live—it's a choice—it's hard to explain."

"So, you think they also have another partner? Especially that young one in Africa. Don't you think she has a handsome playmate to satisfy her when you're not around, you know, someone more her own age?" Sam needled vengefully.

"No, I don't."

"When you're off with your other wife, you don't think she has some healthy young African to amuse herself with?"

"No."

"What? You're so macho, you give her enough satisfaction to last her months at a time?"

"I doubt that, but she doesn't have a *playmate* as you call it. She's not that kind of a woman."

"And how would you know that, Solomon Wilberforce? You're never there!"

The fury in Sam's voice reminded Solomon why he kept his life so private. Most often when he told people he had two wives, it angered them. If it didn't anger them, it intrigued them for all the wrong reasons. As if having two wives made him a sex fiend, or a male chauvinist, or some kind of cultist.

"Do they even know about each other? These two wives?" Sam probed, her voice calmer.

"Of course they do."

"Don't give me *of course*," she flared again. " 'Cause I figured *of course* you're not married! *Of course* it would have come up in one of our many conversations, like when I confided in you about my broken engagement! Or Andréa's divorce! Or my cousin's disastrous wedding! So don't you *dare* give me *of course*, like you tell everybody everything! Like you're oh-so-Mr.-Honest. For goodness' sake, Solomon, if you'd told me you were married, don't you think I'd have locked up my heart? I mean, do you really think after all the miserable relationships I've been through, I'd really be standing here half-naked in your apartment if I knew you were married?"

"It's just always so hard to explain."

"Try 'I'm married'!" Sam yelled.

Solomon took a deep breath and held his peace. Sam finished dressing hurriedly and dug furiously under the couch in search of her shoes. Finding them, she headed out, slamming the front door behind her.

The sound of the door slamming triggered a recollection in Solomon's mind. Hadn't he heard a door slam earlier that day? Where was it? At Miriam's? At Cape Corcos Airport? On the plane? Where was it? At his father's house? Yes. Yes, it was at his father's house. He had walked out the front door, and someone had slammed it shut on his back. My goodness, was this all really one day? Where was his guardian angel? Everything was out of rhythm. He was so unprepared. It was winter; he was not supposed to be here. He had not had time to brace his emotional system to deal with America. He was supposed to be on Cape Corcos. Maybe that's why the day had been so brutal. His guardian angel was still fluttering around Miriam's adobe, wondering where his mortal had gone.

He looked around the room and spotted Sam's purse and coat lying behind the wooden rocking chair. He figured she wouldn't go very far without them, not in this weather and at this time of night. It was nearly one o'clock in the morning. Was she expecting him to chase after her? Perhaps he should just go to bed and sink into oblivion. But then again, what if something happened to her?

Mustering up the little energy he had left, he stood up, buttoned his shirt, buckled his belt, threw on his sweater, grabbed his overcoat off the peg in the foyer, and went outside.

Snow! It was snowing. *How many years has it been*, Solomon wondered, *since I actually saw snow falling from the sky?* Plunging his hands into his pockets, he crossed Riverside Drive and hurried along the deserted sidewalk. Gazing up at the dark leafless trees, he admired the way they bore the weight of the falling snow with patient grace, balancing the snowflakes along their branches as carefully as a dancer balances air. *If only man could bear his load with such poise*, he mused. *I guess the trees trust that the sun will soon melt their burdens away*. "It's gonna be all right," Solomon whispered to himself, receiving the message from the trees. "Everything's gonna be all right."

"Why did you invite me here?"

Sam's voice startled him. He turned to see her standing on the grassy embankment. "Sam!" he exclaimed. "I was looking for you."

"I want to know why you invited me over, Solomon." Sam huffed, pumping steam into the cold air.

"I wanted your company."

"Why?"

The question rendered him speechless. As he was standing there, figuring out the answer, Sam looked at him disgustedly and went marching up the road. Solomon chased after her. "My father died," he announced and stopped walking.

His words took him by surprise. He didn't know why he told Sam. Maybe to make her stop walking and come back up to the apartment, because enough was enough, and he had participated in enough drama for one day. Or maybe subconsciously it was the answer to her question of why he had invited her over. He had thought his invitation was a spontaneous act, but maybe he had somehow engineered the situation. After all, he had no work objective for going to the agency. Driving around after his minor accident, he had found himself headed there for no particular reason except to see Sam and have her talk to him, perhaps help him make sense of his muddled life before he headed back to Cape Corcos—the way she helped him edit and simplify his stories before publication.

"I flew in this morning for his funeral," he said. And then he turned around and walked back toward his apartment. It wasn't that he was angry, it was just that the day had been too long. He cared for Sam, perhaps more deeply than he realized, but he just didn't have the emotional energy to add her to the pile already sitting on his shoulders.

Sam ran after him. "I'm sorry," she said quietly as she clutched his arm and walked along beside him. "I had no idea. I'm really sorry."

They walked a little way in silence, their friendship closing in again like a boat gently coming back to harbor. Solomon looked up at the trees as they passed beneath their branches. *Thank you*, he murmured to them in his heart.

"Ow, Solomon," Sam groaned suddenly. "I'm ffffreeeezing." She shuddered, the cold slicing through her thin clothing.

"That's what you get for being so hotheaded," Solomon teased.

"For real, Solomon, my arms, my feet, ow, ouch, my feet!" Sam stopped, cold tears dripping out of the corners of her eyes. "I think my feet are going to drop off," she said, shaking each leg in a panic.

"Silly woman, you probably got frostbite," Solomon scolded as he scooped her up and cradled her like a baby. "Didn't your mama teach you nothing?" Carrying her in his arms, he continued walking back to his apartment.

Sam hugged her arms around his neck, pressed her body close to his warmth. "What's my mama got to do with it?" she asked, shivering through clenched teeth.

Solomon could feel her body becoming like cold lead. Concerned, he broke into a labored jog. "She should have learned you how to act right," he panted. "And not go running out on good people. Especially not in the middle of the night, in New York City, in the dead of winter with no coat on!"

Sam laughed and then shivered again. She unbuttoned the top of Solomon's coat, slithered one arm inside and wriggled her body in tighter against his body. "Aaah, Solomon, I'm cold! I'm so cold." She nuzzled her face into his neck. Solomon found himself wishing once more that she were not so attractive, or that he wasn't so affected by her cold hard nipples pressing against his chest, or her soft warm mouth against his skin. With each jogging step her body rubbed against his, up and down, up and down, sending waves of heat rippling through his blood. He tried to focus on something other than the woman in his arms, other than the hot fiery sparks being stimulated between them.

Nothing else came to mind.

This was a very different Sam than Solomon had ever encountered. Snuggled down in his bed in his oversized T-shirt, his *kente* cloth bedspread pulled all the way up under her nose, she looked unrecognizably vulnerable. Freshly out of her warm bath, her face scrubbed clean of all her expertly applied makeup, she appeared much younger than her thirty-four years as she peeked out at him over the quilt like a mischievous child.

"Anything else, ma'am?" Solomon asked with a smile, placing a tray of milk and oatmeal cookies on the nightstand beside the bed.

"You really got me milk and cookies?" Sam's eyes flashed with pleasure. "Thank you."

"You're welcome."

There was a moment as he straightened up from bending over the nightstand that Solomon found himself caught in Sam's eyes. He noticed, as she stared at him, how entrancing they were, multicolored see-through brown, like pieces of broken bottles. "Night, Sam," he said, looking away to release himself from the captivity of her gaze. Preparing to leave the room, he reached out his hand and retrieved his locket off the dresser.

"Sorry I broke your chain." Sam fixed her eyes on him with cat-like curiosity. "Who's in the locket?"

"I don't tell people."

"I'm not people."

"It's just one of those things I don't tell anyone."

"I'm not anyone."

Solomon rolled the locket in his fingers.

"Tell me," Sam coaxed, "what lucky woman do you keep next to your heart?"

"My mother."

"Sure!"

"My mother. Really!"

Gentleness touched the room. Sam sat up in the bed. "Can I see?"

"I only open it on her birthday."

"When's her birthday?"

"April fifth."

"I bet she was beautiful."

"Yes, she was. Inside and out."

"Like her son."

Sam gazed at him with her broken-glass eyes. They looked to Solomon more inviting than ever before. Accepting the invitation to come closer, he stepped inside and found the sweet little girl that lived behind them. "Get some sleep," he encouraged, backing out again for fear of cutting himself.

"With you in the house, it won't be easy," the little girl beckoned as he moved farther away from her.

Solomon kept walking, determined not to turn around. Out in the hallway he closed the bedroom door and leaned against it. He felt a sense of victory. He had made it—he had resisted temptation. The sun-blue skies of Cape Corcos suddenly seemed but a wingspan away.

Chapter 7

✦

"*A*YIEE! SOLOMON! WHAT ARE YOU DOING HERE?"
Hurriedly knotting the thread on the twisted plait of her customer's hair, Ashia wiped the grease off her fingers and ran to greet Solomon. "What a surprise! What a big, big surprise." She giggled as she pulled an old head scarf off her hair. Stroking her hand down the front of her wrinkled cloth, she apologized for her messy appearance. "Excuse," she said, giving a little curtsy, offering him her wrist to shake instead of her soiled hand. "Please excuse. I was just plaiting hair." She ran to remove from the wooden stool the greasy newspaper she had wiped her hands on. "Please sit. Ayiee! Solomon! What a surprise. What a big, big surprise," she repeated in her nervous excitement.

"I couldn't wait till summer," Solomon said, easing himself down onto the stool in the dappled shade of the old courtyard tree. He leaned against its low bent bark and took his first good look at Ashia. Sweaty and unkempt, she looked more beautiful than ever.

"Let me fetch you water," her voice sang as she almost skipped into the bedroom. The customer whose hair was being plaited rose off the mat she'd been sitting on and followed Ashia inside.

Solomon could hear the two women speaking very fast in Twi amid excited giggles. He looked around the peaceful courtyard and marveled that he was actually there. And to think that less than twenty-four hours ago he was cramped up on his couch in his Harlem apartment, with Sam asleep in his bed. Thinking of Sam, Solomon touched his T-shirt pocket in a reflex action and pulled out her note.

Morning Solomon,

I know it's been a rough and sleepless two days for you, so I didn't want to wake you. I'm leaving early to go home and change before work. I'm really sorry about your father, and for my going off on you last night. I was just hurt that, close as we've been all these years, you kept from me that you were married. That got me to questioning myself this morning as to whether there was anything significant I've also kept from you. As close as I am to you, I realize there is. Watching you deal with your father's death is a reminder to me that one day the people I love may no longer be around for me to let them know how I feel, and that holding back really isn't worth it—so here goes:

Solomon, have you ever wondered what it would be like to have one woman with whom you could share everything? All the different aspects of you and your life? Your work—your travel—your politics—your heart? It's not impossible, you know. You're complex, but not impossible—and you're certainly worth the effort it would take to really encompass all of you. At least, that's what this woman believes. I believe I could do it. I believe it could be incredible. For both of us. I wanted to let you know how I feel while I have the courage to say it—before you fly away again.

Much love, Sam

Solomon folded the note and put it back in his pocket. It seemed so far away—Sam . . . their walk in the snow. Time and space was a funny thing. Strange, with a direct flight he had got here in less time than it was going to take him to get back to Cape Corcos, even though Ghana was so much farther away from New York than the Caribbean.

He had promised Miriam he would come back after the funeral to complete his winter season with her, and yet here he was in Africa. The image of Miriam dressed in white, standing at the airport, twinged his conscience. He had fully intended to return to her, but picking up the phone to ask his travel agent to book a flight to Cape Corcos, questions about Ashia had crept into his mind, and the next thing he knew, he was sitting on a plane headed for Ghana.

Ashia came out of the bedroom holding a tray with a long glass and a decanter of ice-cold water. Solomon watched her walk carefully toward him, watched her place the tray respectfully at his feet. The image of Miriam—of Sam—was wiped from his mind.

Chilly droplets splashed onto his fingers as ice cubes tumbled out of the decanter into his glass. He took a sip of the cool water and poured the remainder over his head. Ashia laughed and asked him if he'd like to freshen up. Solomon stripped off his shirt and said sure, but only if she'd join him. Overhearing their conversation, the female customer hurried across the courtyard, three sleepy children in tow and a pile of rolled-up mats under her arm. With an embarrassed grin, she mumbled to Ashia and Solomon that she would deposit the children at Mr. Opoku's house and let everyone know that the Big Man was back, so they should not come to sleep there for a while.

"Who?" Solomon inquired.

"Some of the women and children sleep here sometimes when you are away," Ashia told him tentatively. "You know in our culture I cannot keep all this space for myself."

The customer shuffled out, asking Ashia to send for her whenever she had time to finish threading her hair.

As soon as she left, Solomon and Ashia filled two buckets with water, dragged them behind the semicircle of stones, took off their clothes, and bathed each other. Solomon played away Ashia's shyness, teasing and tickling her until she was comfortable again with their nakedness. Despite the unexpectedness of his visit, everything flowed smoothly. That is, until the weekend.

It was not anything major, but on reflection Solomon realized it was the first outward sign of the cracks in the wall that the hammer of Sam's tongue had inflicted on his mind.

It was a peaceful Saturday morning. He was sitting under the tree in the courtyard at a small wooden table, writing a new story concept in his notebook. Ashia was in the bedroom gushing over some fuchsia-and-gold handwoven silk he had stopped to buy her as a gift from an Indian store in New York, on his way to the airport. He could see her through the lace-net curtain, standing in front of the long mirror in her bra and panties, wrapping and unwrapping the fabric around her body, creating different styles. He was watching her and at the same time trying to figure out how to get Beento

Blackbird out of a scrape, when a deep voice filtered in from the front of the house. Recognizing the voice, Solomon strode out of the courtyard, into the bedroom.

Noticing his reflection in the mirror, Ashia struck a pose. "Look—Cleopatra!" she declared, pulling some of the silk sari that was twisted tightly around her body up over her head and across her mouth like a vixen.

"Your friend's here," Solomon announced without hiding his displeasure.

"Who?"

"The happy college student."

"Olu?" Ashia asked nonchalantly.

"Has he been staying here?" Solomon questioned.

"Sometimes he has been visiting."

"I told you I like us to stay alone, Ashia."

"I am thinking, only when you are here."

"What's that supposed to mean?"

"Only when you are here I have told them nobody can stay, because I know you want me all for yourself. You see how the day you came, when they returned from the farm, everybody took their things and went and moved into the big house? That's why usually when I know you will be arriving, you come and find nobody sleeping here. But I did not know."

"You didn't know what?" Solomon queried, irritated at the odd way she was stringing her words together.

"I did not know you were coming."

"So you mean when I'm not here—" Solomon stopped at the sound of Olu's jovial voice outside the curtain.

"Madam Ashia!" boomed the deep voice. "Princess of Aburanoma, where are you hiding yourself?" Olu came bounding into the bedroom all friendliness and high energy. "Ayiee, Solomon!" he exclaimed, surprised. "What brings you here at this time of year? Has your Western world grown too sour for you?" Without waiting for a reply, Olu strutted over to Ashia. "Nature's finest," he proclaimed, embracing her longer than Solomon felt was necessary. "I've been dreaming of your okra soup. You must pound fufu for me today, those spoiled city girls in Accra don't like to make it anymore."

The fabric wrapped around Ashia's body slipped under the pressure of Olu's tight hug. Solomon noticed the exposed top of her low-cut yellow lace bra (the one he had bought for her in Paris on his way to Dakar) and wondered with indignation why she didn't cover herself up in front of Olu. To make matters worse, Olu plunked himself down on the bed as if he had a right to be in their bedroom. "You need to give us a minute," Solomon asserted. "She's got to get dressed." Olu bounced up, threw a comment to Ashia in Twi, and bounded out of the room.

"What was that about?"

"Please, what are you asking me?"

"I'm asking what that was about."

"Please excuse me, but I am not understanding you."

"What did Olu say? When he walked out, what did he say to you?" Solomon enunciated, finding Ashia's lack of comprehension and excessive politeness suspicious and increasingly annoying.

"He said he was going to go and greet the old folks, that he would go and come." Ashia answered.

"Why couldn't he say that in English?"

"English is not his language," Ashia stated simply.

"What's the big deal, Ashia? Why does he have to come here, anyway?"

Ashia unraveled the silk from her body, spread it out on the bed, and folded it carefully. Solomon watched her, waiting for a reply.

"Why does he come here, Ashia?" he repeated.

"He likes to get away from the city."

Ashia's voice was so sad and small, it made Solomon feel ashamed of himself. He wanted to leave her alone and go back to his writing, but he was gripped with the fear that what he had always thought was Ashia's submissiveness was in actuality a form of slyness. Perhaps she was more like her mother than he realized. Perhaps like her mother she was capable of allowing her body to exist in one place while her heart and soul lived somewhere else entirely. Or perhaps like her grandmother she was impenetrable, her motives undecipherable, her actions imperceptible, yet full of purpose, carving out their own agenda. Suddenly unsure of who Ashia was, or what she was capable of, Solomon pushed on, his suspicion mounting. "He hasn't anyplace else to go?"

"Why should he go somewhere else? He is my brother," Ashia pleaded, close to tears.

"He's not your brother, Ashia; he's your stepfather's cousin's nephew, or whatever. You haven't got one drop of blood in common!"

"In our society he is still my brother." Ashia's voice was almost inaudible.

"Well, in my society he's just a city slicker trying to get next to you in my house, and I'm not going for it, Ashia. Tell him he can't stay here anymore. That's final."

"When he comes, he coaches me for my exams," Ashia retorted with a forceful passion that took Solomon by surprise. "I have told you all that I want to go to college in London, that is my dream. I have told you, but only Olu takes me seriously."

Ashia placed the silk fabric back in the colored paper it had been wrapped in and sat on the bed with her hands folded in her lap. Solomon stood not knowing what to do. He watched her as she gazed down at her feet and ensconced herself in a thick hermetic silence. She had never quarreled with him before, and he couldn't tell whether this was the end of her argument or the beginning.

Finally she looked up at him with disappointment in her eyes and asked, "What is it, Solomon? Why are you so vexed with me? Why did you travel here so unexpectedly? Is it to tell me you do not want me anymore?"

Solomon was taken aback. How on earth could she ask such a question? Was he behaving so differently? Did he seem as if he might not want her anymore?

"I'm not vexed with you," he said, sitting beside her on the bed. "I'm not vexed, Ashia, I'm just—I don't know, I'm just—"

What? What am I? Solomon searched his mind. "I'm just thinking that maybe I'm not here enough for you. Seven months is an awfully long time to do without a playmate, you know . . . to satisfy you. I just wonder what you do all that time when I'm not around."

Ashia lifted her eyes off her feet and fixed them on Solomon's face. "I wait," she said, with a quiet fire that burned into his soul. "I live this life God gave me and I wait."

For the most part, that was the end of the matter. The rest of Solomon's time in Aburanoma was spent in the usual manner: playing with the children, collecting bits and pieces of folklore to weave into his stories, writing, teaching now and then at the village school, feasting on Ashia's cooking, drinking in her sweetness, and generally recuperating from the ravages of Western society. It was only two weeks later, on the afternoon before his flight back to the States, that the issue of Ashia and Olu resurfaced.

Delighted that he had come unexpectedly, but sorry he was leaving so soon, Ashia's grandmother, Nana Serwah, had insisted on arranging a big feast for Solomon before he departed. Many family members had gathered at Mr. Opoku's house to pay their respects and bid him bon voyage. Ashia's mother, Akua Gyamma, and Mr. Opoku's two other wives, Afua and Awuradjua, were helping Nana Serwah and several female relatives prepare a lavish meal on the large open portion of land at the back of the house. A young girl was helping Ashia pound fufu, deftly turning the sticky substance with her hand in a large wooden bowl while Ashia beat it with a thick six-foot wooden pole, pounding down with all her weight in a hypnotic rhythm. Turn, pound—turn, pound, the two of them working in perfect synchronization. One missed beat and the girl's hand would be crushed under the pole. Olu, who had come from Accra for the weekend, was squatting down on the ground near Ashia's feet, cooly sipping a glass of ice water, watching her every move.

Solomon was seated on a wicker chair in the shade of a cloister of trees not far from the women. A group of enthralled children sat at his feet, listening to him read from his new manuscript, *African Warrior Queens*. Ashia's blind sister, Amamaa, was seated on Solomon's knee, a proud smile on her face, her brother Kummaa on the ground beside her.

"After that day the British governor sent a troop of three hundred and fifty men with big guns to hunt Queen Mother Yaa Asantewa down, and . . . um . . ." Solomon's voice faltered as he noticed Olu's eyes following the rise and fall of Ashia's breasts as she heaved and pounded the fufu with her stick. ". . . and I, Beento Blackbird, hid in the trees and . . . uh . . . I . . . uh . . ." Solomon struggled to stay focused on the words as he watched Olu get up in full view of everyone, pick an ice cube out of his glass and run it along Ashia's bare sweaty shoulders. He couldn't hear what Olu said to her, but whatever it was, Ashia shrugged his ice-cubed fingers off her back without missing a pounding beat. Olu laughed, squatted back down at her feet, and admired her, undeterred.

"I aimed my . . . um . . ." Solomon tried to continue.

"Aimed my droppings at the governor's head," Amamaa burst out, finishing his sentence for him.

"Don't spoil things, Amamaa, this is Solomon's masterpiece. Let him tell it," Olu shouted from his squatting position.

"It's not a masterpiece, it's just a story," Solomon shouted back with thinly disguised animosity.

"Yes, well, of course," Olu beamed, baring his healthy teeth. "For us, it is an old story, but in your Western world I am sure they will slap you on the back and declare it a brand-new masterpiece."

"Uncle Solomon, may I tell what happens in the end?" Amamaa pleaded, her voice cutting through the wire of tension stretched between the two men.

"Sure, Amamaa," Solomon said kindly. "Go right ahead."

Amamaa held the manuscript in front of her face and continued to tell the story. "Look, Mama, Amamaa is reading," Kummaa laughed, pointing at his sister. The children burst into fits of giggles as Amamaa mimicked reading while telling the rest of the story. Solomon walked over to where Ashia was pounding. He stood behind her, circled his arms around her onto the stick, and helped her pound. At first his movements were awkward, but he soon found her rhythm and kept in time—pound, pound, pound, pound—Ashia's strong back leading him forward.

"You have become an African," she laughed proudly. "You see," she said to Olu kneeling at her feet. "You call him a Westerner, but Solomon is also an African man. He is everything, from everywhere. That is what makes him so wonderful."

Solomon continued to pound, leaning on Ashia's back, rising and dropping with the beat of her heart.

*   *   *

Solomon knew he risked missing the plane by going back to Ashia's house, but he needed his neck charm and locket. The evening before the message arrived informing him of his father's death, Peace had tucked the charm on a leather string inside Solomon's shoes, which he had left on the mat outside Miriam's bedroom door. The following morning, Solomon had packed the shoes and left for America to attend his father's funeral. That night, the chain Solomon had worn for twenty-four years, on which he hung his mother's silver locket, had been broken by Sam. Unpacking his suitcase before going to sleep, Solomon had discovered the charm with a note that read, *For your protection. All will be well. Peace.* Feeling a sense of comfort from finding the hidden gift and message, Solomon had strung the locket onto the leather string next to the charm, and tied them around his neck. *How,* or *if,* Peace had had a premonition about his father's death, or his mother's broken chain, Solomon had no idea. But he did know that they were both precious to him, and he was not prepared to leave them behind.

"You young people like to race life," Mr. Opoku complained when Solomon informed him that he wanted him to turn the car around and go back to their village. Painstakingly, Mr. Opoku turned his old Peugeot around and headed back along the route they had just traveled.

"Maybe you should let me drive," Solomon offered, fearing that as slowly as his father-in-law was driving, he would miss not only his plane but the turn of the century.

Mr. Opoku crawled the car to a standstill in the middle of the red dirt road, got out, sat in the backseat, and announced, "I shall lie here and close my eyes so you do not give me heart attack."

Solomon slid over to the steering wheel, closed the door, pressed his foot on the gas pedal, and sped away.

Ashia was still where they had left her, sitting on the step leading into the front of the house. Solomon never allowed her to see him off to the Kumasi coach station, because he hated sorrowful goodbyes, especially in public places. He preferred his last image of her to be at home. In the rush of his father's death, he had allowed Miriam to come to the airport for the first time in many years, and the image of her sad farewell now haunted his mind.

Ashia's eyes lit up as she watched the Peugeot speeding toward her. Solomon felt bad, realizing she might be hoping he had changed his mind about leaving. To spare her any false hopes, he rolled down the window and shouted, "My neck charm! I forgot my neck charm!"

Ashia leapt to her feet and ran into the house. Solomon screeched the car to an abrupt stop and ran in after her.

Pillows were tossed, bedsheets stripped, baskets overturned—but the charm could not be found. Solomon rifled through a few oddments in a box on the dresser, finding his wristwatch but not the locket and charm. Ashia shook out his dirty laundry piled on the chair.

"Is it there?"

"No," she replied as she dropped to her knees and searched under the bed. She stretched out her arm and felt around on the floor and, unable to reach the entire area, she stuck her head under the brass frame. Peering into the semidarkness, Ashia noticed a small wooden object twisted into the bed springs. Retrieving it, she pulled her head back out into the light of the room.

"Solomon," she said, bewildered. "Look."

"Did you find it?"

"No, but look—a fertility doll hidden under our bed!"

Solomon looked at the doll. Wearing a tiny beaded necklace and gold hoop earrings, it had a flat oval head and wooden arms that stuck straight out of its wooden stump of a body. "How did it get here?" Ashia asked, puzzled.

A wispy recollection of his visit in the summer skirted to the tip of Solomon's brain . . . a wooden object . . . a shadow moving in the darkness . . .

"Solomon!" Mr. Opoku's voice chided from the courtyard, blowing away Solomon's frail strand of remembrance. "If you do not hurry yourself up, mark my words, you will not catch this plane of yours!" he warned, his footsteps fading away as he headed back out to the car.

Tempting, Solomon thought. *Why don't I miss my plane, unpack my bags, and stay put.* He considered it, but as healing as the past two weeks had been, he hadn't been able to shake his sense of disquiet. Wintertime was Miriam's domain, and he felt obligated to return to her and complete his season. When she had consented to his marriage to Ashia, it had been her only stipulation: that he never rob her of her winters. "Come Christmas, you are mine," she had said. "And the New Year. Each New Year's belongs to me."

"Solomon!" Mr. Opoku shouted again. "If you do not make haste, I am going home. I will not let you kill us on the road."

Solomon grabbed his watch and ran out.

"Solomon!" Ashia called urgently. "Solomon!" She chased after him. Solomon ran back, met her in the courtyard. She handed him the charm. "It was under the mirror," she panted. Solomon kissed her quickly on the forehead, cupped her cheeks in his hand, and vowed, "I love you, Ashia. I will always love you. You're forever in my heart. Never forget that. I love you deeply. Take good care of yourself, my beautiful. I'll see you in the summer."

Chapter 8

✦

*D*WELLINGS, LIKE PEOPLE, can bring you down or pull you up. Solomon often referred to his 1930s apartment as his "New York pit stop," his "Harlem changing room," a place to complete his writings, repack his suitcases, and move on. From time to time he contemplated ridding himself of the responsibility of its upkeep—simply staying in a hotel when in New York—but whenever he was on the brink of selling it, he would change his mind and take it off the market. On nights like tonight, charmed by the apartment's quaintness, he was reminded of why he always ended up keeping it.

Dressed in his much-worn jogging pants and favorite old T-shirt, his back leaning against the Moroccan tapestry couch, his bare feet warming in the glow of the fire, Solomon found himself thinking of it more as a home. His home.

The table lamp, a voluptuous Egyptian goddess holding a shaded lightbulb in her hand, shone across the Persian rug onto the wooden floor strewn with illustrations. Sam held up one of the illustrations for him to see. "What do you think?"

"I think, How did you know I was flying in tonight? That's what I think."

"You still trying to figure it out? Give it up, Solomon," she grinned, gloating like the cat who got the cream. "I told you, I know how to get information on anything I want to know."

"Oh, you do, do you?"

"You better believe it. I've discovered your whole routine. Winter in the Caribbean, spring here, summer in Ghana, and fall back here or somewhere exotic, doing research."

"Fascinating. And how did you find all that out?"

"Ingenuity."

"Oh, really?"

"Yes, I'm a very smart woman, Solomon. That's why I'm still single, 'cause it's going to take a very smart man like you to handle me."

Tricky, Solomon thought. *Women are tricky as molasses let out of a jar: wipe them off one place, and here they come, sticking to another.* Sam had agreed they would not go back into personal territory, neither by touch nor by conversation. For an hour or so she had kept her promise, but he could see he would have to keep his wits about him for them not to reenter dangerous territory.

He was glad, however, that she had come. It had given them an opportunity to talk out the drama of her last visit. Each taking a share of the blame, they had agreed to keep their friendship on a platonic and professional basis.

"Let me see that one. That should be the cover," Solomon said, pointing to one of the illustrations, deliberately turning the subject away from them.

"No, this should be the cover." Sam reached across and held up a different illustration.

"Why? I like the other one."

"This one's better for the cover."

"Why?" Solomon challenged.

"Because the queen looks softer, more feminine, and it's good for little girls and boys to know that a woman can be soft and pretty and still be a warrior queen."

"The one with the trees could be good too."

"Not for the cover; inside maybe, but definitely not the cover. It's too busy for a cover and it won't sell as well."

"Okay," Solomon acquiesced, trusting her judgment.

Sam gathered up the illustrations, slipped them back into their plastic covers, and filed them in her briefcase. Solomon moved away from the sofa, stretched himself out on the carpet. Linking his fingers, he extended his arms as far as he could above his head, groaning contentedly at the satisfying pull and stretch of his travel-weary muscles. Sam crawled over and sat on his stomach.

Solomon tensed.

"Relax," Sam said, trying to put him at ease. "I told you I understand, nothing but platonic." She leaned over his chest, her hands kneading the muscles from his neck to his shoulder.

"Come on, Sam, I'm fine. Get off."

"Don't be ridiculous. You're not fine; you're all tied up in knots." Her hands worked through his resistance. "I can feel it all along here. See," she said as Solomon flinched under her fingers, "tight. You're all stressed out."

Ignoring the heat of Sam's body that was spreading into him through the tops of her thighs, Solomon forced his mind to focus on her fingers working his shoulder. "That's it," Sam coaxed, "let it go. Just let it go, Solomon. It's okay." She stayed there awhile, working on his left shoulder until his tension eased a little, then she scratched her nails lightly down the side of his neck, along his shoulder, down his biceps and back up his neck, dragging a thrill through Solomon that relaxed him some more. Something in her touch made him want to cry. Something that he recognized within himself. It was something she was telling him, something real from inside her that he had never heard her articulate but could feel through the language of her fingers. She cupped her hand around his left ear, shifted her weight, and went to work on the other side: stroking, scratching, kneading.

Solomon knew it was time to get Sam off his legs. He knew from experience that there is a ravine between a man and a woman that should never be crossed unless the two people intend to live together on one side or the other. Looking up at Sam, he knew she was crossing the ravine and he needed to stop her. His instincts told him that the very survival of his life as he had come to know it was at stake.

"I fly back to the Caribbean tomorrow," he said, in order to break the poignant message that she was passing and that he was receiving through her massaging hands, by bringing the reality of Miriam back into their consciousness. "I should probably go crash soon, I didn't realize I was so beat."

"If you found a woman who could satisfy all your needs, you wouldn't have to do all this running back and forth, Solomon, and your body could get some rest, not to mention your soul."

"Why are you talking about this again?"

Sam got off him and sat on the edge of an armchair. "Because you're emotionally exhausted, because you're too smart and too strong to be so uncommitted, because you'll never get what you're searching for until you do commit, and because I know I could make you happy."

"I'm already committed and I'm already happy."

"Who are you kidding, Solomon? You're not committed and you're certainly not happy."

"What makes you think I'm not happy?"

"Your miserable lifestyle." Sam leaned back in the chair, her eyes watering. "Your miserable, miserable lifestyle," she repeated sadly.

"Yeah?" Solomon crossed his arms protectively across his chest, as if somehow the gesture could block Sam from his heart. "Well, it works for me."

"It's an illusion," Sam stated. "A typical male fantasy. Only most men don't go so far as to try to live it out. Sooner or later, Solomon, you're going to have to face reality." She said it like a final pronouncement. The way she would say, *That chapter needs to be embellished,* or *That passage has to come out,* and then walk away knowing he would think about it, fiddle with it, realize she was right, and end up doing it her way.

Solomon closed his eyes. He felt a little ridiculous. Lying on the floor, arms locked across himself, eyes shut tight like a rebellious child, he felt silly, and yet he couldn't think what else to do.

"No matter how fast you keep running, Solomon, you can't run away from your destiny." Sam's voice was calm and steady. "There's a reason why you were born in the Caribbean, why your father was an American, and why you were drawn back to Africa. There's a reason why you write the books you do. It's your destiny, Solomon. You're destined to help clean up this whole mess. This whole aftermath of slavery and unequal rights. Your traveling, your multicultural upbringing, had a purpose, Solomon, and I don't believe that purpose was for you to go around collecting exotic foreign wives. All displaced black people can't just run back to Africa; that's unrealistic. What we need is people like you to bring Africa back to our hearts, our minds, our culture. You belong here, Solomon, here in the United States, with all us other displaced Africans. We're the ones that need you as our chief, not the Africans. They already have plenty of chiefs. You belong with us. I shouldn't be telling you all this—you should be telling me. You're the one with the calling."

"Why are you bugging me?" Solomon retorted, unnerved. His heart was beating like a clock with an erratic tick. Since his father's death, things had not regained their rhythm. As an explorer, he was used to the unexpected, but he also knew that when the basic beat of your life loses its rhythm, you are in great danger. Without rhythm, the heart cannot function. Without the heart, the body dies. Solomon realized his instincts had been right: he was fighting for survival of his life, the way he lived it. "Give me a break, Sam," he protested. "I've just got off a plane. Don't you think I deserve a little rest?"

"Okay," Sam said, sliding off the chair and crawling back onto his legs. "I'll be merciful. No more truths for tonight, I promise."

Solomon was relieved. "Good," he said, looking up at her with a boyish pout. "You *ought* to be merciful. After all, didn't you say you just came over to be friendly and fix me a surprise meal?"

"Yes," Sam said. Then crossing her arms and gathering the bottom of her short knitted minidress into her fingers, in one quick move she lifted her arms and stripped it off over her head. "Dinnertime!"

By the time Solomon realized what was happening, Sam's two bare breasts were moving down toward him, her left nipple headed straight for his mouth.

"Don't do that!" His arm shot out to restrain her. "Stop!" His palm pushed against her naked ribs.

"I'm not convinced," Sam whispered like a hypnotist reprogramming his brain. She pressed her body against his palm, pressing herself down, aiming her voice like an arrow into the secret place in his head. "I'm not convinced that you really mean that."

*   *   *

"I mean it. Don't do that." Solomon's voice was troubled, tinged with shame. Miriam rolled off him and lay back on her side of the bed. They lay there in their separateness, the pouring rain calling out to them like a deserted lover.

For a while that's how they remained. Solomon. Miriam. And the rain. None of them touching one another. None of them looking at one another. Three units that used to be inseparably one now separated by something nameless and undefined.

The rain, as if afraid they had not seen or heard it, began to fall harder and harder, until finally it cascaded down from the sky in a loud thunderous roar that would not be ignored.

We're coming, Solomon cried from his heart. *Don't stop pouring, we're coming, we're coming.* He wished he could be *with* it—*of* it—*in* it—plummeting from the sky in one almighty deluge. He yearned to reach over to Miriam, to touch her, caress her, flood her with his love; but he couldn't. Tears welled into the corners of his eyes. He needed to talk to her. He needed her to talk to him. It suddenly seemed that, unlike Sam, Miriam never talked to him. They never really talked. Never really challenged each other to be broader, deeper, better, to reach their goals.

"What do you want out of life, Miriam?" Solomon asked, thinking that if he turned the conversation away from his own self-interests, she might be more willing to talk to him.

"That not the point here, is it, Solomon?" Miriam retorted.

Solomon slid himself off the bed. "Need to dry off," he mumbled and headed for the bathroom.

Solomon's toes touched the slippery wet of the bathroom floor where the heavy rain had reached in through the cracks along the windowpane. Without turning on the light, he reached for a clean towel that he knew would be there. It would be large, white, luxurious, folded neatly along the rail, waiting for his return. Miriam would have hung it there the minute she heard the rain fall, just before she took her bath, knowing he was running, running along the beach toward her.

His hands touched it. Pure cotton. Thick. Soft. Tread softly, Solomon. He slipped the towel off the rail, hung it around his neck. Careful. Soft. One foot behind the other . . . walking . . . a tight rope . . . picking . . . his way . . . through the slippery rain . . . back . . . to the bedroom.

Miriam was lying perfectly still, the smooth white sheets shaped along her naked body like the sculptured garments of a garden statue. She had opened wide the stable doors to let in the moonlight and was watching the subsiding raindrops dance across the surface of the sand.

Solomon moved into the open doorway and inhaled the smell of the sea drifting in on the damp night air.

"I wanna finish talking," he said, anxious to rid himself of his discomfort and return to a rhythmic heartbeat.

"About our lives together being an 'uncommitted fantasy'?" Miriam's mockery was tangible. It defied response. "Who been feeding your brain, Solomon?" Disdain dripped from her lips. "You come back sounding so American."

"I am American." He sounded more sure than he felt.

"Easy, Solomon," Miriam's voice was low, cautioning. "Don't let the energy of that land get into you. It built on too much blood, that's why me refuse to step foot there, me don't want all that confusion crawling up through me feet. If your mama ever heard you say you an American, she'd die."

"My mama's already dead."

"She die again. When children deny their birthright, dead parents die again. You not an American. You a Nubian Island king originated from Africa!"

"Maybe that's it," Solomon exploded in irate revelation. "Maybe that's what I'm trying to say, Miriam. I've got all these cultures colliding inside of me and I'm sick of being made to choose. I'm sick of being treated like an outcast because of it. Here on the Island, I was made to feel guilty that I had an American father. Then in America, I was ridiculed for having a Caribbean accent, a Caribbean mother. And then I felt guilty that I grew to like America. I used to scream inside that you wouldn't come live with me in the United States of 'Babylon,' as you call it. Well, I'm part 'Babylon,' Miriam. I can't help it! I was so grateful when I met Ashia; she made me discover the Africa in me but let me be all the other things as well. Not an American, not a Caribbean, not a black man in a white United States, but just a man. A whole man. She accepted all of me. I didn't have to define and confine myself. I finally belonged. 'Man of the world,' she called me. I came to you, Miriam. I vowed not to be like my father, a man who sneaks around cheating on his wife. So I didn't touch her; I came to you!"

"And me allow you to marry her! What else you want from me, Solomon? Make no mistake—it weren't easy, but me love you enough to allow you to marry her."

"Yes! And Western society wants me to feel guilty for that too!

It's okay to sleep around like my father, to lie and cheat on your wife: society accepts a man like that, but whatever you do, don't try to have two wives! You can abandon your illegitimate kids, but two wives?! Now that's perverted! Absolutely unpardonable!"

"But you did it anyway, didn't you, Solomon? You got what you wanted!"

"I wanted *you*, Miriam! All of you. Maybe I wouldn't have needed Ashia if you'd have come with me, if you'd have stopped clinging to this island."

"This island need me, Solomon!" Miriam rose up from the bed with fury in her eyes. "You know how many mothers and babies die every year through lack of medical care? I needed here, Solomon. This my home."

"Well, it's not mine!" Solomon erupted. "I've been gone twenty-four years, and for nineteen of those twenty-four years I've been coming back here, year in, year out, trying to be loyal to something, trying to hold on to—"

"Solomon, if you needed—"

"Let me finish!" Like a slap, Solomon's impassioned voice slammed Miriam back down onto the bed. He was afraid to let her speak. If he let her speak, she would try to placate him. He could hear it in the changed tone of her voice. She was about to try to use her sensitivity as a healing balm. *Solomon if you needed this—Solomon if you needed that—* Then she would offer him something soothing—a tender phrase, a sweet caress, an emotional promise. If he accepted it, he would have to bury his feelings, bury his words, bury them deep inside like a dormant volcano. He needed to let them out, for better or worse.

"When I flew in this time, Miriam," he enunciated, hot lava bubbling in his belly. "I said to myself, What am I really coming here for, and why? Maybe this is all an illusion."

There was a silence. A short seemingly casual silence.

And then he saw her coffee-cream legs slide across the edge of the bed. Saw her smooth arched feet touch down onto the floor. Saw the swing of her heavy breasts as she moved across the room. He even saw the black mass of her hair tumbling across her face as she bent over her doctor's bag on the little cream dresser. But he didn't see what she was reaching for. Didn't see what she was doing. So when she turned to him with her tear-stained face, he was shocked to see the blood that was dripping down her arm.

"See Solomon," she said, tracing the scalpel along the oozing slash she had sliced across her forearm. "No illusion. I'm flesh and blood."

She tossed the bloody scalpel onto the bed and walked out.

"Miriam . . . ," he breathed.

She was gone.

Chapter 9

✦

*T*HE SALT-SEA AIR blew against Miriam's open wound. She was beginning to feel it, feel the pain, but she didn't mind; it was a welcome sting on her otherwise numb body. Maybe she couldn't feel anything else because Solomon was right, maybe she was an illusion. She ought not to be surprised that he was having difficulty locating her—she was having difficulty locating herself. Except her arm. She was alive in her forearm. She knew she was alive there because she could feel the salty air blowing across a slice of flesh that curved in an arc between her elbow and her thumb, thin as a sliver of a new moon. *I'm not an illusion*, she thought. *I'm one thin sliver of stinging flesh.*

The hotel lobby was crowded with guests going to the midnight buffet. Miriam clutched her flimsy kimono across her naked body, pushed open one of the big glass doors, and stepped inside. One by one, heads turned. Her wind-wild hair, her thinly clad body, her bare, wet, sandy feet would have been spectacle enough to call attention to herself, but there was also the soaked bloody sleeve of her kimono sticking to her wounded arm. Looking straight ahead, her head held high, she walked past the hotel patrons mingling in the lobby.

Like dominoes falling, they halted their conversations, trailing her with a veil of silence as she glided by. Watching with open-mouthed curiosity, they followed her with their eyes all the way up to the front desk.

"Can I help you?" Joan looked suspiciously at the crazy-looking woman standing before her. As soon as she spoke, shock and recognition registered on her face. "Evening, Mama Miriam."

"Evening, Joan. Where your papa?"

Joan took one look at Miriam's bloody arm and rushed off to find her father.

*   *   *

Miriam felt her body coming alive. It started along her shoulder, right underneath Toussaint's cradling arm. She couldn't remember how she had gotten from the lobby back out to the beach, or how she had come to be sitting with him in the moonlight at the edge of the waves, but she knew that life was coming back into her body and she knew it was starting right underneath his protective arm.

She turned to look at him, her eyes focusing for the first time in hours. "Evening." It was the only thing she could think to say.

"And good evening to you." Toussaint smiled affectionately, turned little circles with his plump fingers where his hand rested on her shoulder. "How is the lady feeling?"

"Oh, I'll be all right," Miriam said, subdued.

"Well, how about making me all right by telling me what going on. You know me don't mess in your business, Miriam, but me not going to sit back and watch no craziness. Not to a good woman like you. Me kill someone before me see you hurting."

Miriam surprised herself by telling Toussaint everything. How Solomon wouldn't touch her even though the rain had fallen. How he had come back full of doubts and fears and much psychological talk. How he had blamed her for his taking on another wife. Raised his voice to her. And worst of all, dismissed nineteen years of their life together, calling it nothing but an illusion.

"He'll settle," Toussaint assured her. "He just been stirred, but he'll settle."

"Well, whoever stirring him best be ready 'cause as long as me got breath, me know how to fight."

"This not your battle, Miriam, this Solomon's," Toussaint warned, seeing the Corcos in her rising up.

"Then how come I being wounded?"

"'Cause you standing in the cross-fire. Maybe it time for you to step aside."

Miriam looked out at the glistening blue-black ocean. Spilling out of the midnight sky, it rolled steadily toward them, rocking with each rise and fall of the waves. Each time it reached the sand, instead of touching her toes as she wanted, it quickly withdrew again, pulling the tide farther and farther back, as though the sea were drawing itself in for the night.

"Maybe it's not what you think," Toussaint pondered aloud, cutting into her thoughts. "Maybe it's not a woman."

"It's a woman."

"Maybe Ashia pulling him."

"No, this not Ashia. This someone poisonous. Poisoning his mind."

"You must have scared Solomon half to death!" Toussaint remarked, his voice compassionate. Miriam looked down at her bandaged arm. Who bandaged it? And when? She could not remember. She could not even remember cutting it. The whole thing suddenly seemed so absurd. Toussaint gazed into her eyes. "Ah, Miriam!" The longing was gentle, resigned. "You certainly not an illusion."

"When is love enough?" she sighed. It was a question, a real question. She wanted to know.

Toussaint had the answer. "When it's wanted."

Miriam leaned her head on his shoulder, closed her eyes, and willed the sea to come all the way up to her toes.

Chapter 10

✦

MIRIAM COULD HEAR Solomon hovering outside the bathroom door, a diffident ghost of the man he used to be. She would call him in, but she could not bear to have him enter only to stand like a shadow against the wall. He was no longer in his heaven on earth, and it seemed there was nothing she could do to bring him back.

She turned on the tap and added more hot water to her bath, hoping the heat would help her relax. The weeks of uncertainty had taken their toll. Solomon had spoken very little since the night of her wound. He had not mentioned any of what he had talked about that evening, except to say he was sorry for the pain it caused.

They both spent their days pretending that things were normal, but things were far from normal. They had still not made love since he arrived and very rarely stayed in the same room for long, except to sleep; and even then they would feign exhaustion or appear engrossed in some book or article, so as not to have to interact.

She wanted to say something to at least break the barrier of pretense, but she didn't know what to say. One afternoon she had asked him when he was leaving. "Why leave paradise?" he had replied. She had pointed out to him that she had always called Cape Corcos paradise because for her it was, but that "paradise is where your dreams are." He didn't respond, at least not verbally; he just carried on picking the flesh off his swordfish with his fingers, as if eating it required all his concentration. They had not mentioned it again, neither his staying nor his going. They just continued on as they were, barely speaking, yet pretending that nothing was wrong.

Occasionally they would laugh together just to ease the tension, but their laughter never reached their eyes and never danced together in the air like it used to. Whoever this woman was who had shaken his resolve (and Miriam was still certain that the problem was a woman other than Ashia), battling against her influence was wearing Miriam out.

She dipped her sea sponge into her hot bathwater and squeezed it against her neck . . . wearing her out . . . she slid a little lower into the tub. "Ahhh . . ." She let the hot water float out the tension in her muscles . . . *Rejuvenate*, she meditated. *Rejuvenate 'cause me not going down without a fight.*

*   *   *

Standing outside the bathroom door, Solomon could hear Miriam moving in the water. Would he be intruding on her nakedness if he stepped inside? She had taken to sleeping in a nightgown, as though to protect herself from his eyes. As if by questioning his life, he had relinquished all privileges to her being. There was no talking things out with her, he knew that now. Strong as she was, the weight of his present mind was more than she could bear. He didn't blame her. He was aware that his thoughts had become so heavy that if he didn't come out from underneath them, they would destroy him. He would be nothing but dust.

He closed his eyes. There it was, hovering in the darkness. People would probably tell him he was crazy, but in the darkness of his mind he could feel his father's spirit mocking him, pointing at his conduct, taunting him, telling him how the two of them were just the same. He had thought of himself as different, a man of integrity; but when Miriam showed him her bloody arm, he knew. Knew he was just like his father. Knew that his love was a selfish and painful thing. Looking at all the wounds in Miriam, he wondered how he had never noticed them before. *Has she been so adept at hiding them that they were undetectable? Or have I just been blind? All these years that she's been telling me about her wonderful life here while I'm away. How fulfilling, how peaceful. Did she say it just to shield me from her pain? If I could only open this door, walk inside, and make everything better.*

It's not that simple, he heard his father say. Solomon opened his eyes to be rid of *him*. Solomon knew *he* was still lurking in the shadow of his mind, but he hoped that if he ignored the old man, *he* would go away. Reaching out his hand, he took a step forward. He needed to move forward.

*   *   *

Miriam heard Solomon's hand on the door. She watched the knob slowly turn to the right and then stop. She thought to call his name but didn't want to scare him off. Like the other day, when she'd seen him headed toward her sitting up on a rock, she'd called him to join her. He'd waved, turned around, and walked away.

Fragile. Fragile moments.

*   *   *

Solomon heard the water stop moving. He could tell Miriam had stopped still in the tub. He knew she was watching the door. He wanted to go in but didn't want to scare her. He didn't want her to hurry out like she did yesterday, jumping out of the bath, wrapping a towel around herself, and scurrying off to the bedroom. Fragile. She was so fragile.

With his hand still clutching the knob, he opened the door and stepped inside.

Easing down onto his knees beside the tub, Solomon rested his hand on the rim and looked at Miriam. Miriam reached out with her little finger. Lightly . . . tentatively . . . she touched him . . . the kiss of a butterfly against his wrist. Solomon took her brave little finger and put it in his mouth.

"Mmmmmm," Miriam purred.

Silently, he catered to her. Scrubbing her back, washing her feet, pouring more bubble bath into the water. Not a single word passed from their lips. He knew without being told exactly where and when she wanted to be sponged. Finally he knelt back down, kissed her palm, and popped her little finger back into his mouth.

"Solomon?" Miriam's voice filtered into his pores, gently as the steam misting over the window.

"Mmm-hmm?"

"If it not rained by midnight all those years ago, would you really not have married me?"

Solomon released her finger from between his lips. "I knew it would rain."

"How you know?"

"It had to."

Miriam sank deeper into the warm scented water. "Dear God—" she reminisced. "If it's right for us to be together—"

"—give us a sure sign," Solomon continued, remembering verbatim.

"LET IT RAIN!" Their voices joined together in blissful recollection.

"And down it poured," Miriam said, cherishing the memory. "That was the happiest summer of my life."

"I've forgotten what you look like in summertime," Solomon mused, popping her little finger back into his mouth.

"Apple blossom," Miriam promised.

BOOK SEVEN

✦

Seasons of Change

Blood-Red as the Enduring Earth . . .

Chapter 1

✦

*A*SHIA HELD her peace. She had not spoken or moved from the front step of her house since midafternoon, when she had sauntered into the courtyard to take out the groundnut stew that had been baking in the clay oven since morning. She had come right back to sit in the same position, from where she now sought in her mind to hold back the dusk. If she could only hold the sun up there and stop the dusk from rolling across the sky, then she would not have to admit to herself that May 22 was fast coming to a close—and Solomon was still nowhere in sight.

Even the children were disheartened. Confident that Solomon would turn up early in the day as usual, they had kept vigil since dawn, talking and playing while keeping a watchful eye on the road. For the first time in five years, he had let them down. Their hand-clapping and skiproping long since deserted, they straggled in and out of Ashia's courtyard, reluctant to wander too far away, lest Solomon suddenly show up and they miss out on all the toys and excitement.

Ashia ignored the children. Time and activity passed before her eyes like a slow-moving pantomime. Life seemed like something soundless, something outside her that she couldn't contend. She had awakened that morning with a sense of impending gloom, and although she had dressed and adorned herself in preparation for Solomon's arrival, something told her he would not come.

"Pokua!"

The loud harsh voice penetrated Ashia's thoughts, startling her into awareness. A small girl jumped to attention, signaling for Ashia not to tell on her, as she went running down the red dust road toward the market. Ashia knew that Pokua's mother had sent the girl to buy matches and candles hours ago, but when the angry woman came marching up to the house looking for her daughter, Ashia simply nodded to her and carried on gazing at the darkening sky.

"Pokua!" the mother shouted again, casting a disapproving look at all the idle children. None of them seemed to know where her daughter was, so she went marching back up the road.

The sun finally sank behind the distant grass, and Ashia realized she had lost her battle to hold back the night. She watched the horizon at the top of the road as, one by one, the children traipsed back to their homes, small walking shadows fading into the dusky coral twilight. Only Kummaa stayed to keep her company, a loyal silhouette ambling along the roadside, kicking his feet in the dust, waiting.

Overshadowed by darkness, Ashia struggled for the faith to believe that victory was still possible. After all, it was still May 22. Heralded by headlights and the hum of an engine, Solomon could still come riding home, all smiles and teases for having given her such a scare. "Do you think I would ever give up my summer?!" he would shout, laughing, lifting her and spinning her around in the air. "Woman, are you crazy?"

Ashia tried to feel hopeful, but her heart rejected such optimistic imaginings. Realizing she could not be cheered by her thoughts, she curled up on the step and stared despondently into the blackness. She lay there for a while and might have stayed there all night were it not for Kummaa tapping her lightly on the leg and beckoning her to follow him into the house. Placing her left hand on his small eight-year-old shoulder, she used her right hand to heave herself up. Feet aching, she shuffled stiffly behind him as he led her through the living room, through the courtyard, into her bedroom. Keeping her hand on his shoulder, she lowered herself onto the bed. Easing her head back onto the pillow, she sighed with relief. Kummaa passed Ashia her stuffed kangaroo, kissed her good-night, and ran off to their mother's house.

Ashia felt lonely. She pulled the solid silver heart out of the kangaroo's pouch and read the inscription, TO ASHIA, MY BELOVED WIFE. FOREVER YOURS, S. W. Feeling dejected, she placed the heart back in the pouch. She had so looked forward to telling Solomon the good news. Remembering she was not alone, she placed her hands protectively on her very pregnant belly and told her unborn baby not to be sad, that something very important must have delayed him, but papa would most certainly come tomorrow. And wouldn't he be happy to discover that he was finally, finally going to be a father!

*   *   *

"You all right?" Miriam cooed.

"Yeah," Solomon lied as he leaned beside the open door, gazing out at the sand.

"Good. Me too." She rolled over sleepily in the bed.

Solomon closed the wooden doors and climbed in beside her. Holding her in his arms, he glanced at his wristwatch for the umpteenth time that hour: 3:02 A.M. *Two minutes past midnight in Ghana*, he thought. *May 22 has come and gone.* Pulling back slightly, he shifted his chest away from Miriam, to prevent her from hearing the rapid aching beat of his heart.

He gazed at the large wooden doors closed shut in the space where seconds ago there was moonlight. He missed it, the bright light of the moon. He needed it to shine into his soul.

Solomon crept back out of bed. Unbolted the wooden doors. Bared his chest to the moon. Miriam turned over in the bed.

"I'm all right," he whispered before she could ask.

*   *   *

For the first time in six years, Ashia found June to be a very long month. By the end of it she had come up with a multitude of reasons why Solomon had not come, ranging from death to simple forgetfulness. She had gone through days when she had jumped at the sound of every falling leaf, turning to see if it were him, and days when she had managed to obliterate him from her mind altogether, closing in her world to encompass only herself and her unborn child.

Having prayed for him, called out for him, pictured and willed him to come until her head ached with concentration, she finally decided to follow Nana Serwah's advice and set out a calabash full of water for him at the entrance of her bedroom. "He will get thirsty," Nana Serwah assured her. "He will not be able to quench himself without your presence. Then he will remember you and come drink."

*   *   *

By the end of July, Solomon was no longer trying to cover up his dishevelment. Despite its uneven start, that winter had been the most

glorious he had ever spent with Miriam, and being with her in spring-
time had been pleasant, but the passing summer tolled on him like
gray hairs on an old man's chin. He tried to play off the toll the
months had taken on him, joking that scruffiness and inactivity were
the luxurious benefits of not having to fly off somewhere. He used
the same explanation for why he wasn't writing or sleeping or eating
very much, but he could see in Miriam's eyes that she was not convinced. "Something ailing him," he had heard her whisper to Toussaint after dinner one night. "Me don't know what to do, it like he
dying."

Sitting on the patio, reclining on a deck chair, gazing out to sea,
Solomon looked and felt like a convalescing invalid. His was the kind
of tired that sleep cannot cure. It was a sensation he had never experienced before. A numb weary aimlessness, like a tongue with no
taste buds.

Dangerously dehydrated, he lifted a glass of water to his lips, determined to drink it all down, but his hands trembled so uncontrollably that he was unable to keep the glass steady long enough to take
a sip. It had been this way for over a month, grappling with water as
if grappling a wild ferocious beast. He kept his arm suspended in the
air, watching ripples play across the surface of the water as he shook.
Finally, too weak to continue the battle, he lowered his hand and
placed the glass back on the arm of his chair.

"You write her, Solomon? She know you not coming back?"
Cousin Jezz sauntered out from the kitchen, barefoot, wrapped in a
large towel. Provocative and sassy, her voice was forceful and unafraid, probing with a familiar liberty only blood relatives dare to
take, boldly bringing up the subject others dared not even whisper.
Solomon fixed his eyes on her in a silent duel, fighting with her to
hold her tongue. "Ashia," she enunciated with her perfectly painted
lips, ignoring the unspoken code of silence on the topic. "Have you
contacted Ashia?" Solomon turned to look at Miriam in the kitchen,
checking to make sure she was out of earshot. "Like father, like
son!" Jezz proclaimed, stripping off her towel and walking down to
the sea in her skimpy bikini. "Love 'em and leave 'em. You turning
out just like you old man, Solomon. Must be in the blood!"

*   *   *

If she were not afraid of harming the baby, Ashia would run faster. The news made her want to fly across the grass like one of the many winged insects hidden among its long blades. A local woman had sent Kummaa to tell her that she should hurry over to her mother's house to see an American man who was on his way to meet her there. Who else could it be but Solomon? What other American ever came to Aburanoma village? Except for the old preacherman people sometimes mentioned befriending, but that was before she was born.

Dragging Ashia by the hand, Kummaa's free arm flapped through the air like the wing of a baby bird. Ashia was too busy asking and answering questions in her mind to hear what her little brother was chattering about. Why did Solomon want to meet her at her parents' house? He must have a surprise! And to think that she had feared he was dead! Would the surprise explain the reason for his delay? Kummaa said there was apparently also a woman with him. Who was the woman? Was the woman the surprise?

"Possibly he has brought his first wife to meet us," Nana Serwah suggested as Ashia came gasping up the steps onto the veranda.

The thought scared but thrilled Ashia. To finally meet the other Mrs. Wilberforce! What would she be like? Would she be sweet like Awuradjua? Would they like each other? Were she and Solomon coming to live in Ghana? In Aburanoma? In her house? Would they have to build a second bedroom?

Sitting her down in the ornate living room, Nana Serwah gave Ashia a cool glass of water and told her to calm herself, all her questions would soon be answered.

A car horn beeped in the driveway; Ashia put down her glass and ran out onto the veranda. "Hi," a man called out through the car window. His accent was American, and when he stepped out of the car, he was tall and brown like Solomon but he was definitely not Solomon.

"I'm Jake. Nice to meet you." He walked up to the low veranda wall, stretched his arm across the foliage, offered Ashia his hand. Ashia stared at his muscular forearms framed by green leaves and tiny white jasmine flowers, and the sight of his outstretched brown fingers and pale tan palm, so like Solomon but not Solomon at all, made her take a step back. Stricken with disappointment, she stroked her belly and stared at the *imposter* as though he were the angel of death.

"You speak English?" His voice became slower, more articulated.

"Yes, we speak English," Nana Serwah said kindly, joining Ashia from the living room. She shook the stranger's hand vigorously in an attempt to compensate for her granddaughter's rudeness.

"Great. Nice to meet you." Relief spread across the man's face. "I'm Jake. That's my wife, Wanda."

Wanda rolled down the passenger window and waved. "Nice to meet you," she shouted enthusiastically. "Is she Ashia?"

"Yes, she is Ashia," Kummaa shouted with equal enthusiasm from his vantage point on the veranda steps, his little body hidden from the driveway by all the foliage.

"I figured as much 'cause he told us she was real pretty." Wanda popped a peppermint Tic-Tac into her mouth. "Want a Tic-Tac, whosoever little voice that was?" She smiled. Kummaa poked up his head, jumped down the steps, and asked the lady politely if he might have one for his blind sister also. Wanda gave him the little clear box full of the tiny mints, and he went off rattling them in search of Amamaa. Ashia's heart began to hope again. The woman had said *he*. Who was the *he* that had told them she was real pretty? Perhaps Solomon had sent them with a message.

"May I ask who told you about Ashia?" Nana Serwah inquired, picking the thoughts from her granddaughter's brain.

"When we were in Accra last year, we hooked up with this great guy, Olu, Olu Neean—Nyaanteechaa—I never could say his last name, but he told us if we ever came around these parts, we should look you up and say hi, so voilà! Here we are!" Wanda laughed. Ashia stared at the green Tic-Tac tossing around on Wanda's pink tongue. *Angels of death,* she thought, taking another step back.

"Actually, we were also hoping she would braid my wife's hair. We hear she's the best around." Jake addressed this remark to Nana Serwah, throwing Ashia a smile and a nod that says, *I know you don't understand a word I'm saying.*

"I wanna get those little wrap things. You know, with the thread?" Wanda made raveling motions in the air with her index finger. She looked into Ashia's bewildered looking eyes. "Do you speak English?"

There was a pause. Ashia realized everyone was waiting for her to reply. She opened her mouth to speak, but instead of words, a lamenting call that defied time and space came wailing out of her mouth. Raw and ancient, her cry rose above the treetops and spread itself across the sky, echoing all the way up into the heavens. The heavens heard her cry and sent down angels of mercy, who in turn sent the women of the house running toward the veranda from all directions, their hearts full of sympathy and love.

"Our daughter is calling. Our daughter is calling."

"It is the weight of the child that makes her soul cry."

"It is the weight of her missing husband that makes her soul cry."

"It is labor that makes her cry."

"The labor of life."

"Our daughter is calling. Her soul is calling."

"Hurry, hurry. She weeps, she weeps."

As the women approached, Nana Serwah struggled to keep her granddaughter up on her feet, but the gravity of Ashia's grief pulled them both down onto the floor.

"Do you need a ride?" Jake offered, bouncing on his sneakered feet as he leaped up the veranda steps.

"Like to a hospital?" Wanda joined in, gingerly stepping out of the car.

Crouched on the ground, Nana Serwah kept her arm firmly clutched around her granddaughter's waist. "Stop this grieving," she whispered sternly in Ashia's ear. "You will make your baby blind. Remember when your father died, your mother was pregnant—she grieved so bitterly that when she gave birth, the grief in her belly had made Amamaa blind. Stop it. You must stop it. Cry tears, Ashia. Do not keep them in your belly; let your grief fall from your eyes. Cry tears, Ashia. Cry tears."

Nana Serwah's words sank through Ashia's ears and opened up her heart. In the safe grip of her grandmother's arms, she swung and moaned until hot tears erupted up from her belly and rolled down her cheeks onto her grandmother's hand. Knowing that like sweat to a fever, being the first sign of recovery, tears are the first sign of the expulsion of sorrow, as soon as Nana Serwah felt Ashia's warm wet tears on her fingers, she breathed relief.

"Her grief is breaking," she announced to the surrounding

women. The women nodded their understanding. For most of them, grief was no stranger, and they were well familiar with the sweet relief of tears. They offered Ashia strokes of love and words of encouragement before dispersing back to their various chores, counseling her to be strong. Always to be strong.

"Please don't trouble yourselves," Nana Serwah spoke reassuringly to the American visitors, who were standing on the steps, not knowing what to do. "She will be all right. Thank you very much for your kind concern. Perhaps it is better you come back another time."

The visitors got into their car and backed it slowly out of the driveway. Aunt Lamiley knelt down and wiped Ashia's face with a damp cloth. Akua Gyamma stood back, not knowing what to do. She hated to see her daughter manless at a time like this. She knew what it was like, to spend day after day longing for the man who made you pregnant to suddenly appear. In her experience, it was a void no loving female could ever fill, so she did not try with Ashia. Instead, she stood back and watched her mother hold her daughter, watched her sister wipe her daughter's face, watched her daughter cry out her loneliness, watched with regret that she had not made Ashia wait for a husband all to herself, to save her all this pain.

*   *   *

Two hours' walk from Miriam's adobe, Solomon sighted a sixty-foot-high rock jutting out of the sea like the stony gray tail of a shark. Swimming out several hundred yards from the shore, he climbed on top of the rock surrounded by turbulent waves, and stood with his toes pivoted precariously over the edge. Facing the horizon, he spread his arms like a bird in flight and bellowed from the depths of his being, "ASHIAAAAAAA!"

Four hundred and sixty thousand miles away, round the back of her stepfather's house, Ashia froze midbeat, her fufu-pounding stick held high, as she listened for what she felt was someone calling out her name. Amamaa, who was turning the fufu, removed her hand from the bowl and keened her ear to the echo of a voice floating in the air.

"Ashia, hurry up," first wife Afua shouted from her stool. "Why have you stopped? Papa is waiting for his food."

"What are they doing?" Awuradjua questioned as she jiggled her fussing baby.

"They are listening," Nana Serwah explained.

"What are they listening to?" Awuradjua tried to give her baby her breast.

"He is not hungry, he is sleepy. Bring him here," Nana Serwah said, knowing the answer but changing the subject. Awuradjua handed over her infant son. Nana Serwah laid him face down across her lap and instantly he stopped fussing.

"Ashia has been carrying her baby for nearly ten months." Lamiley lowered more plantain into the sizzling frying pan.

"She is trying to hold on to it until Solomon comes," Akua Gyamma said, sprinkling extra pepper on top.

"That is why I asked her to make fufu," Nana Serwah whispered, removing cooked pieces of plantain with her fingers and placing them on a plate for Kummaa. "The pounding will make the baby drop."

Olu slid the straw hat off his face onto his chest and turned to look at Ashia. The break in the rhythm of her pounding had woken him up. Stretching himself up off the mat where he had been sleeping under the shade of the cluster of trees, he went to take over for her. "Rest," he told her as he beat the stick into the bowl. "Lie down on the mat. I told you, Princess Ashia, I have come to take care of you."

*   *   *

Solomon heard the fluttering of wings. Realizing it was not part of his dream, he opened his eyes and sat up, just in time to see a blackbird swoop over his head and out the open stable doors. Sleep reclaimed him so quickly, it was as if he had never been stirred. "I love you," he murmured, slipping back unconscious into Ashia's arms.

*   *   *

Moving stealthily, Ashia curled her leg over Solomon's thigh, smooth liquid silk sliding over him as she mounted him in her fantasy . . .

*   *   *

"Mmmm . . ." Solomon moaned as Ashia's essence filled his dream.

"Solomon!" Miriam's voice startled his eyes back open. She reached across the bed, placing her hand on his arm. "I dreamed you flew away. You grew wings and flew away."

They both fell fast asleep again, with Miriam's fingers stroking his arm, checking for feathers.

*   *   *

Ashia had held on to her baby for more than ten months. It was so active in her womb that the constant kicking of its legs often prevented her from sleeping. The steel will with which she kept it inside in the hopes that Solomon would show up for its birth caused people to note how she was growing more and more like her mother every day.

Beyond grief or self-pity, she sauntered around swaying her hips defiantly, ignoring all admonitions and petitions to let her baby out. "We are waiting for Solomon," she would say with a stubborn but casual air, as if holding on to a ripe and ready fetus was the most normal thing in the world. "The baby wants to come out and look straight into its papa's face."

Nana Serwah could not fathom where her offspring had gotten it from, this unnatural inclination toward their men, this *idyllic* desire to be the center of their husband's attention. It was impractical, a desire doomed for disappointment; men had more important things to do than focus only on their women—they were supposed to be about the business of subduing the earth. And women certainly had more important things to do than sitting around waiting on their men, more important even than the subjugation of the earth: women were supposed to be about the business of reproducing and nurturing God's greatest love—people.

This unnatural inclination of her offspring had almost robbed Nana Serwah of her granddaughter Amamaa when Akua Gyamma had resolved to starve the fetus to death. And now here was Ashia, holding on to her first great-grandchild as if the baby's life were hers to do with what she pleased. And all for what? So it could "come out and look straight into its papa's face." Nonsense! Sheer and utter nonsense! Nana Serwah purposed in her heart that Ashia would give birth that very day. After all, if she, being the great-grandmother, did not free the poor imprisoned infant, then who would?

Holding a small empty cooking pot and a jar, Nana Serwah wandered off by herself up into the Aburanoma hills. The women watched her sway up the steep incline and disappear into the greenery. One hour and forty minutes later she came marching back down with a pot full of roots and herbs and a jar full of river water. Squatting down at the far end of the compound, she chopped some cassava leaf, goat meat, onion, tomato, and a little pepper, mixed it up with the roots and herbs, boiled it in a pot, and sent Kummaa to take it to Ashia for her evening meal.

Ashia stood in her courtyard washing her underwear beneath the tap on the wall. She was full and sleepy, but she wanted to finish her bucket of laundry before lying down.

All the warnings and descriptions in the world could not have prepared her for that first contraction. Leaning her hand against the wall, she doubled over and called out in panic, "Olu! Olu!" Olu came running from the front room where he had been writing his term paper. He caught one glimpse of Ashia's doubled-up body and went running back through the front room and up the dirt road to Mr. Opoku's house. "Run to the house, fetch the women," Ashia called out weakly, not realizing Olu was already halfway up the road.

Hearing the approaching women's voices, Ashia gave up sliding herself backward along the floor and collapsed just inches away from her bed, which she had been trying to reach.

A windswept forest came blowing into the dark bedroom. That's what the women looked like to Ashia from her position on the floor as they rushed in, their branchlike arms waving about, hastily passing objects from hand to hand. Towels, scissors, a washing bowl, soap, iodine. Ashia heard Nana Serwah call the items out as the women lay them on the dressing table.

Someone held up a lantern that created dancing shadows on the wall. Someone else threw a clean sheet on the bed. Someone else untied her wrapped skirt for her and removed her underwear. Ashia did not know who was doing what. In the dim flickering light, she could not tell one face from another. It was all she could do to hold in her screams and pant out her pain as the women instructed.

Suddenly all the movement came to a standstill. Ashia noticed her body was surrounded by brown ankles and feet. She looked up as the treelike shapes wearing colored fabric bent over her and swooped her up in a sea of hands. They sailed her through the air and lowered her soft as a feather onto the bed, just in time for her to bear down with her next contraction.

Someone bent Ashia's knees, someone else intertwined their fingers in hers, someone spread her legs wider, someone else washed her privates—Ashia knew that was Nana Serwah washing her privates, she would recognize those hands anywhere, gentle but firm, thorough, confident.

"Yaaaaaaay!" Ashia let out her first howl. Lamiley hushed her quiet. Akua Gyamma stroked her big rounded stomach. Awuradjua rubbed her swollen feet. First wife Afua wiped the perspiration off her forehead. The rest of the women lined the walls of the bedroom, keeping out of the way as Nana Serwah coached and coaxed Ashia to let her great-grandchild out. Tap-tap-tap, tap-tap-tap, Nana Serwah patted repeatedly on the back of Ashia's hand. "Bear down." She patted, rapid as a racing heartbeat. "Bear down. You must push and bear down."

*　　　*　　　*

Solomon was nestled up against Miriam's back, deep in sleep. "Push . . . Push . . ." he muttered, his hand gently stroking her stomach.

Miriam did not feel or hear him. She was lost in her dream. Creatures with the face of Solomon, the body of a swan, and the wings of an angel were flying away from her in droves. They were soaring out of her heart into the powder blue sky, rising in perfect formation far beyond her reach. She wanted to go with them, but the Island held her down. Seaweed washed in from the waves wrapped around her ankle like a chain. She kept untangling herself, but every time she tried to rise with the Solomon-angel-birds, the sea would spit out more weeds to chain her down. Sitting in the sand as the Solomon-angel-birds soared toward the sun, Miriam grappled with the clinging weeds to free herself. "*Let me fly,*" she pleaded, clawing at the weeds. "*Let go, even the angel-baby-birds are flying. Let go, I want to fly too,*" she demanded, pulling Solomon's stroking fingers off her stomach. "Let go!" Miriam turned violently in the bed, her eyes opening straight onto Solomon's sleeping face. Afraid to fall asleep again, fearful of her own dreams, she lay still and waited for the dawn.

Lying alone on the bed, Solomon woke to a blaze of sunlight. Already gone on her rounds, Miriam had left the stable doors open wide to the morning glory. Solomon reached out his hand to gather a fistful of the teeming glow. Closing his fingers around the rays that were beaming down onto his face, he clenched them tight. *I have it,* he thought, gripping a piece of the sun in the palm of his hand. *I finally have it. Joy. Inexplicable joy.*

* * *

Ashia held the baby in her arms. Looking into the light of its face nothing mattered to her anymore. The fact that Solomon was not there to witness the birth did not matter. The pain of labor did not matter. Olu standing there in the doorway seeing her all bloody and sweaty and ungainly did not matter. She had a child; that is what mattered. A wonderful, healthy, wide-eyed baby.

"My son," she said like a hymn of praise. "Look at my beautiful son."

The women smiled. They tried to relieve Ashia of the infant, but she would not let him go. They had to wait until she had fallen asleep before they could remove him from her nipple to clean up the two of them. First, they washed the baby. Awuradjua, who considered it an honor, held him in her arms while Akua Gyamma cleaned him with pieces of cotton wool, soused in a special river-water solution Nana Serwah had boiled that afternoon returning from her walk in the woods. Next, they cleaned Ashia. Filling the bucket with warm water from a cooking pot, they wiped her down tenderly . . . smooth delicate strokes, one hand and then the other, one washing, another drying . . . eight gentle hands taking great care not to wake her . . . she had labored strenuously for seven and a half hours . . . so they worked compassionately . . . needful not to wake her. When they had finished, they laid the baby back down on the bed beside her and tiptoed out of the room. All except Nana Serwah, who perched herself on the end of the bed and waited.

Chapter 2

✧

"*A*SHIA SAYS she wants to go find her husband." Nana Serwah lowered her eyes respectfully, folded her hands in front of her, and waited for a reply.

Mr. Opoku looked up from the bed at the two women standing before him. Akua Gyamma with her silent sensuous reserve, and the old fox with her wise humble manner. He motioned Awuradjua out of the room before responding. He didn't want his young bride learning any tricks from these two unconquerable characters. At the wave of Mr. Opoku's hand, Awuradjua got up from the little table where she was busy sewing, picked up her baby from the foot of the bed, wrapped it on her back, and walked out.

"Ashia should wait." Hoping beyond hope that he would not have to say anything more on the matter, Mr. Opoku went back to reading his periodical.

"It is hard for her to wait. At a time like this, a woman needs to be with the man she loves. She needs to be with the father of her baby." Unlike her mother, Akua Gyamma had no respect in her voice, no slight inclination of the head, no lowering of the eyes.

Mr. Opoku felt a seething sense of fury. Had she forgotten? Three months after the birth of their son, Kummaa, when he had sent for her to come to his bed, had she forgotten that she had refused to come out of her bedroom? Did she not send him word that "she begs his pardon but at a time like this, a woman needs to be alone with her infant"? How is it that she has now decided that, at a time like this, a woman needs to be with the father of her baby?

"She knows how to find where he is," Akua Gyamma continued. "I think we should send her to him."

"Nonsense." Mr. Opoku waved his hand in the air dismissively. "Where is the money supposed to come from? Tell Ashia that when Solomon is ready to see her, he will come home."

Akua Gyamma opened her mouth to speak again, but Nana Serwah took her by the arm and led her from the room.

Ashia, Lamiley, and some of the young female relatives who helped run the house crowded around the two women as soon as they came out of the bedroom. "He says Ashia must wait," Nana Serwah announced as she kept on moving down the passageway toward the open compound, the women crowding behind her.

"I disagree with him. I want to send her." Akua Gyamma was more forceful and passionate than Mr. Opoku's relatives had ever seen her.

"You must obey your husband. I am your mother and I am telling you, you must obey and respect him." Nana Serwah's voice was firm. Checking to make sure first wife Afua was nowhere around, she waited until new wife Awuradjua had slipped back into the master bedroom before adding with a mischievous twinkle in her eye, "Me, I am old; I do not have a husband, so I do not have to obey anyone."

"Du Pois. Du Pois Literary Agency. Pardon? Pardon? Yes. Yes, America. New York City. Thank you." Looking around, Ashia was glad to see that in the time it had taken to reach an operator, many of the customers had left, leaving the small, corroded, pale-yellow post office almost empty. That was the biggest drawback about having to talk from the post office telephone: the connection was always so bad that you had to practically shout for the person on the other end to hear you, which made it easy for people to eavesdrop on your conversation. However, it was the only telephone in Aburanoma village, so they had no choice.

Satisfied that no one was listening, Ashia turned to watch Nana Serwah at the counter. Cool as can be, her grandmother pulled out a wad of money and handed it to the post office clerk. Nana Serwah unraveled another wad from a strip of fabric bunched around her waist, and still another from inside the scarf on her head. The clerk meticulously counted out sixty American dollars from a small metal safe on the wall and exchanged them for the first wad of cedis. Nana

Serwah checked the dollars while the clerk counted the next wad of cedis. Ashia heard a voice on the line, blocked one ear with her hand, and focused back on her call.

"Hello. Hello . . . May I speak to Andréa Du Pois, please? . . . Andréa Du Pois . . . My name is Ashia . . . ASHIA . . . I am the wife of Solomon Wilberforce."

Accra was bigger and busier than Ashia had pictured in her mind. As she gazed out the coach window, her nervousness about her upcoming voyage was assuaged by the liveliness of the city. Street sellers lined along the road tapped on the windows of passing cars, touting their wares to those fortunate enough to be riding in vehicles. "Refresh!" "K. P. chewing gum!" "Ice-cold water!" "Paper—paper—paper! *Standard, Statesman, Chronicle!*" the voices cried out in loud solicitation. Skipping ropes, cough sweets, razor blades, bath nets, cassette tapes, and other brightly colored objects that Ashia could not fully identify were dangled in front of closed car windows, as the air-conditioned passengers looked straight ahead with practiced uninterest, ignoring the peddlers until they backed away, hurrying off to more promising prey.

And then there were the beggars. The blind and the maimed, crawling, sliding, or riding in wheelchairs, weaving in and out of traffic—their twisted, stunted, and uneven limbs pitifully on display. Ashia watched in sympathy as they approached the moving cars, their hands outstretched in the hopes of receiving a few coins, their faces set for disappointment. She watched as the tinted window of a black Mercedes-Benz rolled down and a fat hand with a gold wristwatch flung a few coins onto the road. Dodging vehicles, a crippled man hobbled to collect the coins, counted them, and moved to the next car.

There was so much to see, Ashia turned this way and that trying to take it all in. The bright blue, bright red, and yellow billboards. The two- and three-storey commercial buildings, with boldly painted names and garish advertisements. The small dilapidated dwellings, just minutes away from opulent mansions behind big iron gates and ornate walls covered with bright creeping flowers. Everything clean and dirty, pretty and ugly, old and new, all mixed up together. Telephone wires sliced across the sky blue skyline, crisscrossing their way through palm trees sprouting up from concrete pavements. New and battered two-tone yellow-green, yellow-white, yellow-red taxis and rickety multicolored *tro-tro* trucks, crowded full to capacity, bumped alongside chauffeur-driven luxury cars. Ashia read the fancy painted slogans on the trucks as they overtook the coach: IN GOD WE TRUST. AM I MY BROTHER'S KEEPER? TOMORROW THE SUN GO SHINE. Passengers leaning out of the backs waved at her as they passed by, using their other hands to hold on to whatever would keep them from falling out.

Ashia was pivoted on the edge of her seat, her head poking out the open window, her right hand waving back, her left hand firmly planted on the warm bundle beside her. She was trying to remember everything she saw, so she could write and tell Nana Serwah. It was all so enthralling, especially the people. The brightly dressed, radiant-looking people, packed into lorry buses, bursting out of taxi cabs, crowded into marketplaces, laughing, holding hands, strolling, jumping over gutters, peddling bicycles, pushing tin barrows. People large and small, young and old, balancing heavy objects on their heads—boxes, baskets, enamel bowls, piled high with goods—moving their necks to keep in balance as they walked, agile, alert, dodging the swerving trucks and cars, heeding the beeping horns: *Beep!* "Watch out." *Beep!* "Car passing by." *Beep!* "Woman with your big basket on your head, move!" *Beep!* "Let me through." *Beep!* "Come over here." *Beep-beep!* "Look at my fine, fine car." *Beep-beep-beep!* "Get off the street." *Beep! Beep-beep-beep! Beeeeeep!*

Ashia loved it all! The air-conditioning on the coach was broken (the driver explained that the parts needed to fix it were currently unavailable), so all the windows were slid wide-open for the entire journey. Despite the layers of dust that drifted in and coated everything red, Ashia was glad the windows were open—it added to her excitement. Blowing in with the hot humid breeze, the red dusty earth, and the relentless clamor of Accra street life was the tempting smell of food. Small wooden kiosks stacked to capacity with dried and canned goods were dotted between little roadside tables selling peanuts, plantain, and hot skewered meat, cooked over open flames, their tantalizing aromas blending into the air with the curling smoke. Ashia inhaled as she listened to the cacophony of voices shouting, laughing, bargaining, arguing, debating, in Twi, Ga, Hausa, English,

and pidgin English, clashing and intermingling with the din of radios
and cassette players booming through the streets, blasting local
news, traditional drumming, highlife music from West Africa, soul
music from America, and reggae music from the Caribbean.

The Caribbean. Ashia's stomach churned in nervous anticipation.
She looked up, checking to make sure her big suitcase was still where
her stepfather had put it in the overhead rack. Swinging out her leg,
she touched her foot on her smaller case, which Kummaa had tucked
under the seat in front of her. Dear little Kummaa, even though her
case was so heavy, he had insisted on carrying it onto the coach for
her himself. Just before stepping back off, he slipped her a folded
crayon picture he had drawn of the family so she wouldn't "forget
them."

Suddenly Ashia felt homesick. She thought about how first wife
Afua, who was usually aloof toward her, had braided her hair for her
the night before, threading it into an intricate crown, twisting curly
tendrils that spiraled down to her shoulders. And how her mother,
Akua Gyamma, and all the girls of the household had spent the past
two weeks sewing and embroidering new clothes for her to take on
her journey. And of the food Nana Serwah had prepared for her:
jars of dried shrimp pepper, bags of powdered yam, gari, cornmeal,
crushed fish heads for seasoning, and who knows what else her
grandmother had wrapped and tucked into her luggage.

Ashia unclasped her purse with one hand and took out the
smooth stone that Amamaa had given her. It was Amamaa's favorite,
and she had instructed Ashia that whenever she missed the village,
she should hold it in the palm of her hand and "feel home." Ashia
closed the purse, gripped the stone in her fist, leaned back, and resumed looking out the window, her left hand never leaving the precious bundle by her side.

The passing vehicles packed full of people reminded Ashia of her
early morning trip to Kumasi. Her stepfather had borrowed three
extra cars so the whole household could come along to see her safely
onto the coach for Accra. He had acted as if he were against the
whole idea of her traveling and didn't understand why she was so
desperate to find Solomon, yet he had called up an old acquaintance
in Accra, a Mr. Ofori Kumi-Bruce, for whom he had once surveyed
land, and asked him to use his connections at the embassy to get his

daughter a visa, which unless you knew the right people was an almost impossible document to obtain. Despite his apparent disapproval, her stepfather had also given her three beautiful robes to give to Solomon, one of them with matching attire for her and his first wife. To further assist her, he had called his sister's friend in Accra to meet her at the coach station, and then arranged the extra cars so they could all escort her to Kumasi to see her off. On arrival in Kumasi, he had even given her several hundred cedis to pay for food on the trip and to cover taxi fares when she got to Accra. When he embraced her good-bye, she realized that despite his reserve, he was as sad as the rest of the family that she was leaving and as well-wishing that she would find Solomon and happiness at the end of her journey.

The money for her plane ticket had come from the women of the house. Under Nana Serwah's supervision, they had been preparing and selling raw and cooked foods to neighboring villages for the past seven years. The money was kept in a small metal box hidden in a hole beneath Nana Serwah's bed. It was used whenever it was deemed necessary by the committee, which consisted of Mr. Opoku's eldest sister, Nana Mayfee; first wife Afua; and Nana Serwah—who was the only one with the key. Nana Serwah had never approved the money to be used until now.

Ashia fumbled nervously in her purse to make sure no one had stolen her ticket or her American dollars or the directions to Olu's house that he had given her two years ago in case she ever decided to "leave the bush and visit the nation's capital."

Listening to Big Auntie Mercy was like taking a historical trip of Accra. She was as large as her name implied and full of mercy. Ashia had never met her before, but having been with her for fifteen minutes, she already felt at home in her presence. "While you are in Accra, you will be my daughter," Auntie Mercy had said with a smile as she heaved Ashia's luggage off the coach. "Your father's sister, Nana Mayfee, is my very good friend. You look just like your auntie, you know, just like her," she said, laughing. Ashia felt this was impossible, since Auntie Mayfee was her stepaunt, but Auntie Mercy seemed so pleased with the apparent resemblance that she decided to leave the comparison unchallenged.

"Don't mind the smell, it's the Korle Lagoon," Auntie Mercy apologized as the taxi cruised past the Central Mosque into the industrial area. Ashia looked out at the stagnant water covered with green slime. "When I was a little girl, the lagoon was beautiful," Auntie Mercy lamented. "Tilapia fish jumped happily in there. I used to catch them with my sister and bring them to my mother to fry, but that was before it silted up. You see these long grasses?" Auntie Mercy pointed at the long dry rushes growing along the bank. "We use them to make baskets. And that is the old marketplace; it closed down many years ago. Now people sleep there in those small huts. And that over there is Galloway's old sawmill, and look see over there . . ."

Auntie Mercy's voice went on in a low excited lilt, sharing with Ashia her beloved Accra. She had paid the taxi driver extra money in order to hire him for the whole hour without his picking up any other passengers, so they took the long route home, enjoying the many sights.

Amankwa woke from his deep slumber and fussed in his mother's arms. Ashia peeled away his protective bundle of fabrics and held him up to the window to look at the view. He kicked his legs and let out a plaintive little cry that let Ashia know he was too hungry to be amused by passing scenery. Slipping her elasticized top off her shoulder, she loosed her breast out of her bra and fed him. He sucked on her nipple so voraciously that Auntie Mercy laughed, pulled his chubby little leg, and called him "mama's greedy little goat."

The taxi driver drove onto the Hanson Road, which, as Auntie Mercy pointed out, stretched all the way from the cemetery to the sea. "That is the old Methodist Cathedral. And that is the Palladium, Accra's very first cinema." Ashia turned to look through the back window of the taxi. She had watched a few videos on her stepfather's television but had never seen a film projected on a big screen, so to her the old cinema that had once been the toast of Accra still looked exciting and full of promise. "Do they show films every day?" Ashia asked hopefully.

"Long time closed," the taxi driver interjected as he cruised on past Derby Avenue.

"That is where the old corn mill used to be." Auntie Mercy pointed down the avenue. "And this is the Roman Catholic church.

And this here," she stated proudly, "this is Princess Marrie Louise Children's Hospital, where your Auntie Mercy was born. I was the first in my family, you know, to be born in a hospital." Auntie Mercy fell silent and leaned back in the seat, as if having pointed out the place and distinction of her birth, there was nothing more to be noted.

Ashia bent over to focus on Amankwa, who was still sucking hungrily on her nipple. With his legs kicking with pleasure, the energy of feeding induced a sweat on his tiny forehead, which she brushed lovingly with the back of her hand. *Solomon will be glad to see us,* Ashia tried to reassure herself. *He will be glad to discover that he has a son. He has longed for me to bear him a son since the day we got married. He will see now that I was right. I carry nations in my womb. How could he not be glad to see me? To see us both? He will be glad. Of course he will be glad.*

Ashia was awakened by the sound of voices bartering behind the wall. Auntie Mercy's house shared a common wall with the gas station on a busy corner of Zongo Junction where by 6 A.M., traders were out selling their wares, the day already in full thrust. Unable to go back to sleep, Ashia opened her eyes and looked straight at the bleeding head of a ceramic Jesus hanging on the wall at the far end of the room. The crown of thorns was made out of real twigs, and the loincloth was a piece of red-splattered gauze. The figure saddened Ashia, and she wondered how Auntie Mercy could wake up each morning to such a mournful sight. "It reminds me," Auntie Mercy explained as she bowed her head to bless their morning meal, "that Jesus rose up out of that terrible situation and because of him, I too can rise. Whatever burdens I wake up with, I look at that figure and know that because of him nothing can keep me down." She blessed the food and plopped a ball of hot kenke onto Ashia's plate next to a small baked fish and spoonful of crushed tomatoes, peppers, and onion, telling her that she is now in Accra, so she must eat like an Accra girl.

Auntie Mercy shouted for people to hurry up and come to table, and nine bodies ranging from three years old to thirty joined them for breakfast. Ashia was introduced to them all. They were Auntie Mercy's nieces and nephews, sent to her—their unmarried aunt—

for her to guide, educate, and house safely in the big city. Ashia wondered where they had all slept, especially since the small house had only two bedrooms, and Auntie Mercy had insisted on everyone vacating the master bedroom, decreeing that Ashia and Amankwa be left alone in there, so mother and baby could get a good night's rest from their long journey.

Despite the lack of space, breakfast was eaten and cleared away in a concert of deftly moving bodies squeezing in and out of tiny spaces, making room for utensils and one another, where it appeared there was no more room to be made. No one would let Ashia help clean up, so when she had finished eating, she went to sit in the narrow living room adjoining the small dining room.

She laid Amankwa on the rose-patterned couch, but as soon as she let go of him, he fussed. She sat down beside him and wiggled her fingers in front of his face to amuse him.

"Hello, Ashia."

Ashia looked up through the open living room door. Standing outside, behind the mosquito-netted frame, she saw the shadowy shape of a man in the hazy sunlight. Realizing who it was, her heart leaped with such excitement as she moved to open the frame, that her feelings took her by surprise.

Olu stepped inside, spread his arms, smiled a heartfelt welcome, and embraced her. Leaning her head against the warm dampness of his cotton shirt, Ashia smelled the sweet pungency of his musk mingled with his sweat. She liked the way Olu smelled; it came from his pores. No matter what musk or cologne he put on, his own special body scent was instantly recognizable, like a great signature.

"Welcome to Accra." His voice resonated through his muscular chest onto her cheek. Ashia clutched him, relishing the feeling of security it gave her to have a man who cherished her wrap her in his arms. It was the safest she had felt since the beginning of her pregnancy. Olu spread his legs wider for better balance and hugged her so tightly that it was hard for Ashia to tell whose breath it was that was making her head rise and fall ever so slightly against his heart. It reminded her of being with Solomon, of how she could never tell their bodies apart when they made love.

Thinking of making love with Solomon created a surge of resentment within her. He had left her to bear his child without the com-

fort of his presence, or knowledge. She had lived most of her pregnancy on the edge, hoping he would show up, going to bed every
night disappointed—fearful that as with her father, just when she
most needed him, death had come and stolen him away. It had been
several weeks since she found out through his agency, referred to
her by his publisher, whom she tracked from looking at the back of
one of his Beento books, that at the beginning of the summer,
Solomon had been well enough to send them a letter from the
Caribbean. The joyous relief of knowing he was alive was being per-
meated with moments of resentment.

Ashia lifted her head off Olu's chest. Olu kept hold of her as he
stared down at her face. "Brave little Ashia," he said admiringly, his
eyes full of love. Looking up at him, she became aware of the closeness of their lips. Just at that moment Amankwa let out a heart-
piercing wail. Ashia jumped back; stooped down; and, scooping her
son into her arms, proudly showed him to Olu. "We named him
Amankwa," she beamed. "After Mama's grandfather." Olu looked
down and saw Solomon's likeness staring up at him through Ashia's
big brown eyes.

"He has grown. He has your beautiful eyes," Olu said truthfully.

"And his papa's everything else," Ashia complained, not really
minding at all.

"Yes," Olu said wistfully. "And his papa's everything else. He is
Solomon's son, no question. Solomon is a very fortunate man."

Olu had only one day to show Ashia around Accra, so he persuaded
her to leave Amankwa with Auntie Mercy while he whisked her off
to some of his favorite spots. Ashia agreed on the condition that they
stop back at the house between places, so she could feed and check up
on her baby.

Despite Olu's efforts to amuse and dazzle her with Accra's high-
lights, Ashia was distracted. Her mind was on the long flight she was
to take the following day and on what she would find at the end of
her journey. The only time she was really present and excited was
when they climbed the small slope leading to the ruins of a deserted
mansion that the goatherds now used to shelter their animals. As
Olu led her through the jagged remains of the back wall, she beheld
a sight she had never seen before that left her breathless. The ocean.

Delighted by her reaction, Olu took her by the hand. "Welcome to the sea!" he shouted as he ran her along the sand to the tip of the waves. "The linker of continents." He stripped off his shirt and pants, imploring Ashia to at least kick off her shoes.

Ashia looked out, amazed. Water—as far as her eye could see—bluer than the sky—bright foaming white—neverending water. Stepping gingerly behind Olu, she followed him as he led her by the hand, deeper and deeper into the vast overwhelming blue. Submerged to her waist, Ashia squatted down to prevent herself from being drawn away by the current. Immersed in the sea up to her neck, she laughed at the tickle of the soft sand squishing between her toes; and the amazing weightlessness of her body held up by the swaying sea as it undulated through her clothes, lifting them, lifting her, making her laugh.

A large swell rose in the horizon. Ashia watched it as it broke into a wave, spreading across the surface of the water—linking foamy white hands, it forged forward, picking up speed as it rolled toward her. She tried to run from it, her arms thrashing wildly in the water. She screamed, her legs moving fast, moving nowhere—the water was too heavy—she panicked, lost her balance, toppled backward, her feet floating off the sand. Laughing, Olu caught her, held her from behind as the wave came crashing down on top of them. Water flooded their ears, filled their noses, salted their eyes, gushed into their mouths. Ashia thought they were drowning—*Amankwa!*

Water fell out of her face. She could breathe again! She was so relieved, she joined Olu in his laughter. The salty taste of the sea clung to her bright tongue, and she laughed and laughed. Delighted to have Ashia's wet, wriggling, giggling body in his arms, Olu kept her held against him as they waited for the next wave to fall. They played that way for nearly an hour, running, splashing, kicking, barricading against the waves, Olu constantly protecting Ashia from the push and pull of the mighty Atlantic Ocean.

Prompted by the motherly pang in her heart and the weight of her milk-filled breasts, Ashia walked out of the sea and beseeched Olu to take her home to her baby as quickly as possible. "He must be getting worried," she said, speaking more for herself than for Amankwa. "And hungry."

"I was going to take you to Nii Kwate's Tilapia joint for you to enjoy the best fish in town before taking you back." Olu's voice was almost a plea.

"I have to go back now," Ashia said emphatically, as she wrung out the bottom of her cloth.

Disappointed at having to leave, but glad that he had at least managed to make her laugh, Olu got out of the water, stripped off his wet underpants, and put on his dry trousers, which he had left lying in the sand. He made the change so quickly, Ashia barely had time to look away. Embarrassed at having glimpsed his nakedness, she walked on ahead of him while he put on his shirt.

Her soaking wet clothes, clinging to her body, weighed her down, making her steps labored as she plodded through the sand. Reaching the side of the rocky ruins, she brushed the sand off her feet and tiptoed around the edge of the broken wall so as not to tread on the goat droppings littered on the ground. By the time she reached the side of the road, Olu was sitting on a tree stump, waiting for her, a playful smile on his face.

"How did you get here?" Ashia asked, puzzled.

"It's my city," Olu said, hailing down a yellow-red taxi.

The driver refused to let Ashia sit on his cloth-covered seats in her wet clothes, suggesting that they find another taxi. Olu solved the problem by sitting her on his lap. He did it so casually, Ashia felt it would be rude of her to make a fuss and refuse. They both acted as if the close contact were nothing, and yet for the first time since they met at her mother's wedding to Mr. K. K. Opoku, neither one could think of a single thing to say to the other. The intensity of their silence was so strong that even the driver felt it, causing him to peek frequently at them through his rearview mirror.

Olu had the driver pull into the gas station at the back of Auntie Mercy's house, because no car could safely travel on the bumpy dirt path leading to the front. Ashia got out and walked slowly ahead while Olu counted out the money to pay the fare. Watching her through the open door of the taxi, Olu noticed the perfect round of her backside where her wet cloth still clung to every curve and crevice. The driver followed Olu's gaze and chuckled. "Woman she go drive you crazy," he warned.

Auntie Mercy was sitting on a rusty metal chair outside her front door, jiggling Amankwa on her knees. With one flick of the big woman's eyes from her wet clothes down to her bare sandy feet, Ashia felt scolded. "Wash yourself and change before you come and feed your child" was all Auntie Mercy said as she squinted at Ashia's engorged breasts, the damp fabric of her top clinging so tightly that it was impossible not to notice the large swell of her nipples. Feeling naked and embarrassed, Ashia scurried inside to obey.

By the time she had washed, dressed, and hurried back outside, Olu had come and gone, leaving her shoes and a message that he would be back in the morning to take her to the airport.

"Thank you," Ashia said, as she relieved Auntie Mercy of a hungry fretting Amankwa. She sat on a plank of wood laid across two piles of bricks and gave Amankwa her breast, which had already leaked milk all over her clean lilac blouse.

Auntie Mercy stayed to keep Ashia company while Amankwa fed. She was kind and friendly and showed no signs of what Ashia had feared was disapproval for her having gone off and cavorted in the sea, although later that evening while she was sleeping with Amankwa in her arms, Auntie Mercy crept into the room, sat at the bottom of the big double bed, and woke Ashia up, saying she needed to talk to her about Jesus, the Bible, and being a virtuous woman. She warned Ashia to be careful of men, especially foreign ones that she would meet on her trip. Then she knelt Ashia down on the floor beside her and prayed fervently for Ashia's safety and success in finding her husband, for her posterity, and for her safe return home to Ghana.

When Ashia rose up off her knees and climbed back under the bedsheet, she felt a comforting sense of peace and certainty that she would find Solomon and that all would be well. Auntie Mercy placed a maroon leather Study Bible on the pillow next to Amankwa and told Ashia to be sure to take it with her on her trip.

Chapter 3

✧

$\mathcal{A}$SHIA WAS NERVOUS about leaving her luggage, but it wouldn't fit into the little cubicle, so she left her two suitcases leaning against the wall by the sinks. With Amankwa tied to her back, she squatted over the toilet bowl and took a hurried pee. After washing her hands, she looked around to see where she could wash Amankwa and dress him in the princely clothes the women had embroidered for his first meeting with his father. Cape Corcos Airport was limited in its facilities, and the cramped ladies room was no exception. Finding no suitable surface on which to change him, she settled on turning her suitcase flat on the ground and lying Amankwa on top, which blocked the door to one of the three cubicles, much to the irritation of travelers who entered the bathroom before Ashia had a chance to finish dressing her baby.

Apologizing profusely, she lifted up her half-naked son and leaned her suitcase back against the wall. She finished dressing him holding him in her arms and waited anxiously for the bathroom to clear again, negotiating in her mind how she was going to change her own attire. She thought of going back inside the cubicle, but that would mean she would have to lay Amankwa down on her suitcase and leave him outside the door, which was out of the question. She debated staying in the clothes she was in, but she wanted to go straight to the Hotel L'Ouverture—it was the only Corcos address Solomon's literary agency had managed to trace for him, and it was possible that if he were there, which she prayed he was, he would see her before she had a chance to find a place to change. She did not want to disgrace him or herself by arriving in the bedraggled state she was in, especially if he was with his first wife, who had never seen her before.

Ashia looked at herself in the mirror, and the sight of her milk-stained clothes made her panic. She was tired, uncomfortably sticky, and very nervous. The trip had been a long one. There had been three stops, including an overnight in Rome, where they would not let her out of the airport because she did not have a transit visa. So she had spent the night in the harshly lit airport building pacing up and down, trying to appease Amankwa, whose ears and nose were greatly troubled by the air pressure on the flight. She was accustomed to bathing two or three times a day, and the fact that she had not been able to bathe for nearly three days added to her feeling of insecurity.

The bathroom cleared again, except for a young woman who was looking in the mirror applying rouge blush on her cheeks. Ashia turned over her suitcase and, placing Amankwa on top, fought through her bashfulness, stripped down to her underwear, and washed herself with wet paper towels. Removing a bundle she had rolled in her small suitcase, she changed into a beautiful outfit made of the fuchsia-and-gold silk sari fabric that Solomon had given her on his last trip to Ghana. She adorned herself with her mother's long gold earrings and necklace, which she had kept tied in a handkerchief on a string around her waist for fear of losing them. Adding around her eyes a touch of black kohl pencil that had been given to her by Auntie Mercy's teenaged niece, and a touch of Vaseline on her lips, she finally felt good enough about her appearance to leave the airport.

Cape Corcos Island looked beautiful and not as different from Ghana as Ashia had expected. Some of the streets and faces even looked strangely familiar, which gave her a sense of confidence. Only when the airport bus sidled into the opulent circular driveway of the Hotel L'Ouverture did her nervousness return. Kind as he was, the airport driver told Ashia he couldn't wait for her to find out if Solomon were there, because waiting was against regulations.

Now standing there with her luggage next to her, in a strange country, with her baby on her back and all her worldly belongings at her feet, Ashia wondered at the wisdom of having come to Cape Corcos. Perhaps her stepfather had been right, perhaps she should have waited at home for Solomon to come back to her. Once she discovered from his agency that he was alive, she could have sent him a telegram informing him of the birth of his son and asked him to come home as soon as possible. No matter why he had deserted her, having longed for a child for so many years, surely he would have come. Tears welled into Ashia's being as a barrage of *what ifs* flooded her brain. What if Solomon had lied to her, and his first wife did not know she existed? What if he had already left and flown off to another country? What if he was bored with her and had married another woman elsewhere? What if he was there but refused to see her?

Ashia suddenly felt as though she did not know her own husband. Had it not been for the warmth of Amankwa tied to her back, the feeling of fear and isolation would have completely overwhelmed her. His tiny heart beating into her spine was the only thing that prevented her from collapsing right there in the driveway, in a fit of uncontrollable tears. His warm little body was a reminder that she had more than herself to think about; for his sake, she was determined to keep her spirits high and her wits about her. She chastised herself for not asking the kind airport driver how much she should pay for a taxi to a cheaper hotel if she could not locate Solomon right away. Her money was very limited, and even though she had the comfort of a round-trip ticket back to Ghana if all else failed, she wanted to stretch her funds to last as long as possible in order to give herself time to complete her mission, which was twofold: first and foremost, to find Solomon, and failing that, to wait for her correspondence-course exam results and explore the possibility of furthering her education while abroad. Thinking of Amankwa and her ambitions for their future gave Ashia the strength she needed to walk confidently into the lobby, ask for Solomon, and face the outcome.

An irate businessman, with his wife and three unruly toddlers, stood at the front desk trying to hustle Joan into finding them a room. Ashia sidled up next to the wife and waited her turn.

"But we talking 'bout just one night, how could you give away my suite?" the man complained in his mid-Atlantic accent.

"Like I said, we fully booked," Joan insisted. "We only hold unpaid reservations until six P.M."

"Look miss, I will settle for just one room, then in the morning we'll go and look for another hotel."

"I be with you in a minute," Joan assured Ashia. She turned back to the man. "It no use fighting me, there nothing I can do. We fully booked. Better you move along quick and find another hotel, 'fore them fill up as well."

"I will not forget this," the man threatened before walking out in a huff. "I have many important friends who will boycott this hotel when I tell them of your rudeness." His wife smiled a surreptitious apology to anyone within hearing of her husband's fulmination, then followed after him, gathering together their three young sons.

"That a pretty outfit," Joan admired, glad to be rid of those people.

"Thank you." Ashia smiled, feeling shaky inside.

"Sorry, we don't have no more rooms."

Ashia played with her fingers and wished she had stayed out in the driveway a few moments longer, to have better prepared herself for what she might find. *What if? What if? What if?*

"I am looking for one Mr. Solomon Wilberforce," her voice quivered.

"You a friend?"

Ashia hesitated. *Am I a friend?* "Yes, I am a friend."

Joan sized her up. "He over at Miriam's."

Whoosh. That was all Ashia could feel, as a surge more powerful than the wave that had come crashing down on her head only a few days earlier flushed through her body. Olu was not there to protect her, so she placed her hands flat on the cool marble countertop, in case the rush came again and tried to knock her down. "Can I walk there?"

"I wouldn't advise it."

"Oh." Ashia was confused, unsure of what to do next.

"Since you a friend of he, make I get someone to take you over," Joan offered, banging the bell on the front desk.

"Thank you very kindly," Ashia said, more grateful than she could express.

"Where you from?"

"Aburanoma."

"Never heard of it. That's the country you from?"

"It's my village in Ghana."

"That's in Africa?"

"Yes. On the west coast."

"I like that Aburr—what?"

"Aburanoma."

"What do it mean?"

"It means 'bird of the horizon,' a dove."

Joan banged the bell again and moved to serve a guest who was waiting to collect his messages. "I like that, a dove. Me like doves, they be birds of peace," Joan remarked to Ashia as she handed over the messages to the sun-reddened guest. Climbing onto her high stool, Joan looked at Ashia with a wily look in her eyes and said, "So you come all the way from Africa to bring Solomon peace, huh? You and your little baby."

When she first saw it with Olu, it looked awesome but not frightening. Speeding past it now on the back of a moped in the dark blue of night, the sea looked like a terrifying abyss into which Ashia prayed not to fall. *Is this the same sea? The same as the one in Accra? The same as the one I saw from the airplane window?* Speeding alongside it, Ashia let her mind ponder the question while her body focused on keeping her son and herself balanced on the moped. With one arm curved behind her, gripping Amankwa, she used the other to cling to the waist of the young man who was driving them, apparently completely oblivious of the danger of their falling off the road into the water as he curved and sped his way along the shore.

Leo Rap-A-Tap, as Ashia later learned, was not afraid of anything and interested in nothing but politics and rap music, which to him were the same thing. Not yet successful in his chosen profession (although he had won a competition to have his rap love songs played on the radio the previous year, which gave him temporary popularity), he was constantly in need of extra cash, so Joan had come up with the idea of having him work as a messenger for the hotel, and she had managed to get Kawasaki to hire him without her father's knowledge that it was her suggestion. Nor was her father aware that Leo was the boyfriend he had caught her sneaking out to meet.

At one point Ashia tried to ask Leo to please slow down for the sake of the baby, but between the roar of the sea, the loud pulsing track blaring from the small tape recorder tied to the handlebars, and his rhythmic voice rapping over it, her voice was but a futile whisper in the wind. If he heard her, which was unlikely, he certainly ignored her, because the farther away they got from town, the faster he sped, until they were speeding so fast that she had to close her eyes against the slicing wind to keep them from watering.

The moped finally slowed, and Ashia opened her eyes to see a small isolated house just seconds away. Crawling to a complete standstill a few yards from the back stable door, Ashia felt as though they were still racing against the wind.

Peace rose from his mat and walked toward them.

"She come to see Solomon," Leo explained, turning off his loud music. Peace looked at the nervous excitement in Ashia's eyes, saw the baby sleeping on her back, and in one smooth movement lifted her off the bike and placed her feet down safely on the sand. His hands gentle, he rearranged her windswept clothing; he even lifted a ruffle of the soft silk sari off her shoulders and draped it back over her head, as if he knew exactly how she had looked before she got on the moped. He brushed the sand off her face with the tips of his fingers and led her by the hand toward the side of the house. Leo turned up his music and took off back along the shore, leaving the adobe to its sea-song silence.

Rounding the corner to the back patio, Peace placed his arm across Ashia's shoulders and pushed her gently forward onto the marble tile floor of the outdoor dining room. Before she had a chance to ask him any questions, he had disappeared into the night, leaving her standing there, flooded by the light of the moon.

Chapter 4

✦

STANDING THERE in the dreamlike setting, Ashia felt as though she had stepped into a fairy tale—an illustrated page from one of Solomon's Beento Blackbird books. The enchanting outdoor dining room had a moon for a light, stars for a roof, and the silvery blue-black sea as its grand entrance hall. Fairy lights with clinging vine were intertwined around a marble statue, draped across stools of stooping angels, and trailed along hand-painted floor tiles that merged into the soft carpet of endless sand. In one glance Ashia saw it all: the moon, the stars, the cascading lights, the velvet sofa, the glass-topped dining table, the bowl of tropical fruit, the full glass, the empty glass, and the humming woman dressed in white.

Is that her? Is that Solomon's first wife sitting there humming so contentedly? Ashia's nerves erupted again. If that was her, then she was not at all how she had pictured her to be. Solomon had described her as a midwife, a few years older than himself, so she had pictured her to look staid, matronly. But this woman looked lovely, so very lovely . . .

The woman had not yet noticed her, and too nervous to introduce herself, Ashia was filled with the sudden desire to run away. Maybe Solomon had decided that this beautiful woman clothed in white was all he needed, and everything he wanted. In the split seconds that she struggled with what to do, Amankwa woke and let out the faintest of gurgles. Hearing him, the woman at the table flashed her eyes onto Ashia's face.

As soon as their eyes met, no one needed to tell either one of them who the other was. The woman rose to her feet. Ashia stepped forward and offered the woman her hand. The woman took it. Ashia curtsied. "Good evening," she said, inclining her head to the ground. "I am Ashia."

When Ashia lifted up her bowed head, the woman in white was staring down at Amankwa with such intensity that Ashia was not sure what to do—the woman appeared to be sinking to the ground even though her body was still standing perfectly upright. Ashia could feel a tremble quivering through the woman's fingers. It was a tremble so slight, she would have thought it a mere shiver against the breeze, were it not for the flickers of fear and anguish passing in and out of the woman's hazel eyes. Solomon shouted something from the kitchen; the woman withdrew her hand, but neither woman moved. "Hey, Miriam," he came to the doorway. "Miriam, where's the—" Before Solomon could finish his sentence, he saw Ashia.

Standing there in the warm Caribbean breeze, Ashia felt as though she had always known this moment. As if somewhere in her memory it had been prerecorded in all its turbulent stillness, long before she was born: Solomon, standing in the kitchen doorway, in his beige linen pants and thin white shirt, a hint of moonlight in his eyes. Her, wrapped in fuchsia, their baby on her back, her head braided high in a queenly crown, the gold-bordered silk framing her face like a veil. And Miriam, standing between them, robed in white from head to toe, like a forever bride. Ashia felt as though she had lived it all before but could not remember what came next.

*   *   *

Miriam was too busy to move. She was busy trying to tell herself it was just a baby. A baby on a woman's back. The task of convincing herself was a hard one because in her heart it was not just a baby, it was a dagger, an indictment of her womanhood. She fought in her mind to hold on to the hope of the last few months, to the solace of Solomon staying with her on the Island forever, but just as the thought of that was about to soothe her heart, she caught sight of him, his whole being seemingly expanded to full capacity at the very sight of Ashia. Miriam looked at her billowed husband and feared her short-lived dream was coming to an end.

*   *   *

Solomon was ready to leap. He was so overjoyed to see Ashia, so thankful at being able to breathe freely again that he was willing to face whatever consequences her arrival would bring. He would have leaped to embrace her, were it not for the awkwardness of the situation. Would Miriam mind if he did? Would Ashia mind if he didn't? Or maybe Ashia would mind if he did. Would he ever be able to explain to Ashia what had happened? How he had missed her? Why he had remained with Miriam? How he had felt? How he was feeling? Shame kept him standing there in the kitchen doorway, an astonished look on his face.

They stood, the three of them, in the stillness of time, an oil painting of people frozen on the canvas of life. Each waiting for another to make a move.

Amankwa jerked on Ashia's back, reminding her of why she had sojourned to this faraway island. "Good evening, Solomon," she said, prompted by her son's kicking feet. She bent over to balance Amankwa while she untied the cloth that was holding him. "You have a son," she announced, swiveling her infant into her arms. "Amankwa."

The leap that had been repressed within Solomon's muscles broke loose and propelled him toward Ashia with the agility of a leopard with wings. Ashia held the baby out for him to take, but Miriam intercepted. Cradling Amankwa in her arms like a cat with a stolen kitten, Miriam headed for the kitchen. Ashia watched Miriam's movements with the focus of a lioness about to pounce. They were animals; they had all become animals.

Miriam stepped inside the house, and Ashia moved to protect what was hers. Solomon caught Ashia by the arm. "It's okay, leave her. She won't hurt him." Ashia cut her eyes to Solomon as if she had never seen him before. Her eyes darted back to the kitchen. "I promise you, Ashia," Solomon assured her. "Miriam won't hurt him."

This time Ashia looked at Solomon as if she knew him but did not like him very much. She lowered her eyes imperiously to the spot where his hand was still gripping her arm. He promptly released her. "You didn't come," she said, the hurt of betrayal ringing in her voice. "You just didn't come."

Solomon wanted to narrow the gap that divided them, but he didn't know how.

"Why? Why didn't you come?" Ashia's voice faded into a broken whisper. Within her held-back tears, Solomon recognized the child he had met, the girl he had married, and the woman he had deserted.

"I'm sorry," he said, wishing he could find a better way to express his wrenching remorse. "I'm sorry, Ashia. I'm so sorry." The words wavered weakly in the air. Solomon knew they were too feeble to cross the gulf between them. Pained by the distance no words would ever reach, Solomon cast out all self-preserving caution and embraced Ashia, hoping the love he bore for her in his soul would somehow be transmitted through his body into her heart.

"No!" Ashia struggled violently out of his arms. "No!" She pushed him away, shoving his chest with her tiny hands. Solomon was shocked. He would have let her be, but he wanted desperately to reach her and sensed even in her rejection that she wanted desperately to be reached, so he embraced her again, willing his body to be a bridge to close the gap between them. "No!" Ashia resisted, wriggling like an eel as she pried his hands off her. This time she didn't push him away, so they stood, inches apart, staring at each other.

"Ashia," Solomon whispered, "I love you. Every day, Ashia, I thought about you—I didn't come because—I hurt Miriam, Ashia, and I was trying to work it out—she cut herself—I was trying—I didn't know you were pregnant—I didn't know if I was any good for you—I didn't know whether to send for you—I was trying to work it all out. There's nothing I can say that will be good enough, but believe me, Ashia, I love you—I love you, Ashia . . ." Silent tears rolled down his face. Or was it hers? Whose cheek was it that was so wet? He couldn't tell. She couldn't tell. Their faces brushed together, merged—their bodies rocked each other—rocked all the unspeakable words that they would later have to try to utter, to explain all that had happened. But for now, the warm, the wet, the rocking were enough.

Miriam looked through the kitchen window and saw the two locked and swaying bodies. Looking out, she realized that throughout the summer she had been making love to Solomon with Ashia in the bed. She was sure of it now. His body had stayed with her, but when

the torment of separation had gotten too painful for him, he had
brought Ashia over in his mind and laid her down in the bed beside
him. That's why he had taken to staying in bed so long, even though
he hardly ever slept. It was the only place where he could dream
himself in Ashia's arms. He had lain there and imagined and willed
her to come to him so hard and for so long that she had finally come
to the Island to fulfill his desire. There she was! Ashia the beautiful!
The summer of Solomon's existence! Ashia the African queen! All
budding and blossoming and bursting with baby's milk.

Amankwa wriggled his head. Miriam realized she was gripping
him so hard against her chest, he could barely breathe. She laid him
down on the kitchen table. "Sorry, little Solomon," she cooed, wig-
gling his chubby legs. "So sorry. Sorry me couldn't be your mama."
The indictment of her womanhood flooded back into her being. This
time it rushed in too fast and forceful for her to control—washing
over her, drowning her in a torrent of grief.

Stroking her stomach, she remembered all the nights and years of
trying to get pregnant. All the check-ups, the supposed remedies,
the false alarms, the trying again, and the failing. Always the failing.
And then, of course, there were the babies. The endless, endless babies she had guided into this world, some of them unwanted by their
ungrateful parents who didn't appreciate the blessèd gift that God
had given them. Those were the births that hurt her, the ones where
God had bypassed her and given a child to people that didn't even
have the grace to be grateful for it, and here she was, willing yet barren! It was the first time Miriam allowed herself to even think the
word, and it cut her like a knife. *I am a wasteland,* she grieved. *After
all these years of hoping and loving and waiting. I am nothing but a
wasteland.*

Bending over Amankwa at the kitchen table, she covered her
mouth to hold back the tears that longed to fall. *Barren!* This child
was living proof that Solomon was fruitful and she was barren. "So
it's me," she lamented, gripping her stomach as if her very insides
were about to spill out. "It's me, it's me, it's me."

Amankwa felt the splash of her tears fall on his face; he smiled,
reached his hands, tilted his head to the side, and laughed into her
eyes. Miriam laughed with him. Laughed and laughed until she cried

herself a winding rolling river, careening down into a dry and barren land.

Outside under the stars Solomon lifted his wife triumphantly in the air. "I got a son," he yelled, holding Ashia up to the heavens. "Glory hallelujah! I got a son!"

✦

BOOK EIGHT

Stormy Weather

Clamorous Clouds of Gray . . .

Chapter 1

✧

*M*IRIAM LAY on the bed, thinking. She could hear them out there, talking in the kitchen. She had been in the bedroom several hours since Ashia's arrival, and Solomon had still not asked her to come join them. *Maybe he too busy being happy to think about me.* She had seen it through the kitchen window—happiness, spilling out of his pores like water through a sieve. When he had wanted to marry Ashia, he had needed not only her approval but her happiness. "I can't be happy without you, Miriam," he had claimed. So she had fought her will and gotten happy about it. *So how now him not need me to partake of his happiness?* Miriam wondered as she listened to the hushed enthusiasm of his voice filtering into her room.

She rose from the bed. Standing in front of the dresser, she inspected herself in the mirror. Usually the slight sag of her face was not noticeable because her radiant animation kept it all high and moving, but tonight she could see quite clearly that her features had fallen with age. She opened her robe and inspected her naked torso. With a look of defeat, she cupped her hands underneath her breasts and lifted them high. *Like they used to be,* she thought, pushing them up until they plumped into two bulbous mounds. *Like when I was in my twenties, full . . . voluptuous . . . like Ashia's.*

Miriam closed her robe and lay back down on the bed. Thinking . . .

*   *   *

Solomon was not sure how to behave, so he hovered outside the bedroom door, trying to plan things out. If he went in too excited about his new son, it might be painful for Miriam. Yet she knew how much he had longed for a child, so if he hid his joy from her, she might feel patronized. Then there was Ashia. He had thought it would be courteous to ask Miriam if Ashia could move into the spare bedroom; on the other hand, he had considered the ramifications of what would happen if Miriam said no. After all, Ashia was his wife too. So instead of asking Miriam a question he had already made his mind up about, which could only make matters worse, he had sent Peace into town to fetch Ashia's belongings because as far as he was concerned, there really wasn't any other viable alternative to her moving in with them. If it was anyone else, any other visitor, of course he would comply with Miriam's wishes, but Ashia was family and the adobe was their family home. Even though they always called it *Miriam's adobe* (like Ashia's home in Ghana was *Ashia's house*), it was *he* who paid for it, *his* name on the title deeds. Not that he would bring that up; it wasn't the point. The point was that he didn't want to hurt Miriam, but he couldn't turn his back on Ashia—not again—especially not with a newborn child. *His child.* No, there was no viable alternative; they would all have to find a way of living there together—at least until he could sort out what to do.

Solomon tapped lightly on the door and stepped inside. Miriam lay on the bed in her kimono, gazing into space. He edged his way up to the bed. "Been quite a night." His voice was cautious. Miriam shifted her gaze onto his face. Solomon sat beside her, took her hand. He tried to hold it but her hand was too flaccid to be held, so he placed it in his left palm and cupped his right hand gently over it as if it were a delicate petal that could easily be blown away. "You're quite a woman, you know that?"

Miriam's eyes left Solomon's face and focused on the ceiling. He wanted to envelop her, reassure her that no matter what transpired, there was a place in his heart that was hers and hers only, baby or no baby, other wife or no wife; theirs was, would always be, a love that survived—a constant rainfall that made good things grow.

Solomon leaned forward to kiss Miriam on the forehead. She turned her head away and almost imperceptibly, with her free hand, closed her kimono over her exposed thigh. The gesture was small but clear. Solomon pulled back. "Just wanted to make sure you were all right," he said, releasing the petal from his palms.

Heading out to join Ashia in the kitchen, he wondered when the bedroom had gotten so long. He was only halfway across and Miriam already seemed so far away. Trackless footsteps stretching out between them. By the time he reached the little cream dresser with the tiny peach flowers, her body scent was already undetectable. If he walked out of the room without turning back, would her face also fade away? Would he forget the color of her eyes? Solomon clicked the door shut behind him.

Chapter 2

✦

*F*OR DAYS AND WEEKS the women watched Solomon
move—Solomon watched the women move—and the women
watched each other: like intricate moves of chess, each player advancing and protecting, advancing and protecting; edging their way
deeper and deeper into the center of one another's lives; peeking, listening, tasting the atmosphere—licking up the good—spitting out
the bad; smelling each other out—a sniff of fragrance—a whiff of
stench; peeking, listening, feeling their way around.

*   *   *

Miriam sat humming at the breakfast table in a body-hugging, knee-
length dress with a neckline so wide it exposed her smooth, coffee-
cream shoulders. She smiled sweetly at Solomon and Ashia—oh, so
politely, as if to a couple of strangers she had just noticed sitting beside her in a restaurant. One of those quick crinkly smiles where a
person immediately focuses back on what she was doing, which in
Miriam's case was swaying and humming her cheery little song and
pretending she was not aware that her provocative new dress, which
she had just had sewn, was made from the exact same Indian silk
fuchsia-and-gold fabric Ashia had worn the day she arrived—beautiful material, so soft, so comfortable—a gift from Solomon.

Ashia sat looking awkward. She peeked at Miriam's hand to see if
Miriam's wedding ring was also the same as her own. It wasn't.

Solomon noticed a smug curve on Miriam's humming lips. He
contemplated explaining that the fuchsia fabric had been the last of
the bolt, that the Indian merchant had insisted he buy all twelve
yards, and there being so much of it he had decided to give the two of

them six yards each, but that it was the first and only time he had ever given them the exact same gift. He looked at the expression on both his wives' faces and decided it was not a good time for his lengthy explanation. Feeling thirsty, he poured himself a tall glass of water, which he drank down in one gulp. "Ahhh . . . ," he sighed, "that was good. You wouldn't believe it, Ashia, up until last week, I've been having the hardest time drinking water."

"That must have been terrible," Ashia responded, an indiscernible smile creeping across her face. She reached across the table and helped herself to one of Miriam's home-baked buns, savoring it with relish.

. . . peeking, listening, tasting the atmosphere—licking up the good—spitting out the bad . . .

*   *   *

"Maybe you should let Toussaint come fix it," Miriam teased from the hallway as Solomon sat on the edge of the copper bathtub, attempting to repair the hot tap.

"You trying to say I ain't a good handyman?"

Miriam sauntered up to him. "Now, that all depend on what you handling," she said in a flirtatious tone that Solomon had not heard her use since Ashia's arrival.

"You got that right," Solomon boasted, his eyes taking in the invitation on her lips. He stood up and slipped his arms around her waist. Leaning forward, just before he closed his eyes to better enjoy the warmth of Miriam's mouth, he caught a glimpse of Ashia watching him from the hallway through the half-closed door. Her arms holding a pile of dry towels from the clothesline, she stared at him with a look both wounded and embarrassed, before turning and walking away. Solomon closed his eyes and kissed Miriam in the agony of confusion.

. . . smelling each other out—a sniff of fragrance—a whiff of stench . . .

*   *   *

"It is hard to be so quiet."

"You call that quiet?" Solomon whispered, rolling off Ashia's naked body. "Woman, you a wild and crazy African!"

"I am what you have made me," Ashia whispered back, nibbling on his ears. Solomon kissed her on the tip of her nose and rose up out of the bed. He yawned, stretching up his arms, and Ashia watched his muscles making patterns on his naked back. Reaching over to the side table, he retrieved his drawstring pants and slipped them on.

"Where are you going?" Ashia sounded vulnerable, her voice uneasy. Solomon sat down on the edge of the bed. He placed his hand on top of the sheet, stroked her trim leg lying underneath.

"I told you this afternoon, Ashia, that I was going to sleep with Miriam tonight. I haven't spent the night with her since you got here." His voice faltered. "It's not to make love to her necessarily, it's just—"

"Of course," Ashia said, cutting him off.

Solomon wanted to say more, or at least stay with her until she fell asleep. He knew it was a terrible time to get up and go, but it was getting late into the night and he had already promised Miriam that he would spend the night with her. "I miss your company," Miriam had said to him that afternoon when they had kissed in the bathroom. "You can come back to your bed, Solomon. I want you to lay with me tonight and hold me till I fall asleep."

Solomon looked down at Ashia, lying there, watching him think, her big brown eyes beckoning him back into her arms. He thought of his promise to Miriam and forced himself up off the bed. "Ashia, I can't—I ought to give—I mean, I just can't just—" He struggled to find the truth of what he wanted to say. "I ought—no, I *want*—to give Miriam some company. I promised."

Squatting over Amankwa's padded box on the floor, Solomon kissed his sleeping son on the head. "Good-night, little prince," he said dotingly. With Ashia's eyes still fixed on him, Solomon struggled against her voiceless pull and left the room.

It was hard. The leaving was hard, but with Miriam opening up to him, Solomon felt heartened. Things between the four of them were certainly better than over the previous month. On the first few nights after Ashia's arrival, when he grew tired of sleeping outside on the patio couch, he had tried to get back into bed with Miriam— but each time he tried, she had jumped up, stripped off the top sheet, rolled it around herself, and slept on the floor. So he had eventually taken to sleeping with Ashia—until tonight.

As soon as Solomon climbed into bed, Miriam turned over onto her side to face him. He stroked her hair and asked her whether she was sleepy. She said she wasn't. He said he wasn't either, so they lay facing each other, their hands linked on the pillow between their heads, chatting about how the fishermen had reeled in so much swordfish that, according to Mrs. Shackelton, the government was making them dump tons of them back into the sea to keep the prices up; and wasn't it about time they put Cassie in school instead of letting her run wild all over the Island. And believe it or not, Toussaint had suddenly taken up flamenco dancing. Poor Emelia, he was making her practice with him up and down the hotel lobby in full view of everyone! They laughed at the thought of it and then went quiet. That's when Solomon's ears first picked it up—Amankwa's plaintive little cry.

Miriam continued to chitchat, but Solomon became more and more distracted as Amankwa continued to cry. Finally, when his son's cries became interspersed with a painful-sounding cough, Solomon broke hands with Miriam and sat up.

"He not alone, Solomon, he all right," Miriam assured him softly. "You worse than a nervous mama," she teased. Amankwa continued to cry and cough, finally bursting into an almighty howl. Solomon heard the door to the second bedroom open, followed by a light tap-tap on their door.

"Solomon," Ashia's voice was low, cautious. "Solomon." There was another light tap-tap and then the sound of bare feet moving away.

Miriam pushed Solomon back down on the pillow and traced little circles on his chest with her fingertips. "Let me just go and see what's wrong," Solomon beseeched her. Miriam kept on circling, her fingertips light . . . light . . .

"Solomon . . . ," Ashia called again, her voice barely audible.

. . . like intricate moves of chess, each player advancing and protecting, advancing and protecting . . .

Solomon placed the wooden bassinet on the kitchen table and inspected the final layers of polish that he had just let dry in the sun. Pleased with the curve and hue of it, he tapped it with his finger and watched it rock steadily back and forth, back and forth, the tiny bells strung around the rim jingling as it continued to sway. He added a soft white pillow case, which he had already stuffed with lamb's wool, and proceeded to tie a row of white satin ribbons along the big curved handle that made the bassinet easy to carry. While he was tying the last ribbon, Miriam came in from the bedroom. Glad for a witness to his handiwork, Solomon tapped the bassinet to make it rock again. "What you think?"

Miriam glanced at it and placed her basket by the sink without comment.

"For Amankwa," Solomon explained enthusiastically. "Think he'll like it better than that box?"

"I think he too young to notice the difference," Miriam replied tersely. She removed a tin from her basket to fill it with hard-boiled eggs that she had already cooled in a bowl of cold water by the sink.

"Good morning, Mama Miriam," Ashia chirped cheerfully as she swayed into the kitchen from the patio, a basket full of dry laundry balanced on her head.

"Morning," Miriam replied despondently, not looking up from arranging her eggs.

"Oh, Solomon! How beautiful," Ashia effused, noticing the bassinet. "You finished! You are so clever! Mama Miriam, did you see? A new bed for Amankwa. Ayiee! He is going to be so happy! We must put him inside. Come," she beckoned as she lowered the laundry basket onto the floor. "Come, Solomon, let's put him in." Without waiting for a reply, Ashia ran back outside in a flurry of excitement.

Amankwa was lying fast asleep in his box, shaded by Peace's big black umbrella. Putting down the bassinet, Solomon lifted his warm baby into his arms. Without waking, Amankwa emitted a contented sigh as he yielded his head onto Solomon's shoulder, his tiny arm curving automatically around his daddy's neck.

Unadulterated bliss. Those were the only words that sprung to Solomon's mind to describe the sensation of holding his son in his arms. If it were possible to be so full of love that your heart could burst into pieces, Solomon felt sure his would be scattered on the ground like a million grains of sand at the very sight, feel, and smell of Amankwa. Even the dribble Amankwa was drooling on his neck as he slept against him seemed to Solomon like heavenly nectar.

Reluctant to let him out of his arms but prompted by Ashia to try him out in the bassinet, Solomon lowered Amankwa onto the cotton-covered lambskin. Amankwa's little body stirred at the loss of human contact, but as soon as Solomon's hand rocked the bassinet, he settled back into a deep sleep, the tiny bells tinkling by his side.

"I'll be back before dusk," Miriam called out in a tuneless voice as she began to trek along the beach toward town. Solomon watched her go, his heart consumed also with the urge to run after her.

. . . *edging their way deeper and deeper into the center of one an-other's lives . . .*

Chapter 3

✦

"SOLOMON AND MIRIAM WILBERFORCE! WE COME TO TAKE YOU HOSTAGE. YOU MUST COME OUT IMMEDIATELY!"

Solomon pulled on his tapestry boots made especially for him in the north of Ghana, placed a cream and gold-embroidered cap on his head to match his stately cream and gold-embroidered African robes, checked himself in the dresser mirror, and strode out from the bedroom through the kitchen and onto the patio. "I surrender!" he shouted playfully at the two moonlit bodies sitting in the small speedboat that was bobbing at the edge of the water just beyond the patio.

"Prepare to fire," Kawasaki instructed, his voice booming through a hand-held megaphone. Three rocket fireworks went blazing off the back of the boat, showering waterfalls of colored light into the night sky.

"You a mess," Solomon laughed. "You a crazy out-of-your-mind mess!"

"If Mohammed won't come to the mountain, the mountain got to come to Mohammed," Kawasaki declared.

Jezz leaned across him and boomed through the megaphone, "You hereby charged with the crime of being extremely late for you own party, forcing us to come get you. You must get in the boat immediately!"

Miriam emerged from the adobe in a beautiful robe and headdress, her fabric exactly the same as Solomon's, her attitude very different. "Evening," she said in a subdued voice as she moved toward the boat.

Ashia poked her head out of the darkened kitchen window, the gold embroidery of her matching fabric flashing in the starlight. "Solomon, please come," she called softly. Lingering for her on the patio, Solomon walked back to the window. "If you like, I can wait here," she offered.

"Absolutely not."

Ashia closed the window. Solomon heard her little feet hurrying into Miriam's bedroom, which surprised him, because he had never known her to enter it before. Then he heard her say something to Peace about Amankwa, close the stable doors, and then scurry back through the hallway. Meeting her at the kitchen door, he offered her his arm and escorted her to the shore. Tonight was his first outing with his two wives by his side, which made him feel especially protective. "This is my second wife, Ashia Wilberforce," he introduced her as he helped her climb into the waiting speedboat. It was easier to say than he had imagined. He climbed in after her and sat majestically between her and Miriam, resplendent in their regal robes, the king and his royal consorts. Kawasaki smiled. "Fire some more fireworks, Jezz," he ordered. Jezz, who was uncharacteristically speechless, fired off more fireworks as Kawasaki powered the boat toward the horizon.

By the time they got to *The Kawasaki Kruiser*, Solomon's party was already in full swing. As soon as some of the guests recognized Kawasaki's speedboat heading toward them, they notified the band, which broke into a reggae rendition of "For He's a Jolly Good Fellow."

Only her second time at sea, Ashia was nervous about climbing out of the small boat and up the rope ladder, so Jezz and Miriam went first, leaving the two men to climb in front and behind Ashia to hoist and push her up if necessary.

As soon as they were all safely on deck, Solomon was whisked away in a flurry of jewels and colors, as the very merry, very champagned Cape Corcos society ushered him into the main cabin to grace them with a speech. Solomon had not planned to address the people, but since the party was a fund-raiser for the Royal Nubian school, he decided to oblige. The cabin was full of Islanders seated at formally set tables strewn with gold streamers and silver balloons. Climbing onto the stage and looking out, Solomon could tell everyone was in a partying mood, so he kept his speech short, speaking briefly about their being the forgotten tribe of Africa and remembering the majesty from which they came. "My mama taught me as a little boy," he concluded, "that to race ahead, you got to reach back and anchor your foot against the tree of history. 'Solomon,' she used to say, 'that what give you the mighty thrust to run like a champion. Our tree got ancient roots, deep and rich and full of power. When you tired, Solomon, push hard on it, give it all your weight. It can never be uprooted.'"

The room broke into a cacophony of applause, clinking glasses, shouts of approval, and the click-click-click of the drummer's drumsticks as he counted the band back into play. The musicians broke into a rousing reggae rhythm that sent bodies scrambling onto the dance floor devouring each note, letting it infuse them with an energy so potent, they could not help but pump it back out.

Solomon was looking for a way around the writhing bodies when he saw a face in the crowd that startled him. Quick as a flash, the face disappeared from his sight, leaving him uncertain as to whether he had seen who he thought he saw. *Impossible*, he concluded as he weaved through gyrating bodies to get to Kawasaki, who was beckoning him along the side of the dance floor.

A waiter tapped Solomon on the back. "Pretty lady say to give you this." The waiter handed him a letter and rushed off to continue passing out the gourmet goodies on his tray. Solomon tore open the envelope and pulled out a note:

Dear Solomon,

I missed you this spring. We got your rather vague letter at the beginning of the summer, but nothing more. Even Zelda says you've stopped responding to the messages she faxes you.

What's happening with you? How's the new book coming along? We need to talk. As I told you before, whatever's going on, I'm here for you. Remember what I said . . . I believe in you . . . no matter what, you're worth the effort. That's why I've come.

Talk to me, Solomon.

Much love, Sam

P.S. Enclosed is a little gift to replace the one I broke.

Solomon looked in the envelope and pulled out a silver chain with a solid silver clasp. So it *was* Sam he saw! Was she watching him? Had she seen him open the envelope? Had anybody else? With so many people crammed into the main cabin, it was hard for him to tell.

"Sit. You the guest of honor." Kawasaki pointed Solomon to the seat at the head of the captain's table, where Miriam, Ashia, Jezz, Stavos, Toussaint, Emelia, Joan, Cassie, Captain and Mrs. Morrow, and Kawasaki's on-again, off-again fiancée, Miss Candy Spears, were all seated, making polite conversation while eyeing Miriam and Ashia with curiosity. Feeling uneasy, Solomon sat down. "We only set the table for twelve," Kawasaki said apologetically. "We miscalculated."

"They foolishly calculated only one wife per person," Stavos interjected facetiously.

"Evening, Stavos," Solomon said as he flicked his napkin onto his lap, with the distinct feeling that it was going to be a very long complicated night. "I'm surprised to see you at my party. I heard you were my sworn enemy."

"In order to ruin a man, you must break bread with him. It's the only way you will find out his weak spots," Stavos imparted in his thick Greek accent.

"I see," Solomon responded, reaching into his robe to make sure the hurriedly hidden note was tucked securely inside the inner pocket. "In that case, I shall do my best not to divulge any of my shortcomings."

Solomon tried to relax. He was determined not to worry about where exactly on the boat Sam was, or why. It was enough trying to cope with the Miriam/Ashia situation. He could feel the news of his polygamy traveling from table to table as people turned to stare at the three of them, their attitudes toward him changing fast as marbles rolling down a hill. Digging his fork into the crab farci on his plate, he did his best to ignore all the curiosity, hostility, or envy aimed in his direction.

"Me can't believe the man got the audacity to bring him mistress with him all the way from Africa!" a notorious troublemaker griped.

"Never mind jus' bring her, but flaunt her at the captain's table!"

"Blatant."

"All cocky and unashamed!"

"Scandalous!"

"And *he* the one our children supposed to follow?"

"Me no know why you all so scandalized, it our heritage," the notorious troublemaker's husband interjected in defense. "From Africa."

"Yes!" his wife hissed back with a look that threatened poisoned coffee. "But we not in Africa, we on Cape Corcos Island!"

Valuing his life, the lightfooted husband got up from the table and drifted onto the dance floor, leaving his wife and her friends to vent their fury without interruption.

The women discussed the situation at hand. They had warned Miriam over the years that there must be someone else in Solomon's life for him to be gone all those months. Miriam, in her stubborn eccentric way, had never confirmed or denied their suspicions. Even now, looking at her face, it was impossible for them to tell how she was feeling, or whether she had known about this other wife. "Look at her! Sitting up there like that! All dressed up the same as him and her. Condoning it!"

"Giving our men the wrong impression 'bout what a decent woman will and will not put up with."

"It make me mad to watch her."

"And her a midwife and all."

"Scandalous!"

As for "the other one," "the African child," she never once looked them in the eyes. At first they thought she made no eye contact with them because she was too ashamed. They presumed that since her eyes never turned in their direction, they must be cast downward toward the ground. But after a while they realized her eyes were not cast down at all; on the contrary, they were up and open wide. In fact, now that they really looked at her, wasn't her head held just a little too high for a person living in shame and disgrace? And that back! She never once leaned it against the chair. She just sat there with it unsupported, poised, like she was royalty or something!

"Me got it!" the troublemaker said connivingly. "Me was there when that Solomon Wilberforce plant the tree for the new school. All him talk about was kings and princesses and teaching the children how to *behave* like them do in *Africa*. Me telling you the man planning to turn our boys all imperious and polygamous like himself, and him brought his young mistress over here to turn our little girls into man-pleasers. Just look at the way that African child serve him all the time, buttering his bread and what have you. And notice her plump mouth, the way she pout it when he look at her, you can tell by that mouth what she all about!"

The women jerked their heads, looking at one another in horror. "Need I say more?" the troublemaker asked. The silence that met her question was the confirmation she was looking for—what more was there to say?

Making her way over to the captain's table, the troublemaker greeted Solomon and asked him if it was true that he had been appointed headmaster of the new school. Solomon gave her a noncommittal answer, at which point she asked him if he had ever taught or run a school before, and if so, where?

"Solomon a genius," Kawasaki replied. "You name it, he done it. And if he not done it, he capable of doing it. He not here to give nobody him credentials, this a party, Judith Morenzi, go relax yourself."

Judith "Troublemaker" Morenzi wandered back to her tongue-wagging friends with absolutely no intention of "relaxing herself."

"Ah! So Solomon's a genius!" Stavos quipped, sipping his champagne. "Perhaps that's why you can't produce any children, Solomon—your reproductive cells are too busy feeding your brain."

Relief. For the first time in years, the ache of inadequacy and longing that constricted Solomon's being at the mention of his having, or not having, children was not there. Stavos's cruel but supposedly lighthearted gibe left him completely unaffected.

Ashia now focused her eyes on each face as she looked around the table. "He has a son," she announced simply. She spoke so quietly that she could barely be heard above the din of the room. "Solomon has a son," she repeated a little louder for those seated at the captain's table who appeared not to have heard or understood. "His name is Amankwa." Ashia straightened her spine, becoming even taller than before, and withdrew into her wide-eyed, nonfocusing world.

Solomon turned to look at Miriam. She had aged. "*It's as if the defeat of losing you is only just becoming a reality.*" That's what she had said to him while they were dressing earlier that evening. He had assured her that she could never possibly lose him. *"I lost you five years ago when you took on another wife. I just never admitted it to meself until now."* Then with a smile, she had perked up and said, *"Let's have fun tonight. After all, it your party."*

Solomon became aware that he was not the only person staring at Miriam: the entire tableful of people was focused on her, watching for her reaction to Ashia's announcement. Using all the charm and grace she could muster, Miriam raised her champagne glass into the air. "To Amankwa," she toasted, "Solomon's firstborn." Despite her valiant attempt at joy, the defeat in her voice affected even Cassie, who stopped eating and fiddled evasively with the bottom of the tablecloth.

"To Amankwa," Solomon agreed cheerily, lifting his glass in an attempt to save the moment. "Long life and good health." Following his lead, everyone lifted their glasses.

Sam sidled up to Solomon at the head of the table, her glass held high. "Surprise, surprise," she beamed, looking exquisite in her copper-beaded minidress. Solomon looked at her and stood up. Standing there close together by the table, they kept their voices low as Solomon asked Sam what she was doing on Cape Corcos.

The official reason Sam gave for her presence on the Island was to discuss the story line of his next book, which in his letter to the agency Solomon had stated that he felt "unable to write," and also to have him sign the contract, which had been waiting for months, for a scheduled cartoon series about Beento Blackbird.

"But that's not the only reason why I flew all this way; the rest is personal," Sam confessed quietly to Solomon. But even though she kept her voice inaudibly low to anyone but him, her body language was easy for all to hear.

Inquisitive eyes turned again to Miriam, and Miriam's eyes were fixed on Sam.

Like a shrub struggling back up from the dirt in which it had been trampled, Miriam struggled up from her seat. Life was changing. She tore herself from the earth she had come to know and made her way through the crowded cabin. With all her roots dragging behind her, she knew she had to find a hole in which to replant herself; otherwise, she was in grave danger of dying. Hurrying, she headed out onto the deck.

Solomon wanted to call her back, but he restrained himself, knowing she would not like the attention it would cause. So instead, he sat down in his chair and turned to Ashia. "I'd like you to go and fetch Miriam," he requested, his voice full of tenderness. "Ask her to please come back and take her seat." Intending to address Sam, he looked to where she had been standing. Sam was nowhere to be seen.

It had been fifteen minutes since Solomon sent Ashia to fetch Miriam. She had searched everywhere. Only now, back on the smooth polished deck where she started, did she lean over the side and spot a lone figure sitting in the small speedboat. Staring, Ashia realized by the fabric of the woman's dress that it was Miriam. Cupping her hands over her mouth, she shouted down, calling Miriam's name. Miriam either ignored or didn't hear her.

Swinging her leg over the edge of the ship onto the top rung of the rope ladder hanging on the outside, Ashia climbed down toward the speedboat bobbing below on the surface of the pitch-black sea. A rush of adrenaline surged through her body. She felt adventurous. She was glad to be free from the curious eyes and tedious comments. Everything was suddenly quiet, save the sound of the sea. Her body worked like a well-oiled machine as it descended—right hand, left foot, left hand, right foot—inching its way down the ladder.

A wave rose and crashed fiercely against the side of the *Kruiser*. Unnerved by the noise, Ashia looked down into the watery depths and was filled with sudden terror as she imagined herself plummeting into the foamy eruption. The distance between the *Kruiser* and the speedboat suddenly seemed much farther than she remembered. She had been descending for quite a while and yet she appeared to be only halfway down. A gigantic wave crashed again, with a terrible roar. Seized with fear, Ashia's body froze. The blood in her hands drained away, leaving them weak and scarcely able to hold on to the rope, which suddenly felt rough and abrasive against her skin. Using all her faculties, she tried to push through her fear and make herself move. Weighing her options, she decided it was easier to keep on moving down than to hoist herself all the way back up, so she reached out her foot and felt around for the next rung. It was not there. Nothing was there. Panic welled in her throat. A wave crashed again, louder this time, and salty stinging vapor from the sea stung her eyes. Everything turned black; even the deep red paint on the *Kruiser* suddenly looked as blue-black as the ocean beneath her. In the dizzying darkness her anchorless leg became a lead weight that dragged her body downward. Straining under the pull, her bloodless fingers lost their battle to hold on and flew up into the air.

Ashia sailed. In a flash her spine smacked hard against the water, like shattering ice, and her wild petrified eyes shot a pleading look at Miriam. Then her body, face and all, sank down into the impossible, terrifying, unbreathable deep.

*   *   *

Miriam had watched it all. From the moment Ashia had stepped out onto the deck, Miriam had followed her movements. The search, the find, the descent, the hesitation, the fear, and now the fall.

She was about to dive into the water to try to save Ashia from drowning, when a thought occurred to her: what if she waited? What if she just sat there for a few minutes and let the elements have their way? Miriam made a swift evaluation in her mind. Solomon, Amankwa—all hers—exclusively—if Ashia never resurfaced. She looked up onto the deck; nobody had noticed. She looked down at the water. The turbulent ripples where Ashia had hit the surface had already begun to subside.

*   *   *

The anguish was like falling to her own death. Miriam knew that if she were too late, if her seconds of hesitation had cost Ashia her life, then the agonizing cry that wailed from her spirit as she dove into the sea would never leave her. Skillful as a mermaid, she let her body sink deeper and deeper into the water, her eyes combing the depths for signs of life. The sea was her home, she was raised in it, she knew its nature, knew how to behave like one of its own.

After a while Miriam became aware that she needed to come up for air. At the onset of the thought, desperation hit her: if she needed air, then Ashia did too—with her lungs straining, she stayed underwater, determined to find her.

Algae brushed against Miriam's face, caught her hair; she shook it off, and in the movement she saw her—Ashia—her limp body drifting. Gathering graces—Miriam swam to her. Gathering graces—she folded her in her arms. Gathering graces—she held up her face, pulled her up, up, out of the water. Gathering graces—she defied the current, swam to the small boat, and lifted them, lifted her, their sodden clothes pulling against her like a weighty enemy. Gathering graces—she heaved Ashia onto the boat, heaved herself in after her. Gathering graces—she went to work, pumping, breathing, pumping, breathing, mouth to mouth, will to will, life to death, life and death. Gathering graces, gathering graces—mercy, Lord—mercy, mercy Lord—Lord, Lord, Lord, have mercy.

Chapter 4

✦

SOLOMON JOGGED STEADILY along the beach. It had taken him nearly an hour to establish the fact that neither Miriam nor Ashia were on the *Kruiser*, and another twenty minutes to work out that they must have left for the adobe on the missing speedboat.

Trailed by Sam on her way back to the Hotel L'Ouverture, he endured her heartfelt appeals for him to continue his "vocation"—his books and his work with prison inmates and youths in the United States.

"Okay," she panted as she jogged alongside him. "So we'll put aside my note for now. I guess having it delivered at the party and showing up unannounced was a bad judgment call. I apologize. But I'm not apologizing for what I'm saying, because you know I'm speaking the truth. Much as you try to deny it to yourself, Solomon, you're unsettled here, and it's because you're trying to dodge your calling. You're a messenger—the world needs your words. So if you can't write anymore, if you don't have the passion to speak out anymore, if staying on this island does that to you, then you're not supposed to be here!"

Solomon quickened his pace to get away from her but, Sam being Sam, she managed to keep in stride with him. "You're suffering from acute inertia, Solomon," she continued. "It's caused by having spent too much time and energy on the wrong people, and in the wrong place, which for a dynamic visionary like you is akin to death. You need to reflect on your past and think about your future before it's too late. It's essential, Solomon."

Yes it is, and that's exactly what I'm doing, Solomon thought. *How can I be a "messenger," how can I teach and point the way, when I'm so lost myself?* He looked at Sam and wished he could explain it to her but knew if he tried, she would only argue with him. Instead, he hitched the flowing fabric of his African robe onto his shoulders and broke into a sprint.

*   *   *

Sam stopped running to catch her breath. Moving into a slow walk, her sandals in her hand, she watched Solomon racing on ahead of her and wondered why she cared so much, when he seemed at the moment to care so little about *anything*, least of all himself.

He had changed. Since his father's death, he had changed considerably. It was as though some nameless weight were sitting on his shoulders constraining him. Were she not so convinced of his larger purpose, she would leave Cape Corcos as soon as possible and write him off as just another example of wasted talent. But he had a purpose, one that she had committed herself to from the start; and right now, the only way she could assist him was by bringing him back into the reality of his own passion—his talent, his love for mankind. He had a rare gift. Few people were touched with the creative force and vision that Solomon possessed, and she wasn't going to sit back and let the twists of life strangle him to death. Watching him in the light of the full moon, silhouetted against the Caribbean Sea, she realized the long way they had come since their chance meeting in the New York subway.

It had been nearly eleven years ago. She had just been appointed as Andréa's personal assistant and was looking for literary talent to prove to Andréa that she would make an excellent agent. In the midst of this quest, she chanced upon Solomon, on the open platform of the 125th Street subway station in Harlem, reciting his twelve-page poem "Ode to the ChoKolate-Kolored Kiddies," and handing out handwritten copies. Listening to his passionate recitation, she had been so enraptured by his words that she let several trains go by just to hear how the story ended and to secure one of the copies. She handed him her card, and Solomon thanked her for her enthusiasm and invited her to attend a dramatic reading of two of his stories at a youth club the following afternoon. She went, and from that day on, she began a relentless campaign to bring Solomon under the agency's umbrella as her own personal project. Three months later Andréa gave her approval.

Struggling with a faltering relationship with Bob, her live-in fiancé, she had been only too glad to stay late at the office and work on *the Solomon project* on her own time. She read his stories, made suggestions, and wrote up endless proposals for him to receive research money to travel through Africa. On his first trip back from the continent, with his new work, she found him an editor and a publisher for his books. She canceled her wedding, but her work was a success. Within four years she had built Solomon into the agency's biggest money-maker and had become a well-respected agent.

Reflecting on their beginnings made Sam all the more determined to get Solomon back to work. His detachment meant much more to her than just the loss of a large commission. Like Solomon, she believed that if the inequality between black and white education was not tackled at a childhood level, the racial situation in America would never be rectified. Being a part of bringing Beento Blackbird to black children, being a part of bringing them their heritage, and also of educating nonblack children about the history and origins of black people brought her great satisfaction. Losing that, watching it being thrown away now, would be like losing a major part of her work, her life, her own history.

*   *   *

Solomon suddenly felt a deep affection toward Sam. As he turned back to look at her way down the beach, what she had spoken while jogging beside him moved from his intellectual memory and touched his heart. She knew him well, faults and all, and she always had the courage to voice the truth. It was that smart courageous side of her personality that attracted him. Sam challenged and inspired him to write. She understood the power and importance of the written word and encouraged him to reach out into the world, to fulfill his dream of making a difference in the lives of millions of so-called *minority* children, lifting their self-esteem, enlightening them with books full of untold stories of heroic *minority* people like themselves. For him, it was Sam's ability to inspire that made her so compellingly attractive, her physical beauty notwithstanding. She was a comfort to his intellect, which in turn comforted his soul. Glancing back again, Solomon noticed Sam curving away from the shore, heading west toward the Hotel L'Ouverture, where he knew she was staying. "Sam!" he called out, running back toward her. He felt a sudden urge to let her know he was grateful that she had come. "Sam!"

Hearing his call, Sam stopped walking and waited for Solomon to reach her.

"I hear you," he said, coming to a stop in front of her in the sand. "I'm not saying much. I don't want to say too much," he panted, "but I hear you. Give me time to think."

"Sure." Sam smiled and then continued walking toward the hotel. Solomon watched her go.

"Sam!" he called out again before she had gone too far. "What made you come?"

Sam turned to face him, tears glistening in her eyes.

"I guess you said it in your note, right?" Solomon asked, the gentleness in his voice like a caress. "Well, I'm glad you did. Thank you."

"That's what friends are for," Sam replied, the agony of love in her voice.

Solomon watched her go; he would have escorted her to the hotel but he was eager to return to the adobe. He set off sprinting along the beach to find Miriam and Ashia, filled with an ominous sense of foreboding.

Standing by the wide-open stable doors, Solomon was so relieved to see his two wives that he surprised himself by laughing. They looked so tranquil, sprawled out asleep on the bed like washed-up jellyfish, that he couldn't imagine what it was that had given him such a sense of doom. Miriam looked more serene than he had seen her in a long time, and Ashia, with her fingers entwined in Miriam's wet hair, looked like the innocent child she was when he first met her. The only telltale sign of her present womanhood was Amankwa's mouth resting limply on her nipple, where he must have drunk himself to sleep.

Looking down at Amankwa, Solomon heard Sam's words echoing in his mind. "Come back to the States, Solomon, fulfill your purpose. You owe it to yourself. You owe it to your son. *Bring him with you . . .*"

Mindful not to wake the women, Solomon lifted Amankwa off the bed. His son. Every time he looked at him, the miracle struck him anew. Cradling him in his arms, he walked out, quietly closing the door behind him.

When he woke a few hours later, there was a blessedness that had settled on the house as fine as a layer of the golden sand that surrounded it. Stretched out in the second bedroom, Amankwa was playing quietly beside him on the bed. Sitting Amankwa on his shoulders, Solomon wandered outside and was surprised to find Miriam and Ashia sitting at the table, eating a light brunch and laughing together—warm and familiar as childhood friends. They told Solomon they had decided to prepare a special dinner. Ashia would need certain foods and African spices, so Miriam requested that as soon as he finished his brunch, he head out in search of the various items.

Cruising on his motorbike along the coast toward town, Solomon reflected on how last night he had thought his life was complete turbulence, yet today it appeared as though things were calm and in order. *In fact*, he mused with pleasure, *things are more calm and in order than they have been since my father's death, and that was what? . . . Almost a year ago now.*

Lost in his own thoughts, Solomon did not notice Leo Rap-A-Tap or the immaculately dressed woman clinging to him from the backseat of his moped as they zoomed past him in the direction of Miriam's adobe.

Chapter 5

✦

*H*I, IS SOLOMON HOME?"
Miriam did not bother to look up from the sink. She did not need to see her to know that Miss Americana, walking uninvited into her kitchen, meant trouble. There was no doubt in her mind that this hair-straightened, cat-eyed creature was the selfsame hussy who had thrown Solomon into his whirlwind of confused self-analysis. As far as Miriam was concerned, the end result of such self-indulgent introspection was always discontent, leading people to blame and attack those who love them, the way Solomon had attacked her on his return from his father's funeral, calling their lives together "an illusion."

"Is Solomon home?" Sam repeated.

"No."

"When do you expect him back?"

"Solomon come and go as he please."

Miriam continued wiping her surgical instruments. She held her breath against the synthetic sweetness of Sam's perfume. Sam fumbled around in her cream leather purse. "I'd like to leave him a note." She held out a letter on Hotel L'Ouverture stationery. Miriam flashed her eyes at the sealed envelope and carried on wiping. Sam looked around for a place to leave it. She leaned it against a jar of mango jam on the kitchen table and asked if she might have a glass of ice water.

"When you leaving?" Miriam quizzed, without attempting to disguise the hostility in her voice.

"I've only just got here," Sam retorted.

"Me no ask you when you got here, me ask you when was you

leaving," Miriam clarified cooly, handing her a glass of tepid tap water.

"I'm here on business. I'll leave when I've accomplished what I came to do," Sam replied, equally as cool. "But if you want me out of your house, just say so."

"I just did," Miriam bristled.

"Thank you for the water," Sam said, taking one sip and handing it straight back.

"You need to go home, Miss St. Jude," Miriam asserted, standing the glass in the sink. "Solomon don't want you."

"The name is St. *James*. Sam St. James." Sam removed her sunglasses from her hair and slid them over her eyes. "And Miriam," she remarked as she headed for the door, "when I do go home, I'm taking Solomon with me."

"I don't think so, Sam," Miriam retorted.

"But you're not sure, are you, Miriam?"

Chapter 6

✦

SAM COULD TELL by the jingle of keys and the light tap-tap on wood that the little girl who helped around the hotel was outside the door of her suite. "Hey, sweetie," she smiled as she opened the door onto Cassie's bright face.

"Uncle Toussaint say, Sergeant Vincent say, Captain Morrow and him here with the police car to go give you ride, and him go help you catch the plane," Cassie recounted, concentrating hard in order to relay the message correctly.

Sam hesitated, debating what to do. Since the sudden collapse of Corcos Airlines, on which she had a return ticket, the few flights from Cape Corcos to the States were so heavily overbooked that she had been told she might not get a seat for another ten days—not even if she were prepared to pay the hefty bribes desperate travelers had been forking out to get on board. When she came in from reading on the beach that afternoon, the hotel manager had informed her, as he handed her the keys to her suite, that he had managed to confirm her on a plane to Miami, leaving at 10 P.M. that evening, with a connecting flight to New York. A little panicked at the thought of leaving so quickly, with the situation with Solomon unresolved, Sam had thanked the manager for his efforts but explained that since it was already five P.M., she probably would not be able to make the flight. In light of that, she was surprised by Cassie's message. He was obviously still trying to orchestrate her departure.

Following Cassie down the atrium stairs, Sam noticed the manager, or "Uncle Toussaint," as Cassie called him, whispering suspiciously with Captain Morrow at the front desk and slipping him what looked like a large wad of money. She also noticed that the manager, who had been very cordial when she first arrived on the Island, was now avoiding looking her in the eye—the way she used to avoid looking at her daddy when she was a little girl and she knew she had done something wrong. "Look at me, Sam," her daddy used to insist. "Look me in the eye." She would fight not to, because whenever she looked him in the eye, she would admit her guilt. "Like I coach my legal associates, never look away from anybody," he told her when she was leaving home for college. "Whatever you feel inside, always look a person in the eye. It inspires confidence. Confidence, Sam!" her daddy would drill, whenever she doubted herself. "Success in life is just a matter of confidence. Act like you've got confidence, even when you don't. By the time you need to draw on it, you'll have been acting it for so long, folk will believe you; and when folk get to believing in you, Sam, why then you get to believing in yourself."

"But don't forget God now, Samantha," her grandmother Etta used to add, fearing that her granddaughter would grow up too much like her daddy and mistake a desk for a pulpit, and a courtroom for a church.

Confidence, Sam repeated in her mind as she reached the bottom of the stairs. Remembering her father's words gave her a new resolve. She had intended not to take the flight, but remembering who she was, and what you could get in life if you had the confidence to try, she decided to aim for what she really wanted: which was to be on the plane that night, with Solomon onboard beside her.

"Good evening," she said pleasantly, shaking Captain Morrow's hand. "I understand you gentlemen have arranged a way for me to catch that flight to Miami. I really appreciate it."

"No problem," the captain said with a grin, remembering he had found Sam *stunningly beautiful*, enough to impel him to stand up when she arrived at Cape Corcos Airport.

Sam was mystified as to why she was getting such preferential treatment, until on walking out half an hour later with the captain carrying her suitcase, she overheard Emilia Joseph's loud whisper, and the reason became clear.

Sam slid into the waiting police car, the words running through her brain. "Congratulations. Miriam should be well pleased," the manager's wife had muttered to her husband disapprovingly. "What you going to do next? Poison Ashia?"

Chapter 7

✦

THERE WERE FLOWERS surrounded by seashells that Ashia had collected and arranged on the patio table. She had insisted on preparing dinner herself, banning Solomon and Miriam from entering the kitchen. Happy to comply, they sat outside while she cooked. No one had mentioned Sam's visit, or the letter she had left for Solomon. Spotting it on the kitchen table while unpacking the groceries, he had read it and headed straight back into town and back home again without mentioning a word.

Ashia entreated Peace to join them for dinner, and he accepted. He put on his best garments and found a giant delicate pink shell as a gift, which he placed on the table to add to her collection.

"Thank you, Peace, it's beautiful," she said, stepping from the kitchen, holding a crystal bowl of lemon water for Solomon to wash his hands.

"My goodness, Ashia, this is quite a banquet," Solomon complimented, dipping his fingers in the bowl.

"Every meal of a king is a banquet," Ashia replied graciously.

Miriam closed her eyes.

"Are you sleepy, Mama Miriam?"

"No, Ashia, I'm not sleepy. I was just thinking how lovely everything looks, and what a beautiful evening this is."

Ashia smiled, pleased with herself. She thanked Miriam, disappeared into the kitchen, and came back with a clean bowl of water for Peace to wash his hands.

Peace hesitated. It had been years since anyone served him, especially a woman. His fingers trembled ever so slightly as he lowered them into the water. "Thank you for eating with us," Ashia said in a hushed voice. He nodded, bowing his head over the bowl.

Peace was deep in thought. She reminded him, this woman-child from Africa, of his child-bride from Balanique. Meeting Ashia was the first time he had seen his dead wife in another person's smile, or conjured up in another person's gaiety. The way Ashia laughed and played in the sand and picked up shells as if collecting precious gems reminded him of Rafael, of how she used to stay and play in the woods while he went out with his comrades. The women all complained that Rafael was too childish, yet they had loved and protected her like a daughter. Like Miriam with Ashia. Miriam loved Ashia more than she realized. He had watched her, watched all of them, all four of them—Miriam, Solomon, Ashia, and Amankwa—their love was thick like Rafael's chocolate rum cake, the cake she had been going to make for him the day . . . the day he took her life . . .

Ashia handed Peace a small hand towel and smiled into his sad reflective eyes. She tossed the water into the sand, and disappeared again into the kitchen. Solomon poured them all coconut juice from the large decanter on the table. Almost immediately, Ashia reappeared with more clean water and stood before Miriam. "Would you like to wash your hands, Mama Miriam?"

Miriam looked down at the bowl. As often as Ashia had offered it to Solomon, it was the first time she had ever offered it to her.

"Yes, thank you," she said finally, dipping her hands into the water. The two women stared at each other. They stared and then smiled and then laughed, laughed fully, their laughter taking over their entire bodies. Ashia tossed the water into the sand, wiping tears from her eyes. Solomon asked what had happened, what it was that had been so funny.

"Life," Miriam replied. "Just life."

Dinner was a delight. Everyone was content and of one accord. The sea lulled quiet and easy, as the frail sun shed a delicate orange haze that stroked their heads, feathered their faces, and tinged the tips of their clothing. Amankwa, who Peace had laid in his bassinet by the kitchen door, had sucked happily on one of the white satin ribbons Solomon had tied to its handle, and fallen right to sleep.

In the sensory silence that ensued, Ashia noticed that Peace was watching her. She didn't mind. His eyes were kind and unobtrusive. It was part of the enchantment of the evening; everyone watched everyone, and no one minded or looked away. There were moments of excited chatter, moments of laughter, moments of calm conversation, and moments of silence. Whatever the moment, there was a constant underlying harmony that kept the evening sweet. They might have sat there for hours, had their tranquility not been shattered by the sudden sound of a siren blaring.

"Wilberforce," Captain Morrow called to Solomon as he leaped out of the police car, "we have a lady here in urgent need of her passport, which apparently is in your possession. She say you took it to try to get plane tickets back to America, is that correct?"

Solomon took a quick inventory of the situation. He was surrounded. Everyone had jumped up from the table and headed to the front of the house to see what the emergency was. Even in the evening haze, he recognized instantly that it was Sam seated in the back of the police car. Glancing to his left where Miriam had been walking by his side, he noticed she had come to a standstill several yards away from him. Peace, standing just behind his right shoulder, took a few paces backward and lowered himself into a squat on his mat by the big wooden doors. Ashia rounded the corner last and stopped abruptly. Everyone watching and waiting for him. It was his move. They were back at it. Championship chess. He was the king in serious check.

"Yes. That's correct. I've got her passport in the house," he said as casually as he could. "What's going on?"

"Evening. Solomon, sorry to interrupt you like this," Sam apologized as she stepped out of the car. "I didn't realize our entrance was going to be quite so dramatic. Could I talk to you for a minute?"

Solomon looked around awkwardly at their silent audience. "Sure," he said, taking a few steps toward her. Sam turned away from him and walked into the sand away from the adobe, obliging Solomon to follow.

"Toussaint managed to get me a flight to Miami. It's leaving out of Barbados in a few hours, so we're in a bit of a hurry; hence, the intrusion," Sam explained. "Of course, I need my passport, but I also wondered if you've considered what I said," she queried softly. "I mean about coming back to the States with me. Maybe being in New

York will trigger you to write again. You know, being around all that energy. Maybe it will take your coming back to remind yourself of how much what you do is needed. Besides, look at you—I can tell you're craving soft warm chestnuts. Chestnut deprivation is written all over your face," Sam smiled.

Ashia disappeared around the side of the house in response to Amankwa's cries. Miriam and Peace kept their vigil, watching Sam and Solomon talking quietly as they stood in the sand.

Striding back after a few moments, Solomon leaned into the window of the police car and asked Captain Morrow to wait just five more minutes, thanking him profusely for taking so much trouble to assist Sam.

"I'll be right back," Solomon said as he went running into the house. Grabbing his leather satchel from the bed, he looked up to see Sam standing barefoot in the sand whispering something to Miriam. Whatever it was Sam said to her, Miriam's face registered defeat.

Uneasy, Solomon hurried back out. "I'm here, I'm ready," he said. "Let's go." Sam slid into the backseat of the car.

"I'm going to the airport," Solomon announced to Miriam as he slid in beside Sam. Sergeant Vincent jumped into the driver's seat and sparked the ignition.

"Solomon? . . ." Miriam called out in thinly disguised panic. Unheeded, she dodged out of the way as the sergeant turned the police car around and sped off, lights flashing, its siren blaring. *As if heralding the end of the world,* Miriam thought.

"Do you really want a man like Solomon confined to a place like this? It would kill him," Sam had whispered. "Don't kill him, Miriam. Don't make him stay here and die for you. Let him go."

Chapter 8

✦

NIGHT WAS NEVER going to fall. That's how it seemed. The sky was holding daylight in its arms and would not let it go. Frail as the sun had appeared during dinner, Miriam sat beneath the still-defiant rays staring out to sea. She had walked until her body was so numb that she couldn't feel the dampness of the sand beneath her. Even the weight of the sharp sterile scalpel she held tightly in her fist seemed overwhelming. She would put it down—lay it next to her in the sand—but she couldn't—she was unable to release it. As she passed through the kitchen, the siren of Solomon's departure still ringing in her ears, it had caught her attention, lying there on cotton wool by the sink where she had left it. She had tried to walk past it, but the shiny steel blade had called out to her.

Gripping it in her fist, she felt protected. As she wandered far from the adobe along the deserted part of the beach used only by the occasional fisherman, the scalpel gave her a strange sense of comfort. It was an assurance that she didn't have to suffer anything she didn't want to endure. She had used it to assist in bringing life into the world, so why not use it to assist in bringing death? If pain became too unbearable, she could put a stop to it. An easing. A releasing. A letting of blood. Slow, soothing—light as a hum. A blade of light piercing through her—all she would have to do is flow . . . let her blood flow like water . . . it would be so easy . . .

Miriam sat gripping the scalpel.

Seabirds made their final flight for the day, disappearing into their secret hideaway, and still Miriam sat, gripping the scalpel.

It would be so easy.

But sitting there, gripping onto the scalpel, something stood in front of her. She wanted the shadow to move, but it didn't. It bent over her, tried to steal her scalpel. She grappled, fought it, fought the shadow.

But it won. Snatched it away. The cruel shadow snatched away her scalpel.

"I don't have the years to start again," she cried. "Where am I going to find the years to start again."

Peace squatted down by her side. Miriam continued to cry. He placed the scalpel behind him. Stroked her back, watched her. Keeping guard.

Darkness fell. A welcome cloak for the nakedness of her sorrow.

*   *   *

Peace walked to meet Solomon as he came toward them; he placed his hand on Solomon's arm, reached into his robe, and pulled out the scalpel he had grappled from Miriam. Solomon understood. Without any words, he understood. It was the same scalpel she had used to cut an incision on her forearm when he had returned to the Island late last winter. Peace tucked it back into his robe, gave a tender parting look to Miriam, and walked back across the sand to the adobe.

Solomon approached Miriam as cautiously as a candle bearer approaches an altar. He knelt beside her body curled up in the cold sand. "I been looking for you, gorgeous." His fingers ran through her hair like feathers through water.

Miriam shivered and opened her eyes. "Solomon?" She looked at him as if he were an apparition. She closed her eyes again, laid her cheek back down on the cold sand. "I thought you'd gone," she murmured. "I really thought you'd gone."

Chapter 9

✦

THERE WAS NO WAY they could go back to the manner in which they lived before. Not now that he knew what his dreams had cost. Solomon debated what to do, searched for the answer. How to handle Miriam. How to handle Ashia. How to handle himself. Just as he was beginning to despair of ever coming up with a livable solution, the letter arrived.

He sat on the bed with the letter in his hand, waiting for Ashia. Since the day of Sam's departure, Ashia had taken to wandering off with Amankwa for hours and hours at a time. Solomon had no idea when she would return but guessed she would come soon, because she always returned before dark. He was anxious for her to come home. Every time he got up to do something, he was unable to concentrate on whatever it was and he would end up back on the bed, waiting. He wanted to make it a happy moment, a welcome surprise. After all, it would be the fulfillment of a dream. Not his, but hers. *That's what counts*, he told himself, his heart already aching, *her ultimate well-being. It's the best solution for everyone.*

Sitting on the bed, facing the sliding doors, Solomon saw Ashia coming toward him from the patio with Amankwa tied on her back. She was holding the bottom of her skirt in her hands, using it as a basket. Her exposed legs were wet with seawater, glistening with sand. Seeing him looking at her, she smiled and quickened her pace.

Panic rose in Solomon's heart. Perhaps he should not have packed until he had told her. Perhaps he should have told her two days ago when he first got the letter. He had been worried that if he told her before he had a chance to think about it or call and make arrangements, she would talk him out of it, or he would talk her out of it.

Now, suddenly, all that rationale seemed unreasonable. He should have given her the letter when it arrived, but it was too late.

Ashia stood at the door of the second bedroom in speechless bewilderment. Everything of hers was gone. She stepped gingerly into the room. Even her sun-dried laundry that she had brought in just before taking her walk and left folded on the small side table was nowhere to be seen.

Solomon sat in nervous silence as she opened up her skirt and tumbled a pile of colored seashells onto the bed. Rubbing her hands together, she brushed off tiny grains of sand as she continued to glance around the room in alarm. Solomon reached for her hands, finished wiping them clean with his own, and pulled her down onto his lap.

"Toussaint gave me this," he said, handing her a letter that had been mailed to her via Mr. Opoku's post office box in Ghana and redirected to *Mr. Solomon Wilberforce* at the *Hotel L'Ouverture.*

"They said yours were the highest test scores and the most imaginative essay." *Light,* Solomon told himself, *keep your voice light.* "They've been trying to contact you for months. Enrollment was actually last week, so you missed it, but there's a direct flight at ten A.M. tomorrow morning that would get you there in time for orientation. I spoke to them today, and they said that with you being a foreign student, orientation was especially important. So when I couldn't find you, I thought I'd get you ready, just in case."

"What are you talking about?" The tone of Ashia's voice heightened Solomon's nervousness.

"You passed your entrance exams, Ashia," he clarified, making his voice lighter than ever. "You got into the college in London."

"What on earth are you talking about?" Ashia rose up from his knee, backed away from him as if he had a disease she did not want to catch. "How can I go now?" she asked, incredulous. "I have you. I have my baby."

"Amankwa's not a problem, Ashia, I'll take care of him."

"Stop it, Solomon. What are you saying?"

The startled look on Ashia's face made Solomon want to weep. "I'm just saying I'll take care of Amankwa. Ashia, this was your dream, it's what you wanted, to go away to college—in London."

"I have not done anything wrong. I will not be banished!" Ashia stood before him, adamant. Ancestral warriors lined up behind her, armed and ready to fight. Solomon looked at her, standing defiantly in the middle of the room, her letter of acceptance discarded on the floor. *Banished!* Is that how she saw this? If she could only be inside his head, inside his heart, she would understand. Banished? No— loved, unbound, encouraged, but never banished.

"Don't do this, Solomon." Ashia's voice surrounded him like a lasso. "Don't punish me. Don't punish me by sending me away." She pulled the rope and tightened the knot.

"Stop it, Ashia! I'm not punishing you," Solomon struggled, try- ing to loosen himself. He needed to stay focused on her future. "I'm not sending you to prison, Ashia! I just want to support you to put you through college."

"A wife cannot be sold away like cattle!" Ashia derided. "What did I do to you, Solomon? What did I do wrong?"

"You didn't do anything wrong."

"Then what are you saying?"

"Don't you understand? You're young, Ashia, and bright, and I don't want to eat up your life anymore."

"You are not eating up my life. Now that we can be together all the time, it's better."

"No, Ashia, it's not."

"Why? Why do you say that?"

"Things are so different here, can't you tell? Our love makes people mad."

"If people are mad, so what?" Ashia scoffed, raising her voice.

"So if we're unhappy ourselves, then none of this makes any sense," Solomon shouted back in frustration.

"But we are not unhappy!" Ashia argued with force. "The other time Miriam and I were very upset only because we thought you wanted to leave us. We thought you wanted Sam. We thought you were going away with her. We did not realize you only wanted to help her catch a plane. You stayed with us, and we are all right. I am all right, Solomon," she appealed. "Miriam is all right."

"Miriam's not all right!" Solomon erupted. "It's killing her!" Heated, he sprang to his feet. The foundation of his world was quak- ing. He stood burning in the molten lava of a volcano he now real- ized had been simmering for years. "Go to college, Ashia. Please! Please! Go and be who you're supposed to be."

"I am who I am supposed to be. I am your wife," she insisted. "I am your *wife*, Solomon! Don't you want me?"

"YES! YES! I WANT YOU! I WANT YOU, BUT THE PRICE IS TOO HIGH! DON'T YOU UNDERSTAND, ASHIA? THE PRICE IS JUST TOO HIGH!" Molten lava singed his temples, scorched his clothes. He was burning, burning alive.

"Then, why? Why did you marry me to throw me away? I bore you a son. Now you want to throw me away. Why? Why, Solomon?"

"STOP!" Solomon smashed his fist against the sliding door, the broken glass shattering to the ground. He was back in the shed again, back in Aunt Josephine's musty wooden shed, fists slashing through the air, breaking glass, defending—trapped—defending—his indefensible self.

"I'm sorry," he whispered.

In the silence that washed over them, Solomon heard the sea. The soothing sound of the waves rolled with the silence into the room, helped drown the echoes of their shouted voices, flushed clean the crash of broken glass. In that silence Miriam appeared in the bedroom door, unheard and unseen. She stood looking at the carnage of all that had been left unsaid throughout the years. All the hurt they had never passed through. All the pain they had never declared.

Ashia saw Miriam standing in the doorway and looked to her for help. "Tell him, Mama Miriam," she coaxed. "Tell him we are all right as we are. He thinks we are unhappy, tell him we are not unhappy. Tell him we love each other, and it is better for us all to be together than apart."

Hope returned to Solomon's heart at hearing the faith in Ashia's voice. Maybe she was right. Maybe they truly were all right as they were. It was different, but maybe their all being together was just another level to their love. The way they should have first begun—instead of his fragmenting himself across the globe. Maybe this was the way—the way of his ancestors—united under one roof. Maybe that would allow him to work again. Create again. Soar again.

Holding the wrist of his grazed hand, Solomon turned to Miriam in the doorway, waiting keenly for her response.

"Tell him, Mama Miriam, tell him we are not unhappy," Ashia urged.

Her wild, petrified eyes shot a pleading look at Miriam. Then her body, face and all, sank down into the impossible, terrifying, un-breathable deep.

"Tell him we love each other."

Miriam turned her back and walked away.

Chapter 10

✦

*I*T BOTHERED SOLOMON that Ashia had not let him accompany her to the airport. He wondered if it was in retaliation for his never letting her escort him to the Kumasi coach station. He had always felt it was less wrenching to part at the house, so their parting image of each other would be in a setting where their love abounded, rather than in a crowded bus station or at the gate in an airport full of strangers. But now, as the one left behind, he understood why she had always wanted to see him off. It didn't feel right not escorting a loved one as far along the journey as one could. He was glad that Ashia had at least allowed him to have Kawasaki send his driver, Tobias, to take her to the plane. Solomon looked up at the sky. He thought he heard the sound of an aircraft, but the only things flying were seabirds. "Look, Amankwa," he said, pointing heavenward. "Birds, seabirds." He had always been careful with Amankwa, but this morning he held him more tenderly than ever before. It was as though he were holding not only his baby but also Ashia's trust, which was sacred to him. It had not been easy for her to leave her son behind. Even though she had not said much, he knew it had not been easy. He had pointed out to her that she was going to a new country, to live in an apartment by herself, to attend college and study for a degree. How would she cope with all that and a baby too? She would end up having to leave him in the care of strangers in a strange land. Why do that when he had a father who would delight in taking care of him? Who was desperate not to be separated from him? Who would raise him with all the love and care he could give? Whether he ended up on the Island or in the States, Amankwa would have a good home, he promised Ashia. He also promised to fly her to wherever they were, to spend her vacations with them whenever she wanted. She had not said much but must have seen the wisdom of his reasoning, because she had left Amankwa with him.

Ashia had walked out that morning in a knee-length ash-gray suit that Jezz had apparently given her. It looked strange to Solomon; he had never seen her wear European clothes before. She had even braided her numerous twists into one and suppressed it under a black beret. It was as if the free spirit-child he had met all those years ago weeping and dancing in an open field had vanished overnight and been replaced by a controlled somber woman with the body of Ashia but the essence of a stranger. She had said very little since the previous evening, when she had gone tiptoeing through the broken glass, clutching the maroon leather Bible Auntie Mercy had given her. With Amankwa still wrapped on her back, she had walked along the shore to the old canoe and sat in it, singing in her native tongue. Long past midnight she stopped singing, walked inside, and told Solomon she would go to London. He had told her they could book a later flight if she needed more time, but she had said no, she would like to go as soon as possible, and that he was right about Amankwa. She would leave Amankwa in his care, at least until she got settled.

Solomon eased himself from the patio sofa, jiggling his arms to keep Amankwa from fussing.

"You really think you should take that baby out walking?" Miriam called from the kitchen.

"Yeah."

"You don't think the sun going to get too high, Solomon? Maybe you should leave him here with me."

"No, it's okay. I'll put his big hat on him."

Going into the second bedroom to find Amankwa's hat, Solomon noticed the kangaroo he had given Ashia lying on the bed. He had packed it for her in her suitcase to take to London, but she must have taken it out just before she left. Looking into its glassy eyes, he wished it could tell him if she had left it behind in anger or in love.

Solomon stepped off the patio into the sand. He was eager to walk. He needed to think. Had he made the right decision? Was Ashia going to be all right? What about Miriam? Sam? His future?

He looked down at Amankwa and made sure the wide-brimmed hat shaded his body from the early morning sun. Peeling open the African fabric he was wrapped in, which Ashia had used to tie him onto her back, he exposed Amankwa's skin to the warm sea air. "You love the sunshine, don't you, little man? Like your mama, and your daddy. We're Africans." Solomon felt a pang of sweet sorrow. "That's from your mama," he cooed, bending over Amankwa's chubby little body and kissing his forehead as though it were a holy relic. Amankwa smiled through his Ashia eyes and grabbed onto his daddy's nose. "Ouch," Solomon flinched, feigning pain, as the tiny nails pressed into his flesh. "Ouch-ouch-ouch-ouch, ouch." Amankwa grabbed harder, which made both of them laugh.

Walking along the tide, pointing out seabirds to his son, Solomon barely heard Kawasaki's cream Rolls-Royce hush along the shore behind them. By the time he became aware of it, it was coming to a stop a few yards away from him. Ashia jumped out of the backseat, hobbling in her high-heeled shoes as she ran through the sand toward him. "What happened?" Solomon asked anxiously, a myriad of scenarios running through his mind.

Ashia reached for Amankwa. Solomon stiffened his grip around his child. "What are you doing? Ashia, what happened? What's wrong?" Ashia didn't answer him. Instead, she tried forcefully to unfold his arms from around Amankwa. "Ashia, what is it? What are you doing? What's going on?" Fear entered Solomon's stomach like an ominous wind, propelling him to take a backward step.

"I want my son." Ashia lurched forward, digging her fingers into his forearm. She was the center of the earth, the sand that made the rocks, the land that holds back the sea, she *could* not, *would* not, be dissuaded, distracted, or denied. "Give him!" Bending Solomon's fingers backward (careful, careful not to harm her baby), she pried open his hand, pulling on it, peeling his arm off Amankwa's back. Solomon clamped it back around again, firm, protective, cradling (careful, careful not to harm his baby). Ashia squeezed her fingers into Solomon's tight embrace and lifted Amankwa out of his father's clutches. It was not her strength that overpowered him, it was the force in her eyes. He could see them, standing there, reflected in her dark brown pupils, *Ancestral warriors lined up behind her, armed and ready to fight . . .* They were small but mighty, hundreds of brave African women brandishing their spears, zealously protecting their daughter.

Solomon appealed to them, would have knelt at their feet, groveled if need be—anything to win back his son. "Don't do this, Ashia," he pleaded, holding on to Amankwa's tiny fist. "We decided. We decided last night. Let him stay, Ashia. It's better this way."

"It is not better."

"Don't, Ashia. Don't do this."

"I am his mother."

"And I'm his father."

"Release him!" Ashia commanded.

Solomon gripped his hand firmer around Amankwa's fist.

"Solomon! Let him go!"

He couldn't. Solomon thought about it, but he couldn't. Standing there, holding on to Amankwa's fist, it was as though the entire world around him were obliterated and the only thing with any life worth having was that tiny little fist in his hand.

"I won't leave without my son."

They were Ashia's final words. Even though Solomon didn't let go of Amankwa's fist right away, he knew in his heart that the battle was over. Where were his protectors? Where were his ancestors? *Do any of them know me?* Solomon wondered. *Have they in their spirit forms kept an eye on their children's children's children to see who we are and where we have been scattered?* "Wilberforce," he murmured under his breath, hoping one of the spirits would recognize him by name. "Solomon Eustace Wilberforce . . ."

Ashia touched Solomon's wrist. There was no resistance left. Lifting his hand up gently, she removed it from around Amankwa's fist. Hoisting up her little son's body, she rested his head on her shoulder. The African cloth that was covering him fell onto the sand and she left it there; stepping over it, she walked back to the car. Tobias jumped out from the driver's seat, opened the back door for her, jumped back in, and eased the car away.

Solomon stooped down, picking up the fallen cloth. Holding it to his nose, he inhaled the essence of Ashia mingled with the sweet baby scent of Amankwa. Triggered by the smells, he turned around and followed the Rolls-Royce gliding through the sand. As if in a daze, he threw the cloth around his neck and broke into a steady jog. Ashia turned her head and watched him through the back window, Amankwa's eyes peeking over her shoulder. Spurred by his son's innocent gaze, Solomon burst into a sudden sprint. Pumping his feet into the sand, he raked through the air with his arms, gathering emptiness with every stride. Terrified that there would be no end to the nothingness he was amassing, he pushed himself faster and faster, inching closer and closer to the cream metal car that was sliding along the beach like an enemy submarine, stealing away his armload of joy.

"AMANKWAAAAAA!" His penetrating cry was lost in the vast indifference of the morning air. Lunging forward, he stretched out his arm and grabbed the handle of the back door. The car accelerated. Solomon felt the ache in his thighs, the rawness in his throat, the burn of friction on his hand as he clung on, running, fighting, screaming for his son.

Ashia waved her hand over the back window, tears streaming down her face. Lips moving, she was trying to tell him something, but he couldn't hear her, couldn't read what her lips were saying. He wanted to tell her he was sorry, he was wrong, he had made a mistake. He didn't know exactly when he had made it, but he knew by the swords clashing inside him and the tears streaming down her cheeks that somewhere along the path of life, he had made a terrible, terrible mistake.

With a final burst, he ran with all his power, muscles stretching, lungs expanding—it was not enough. He had let it slip. Looking along the beach, he realized the car was way, way ahead of him. He had let it slip. Winded, panting desperately, he doubled over; noticing something jutting out in the sand, he staggered to lean on it in the hopes of catching his breath. With his face to the ground, he inhaled great rasping gulps as he clutched his aching rib cage and instructed his mind to breathe, simply breathe. When he had steadied himself a little, he realized he was leaning on the old canoe that Cassie loved to play in. Dragging it into the water, he climbed inside and collapsed.

With nobody to paddle the oars, the sea took control, drifting him on the current of its waves as it rocked the canoe farther and farther away from the shore. Rock-a-bye Solomon, rock-a-bye. Somewhere in him he knew—somewhere in him he could feel himself being taken away. He was glad—glad to be washed away. Rock-a-bye, Solomon, rock-a-bye-my-baby . . . Annetta Anika Wilberforce was rocking him in her arms.

BOOK NINE

✧

Winter—Full Circle

The gift . . . The promise . . . The rainbow . . .

Chapter 1

". . . MEANWHILE in the Caribbean, on the island of Saint Germaine, a man living in a cave has been identified as Mr. Solomon Wilberforce . . ."

Ashia was still sitting on the couch absentmindedly fiddling with her wedding band. It had been nearly an hour since Olu took Amankwa out for a walk in the park, and she had done nothing but sit there trying to unscramble and digest the information the BBC had reported on the news.

". . . A former resident of Cape Corcos Island, Mr. Solomon Wilberforce was reported missing five months ago when he went for a jog on a Cape Corcos beach and never returned . . ."

The wild-looking picture they had shown of Solomon standing bare-chested in the mouth of a cave haunted her mind.

". . . Mr. Wilberforce, who wrote under the pseudonym Beento Blackbird, is the author of the widely acclaimed bestselling children's novels, The Adventures of Beento Blackbird *. . ."*

Had he suffered a breakdown? Was he in an accident? Did he suffer some sort of concussion and lose his memory?

"Until this recent sighting, Mr. Wilberforce was missing, presumed dead . . ."

Ashia's mind was crowded with unanswered questions, but she knew it would not be good for Olu to come back with Amankwa from the playground and find her still sitting in front of the television in a stupor, so she forced herself to get up. At least if she finished making notes on the article she was studying, she would be able to sit down with Olu and have a nice breakfast, which would dispel the thin bright-red twinge of temper he had left hanging in the air when he walked out of the flat slamming the door behind him. He had mentioned several times that his biggest fear was her abandoning their relationship if Solomon were found. She needed to compose herself and let him know that wouldn't happen.

Passing through the narrow hall on her way to the bathroom, Ashia noticed a brown paper package sitting on the small telephone table. As soon as she saw it, she realized that it must be the package Olu had gone to collect from her former landlady. Picking it up, she noticed the bright Caribbean stamps and the black italic letters: *MRS. ASHIA WILBERFORCE.* There was no doubt in her mind that the package was from Solomon. She recognized his handwriting immediately. "Solomon," she whispered to herself. Just seeing his scrawly black swirl brought his presence into the hallway, as if his tall earth-brown body were pressing up against her in the cramped space. She could feel him all over her. There wasn't enough room for his long legs, not enough room for his smooth broad chest or his strong expansive arms. She found herself struggling with the urge to apologize to him for the inconvenience of the crush. She knew this was not the kind of London flat in which he would expect to find her.

He had prepaid her board and tuition for a year, arranging for her to live in a spacious two-bedroom flat overlooking Hyde Park. She had loved it, but as soon as Jezz telephoned her to let her know that "Solomon disappeared," she had panicked and written to Olu, saying she was thinking of quitting college in order to find a full-time job. Having graduated himself, Olu, determined that she should not drop out, had flown to London to help. One of the first things he had done was find himself a night job cleaning vending machines so he could support himself and still be free to watch Amankwa for her during the day, saving her the cost of a baby-sitter. He had also persuaded the owners of her building to apply her rent to one of their smaller less expensive properties in order to stretch her funds. That's how she had ended up in this meager dwelling, for which she was grateful, but in which Solomon's invisible presence had barely enough space to maneuver.

Forgetting she had been on her way to the bathroom, Ashia rushed into the kitchen in search of a sharp knife to cut the strings and open the package.

There was no letter. Ashia's heart sank. She riffled through the layers of brown paper, but there was no letter, just half a dozen sand-painted illustrations and a handwritten manuscript entitled *Freedom Flight* by Beento Blackbird. Throwing her own books on the floor, she sat down, turned the first page of the manuscript, and began to read the story . . .

Ashia's heart leaped. There it was, inserted between pages six and seven, the letter she had been hoping for, written in minute characters almost too small to decipher. She lifted it closer to her eyes, her nose picking up the scent of burnt wood smoked into the paper. With her heart nervously racing, she read:

My Darling Ashia.

I am writing this letter to you from a cave, where I have been secluded for the past five months. I ended up here on the day you left Cape Corcos with our son, and have been unable to emerge. My only contact has been with a local fisherman who has kindly provided me with what little I have needed that nature did not already provide.

Ashia, I have had so much time to think things over, yet I barely know how or where to begin. I know I can never rectify all that I have done to you. I can never explain to you my behavior since the first day I met you. While in this cave, I wrote everything down: pages and pages of my love, my life, my feelings, delving back as far as I can remember. I was going to send it all to you, but on reading it, I found it not worth the paper it was written on. Its most valuable use is to fuel fire. So, instead, I send you fragments of explanations of my life by way of a child's story. Please read the enclosed manuscript, and also read it to Amankwa. He will understand it differently as he grows. I believe now that Beento Blackbird is the only good thing to come out of me. Other than Amankwa, of course, whom I credit mostly to God and you. Wonderful Amankwa, to whom I hope to give better in the future than I have given in the past. It is the future, Ashia, that I need to talk to you about. I am not a perfect man; I cannot be a perfect father. But I believe I can be a good father. I never had the benefit of a father in my own life, not of any significance. I survived without one, but there are many things that I missed. Things I do not want my son to be deprived of. Ashia, no matter what happens between you and me, I believe in my heart we can find a way to raise our son together, in a way in which everybody benefits—most important, him. When I see you, which I pray will be soon, we can collaborate on how best to raise him jointly. I have thoughts, but I want to also hear yours.

Meanwhile, Ashia, I have signed all royalties for Beento Blackbird books to be divided equally between Amankwa and you. It is not to "sell you away," or buy your forgiveness, it is to reassure myself that irrespective of what transpires between us, you will both always be well housed and well fed. On the day I came to ask for your hand, I promised your mother that I would never let you down, and yet I have. I promised to be yours till death do us part. I know now that I was wrong to do so. I have made mistakes, Ashia, committed irreparable wrongs. If by dying, I could undo the pain I have caused you, I would; but the past is irredeemable, so I live for the future, praying constantly for guidance. Whatever happens, Ashia, know this one thing: you have been the joy of my loneliest hours, my most passionate love, my teacher, my pupil, and my friend. You are one of the finest human beings I have ever encountered on God's earth. The pride I feel at having fathered a child mothered by you is inexpressible. The life-giving love that you have poured into me throughout the years runs constantly through my veins. You are in my blood, Ashia; you are in my heart; you are in every breath I take. I will never stop loving you.

Yours throughout eternity,

Solomon

Chapter 2

✦

SAM HAD BEEN STRUGGLING with the manuscript on her desk for one whole hour, but had not managed to take in a single word of Gail Alexander's new novel. It was unlike her to be incapable of focusing on her work at will, but her mind was still on the article. As soon as her assistant, Debra, had walked out of her office and closed the door, Sam had rushed from the window to read the newspaper that Debra had left on her desk. The caption read FAMOUS WRITER FOUND IN CAVE. It gave a lot of information about Solomon's professional past: his books, his speeches, his Power Program, but no information about his present, except to say that he was alive and that he was sequestered in a cave on Saint Germaine, an island in the Caribbean.

Sam put aside Gail's manuscript and conceded defeat. No matter how hard she tried, she could not concentrate on anything other than the fact that Solomon had been found. *Has he been lost or in hiding? Is he in his right mind? Is he living in the cave with someone? Does he have any idea what he's put people through? His fans? His agency? Me?*

Riding down in the elevator, Sam realized that she had never really "gotten there" with Solomon. Wherever it was that she had thought they could get to, whatever she had with him, or wanted to have, she had never really gotten there. If she had, she wouldn't have so many unanswered questions. She wouldn't know so little about his life, his needs. She wouldn't be so unimportant to him that she had to read the fact that he was alive in a newspaper!

"Everything all right?" Jerry, the doorman, asked, swinging the glass door open as Sam charged out of the building.

"Yes, thanks, Jerry," she replied, flashing him her Miss Teen Maryland smile as she breezed past him. A few strides down the street, she turned around and walked back to him with tears welling in her eyes. "Actually, it's not, Jerry. Do you think you could hail me a cab?"

"You got it," Jerry replied, raising his whistle. Sam followed him to the curb. By the time she got there, he was holding a taxi door open for her. "Whatever it is, my angel," he said affectionately, "just remember, life only gets worse to get better." The kindness in his voice jolted one of the tears that were clinging to Sam's eyes into trickling down onto her cheek. She used the tip of her little finger to slide it back up and wipe it away, hoping no more would follow.

"Where you wanna go?" the cab driver asked impatiently.

"Forty-eighth and Lex," Sam replied, sliding into the backseat of the cab and holding out a five-dollar tip through the window for Jerry.

"Wouldn't dream of it," Jerry said, refusing the tip as he backed up to his post at the door.

The taxi pulled away. Sam put the five-dollar bill in her purse and determined she wasn't going to cry. At least not now. Not until she was ensconced safely in her bed. She felt a little guilty about going back to her apartment so early in the day, especially since she had purposed that morning to close the Brooks deal by lunchtime. But tussling with Mr. Phalen, Jean Brooks's charming but quick-minded attorney, was more than she could handle; in fact, dealing with any business at all right now was more than she could handle. All she wanted to do was get into bed. Sam closed her eyes and pictured it— bed, her real bed, the one with blue clouds and leaping lambs painted on the wooden headboard. The one in her real bedroom, next to her Grandma Etta's room, back in Maryland. Suddenly, that was the only place in the world she wanted to be, home. "Excuse me? You know what?" She leaned forward and tapped on the dividing glass to get the cabbie's attention. "Excuse me, I've changed my mind. Just drop me off at Penn Station."

Sam was glad to be leaving the city. *Anyway*, she remembered, *Lawrence is probably still in my apartment, in my bed, and I certainly don't need him asking me what's wrong.* She calculated everything in her head. If she rented a car when she got off the train, she would be able to get home and tell her grandmother everything be-fore her father got back from the office. Not that she wanted to keep secrets from her daddy, but if she told him how she was feeling right now, he would tell her that she was "the best" and that anyone who couldn't see that she was an "absolute prize" was simply not worthy of her emotions, which she should "conquer" and "ride victori-ously" because she was "a winner." Right now she needed to talk to her grandma, because right now she needed the relief of finally ad-mitting to someone that she was hurting. That for more than a decade she had loved a man who didn't love her back in the same way. That her love for him had chained her. That though she had never admitted it to herself, it had prevented her from giving any other man a real chance, because in her heart of hearts she had never given up the hope of ending up with Solomon. Sam felt tears welling in the corners of her eyes.

Not now, she thought. *Not now, not now. Wait for Grandma, Samantha. Wait for Grandma.*

Chapter 3

✦

WALKING HOME along the sand, Miriam noticed a fisherman asleep in a boat covered with flowers. Before she could get very far, he opened his eyes and called out to her, saying that he urgently needed her to come and see his pregnant wife who was "already in labor." Miriam ran into the house and came straight out carrying her leather doctor's bag.

Climbing into the boat and watching the fisherman drag it into the water, Miriam reflected on how calm she felt. Leaving the airport, seeing Captain Morrow board the helicopter, she had expected to be filled with anxiety over the apparent crisis that surrounded Solomon on Saint Germaine. But much to her own surprise, she was not. Solomon was alive, that much she now believed. Captain Morrow had shown her a copy of a recent photograph of him that had been turned in to the authorities.

As excited as she was at the prospect of seeing him in the flesh, as grateful as she was for his being alive, the quiet inner voice by which she lived directed her not to board the helicopter to Saint Germaine. At first she had thought it was her dread stopping her, her reluctance to travel, her fear of airplanes; but as the voice continued to whisper, she realized it was definitely not fear, it was her inner voice coaxing her to return home. So she had walked back home from the airport, certain that in opting not to fly, she had made the right decision. Life had taught Miriam that you should always obey your inner voice and that when you are not sure what to do, the best thing to do is wait.

Birthing babies, however, was not a waiting matter.

Leaning back in the boat, Miriam relaxed and enjoyed the motion of the fisherman's steady rowing. The fragrance of the intertwined flowers drifted along with them, blending in with the sea air. *How sweet*, she thought, presuming the fisherman had intertwined the flowers in celebration of the birth of his expected baby. *What a good thing me came back home . . .*

*   *   *

The fire inside the cave burned out. Feeling the absence of the flame flickering near his face, Solomon stirred from his semiconscious sleep and opened his eyes. The last of his handwritten papers lay in cinders in the burned-out fire. He was glad. Writing the events of his past, and burning it, was like a purification. He splashed his face with water from a large shell, relit the fire, and sat near the mouth of the cave to look out for the boat. He was anxious for Miriam to arrive.

He wanted to see her, coming over the horizon, floating toward him, surrounded by flowers.

*   *   *

Miriam woke to the bump of the boat being dragged along the sand. The journey had been so long that she had fallen asleep. Looking around, she recognized that she was not on Cape Corcos Island. "Where you bring me?" she inquired, disoriented. Straining to drag the boat far enough ashore to keep it from being drawn back into the sea by the waves, the fisherman ignored her question. Walking her to the mouth of a nearby cave, he beckoned her inside. Miriam hesitated.

"Please go in," he implored. "Me mean you no harm. It better me wait out here."

"Your wife is inside?"

"Please, ma'am, hurry."

Miriam stepped cautiously into the cave. Traveling through a corridor of rock, she followed its curve into a dark passage beyond the light of the sun. Apprehensive, she was about to turn back, when she saw a glow of firelight coming from deeper inside. Treading tentatively along the narrow opening, her fingers touching the cold mossy wall, she walked toward the light, which became brighter and brighter, leading her into the domed center of the cave.

Looking around her, she felt as though she had been transported to another world, a world with a strange and eerie beauty. The core of the cave was a dark, spacious, almost perfectly round hollow, surrounded by a wall of black and multicolored rock. Pushed into cracks in the rock, delicate tree branches draped with drying seaweed dangled off the walls like weeping willows over water. Not far from the fire that was burning in the middle of the floor was an old canoe stuffed with bunches of the dried seaweed. It was used, Miriam guessed, as a bed. She recognized the canoe. She also recognized the maroon leather-bound Bible lying on the ground beside it. *He's in here*, she thought, feeling strangely calm.

As Miriam's eyes adjusted to the dim glow, she began to see her surroundings more clearly. *Amazing!* What she had thought was multicolored rock was not rock at all. It was colored sand. The walls had been covered with beautiful sand paintings of multicolored birds in flight. Awed by the detail, she traced the intricate wing of a bird with the tip of her finger.

Solomon stepped out from a tunnel in the rock, into the shadowy mouth of the dome. She heard him, smelled his scent. She wasn't ready to see him, so she kept her back to him, tracing the feathers with her fingers. "I couldn't feel you." The echo of her voice took her by surprise. "All those months," she continued, listening to her voice resounding off the walls, "all those months I couldn't feel you. I guess this rock too thick, held you in."

Miriam turned to look at Solomon with all her yesterdays sitting along the rims of her eyes, tears threatening. She held on to them as tenaciously as she had held on to their marriage, determined not to let them fall into a darkened cave devoid of sunlight.

Standing there in the semidarkness, Solomon seemed taller. Stronger than she remembered. His appearance was wilder. His persona more peaceful.

"I was afraid you were dead." Miriam's whisper echoed around them.

Solomon walked out of the shadows toward her. "I'm alive."

She couldn't believe she had done it. Running, stumbling back through the dark passageway, Miriam couldn't believe she had slapped him. She could hear the sound of her palm against the hollow of Solomon's cheek echoing along the tunnels of the cave as she ran. *I'm alive.* He had said it as if it were the simplest of statements. *I'm alive.* As if her nights of burrowing down in the bed, choking back her fears, were of no account. *I'm alive.* As if she hadn't waited, struggled, mourned, travailed. *I'm alive.* As if nothing else mattered but the fact that he was alive. What did he think? Did he think he was the sun? The moon? The center of the universe? The beginning and the end? Was the mere fact that he was alive supposed to eradicate or supersede anything and everything that had taken place in the past five months?

Miriam ran out into the light. "I'm alive too," she panted. Leaning against the mouth of the cave, she could hear Solomon's rapid breathing echoing behind her. Eager to escape, her eyes combed the area, looking for the fisherman to take her back home. He was nowhere in sight, and his boat had been removed from the shore. Scouring the horizon, she checked the surface of the sea. Nothing. No fisherman. No boat. There was nothing.

Before she had time to think where to hide, Solomon came running out the mouth of the cave and in the same split second, there was a loud rumble in the sky. Startled by the sound, Miriam looked up. Gray stormclouds swept across the sun, shadowing its light. Thunder struck again and the clouds opened up their hearts, emptying themselves over the earth in a torrent of rain.

Miriam felt herself being pulled . . . pulled down onto the sand. "Miriam." Solomon's soft lips spread her name over her face with kisses—"Miriam, Miriam"—slid her name up her dress—"sweet Miriam"—stroked it down her back—"Miriam, Miriam, Miriam." He enfolded her in his arms and rolled her over him, under him, over him, under him, over and over and over, pressing, probing, stroking, kissing, prying. "Open your mouth, baby, open your mouth." Gasping for breath Miriam opened, Solomon entered, writhing, pulling, calling, trying to claim her back, back from that faraway place, back from that place where she had purposed to live without him. "Come, Miriam, come." He was overflowing, flowing into her, pouring like rain into her eyes, washing over her hair, flowing through her mouth, filling up her ears, streaming down her neck, engulfing her breasts. She was soaked, saturated; she couldn't move, her sodden clothes were weighing her down, the sand was sucking her down, Solomon was pushing her down—down into the sand, down into the hole—the rain was beating around her body, the rain was beating a hole for her body, she was being buried, buried alive in a sandy grave.

Chapter 4

✦

*A*SHIA SAT HUNCHED over the table, reading the final page of the manuscript. Completely engrossed in the story, she spoke the words softly to herself.

"So I pass it on to you, Amankwa," Beento said, carefully placing the enchanted flower of time into his son's beak. "You must handle it with care. The riches of the past lie within its roots, the present blooms in its pale green stem and shines bright in its golden petals, the future is hidden in its tiny black seeds. It can never die, but it can be wasted or stolen away, so you must protect it and use it wisely. With its power you can fly wherever you dream and watch the world from way up in the trees, or higher than the clouds, above the sun even, if you water the seeds with faith and dream vast enough. But remember, my son, there are three conditions:

"First, whatever you see from high up, you must tell it down below. You must reach down and lift others up to join you. You must not live so lofty that you forget your fellow flock. You must remember everything you learn and write it down, write it down and pass it on to all the children of the world. Write until every last child is flying by your side, high . . . high . . . above the sun.

"Second, in all the excitement of discovering your new horizons, you must not forget your family. There is no greater gift to create or receive than a loving home and family. Never neglect them; they are a part of you. When you neglect them, you neglect yourself. Treasure them always.

"Third, last, and most important, never forget, my son, no matter where you travel or how high you soar, you will always be lower than

God and the heavens, so you will always have something to look up to
and reach for to pull you higher.

    "Remember these three things and take wing, my son . . . Spread
your feathers wide and take wing . . ."

With love and everlasting joy,
your father and friend,
Beento Blackbird.

Ashia closed the manuscript. Olu stepped in from the hallway.
"Will you go to him?"

Ashia looked up, surprised. She hadn't heard him come back into
the apartment. "Where is Amankwa?"

"He fell asleep on my back on the way home. I've laid him on the
bed." Olu pulled out the plastic-covered dining chair and sat down
opposite her. Ashia picked her books off the floor, put them back on
the table. She could feel Olu's probing eyes watching her. "Ashia,"
he said after a brief pause, "will you go to him?"

"No," she said without hesitation. "I will not go to him."

"What if—"

"No. When I had Amankwa, I went. This is the second time he
has deserted me. I will not go."

"Are you certain?"

"Yes, Olu, I am certain."

Reaching across the table, Olu slid the gold wedding band off
Ashia's finger and laced his fingers with hers. "I promise you,
Ashia," he vowed, "I will make you thank God you did not go."

Chapter 5

✦

SHE HAD COME—just as he had dreamed—floating in the flower-covered boat. It had rained—by the grace of God. They had made love in the pouring rain—cuddled naked in the cave, their clothes drying by the fire. They had eaten fresh fish roasted on burning hot rocks. She had slept; he had gone to fetch the fisherman to take them home. And then—*and then what?* It was in that time when he was gone that something must have happened, but what? *What happened?*

The fisherman had been busy trying to convince a crowd gathered outside a cave that the famous author they thought was still hidden inside had escaped in the night and fled to Jamaica. Looking down from his hiding place above the rocks, Solomon had watched the pandemonium and was grateful to the fisherman for having thought quickly enough when first questioned by authorities as to the "famous author's" whereabouts to lead them to the wrong set of caves.

Whistling their code signal, Solomon had caught the fisherman's attention. Leaving the disappointed crowd, the fisherman had jumped into his boat and rowed back around the rocks to meet Solomon on the other side.

"I'm going home, back to Cape Corcos."

The fisherman had nodded knowingly at Solomon, as though he understood all that this simple statement entailed.

"I'd be grateful if you could take us."

"No problem."

The two men embraced, holding on to each other for those few seconds that say, *I'll miss you, my friend,* and then broke apart, Solomon returning to fetch Miriam, the fisherman checking the boat for the long trip back.

Solomon woke Miriam, who had dressed and fallen back asleep by the fire, and led her outside. Stepping into the boat covered with wilted flowers beaten petalless by the rain, their sweet fragrance turned to a sour stench, Miriam sat down on the wooden plank and announced, "I afraid you can't come home with me, Solomon. I have a new life now, me and the special person living with me."

The words echoed inside Solomon all night long as he lay sleepless inside the pitch-black cave. *I afraid you can't come home with me Solomon . . . I afraid you can't come home . . .*

Morning found him spiritless and defeated. Against his will, he forced himself to kneel and pray. Forced himself to recite a few words he had memorized in his months of isolation, hoping to discourage his discouragement. "Whatever things are true, whatever things are noble, whatever things are just, whatever things are lovely, whatever things are of good report, if there is any virtue and if there is anything praiseworthy—meditate on these things . . ." He repeated the words over and over again, "Whatever things are lovely, whatever things are of good report . . ." He kept it up all day and night, meditating—speaking life, meditating—speaking light into his darkness.

With nothing but the clothes on his back, his Bible, a mind full of beauty, and a heart replenished with hope, Solomon rowed the old canoe through calm waters, headed toward Miriam's adobe. For months and months he had read nothing but the Study Bible which he had found at the bottom of the canoe on his first day on Saint Germaine, left there, he presumed, by Ashia on the night she departed for London. Confused and lonely, he had studied it from cover to cover, gathering wisdom, renewing his broken spirit. There were so many things he had learned, so many things he wanted to share with Miriam. Most of all, he needed to let her know how he felt about their marriage. And he wanted to know what she had gone through, wanted her to have the release of telling it all. He had meant to share all this with her when she came to the cave, but then she ran out and the clouds erupted and the rain poured down and all his desires came tumbling out, wordless and uncontrolled.

The adobe looked quiet as Solomon approached. He sat on the edge of the canoe and watched the windows, waiting for signs of life.

Just before 6 A.M., when the sky was still dawn pink, he saw Miriam walk into the kitchen, and his heart leaped. She looked new, priceless, a thing of beauty. He stood up in the boat, gazing at her.

As if sensing his gaze, Miriam looked out the kitchen bay window, and their eyes met. Solomon stood still, his arms by his side. Miriam studied him. Instead of the African fabric he had been wearing around his waist, which once wrapped Amankwa, he had put on the clothes he had been wearing the day he drifted out to sea. His feet were bare, his shirt worn and crumpled, his trousers faded and frayed at the bottom, but he knew it was not important. What mattered was the state of his heart.

Cassie came bursting out of the kitchen door, brimming with excitement. "Uncle Solomon! Uncle Solomon! Mama Miriam, Mama Miriam, look, look, it's Uncle Solomon!" She leaped into his arms, firing a million questions at him: How come he had gone away? Where had he been? Why were his clothes so raggedy? Was he staying forever now? Was he coming to teach at the Royal Nubian?

"Cassie Wilberforce!" Miriam shouted through the open kitchen window. "Come bathe yourself and get yourself dressed."

Cassie stayed chattering to Solomon a little while longer, and by the time she finally ran inside to bathe, Solomon knew that she was attending the new school, that she had the highest marks in her class for "most everything, even African dance and drumming," and that she no longer had to "put up with Joan's meanness," because Mama Miriam had adopted her and she lived with her now, which was more fun, and much better, because sleeping with Mama Miriam, she didn't have to keep her eyes on the night anymore because Peace was there, and that was his job, he was the night watchman. "Mama Miriam, she the best person in the whole wide world! You also," Cassie added reassuringly.

Solomon's heart soared. So Cassie was the special person Miriam had been referring to! Of course! Filled with a deep sense of relief, he sat back down on the edge of the boat and watched Miriam busy herself in the kitchen while Cassie got ready for school.

Around seven-thirty the two of them came out onto the patio, Cassie wearing the colorful African uniform of the Royal Nubian, Miriam in her flowing white robes. Walking hand in hand across the trackless sand, they waved good-bye to Peace, who was sitting at his post outside Miriam's bedroom, and headed along the beach toward town.

Solomon first sat in the boat waiting for Miriam to return. Then he figured it wouldn't do any harm if he made himself comfortable on the patio couch.

Edging his way onto the marble tiles, he felt strange, like an intruder. Everything seemed so delicate, so pretty. Easing himself down onto the sofa, he was flooded with the memory of the last time he had sat there, cradling Amankwa in his arms, jiggling him to and fro to prevent him from fussing. In his mind's eye he could see Amankwa's little face as they set off on their walk, the happy smile that had broken out when he kissed him on the forehead. He could memory-feel his tiny sharp fingernails pressing on his nose and recall his bright gurgling laughter, soaring above the sound of the seabirds.

Longing washed through Solomon. He missed his son. *Is Amankwa walking now? Talking? Crawling certainly — I'm sure he's crawling — he must be nearly one. Does he know how to say 'Mama'? 'Papa'?* Solomon looked at the empty chair at the head of the table and remembered the first time Ashia had sat in it, draped in gold-and-fuchsia silk, her movements so unsure, the love in her eyes so certain. Ashia, who flew halfway around the world in search of him, who brought him his only child. Ashia, who gave so much and took so little.

Solomon bowed his head. Secluded in his dark cave, he had asked for forgiveness a million times. He had fallen to his knees and wept to a forgiving God, asking him to right all his wrongs, to bless those he had harmed, to replenish and protect them. He had prayed and sung songs of praise he didn't even know he knew, songs he made up as he went along, songs that came straight from his spirit. Sitting on the patio couch with his head bowed, Solomon hummed a new song, a song he heard wafting through the air, pealing in the wind chimes, resounding in the chambers of his heart. His new song lulled him into a restful sleep, his body collapsing onto the soft cushions, his legs floating off the ground as if lifted onto the couch by an angel.

A shadow fell over him, and Solomon opened his eyes and looked up. "Miriam—" he rose to his feet. Miriam hurried to the kitchen door. "Miriam, if it's all right by you, I'd like to speak to you whenever you're ready." Miriam hesitated, her back to him, her fingers on the latch. Solomon wanted to touch her so badly, it ached his soul. "I can wait," he assured her. "I won't rush you. I'll wait until you're ready to hear me out." Miriam stepped into the kitchen, closing the door behind her.

Solomon felt awkward, as if he were taking up too much space, as if his presence on the patio was somehow pushing against the kitchen door, locking Miriam inside. He wandered back to the canoe to allow her freedom of movement.

That night was difficult. He felt cramped and uncomfortable inside the canoe without all its dry seaweed padding. He would have slept on the sand but it was too damp. Somewhere in the early hours of the morning, Peace gave him a mat to sleep on and a small pillow for his head. It helped, but he was still uncomfortable.

Clang-clang-clang, clang-clang-clang. Cassie banged her metal spoon against a tin plate. "Uncle Solomon, why you sleeping outside?" she asked innocently as she woke him up and handed him the plate of food. Solomon took the plate. "From Mama Miriam," Cassie explained. Solomon looked up at Miriam in the kitchen window. He had been sleeping outside the adobe now for eleven nights, and it was the first time Miriam had offered him something to eat. He had been surviving on fruit gifted him from the occasional seller at the far end of the beach, and fish that Peace had tossed him on the occasions he had gone out to sea.

"Thank you," Solomon mouthed to Miriam behind the glass. She nodded slightly in response.

That's how the days passed: a nod here, a gesture there, watching, measuring, waiting, no one speaking to anyone—except for Cassie, who conversed freely with each of them. In her own way, she kept Solomon informed about what Miriam was doing, thinking, and feeling. She kept Miriam informed about what was going on with Solomon. And she kept Peace informed about both of them.

"Uncle Solomon, you never tell me why you sleeping outside?" Cassie inquired again late one night as she snuggled under the blanket with Solomon, the two of them gazing up at the stars. Solomon took a bite of the slice of chocolate cake that she had sneaked out of the house under her nightie because sometimes when she asked for food for Solomon, Miriam would say no. "How come you and Mama Miriam not talking?" Cassie persisted.

"I let her down, Cassie."

"That the same as breaking a promise?"

"In a way."

Solomon swallowed his mouthful of sugary dessert.

"Yeah, Cassie, I guess you could say I broke a promise." He explained to Cassie that he broke the promise a long time ago without realizing it, but assured her that his promise to her that she would never again be homeless still stood firm, as did all the future promises he would make in his lifetime. Cassie went to her bed and fell asleep reassured. Solomon stayed up, as he often did of late, pondering whether he had left Miriam alone too long, put her through too much, and whether, tired of waiting for him, she had moved beyond his reach. Finally dozing off to sleep, he woke with the seabirds as they coasted in the early morning sky. He bathed in the sea, stretched his body by the waves, and sat on his mat reading the Bible in the coral pink sunlight.

For thirty-three days Solomon kept it up. Thirty-three days of living by the canoe, sleeping in the sand, eating sparingly, reading his Bible, watching Miriam, waiting and hoping she would tell him she was ready to hear what he had to say. He made her little gifts—miniature blackbirds carved out of driftwood or sand-painted onto smooth pebbles he collected along the shore. Necklaces made from seashells. Small sculptures put together from oddments that had been washed up by the sea. He feathered, painted, carved, read, watched, prayed, waited, and slept.

"I'm ready."

Solomon woke at the sound of the voice and looked up from his mat into the cloudless sky. Blinded by the light, he closed his eyes and shifted his head away from the glaring rays of the sun. Before he could open his eyes again, his face was showered with sand as Miriam turned and walked away. He was so taken aback that she had finally spoken to him, he didn't know what to say. Through the days and weeks of waiting, he had stored so many things he wanted to tell her that in trying to recall them all, his mind flooded and went blank. Instantaneously, everything he had wrung from his soul, unearthed from his heart, gathered in his brain to speak forth, fused together in one combustive explosion, burning down to one pure microscopic crystal.

He jumped up and chased after Miriam with that crystal clenched in his mouth. He caught up with her, walking barefoot along the edge of the tide. He walked alongside her for a while, trying once more to retrieve some of the things he had gathered in his mind to say. Beads of remembrances skirted around the tip of his brain, waiting to be strung together. Months and months of gathering thoughts—and suddenly he could not string any of them together. He stopped walking. Stopped fearing. Stopped thinking. Miriam turned to face him. He gazed into her eyes. Opening his mouth, he offered her the one pure crystal that remained.

"Hello."

Miriam smiled.

Solomon saw in her smile that she understood the decades he had traveled and the explosion it had taken to purify him to that "hello."

"You had something you wanted to say?"

"Yes." Solomon paused for a while. Nothing else would come out of his mouth, so they resumed walking in silence. He calmed himself, took in the sea air, gave his mind the space to breathe. "I've been thinking, Miriam." The words came out easy as honesty. "Do you believe—" Solomon stopped midsentence. His mother's hand covered his mouth; he could feel her, hear her—"*Careful, Solomon . . . don't love too deep . . . love, but don't attach to anyone . . . love, but don't attach . . .*" Lovingly, he moved his mother's hand away, her small, trembling, fearful little hand. No matter what the consequences, he needed to speak. He needed to go on. He needed to open his heart and dare to be deserted. "Do you believe a husband and wife can become one flesh?" he continued in the freedom of his convictions. "I do, Miriam. I believe we can become one flesh. I've been reading about it, but even before I read it, I knew it, somewhere in my heart, in my spirit. A husband and wife can become one flesh. But the point is, if one of them goes and makes love to another person, then that one flesh gets torn apart. It's not something you can see, it's just . . ." Solomon stopped walking. He looked into Miriam's eyes. He couldn't read them, couldn't tell how she was feeling. "I don't want to tear us apart anymore, Miriam. I want us to be one flesh." He still couldn't read what her eyes were saying. "I want to be a good husband. To you. Just you, Miriam. I mean, if you're willing." He paused. Miriam said nothing. Maybe she didn't want him. Maybe she didn't believe him. Even if she didn't want him anymore, he needed her to believe how much he loved her.

"You don't need me," Solomon said quietly, more naked than he'd ever been in his life. "I don't need you either, Miriam, but I want you. I really, really want you. I hadn't even realized until these last few months how much your love has stretched me, not by the things you say but by the loyalty with which you've loved me. A lot of things I've been through, a lot of the things I've achieved, I've been able to do because, no matter what happened, whether I failed or whether I succeeded, I knew you would always be here for me. I would always be a king in your eyes. I've come back to you broke, broken, bullied, disillusioned, successful, arrogant, charming, inconsiderate—yet your faith in me never faltered, your vision never changed. It was your vision of me that gave me the courage to go out into the world and behave the way you saw me, the way you've always treated me, like a king, worthy of great sacrifice. Because of you, I dared to believe I was enough; and the world gave me homage for that. For thinking my thoughts. For writing my words. God gave me my gifts, and I thank him for it. But all good gifts need nurturing, and I thank you for nurturing them. I'm at the end of my forest, Miriam. I can see the meadow beyond the trees, the meadow I've always dreamed of. I could walk on from here without you, because you didn't cling to me, you left me alone to grow whole, to fly free and discover whatever I needed to discover. Well, what I've discovered,

Miriam, is that I love you. I want you with me; I want to be a good husband to you; I want to fulfill my vows to you, if you're willing to give me another chance."

"I'll be back before dusk" were the only words Miriam uttered in response.

Lying in the bathtub, Solomon wondered how many hundreds of times he had heard Miriam say that. She called it out like a theme song whenever she was leaving on her rounds: *I'll be back before dusk.*

He ducked his head under the water and washed the shampoo off his scalp. He felt liberated. He didn't mind that she hadn't said anything more. The thought of never being allowed the opportunity to express himself to her had chained him. Now that he had spoken, he was free. He had said what he needed to say. He couldn't control what she did with the information. That was up to her and God.

The water gulped loudly as it drained out of the tub. Solomon smiled; he'd forgotten how noisy the old tub was. Sometimes he could swear the tub was talking to him, like now, it was as if it were trying to pass on thoughts that Miriam had let slip through her pores while lying inside it.

Walking past the mirror by the sink as he dried himself, he was surprised to see how much weight he had lost. He stepped back and turned sideways, scrutinizing his reflection. He looked strange to himself. He'd lost too much weight. He knew the perfect person to help him put it back on.

Toussaint piled another spoonful of rice into Solomon's bowl. "Well, I glad you finally opened your eyes, Solomon, me been telling you for years to walk soft 'cause she a real treasure."

"I've always known that," Solomon said quietly. "I think she knows I've always known that."

"Course it's different for you," Toussaint said, a little wistfully. "A man like you got so much choice." He sucked the meat out of his crab leg.

"Listen, Toussaint," Solomon said leaning across the table, "I don't want to talk about Miriam anymore. I know you've always questioned why she stuck it out with me all these years. I know you've questioned whether I truly love her, but I do. I truly love her. And I love you for loving her so much that you've always tried to help me do right by her. Whatever's meant to happen, will happen. I absolutely believe that. God's working it out. I don't want to talk about it anymore 'cause I don't want to mess with what God's doing. I'm one of his kids, so I know he's got my back. I want to talk to you about something else," Solomon continued. "I've been studying up on it. I have to write it, I really have to write it—it's an idea I've got for a great new book." Solomon's eyes lit up with excitement.

Toussaint laughed. "A book? A new book? Well, Solomon," he continued, laughing, "now me really know it you. For a minute me thought an imposter taken over your body."

"No. It's *me*," Solomon said with an energy he couldn't contain. "And I'm going to write this new book as *me: In the Beginning* by Solomon Eustace Wilberforce. And I'm gonna go out there and speak about it."

"You got to learn to eat and talk at the same time," Toussaint teased, noticing Solomon had been too impassioned to eat a single mouthful. He ladled more crab soup into Solomon's bowl. "That'll heat the rest up, now eat!"

Solomon smiled, leaned back, and cracked open a crab leg. "That better," Toussaint encouraged. "Now go ahead, Mr. Pulitzer Prize, tell me 'bout this great new book."

*   *   *

"When people admire something, they want to steal it from you and say it's theirs. If you don't know any better, you believe them. The Europeans have tried to steal everything good and claim it is white. They even tried to steal Jesus and say He's white." Solomon looked out at the crowd of more than one thousand people listening to him in rapt attention. Gathered in the assembly hall of the Royal Nubian school, they were packed along the benches and crowded against the walls. Even with the overhead fans blowing, the room was steamy with all the people. But they didn't seem to mind, and neither did he. He was charged. He had forgotten what it felt like standing up in front of people, being inspired, inspiring them, letting the Spirit inside him lead the way.

"Jesus was born in a land of brown- and black-skinned people," he boomed passionately through the microphone. "He was born from

the root of King David, who's great-grandmother, Rahab, we know
for sure was a full-blooded black African woman, and yet they say
Jesus was white." Solomon looked out and saw Toussaint, who had
heard it all the night before, sitting at the end of the front row, smiling up at him. He smiled back and continued to talk. "The Virgin
Mary and her cousin, Elizabeth, were descended from black people,
and yet they say Jesus was white. The black presence throughout the
Bible is unquestionable, and yet many black people have been so
completely brainwashed that they call Christianity 'the white man's
religion,' acquiescing to the image propaganda of a blue-eyed Christ,
surrounded by Caucasian disciples. Europeans have always painted
Him as they need to see Him, white like themselves, so we throw up
our hands and say we can't relate to Him. 'It doesn't matter what
color Jesus is,' they say now, yet biblical images have been manipu-
lated for centuries, to the detriment of people of color. I agree that
color doesn't matter to God: black, white, blue, or polka-dot, He
loves us all the same. But it matters to our children. It matters to
them that time and time again, no one holy, not even an angel, is de-
picted with brown skin. What am I saying? I am saying that we are
all God's children, and we need to acknowledge and honor that. I see
some of you out there rolling your eyes. Perhaps you're like me and
grew up saying you weren't interested in religion. Or if you're interested in religion, then perhaps you're not interested in what color
anybody was, especially not Jesus. In a perfect world, skin color
shouldn't be an issue. But with the pressures of prejudice driving so
many of our children to follow any old thing that makes them feel
better—a temporary 'high' from drugs, or a 'superiority high' from
black gangs that perpetuate reverse racism or self-hatred and self-
annihilation—we need to realize that it's time to know where we
come from and hold fast to who we are, so we are not blown about
with every evil wind that comes our way. To love, we need to feel
lovely—be lovely. We are not the bottom rung of the ladder. We are
not the third world, we are the first. Abraham, a brown-skinned
man, was the father of all nations. Father Abraham had six sons with
Keturah, a black woman, and also with Hagar, an Egyptian woman.
Jacob, Abraham's grandson, had four sons with two black women,
Bilha and Zilpah, and those sons became four of the leaders of the
twelve tribes of Israel. Jethro, the priest of Median, a black man, was

father-in-law to Moses, and for forty years Jethro taught and coun-seled Moses under God's guidance, preparing Moses to lead his people out of captivity. Zipporah, Moses' black wife from Ethiopia, was so loved by God that when Moses' older sister Miriam tried to interfere with Moses' marrying her, Miriam was given leprosy. The man I am named after, the great King Solomon, married the black beauty Abishag, for whom most of the Songs of Solomon were writ-ten." Solomon paused, as the image of Ashia standing by her bed, reading from the lectern, flashed through his mind. "Solomon's own mother was black," he continued, forging onward. "Solomon was also the son of King David, whose grandmother Rahab was black, in the lineage of Abraham flowing directly down to Jesus Christ, which brings me back to where I started."

Miriam was the first to rise to her feet. Until she stood, Solomon didn't know she was in the room. Watching her standing there clap-ping, he realized how much her applause meant to him. She hadn't responded to his proposal to try again; in fact, she hadn't spoken to him much at all, even though he was sleeping in the house, in the second bedroom.

People crowded him, welcoming him back, asking him ques-tions about his speech. While he conversed with enthusiastic well-wishers, he tried to keep sight of Miriam, but he lost her in the crowd. He walked Cassie into her next class, shaking hands with her mathematics teacher and with some friends as she proudly intro-duced him as her "Uncle Solomon." Settling Cassie at her desk, he went back into the assembly hall, hoping Miriam would reappear. When she did not, Solomon said good-bye to Toussaint and Kawasaki and set out alone on his long walk back to the adobe.

"Hello, stranger," Miriam cooed, sneaking up to him from behind as he walked along the beach on his way back. "Do I know you?"

"Yes," Solomon replied, delighted to see her. "You know me. We met so long ago that you may not remember."

"Ancient days, huh?"

"Before the world began."

"Has it been that long?"

"Sure has," Solomon said fondly.

"Good. That mean it were made for us."

"What?"

"The world. If we met before it began, then it mean the whole world were created for us. All the trees, all the animals, all the people, everything jus' for us."

"You got a point there," Solomon smiled.

"So let's take a trip and survey our property."

"The world?"

"Every corner of it," Miriam said, her voice sing-songing. "Let's fly around the world, Solomon, everywhere you been and everywhere you not."

"You mean you want us to travel?"

"Cassie too," Miriam enthused. "Me want to show her there's more to the horizon than sea and sky. Me want her to know there a big wide world out there, and me don't want her to be afraid of it. Me not afraid of it either, Solomon. Me ready. Me ready to go. Me won't let you stay with me if it mean you staying on this island. The seaweed tried to chain me down. Me dreamed it, but me not going to let it happen. Me a bird too, Solomon. Me got wings to fly."

"You're not serious."

"I am, I am, I am," Miriam sang as she spread her arms wide like a bird and ran along the beach. Solomon ran alongside her. "I want to fly with you, Solomon Wilberforce."

Arms outstretched, hands linked, they laughed, running, leaping, splashing through the frothy tips of the waves.

"First, we'll go to London," Miriam called out as they ran. "See Ashia, take care of whatever you need to take care of to settle your ache about your son, 'cause me know your heart aching, Solomon. Then after London me want you to take me to—"

"Egypt," Solomon called out.

"Yes, Egypt!" Miriam elated. "And after Egypt, Sudan."

"After Sudan, Mali."

"After Mali, Tanzania."

"After Tanzania, Kenya. I've got to take you to Kenya," Solomon said, seeing the Masai Marra plains spreading before them like a heavenly landscape.

"After you've taken me to Kenya, me want to see Senegal."

"Goree Island!" Solomon called out as they ran. "And after Senegal, Nigeria."

"After Nigeria, the Ivory Coast."

"After the Ivory Coast—" Solomon hesitated. *Ghana*, he thought, *after the Ivory Coast we should go next door to Ghana.* He was hesitant to say it.

"Benin," Miriam called out, running over his hesitation.

"Yes, Benin," Solomon agreed, pushing homesickness out of his soul, sacrificing, for the sake of devotion. "I'm devoted to you, Miriam Wilberforce!" he shouted.

"Till death do us part!" she replied.

A large unsightly-looking pile of seaweed and refuse lay strewn across the sand directly in their path, debris the sea had regurgitated onto the shore. Hands linked, they kept on running toward it. "One, two, three, JUMP!" Solomon shouted. They leaped together into the air, flying, sailing, soaring over the waste that lay before them. They laughed as they landed safely on the other side and kept on running without skipping a beat.

"One, two, three—JUMP!" they shouted together, leaping again just for the fun of it, just for the lift of it, just for the love of it.

Love lifted them, held them in the air, reassembled them. JUMP! JUMP! JUMP! Higher than happy, they jumped and felt the shattered pieces of their lives change nature. Old wounds and tragedies shifted from ugly painful scars to beautiful carvings of their life, fully lived. A kaleidoscope of joy, they saw themselves and rejoiced, thankful to God that they had finally found the one thing they had always looked for—to give, to get, to hold, to be—Love, the miracle of creation.